The Library
of
Indiana Classics

Laddie

A True Blue Story

Gene Stratton-Porter

Introduction by Mary E. Gaither

Indiana University Press
Bloomington and Indianapolis

First Midland Book Edition 1988

The Library of Indiana Classics is available in a special
clothbound library-quality edition and in a paperback edition.

Introduction

Manufactured in the United States of America

Library of Congress Cataloging-in-Publication Data
Stratton-Porter, Gene, 1863-1924.
Laddie : a true blue story.
(The Library of Indiana classics)
Reprint. Originally published: New York : Grosset
& Dunlap, 1917. With new introd.
I. Title.   II. Series.
PS3531.07345L33 1988 813'.52   87-4009
ISBN 0-253-33113-7
ISBN 0-253-20458-5 (pbk.)

5   6   7   8   9   05   04   03   02   01   00

CHARACTERS

LADDIE, Who Loved and Asked No Questions.

THE PRINCESS, From the House of Mystery.

LEON, Our Angel Child.

LITTLE SISTER, Who Tells What Happened.

MR. and MRS. STANTON, Who Faced Life Shoulder to Shoulder.

SALLY and PETER, Who Married Each Other.

ELIZABETH, SHELLEY, MAY and Other Stanton Children.

MR. and MRS. PRYOR, Father and Mother of the Princess.

ROBERT PAGET, a Chicago Lawyer.

MRS. FRESHETT, Who Offered Her Life for Her Friend.

CANDACE, the Cook.

MISS AMELIA, the School Mistress.

Interested Relatives, Friends, and Neighbours.

Contents

Introduction ix

I. Little Sister 1
II. Our Angel Boy 23
III. Mr. Pryor's Door 50
IV. The Last Day in Eden 73
V. The First Day of School 91
VI. The Wedding Gown 106
VII. When Sally Married Peter 120
VIII. The Shropshire and the Crusader . . . 148
IX. "Even So" 168
X. Laddie Takes the Plunge 192
XI. Keeping Christmas Our Way 219
XII. The Horn of the Hunter 236
XIII. The Garden of the Lord 265
XIV. The Crest of Eastbrooke 296
XV. Laddie, the Princess, and the Pie . . . 316
XVI. The Homing Pigeon 332
XVII. In Faith Believing 358
XVIII. The Pryor Mystery 388

Introduction

OVER sixty years after her death, Gene Stratton-Porter continues to be widely read, especially in Indiana, and many older adults, when asked, recall with nostalgic pleasure their early reading of the Limberlost novels in particular, that is, *Freckles* (1904), *A Girl of the Limberlost* (1907), and *The Harvester* (1911). These novels and *Laddie* (1913) carry a significant part of their appeal through the integrity of their observation of nature. Known as the Bird Woman and the Lady of the Limberlost to her friends and a host of readers worldwide, Stratton-Porter started her career as a photographer of nature and then as a writer about nature before she wrote the popular novels that brought her fame and, not incidentally, fortune. Her lifelong study of birds, flowers, trees, land, and water is reflected in a dedicated conservancy that is central to almost everything she wrote. This concern for and love of nature is revealed in her fanciful stories of the once great Indiana swamp, the Limberlost, which she came to know intimately at firsthand, and also in the tamer but no less appealing story of post–Civil War farm life told here in *Laddie*.

Born in 1863 in Wabash County, Indiana, the youngest of twelve children, of whom nine were living at her birth, Geneva Stratton was tutored and lovingly guided by her earnest farmer father to know and love the land. Through him she early learned lessons in ecology and conservation that led to her later naturalist activity. Some of this knowledge is rather proudly displayed by Little Sister in *Laddie* when she corrects the literal inaccuracies she finds in the poetry and songs she recites and sings, for example, daisies don't bloom "mid frozen grass," bobolinks sing not in "maples high" but no "higher than a fence post." One such correction resulted in her humiliation by the new school mistress when Little Sister attempted to argue, on the basis of careful observation, that "birds in their nests [do not] agree."

In 1886, Geneva Stratton married Charles Dorwin Porter, a successful druggist. When they moved from Decatur to Geneva, both in Adams County, Gene Stratton-Porter began her love affair with the great Limberlost swamp, daily tramping its trails, observing its variety of wildlife, especially the birds, and recording her findings. In 1895, the now prosperous Porters built a large fourteen-room log "cabin" near the swamp, naming it Limberlost Cabin. This cabin was to figure prominently in *The Harvester*. They remained here until 1913 when, with the profits from her writing, Gene Stratton-Porter bought land on Sylvan Lake near Rome City in Noble County and established there a wildflower conservancy program. Wildflower Woods today is a memorial to her and her conservancy efforts. Beginning in 1919 she started making trips to California and in 1923 permanently made her home in the Los Angeles area. Embarking upon nature studies in California and founding a movie company to film her novels as she felt they should be interpreted, she was beginning a new phase of her writing career that was cut short when she was killed in a car accident in 1924, only a year after taking up her new home.

Stratton-Porter's first published writings were magazine articles on birds illustrated with her own photographs in *Recreation* (1900–1901) and *Outing* (1901–1902). Her first book was *The Song of the Cardinal* (1903), an anthropomorphic account of the life of a pair of cardinals, again illustrated with her own photographs. These writings and other published titles about birds, including *What I Have Done with Birds* (1907), *Birds of the Bible* (1909), and *Friends in Feathers* (1917) are responsible for her Bird Woman epithet taken from a character in *Freckles*. Yet despite her widely published nature articles and the popular "Gene Stratton-Porter's Page" in *McCall's Magazine*, gathered and published posthumously as *Let Us Highly Resolve* (1927), she is best known for the Limberlost novels named above. *Freckles* and *A Girl of the Limberlost* sold well over two million copies each, and *The*

Harvester was listed as a best-seller with a million and a half copies sold. This is an impressive sales record and amply proves her popularity. Later novels, particularly *The Keeper of the Bees* (1921) and *White Flag* (1923), were well received but were not as popular as the earlier Indiana novels, including *Laddie*, which was listed as the third place best-seller for 1913, its year of publication.

Laddie, A True Blue Story is indeed that. First, as an autobiographical novel it tells with considerable faithfulness to fact the true story of a year in the life of Stratton-Porter's family when they lived on Hopewell farm in Wabash County. All the chief characters were real people and most of the events actually occurred. The author herself admitted that "[t]here was no such person as 'Mrs. Freshett' and a few of the things told never really happened; but three-fourths of it is exact truth. If you will read 'Stratton' for 'Stanton' and 'Northbrooke' for 'Eastbrooke' you will have the truth in the case as straight as I can tell it" (cited by Bertrand F. Richards, *Gene Stratton Porter*, 1980, p. 80). Writing largely from an actual life carries with it a certain risk—can the real life be as exciting and well plotted as a fiction which knows no limitation on facts or events? Stratton-Porter takes this risk confidently, and the result is an unusually well-told tale about actual people who emerge from the pages as well-rounded, consistent, and believable characters.

If the plot seems less unified than those of Stratton-Porter's earlier novels, interest still rarely lags; one wants to know if Laddie will be successful in his rather unusual efforts to change the Princess's mind, what lies at the root of the mystery that surrounds the Pryors, what went wrong with Shelley in Chicago. Undoubtedly some of the apparent disjointedness of the plot may be explained by the fact that two of the chapters were published ten years earlier as short stories in *Metropolitan* magazine, Stratton-Porter's first published fiction. Yet the orderly progression of the seasons over a year from one late summer to the following lends a unity that makes up for any lapse in the development of plot. It should be noted here that Stratton-Porter's description of all the natural seasonal changes—weather, trees, flowers, birds—as well as the attendant human activity is the most evocative of her writing. In the chapter "Garden of the Lord" as spring begins to make itself felt and finally comes on in full sway, the reader falls under the spell of accurately detailed scenes and the graphic prose to feel as does Little Sister that "spring came pushing until you felt shoved" (275).

A second aspect of "a true blue story" that is central to the unfolding of the lives of the Stantons is the "true blue" quality of their character and personality. Truly a paragon of virtue, Laddie is superior to everyone in his courage, loyalty, deep faith, charitableness, familial love, and intellectual and physical attainments. A man as good and deserving as Laddie cannot possibly fail to win the worthy object of his affections. Mr. and Mrs. Stanton are proud, hard-working, far-sighted, charitable in thought and deed, and truly pious believers in the efficacy of prayer and in a God who reveals himself in wondrous ways. No task is too hard, no problem insurmountable for these early Hoosier settlers whose lives, however simple, are as rich and productive as the acres they till and reap.

In respect to the expression of positive moral values, *Laddie* follows its Limberlost predecessors with its strong emphasis on courage, strength of purpose, idealistic vision, and the implicit teaching of spiritual as opposed to material values. This latter theme is, as in *The Harvester*, strongly tied to an appreciation for nature and the land. When Laddie announces that he will "stick to the soil" and not go into law, Mr. Stanton is overjoyed and delivers himself of a miniature sermon on the positive values of a life away from the city and men's discords, concluding, "after all, land and its products are the basis of everything; the city couldn't exist a day unless we feed and clothe it. In the things I consider important, you are a king among men, with your feet on soil you own" (274).

The narrative mode of *Laddie* may prevent an easy suspension of disbelief to some readers. It is told in the first person by the eight- or ten-year-old Little Sister (Geneva Stratton herself) but from the later position of adulthood. Her seemingly total recall as well as her incredibly fortuitous presence at the scene of all the action and hence an audience to all the discussions may strain credulity. But we must remember that this is a fiction and that it is not all truth—poetic license is easily granted. Too, the precocity of Little Sister may be a problem to some. However, Stratton-Porter succeeds in creating a believable and reliable narrator in making Little Sister both childishly wise and childishly naive at the same time. She is quick to note her own shortcomings and misjudgments, thus finding a sympathetic reader. At one point Stratton-Porter almost breaks the spell of credibility she has created by bringing us to the present moment in telling us she can hardly see the paper she is writing for the tears evoked by recalling a particularly poignant episode (334). But we respond to the emotion of the situation, accept the author's lapse and go on without a ripple. Choosing to filter the story of this warm, closely-knit family through a child's eyes, that child being also a significant character, gives it a freshness of viewpoint and a liveliness that a third-person narration would lack because of its distance and, considering the moral emphasis, easy tendency to dullness. The intense personal experience recorded by Little Sister is a chief element in the novel's appeal.

In *Laddie*, Stratton-Porter has written not only an appealing story of farm and small town life in post–Civil War Indiana, but she has also written a paean to the strong values of home life and the "wonderful thing it is to own land and love it" (293). She has, in addition, offered a personal celebration of the family members whom she loved and who started her on the path to the active and satisfying life she came to know. Her love and generosity of spirit are central in this autobiographical novel that surely ranks as one of her best.

Mary E. Gaither
INDIANA UNIVERSITY

CHAPTER I

Little Sister

"And could another child-world be my share,
I'd be a Little Sister there."

HAVE I got a Little Sister anywhere in this house?" inquired Laddie at the door, in his most coaxing voice.

"Yes sir," I answered, dropping the trousers I was making for Hezekiah, my pet bluejay, and running as fast as I could. There was no telling what minute May might take it into her head that she was a little sister and reach him first. Maybe he wanted me to do something for him, and I loved to wait on Laddie.

"Ask mother if you may go with me a while."

"Mother doesn't care where I am, if I come when the supper bell rings."

"All right!" said Laddie.

He led the way around the house, sat on the front step and took me between his knees.

"Oh, is it going to be a secret?" I cried.

Secrets with Laddie were the greatest joy in life. He was so big and so handsome. He was so much nicer than any one else in our family, or among our friends, that to share his secrets, run his errands, and love him blindly was the greatest happiness. Sometimes I disobeyed father and mother; I minded Laddie like his right hand.

"The biggest secret yet," he said gravely.

"Tell quick!" I begged, holding my ear to his lips.

"Not so fast!" said Laddie. "Not so fast! I have doubts about this. I don't know that I should send you. Possibly you can't find the way. You may be afraid. Above all, there is never to be a whisper. Not to any one! Do you understand?"

"What's the matter?" I asked.

"Something serious," said Laddie. "You see, I expected to have an hour or two for myself this afternoon, so I made an engagement to spend the time with a Fairy Princess in our Big Woods. Father and I broke the reaper taking it from the shed just now and you know how he is about Fairies."

I did know how he was about Fairies. He hadn't a particle of patience with them. A Princess would be the Queen's daughter. My father's people were English, and I had heard enough talk to understand that. I was almost wild with excitement.

"Tell me the secret, hurry!" I cried.

"It's just this," he said. "It took me a long time to coax the Princess into our Big Woods. I had to fix a throne for her to sit on; spread a Magic Carpet for her feet, and build a wall to screen her. Now, what is she going to think if I'm not there to welcome her when she comes? She promised to show me how to make sunshine on dark days."

"Tell father and he can have Leon help him."

"But it is a secret with the Princess, and it's *hers* as much as mine. If I tell, she may not like it, and then she won't make me her Prince and send me on her errands."

"Then you don't dare tell a breath," I said.

"Will you go in my place, and carry her a letter to explain why I'm not coming, Little Sister?"

"Of course!" I said stoutly, and then my heart turned right over; for I never had been in our Big Woods alone, and neither mother nor father wanted me to go. Passing Gypsies sometimes laid down the fence and went there to camp. Father thought all the wolves and wildcats were gone, he hadn't seen any in years, but every once in a while some one said they had, and he was not quite sure yet. And that wasn't the beginning of it. Paddy Ryan had come back from the war wrong in his head. He wore his old army overcoat summer and winter, slept on the ground, and ate whatever he could find. Once Laddie and Leon, hunting squirrels to make broth for mother on one of her bad days, saw him in our Big Woods and he was eating *snakes*. If I found Pat Ryan eating a snake, it would frighten me so I would stand still and let him eat me, if he wanted to, and perhaps he wasn't too crazy to see how plump I was. I seemed to see swarthy, dark faces, big, sleek cats dropping from limbs, and Paddy Ryan's matted gray hair, the flying rags of the old blue coat, and a snake in his hands. Laddie was slipping the letter into my apron pocket. My knees threatened to let me down.

"Must I lift the leaves and hunt for her, or will she come to me?" I wavered.

"That's the biggest secret of all," said Laddie. "Since the Princess entered them, our woods are Enchanted, and there is no telling what wonderful things may happen any minute. One of them is this: whenever the Princess comes there, she grows in size until she is as big as, say our Sally, and she fills all the place with glory, until you are so blinded you scarcely can see her face."

"What is she like, Laddie?" I questioned, so filled with awe and interest, that fear was forgotten.

"She is taller than Sally," said Laddie. "Her face is oval, and her cheeks are bright. Her eyes are big moonlit pools of darkness, and silken curls fall over her shoulders. One hair is strong enough for a lifeline that will draw a drowning man ashore, or strangle an unhappy one. But you will not see her. I'm purposely sending you early, so you can do what you are told and come back to me before she even reaches the woods."

"What am I to do, Laddie?"

"You must put one hand in your apron pocket and take the letter in it, and as long as you hold it tight, nothing in the world can hurt you. Go out our lane to the Big Woods, climb the gate and walk straight back the wagon road to the water. When you reach that, you must turn to your right and go toward Hoods' until you come to the pawpaw thicket. Go around that, look ahead, and you'll see the biggest beech tree you ever saw. You know a beech, don't you?"

"Of course I do," I said indignantly. "Father taught me beech with the other trees."

"Well then," said Laddie, "straight before you will be a purple beech, and under it is the throne of the Princess, the Magic Carpet, and the walls I made. Among the beech roots there is a stone hidden with moss. Roll the stone back and there will be a piece of bark. Lift that, lay the letter in the box you'll find, and scamper to me like flying. I'll be at the barn with father."

"Is that all?"

"Not quite," said Laddie. "It's possible that the Fairy Queen may have set the Princess spinning silk for the caterpillars to weave their little houses with this winter; and if she has, she may have left a letter there to tell me. If there is one, put it in your pocket, hold it close every step of the way, and you'll be safe coming home as you were going. But you mustn't let a soul see it; you must slip it into my pocket when I'm not looking. If you let any one see, then the Magic will be spoiled, and the Fairy won't come again."

"No one shall see," I promised.

"I knew you could be trusted," said Laddie, kissing and hugging me hard. "Now go! If anything gets after you that such a big girl as you really wouldn't be ashamed to be afraid of, climb on a fence and call. I'll be listening, and I'll come flying. Now I must hurry. Father will think it's going to take me the remainder of the day to find the bolts he wants."

We went down the front walk between the rows of hollyhocks and tasselled lady-slippers, out the gate, and followed the road. Laddie held one of my hands tight, and in the other I gripped the letter in my pocket. So long as Laddie could see me, and the lane lay between open fields, I wasn't afraid. I was thinking so deeply about our woods being Enchanted, and a tiny Fairy growing big as our Sally, because she was in them, that I stepped out bravely.

Every few days I followed the lane as far back as the Big Gate. This stood where four fields cornered, and opened into the road leading to the woods. Beyond it, I had walked on Sunday afternoons with father, while he taught me all the flowers, vines, and bushes he knew, only he didn't know some of the prettiest ones; I had to have books for them, and I was studying to learn enough that I could find out. Or I had ridden on the wagon with Laddie and Leon when they went to bring wood for the cookstove, out-oven, and big fireplace. But to walk! To go all alone! Not that I didn't walk by myself over every other foot of the acres and acres of beautiful land my father owned; but plowed fields, grassy meadows, wood pasture, and the orchard were different. I played in them without a thought of fear.

The only things to be careful about were a little, shiny, slender snake, with a head as bright as mother's copper kettle, and a big thick one with patterns on its back like those in Laddie's geometry books, and a whole rattlebox on its tail; not to eat any berry or fruit I didn't know without first asking father; and always to be sure to measure how deep the water was before I waded in alone.

But our Big Woods! Leon said the wildcats would get me there. I sat in our catalpa and watched the Gypsies drive past every summer. Mother hated them as hard as ever she could hate any one, because once they had stolen some fine shirts, with linen bosoms, that she had made by hand for father, and was bleaching on the grass. If Gypsies should be in our west woods to-day and steal me, she would hate them worse than ever; because my mother loved me now, even if she didn't want me when I was born.

But you could excuse her for that. She had already bathed, spanked, sewed for, and reared eleven babies so big and strong not one of them ever even threatened to die. When you thought of that, you could see she wouldn't be likely to implore the Almighty to send her another, just to make her family even numbers. I never felt much hurt at her, but some of the others I never have forgiven and maybe I never will. As long as there had been eleven babies, they should have been so accustomed to children that they needn't all of them have objected to me, all except Laddie, of course. That was the reason I loved him so and tried to do every single thing he wanted me to, just the way he liked it done. That was why I was facing the only spot on our land where I was in the slightest afraid; because he asked me to. If he had told me to dance a jig on the ridgepole of our barn, I would have tried it.

So I clasped the note, set my teeth, and climbed over the gate. I walked fast and kept my eyes straight before me. If I looked on either side, sure as life I would see something I never had before, and be down digging up a strange flower, chasing a butterfly, or watching a bird. Besides, if I didn't look in the fence corners that I passed, maybe I wouldn't see anything to scare me. I was going along finely, and feeling better every minute as I went down the bank of an old creek that had gone dry, and started up the other side toward the sugar camp not far from the Big Woods. The bed was full of weeds and as I passed through, away! went Something among them.

Beside the camp shed there was corded wood, and the first thing I knew, I was on top of it. The next, my hand was on the note in my pocket. My heart jumped until I could see my apron move, and my throat went all stiff and dry. I gripped the note and waited. Father believed God would take care of him. I was only a little girl and needed help much more than a man; maybe God would take care of me. There was nothing wrong in carrying a letter to the Fairy Princess. I thought perhaps it would help if I should kneel on the top of the woodpile and ask God to not let anything get me.

The more I thought about it, the less I felt like doing it, though, because really you have no business to ask God to take care of you, unless you *know* you are doing right. This was right, but in my heart I also knew that if Laddie had asked me, I would be shivering on top of that cordwood on a hot August day, when it was wrong. On the whole, I thought it would be more honest to leave God out of it, and take the risk myself. That made me think of the Crusaders, and the little gold trinket in father's chest till. There were four shells on it and each one stood for a trip on foot or horseback to the Holy City when you had to fight almost every step of the way. Those shells meant that my father's people had gone four times, so he said; that, although it was away far back, still each of us had a tiny share of the blood of the Crusaders in our veins, and that it would make us brave and strong, and whenever we were afraid, if we would think of them, we never could do a cowardly thing or let any one else do one before us. He said any one with Crusader blood had to be brave as Richard the Lion-hearted. Thinking about that helped ever so much, so I gripped the note and turned to take one last look at the house before I made a dash for the gate that led into the Big Woods.

Beyond our land lay the farm of Jacob Hood, and Mrs. Hood always teased me because Laddie had gone racing after her when I was born. She was in the middle of Monday's washing, and the bluing settled in the rinse water and stained her white clothes in streaks it took months to bleach out. I always liked Sarah Hood for coming and dressing me, though, because our Sally, who was big enough to have done it, was upstairs crying and wouldn't come down. I liked Laddie too, because he was the only one of our family who went to my mother and kissed her, said he was glad, and offered to help her. Maybe the reason he went was because he had an awful scare, but anyway he *went,* and that was enough for me.

You see it was this way: no one wanted me; as there had been eleven of us, every one felt that was enough. May was six years old and in school, and my mother thought there never would be any more babies. She had given away the cradle and divided the baby clothes among my big married sisters and brothers, and was having a fine time and enjoying herself the most she ever had in her life. The land was paid for long ago; the house she had planned, builded as she wanted it; she had a big team of matched grays and a carriage with side lamps and patent leather trimmings; and sometimes there was money in the bank. I do not know that there was very much, but any at all was a marvel, considering how many of us there were to feed, clothe, and send to college. Mother was forty-six and father was fifty; so they felt young enough yet to have a fine time and enjoy life, and just when things were going best, I announced that I was halfway over my journey to earth.

You can't blame my mother so much. She must have been tired of babies and disliked to go back and begin all over after resting six years. And you mustn't be too hard on my father if he was not just overjoyed. He felt sure the cook would leave, and she did. He knew Sally would object to a baby, when she wanted to begin having beaus, so he and mother talked it over and sent her away for a long visit to Ohio with father's people, and never told her. They intended to leave her there until I was over the colic, at least. They knew the big married brothers and sisters would object, and they did. They said it would be embarrassing for their children to be the nieces and nephews of an aunt or uncle younger than themselves. They said it so often and so emphatically that father was provoked and mother cried. Shelley didn't like it because she was going to school in Groveville, where Lucy, one of our married sisters, lived, and she was afraid I would make so much work she would have to give up her books and friends and remain at home. There never was a baby born who was any less wanted than I was. I knew as much about it as any one else, because from the day I could understand, all of them, father, mother, Shelley, Sarah Hood, every one who knew, took turns telling me how badly I was not wanted, how much trouble I made, and how Laddie was the only one who loved me at first. Because of that I was on the cordwood trying to find courage to go farther. Over and over Laddie had told me himself. He had been to visit our big sister Elizabeth over Sunday and about eight o'clock Monday morning he came riding down the road, and saw the most dreadful thing. There was not a curl of smoke from the chimneys, not a tablecloth or pillowslip on the line, not a blind raised. Laddie said his heart went—just like mine did when the Something jumped in the creek bed, no doubt. Then he laid on the whip and rode.

He flung the rein over the hitching post, leaped the fence and reached the back door. The young green girl, who was all father could get when the cook left, was crying. So were Shelley and little May, although she said afterward she had a boil on her heel and there was no one to poultice it. Laddie leaned against the door casing, and it is easy enough to understand what he thought. He told me he had to try twice before he could speak, and then he could only ask: "What's the matter?"

Probably May never thought she would have the chance, but the others were so busy crying harder, now that they had an audience, that she was first to tell him: "We have got a little sister."

"Great Day!" cried Laddie. "You made me think we had a funeral! Where is mother, and where is my Little Sister?"

He went bolting right into mother's room and kissed her like the gladdest boy alive; because he was only a boy then, and he told her how happy he was that she was safe, and then he *asked* for me. He said I was the only living creature in that house who was not shedding tears, and I didn't begin for about six months afterward. In fact, not until Shelley taught me by pinching me if she had to rock the cradle; then I would cry so hard mother would have to take me. He said he didn't believe I'd ever have learned by myself.

He took a pillow from the bed, fixed it in the rocking chair and laid me on it. When he found that father was hitching the horses to send Leon for Doctor Fenner, Laddie rode back after Sarah Hood and spoiled her washing. It may be that the interest he always took in me had its beginning in all of them scaring him with their weeping; even Sally, whom father had to telegraph to come home, was upstairs crying, and she was almost a woman. It may be that all the tears they shed over not wanting me so scared Laddie that he went farther in his welcome than he ever would have thought of going if he hadn't done it for joy when he learned his mother was safe. I don't care about the reason. It is enough for me that from the hour of my birth Laddie named me Little Sister, seldom called me anything else, and cared for me all he possibly could to rest mother. He took me to the fields with him in the morning and brought me back on the horse before him at noon. He could plow with me riding the horse, drive a reaper with me on his knees, and hoe corn while I slept on his coat in a fence corner. The winters he was away at college left me lonely, and when he came back for a vacation I was too happy for words. Maybe it was wrong to love him most. I knew my mother cared for and wanted me now. And all my secrets were not with Laddie. I had one with father that I was never to tell so long as he lived, but it was about the one he loved best, next after mother. Perhaps I should never tell it, but I wouldn't be surprised if the family knew. I followed Laddie like a faithful dog, when I was not gripping his waving hair and riding in triumph on his shoulders. He never had to go so fast he couldn't take me on his back. He never was in too big a hurry to be kind. He always had patience to explain every shell, leaf, bird, and flower I asked about. I was just as much his when pretty young girls were around, and the house full of company, as when we were alone. That was the reason I was shivering on the cordwood, gripping his letter and thinking of all these things in order to force myself to go farther.

I was excited about the Fairies too. I often had close chances of seeing them, but I always just missed. Now here was Laddie writing letters and expecting answers; our Big Woods Enchanted, a Magic Carpet and the Queen's daughter becoming our size so she could speak with him. No doubt the Queen had her grow big as Shelley, when she sent her on an errand to tell Laddie about how to make sunshine; because she was afraid if she went her real size he would accidentally step on her, he was so dreadfully big. Or maybe her voice was so fine he could not hear what she said. He had told me I was to hurry, and I had gone as fast as I could until Something jumped; since, I had been settled on that cordwood like Robinson Crusoe on his desert island. I had to get down some time; I might as well start.

I gripped the letter, slid to the ground, and ran toward the big gate straight before me. I climbed it, clutched the note again, and ran blindly down the road through the forest toward the creek. I could hurry there. On either side of it I could not have run ten steps at a time. The big trees reached so high above me it seemed as if they would push through the floor of Heaven. I tried to shut my ears and run so fast I couldn't hear a sound, and so going, I soon came to the creek bank. There I turned to my right and went slower, watching for the pawpaw thicket. On leaving the road I thought I would have to crawl over logs and make my way; but there seemed to be kind of a path not very plain, but travelled enough to follow. It led straight to the thicket. At the edge I stopped to look for the beech. It could be reached in one breathless dash, but there seemed to be a green enclosure, so I walked around until I found an entrance. Once there I was so amazed I stood and stared. I was half indignant too.

Laddie hadn't done a thing but make an exact copy of my playhouse under the biggest maiden's-blush in our orchard. He used the immense beech for one corner, where I had the apple tree. His Magic Carpet was woolly-dog moss, and all the magic about it, was that on the damp woods floor, in the deep shade, the moss had taken root and was growing as if it always had been there. He had been able to cut and stick much larger willow sprouts for his walls than I could, and in the wet black mould they didn't look as if they ever had wilted. They were so fresh and green, no doubt they had taken root and were growing. Where I had a low bench under my tree, he had used a log; but he had hewed the top flat, and made a moss cover. In each corner he had set a fern as high as my head. On either side of the entrance he had planted a cluster of cardinal flower that was in full bloom, and around the walls in a few places thrifty bunches of Oswego tea and foxfire, that I would have walked miles to secure for my wild garden under the Bartlett pear tree. It was so beautiful it took my breath away.

"If the Queen's daughter doesn't like this," I said softly, "she'll have to go to Heaven before she finds anything better, for there can't be another place on earth so pretty."

It was wonderful how the sound of my own voice gave me courage, even if it did seem a little strange. So I hurried to the beech, knelt and slipped the letter in the box, and put back the bark and stone. Laddie had said that nothing could hurt me while I had the letter, so my protection was gone as soon as it left my hands.

There was nothing but my feet to save me now. I thanked goodness I was a fine runner, and started for the pawpaw thicket. Once there, I paused only one minute to see whether the way to the stream was clear, and while standing tense and gazing, I heard something. For an instant it was every bit as bad as at the dry creek. Then I realized that this was a soft voice singing, and I forgot everything else in a glow of delight. The Princess was coming!

Never in all my life was I so surprised, and astonished, and bewildered. She was even larger than our Sally; her dress was pale green, like I thought a Fairy's should be; her eyes were deep and dark as Laddie had said, her hair hung from a part in the middle of her forehead over her shoulders, and if she had been in the sun, it would have gleamed like a blackbird's wing. She was just as Laddie said she would be; she was so much more beautiful than you would suppose any woman could be, I stood there dumbly staring. I wouldn't have asked for any one more perfectly beautiful or more like Laddie had said the Princess would be; but she was no more the daughter of the Fairy Queen than I was. She was not any more of a Princess. If father ever would tell all about the little bauble he kept in the till of his big chest, maybe she was not as near! She was no one on earth but one of those new English people who had moved on the land that cornered with ours on the northwest. She had ridden over the roads, and been at our meeting house. There could be no mistake.

And neither father nor mother would want her on our place. They didn't like her family at all. Mother called them the neighbourhood mystery, and father spoke of them as the Infidels. They had dropped from nowhere, mother said, bought that splendid big farm, moved on and shut out every one. Before any one knew people were shut out, mother, dressed in her finest, with Laddie driving, went in the carriage, all shining, to make friends with them. This very girl opened the door and said that her mother was "indisposed," and could not see callers. "In-dis-posed!" That's a good word that fills your mouth, but our mother didn't like having it used to her. She said the "saucy chit" was insulting. Then the man came, and he said he was very sorry, but his wife would see no one. He did invite mother in, but she wouldn't go. She told us she could see past him into the house and there was such finery as never in all her days had she laid eyes on. She said he was mannerly as could be, but he had the coldest, severest face she ever saw.

They had two men and a woman servant, and no one could coax a word from them, about why those people acted as they did. They said 'orse, and 'ouse, and Hengland. They talked so funny you couldn't have understood them anyway. They never plowed or put in a crop. They made everything into a meadow and had more horses, cattle, and sheep than a county fair, and everything you ever knew with feathers, even peacocks. We could hear them scream whenever it was going to rain. Father said they sounded heathenish. I rather liked them. The man had stacks of money or they couldn't have lived the way they did. He came to our house twice on business: once to see about road laws, and again about tax rates. Father was mightily pleased at first, because Mr. Pryor seemed to have books, and to know everything, and father thought it would be fine to be neighbours. But the minute Mr. Pryor finished business he began to argue that every single thing father and mother believed was wrong. He said right out in plain English that God was a myth. Father told him pretty quickly that no man could say that in his house; so he left suddenly and had not been back since, and father didn't want him ever to come again.

Then their neighbours often saw the woman around the house and garden. She looked and acted quite as well as any one, so probably she was not half so sick as my mother, who had nursed three of us through typhoid fever, and then had it herself when she was all tired out. She wouldn't let a soul know she had a pain until she dropped over and couldn't take another step, and father or Laddie carried her to bed. But she went everywhere, saw all her friends, and did more good from her bed than any other woman in our neighbourhood could on her feet. So we thought mighty little of those Pryor people.

Every one said the girl was pretty. Then her clothes drove the other women crazy. Some of our neighbourhood came from far down east, like my mother. Our people back a little were from over the sea, and they knew how things should be, to be right. Many of the others were from Kentucky and Virginia, and they were well dressed, proud, handsome women; none better looking anywhere. They followed the fashions and spent much time and money on their clothes. When it was Quarterly Meeting or the Bishop dedicated the church or they went to town on court days, you should have seen them—until Pryors came. Then something new happened, and not a woman in our neighbourhood liked it. Pamela Pryor didn't follow the fashions. She set them. If every other woman made long tight sleeves to their wrists, she let hers flow to the elbow and filled them with silk lining, ruffled with lace. If they wore high neckbands, she had none, and used a flat lace collar. If they cut their waists straight around and gathered their skirts on six yards full, she ran hers down to a little point front and back, that made her look slenderer, and put only half as much goods in her skirt. Maybe Laddie rode as well as she could; he couldn't manage a horse any better, and aside from him there wasn't a man we knew who would have tried to ride some of the animals she did.

If she ever worked a stroke, no one knew it. All day long she sat in the parlour, the very best one, every day; or on benches under the trees with embroidery frames or books, some of them fearful, big, difficult looking ones, or rode over the country. She rode in sunshine and she rode in storm, until you would think she couldn't see her way through her tangled black hair. She rode through snow and in pouring rain, when she could have stayed out of it, if she had wanted to. She didn't seem to be afraid of anything on earth or in Heaven. Every one thought she was like her father and didn't believe there was any God; so when she came among us at church or any public gathering, as she some-times did, people were in no hurry to be friendly, while she looked straight ahead and never spoke until she was spoken to, and then she was precise and cold, I tell you.

Men took off their hats, got out of the road when she came pounding along, and stared after her like "be-addled mummies," my mother said. But that was all she, or any one else, could say. The young fellows were wild about her, and if they tried to sidle up to her in the hope that they might lead her horse or get to hold her foot when she mounted, they always saw when they reached her, that she wasn't there.

But she was here! I had seen her only a few times, but this was the Pryor girl, just as sure as I would have known if it had been Sally. What dazed me was that she answered in every particular the description Laddie had given me of the Queen's daughter. And worst of all, from the day she first came among us, moving so proud and cold, blabbing old Hannah Dover said she carried herself like a Princess—as if Hannah Dover knew *how* a Princess carried herself!—every living soul, my father even, had called her the Princess. At first it was because she was like they thought a Princess would be, but later they did it in meanness, to make fun. After they knew her name, they were used to calling her the Princess, so they kept it up, but some of them were secretly proud of her; because she could look, and do, and be what they would have given anything to, and knew they couldn't to save them.

I was never in such a fix in all my life. She looked more as Laddie had said the Princess would than you would have thought any woman could, but she was Pamela Pryor, nevertheless. Every one called her the Princess, but she couldn't make reality out of that. She just couldn't be the Fairy Queen's daughter; so the letter couldn't possibly be for her.

She had no business in our woods; you could see that they had plenty of their own. She went straight to the door of the willow room and walked in as if she belonged there. What if she found the hollow and took Laddie's letter! Fast as I could slip over the leaves, I went back. She was on the moss carpet, on her knees, and the letter was in her fingers. It's a good thing to have your manners soundly thrashed into you. You've got to be scared stiff before you forget them. I wasn't so afraid of her as I would have been if I had known she *was* the Princess, and have Laddie's letter, she should not. What had the kind of girl she was, from a home like hers, to teach any one from our house about making sunshine? I was at the willow wall by that time peering through, so I just parted it a little and said: "Please put back that letter where you got it. It isn't for you."

She knelt on the mosses, the letter in her hand, and her face, as she turned to me, was rather startled; but when she saw me she laughed, and said in the sweetest voice I ever heard: "Are you so very sure of that?"

"Well I ought to be," I said. "I put it there."

"Might I inquire for whom you put it there?"

"No ma'am! That's a secret."

You should have seen the light flame in her eyes, the red deepen on her cheeks, and the little curl of laughter that curved her lips.

"How interesting!" she cried. "I wonder now if you are not Little Sister."

"I am to Laddie and our folks," I said. "You are a stranger."

All the dancing lights went from her face. She looked as if she were going to cry unless she hurried up and swallowed it down hard and fast.

"That is quite true," she said. "I am a stranger. Do you know that being a stranger is the hardest thing that can happen to any one in all this world?"

"Then why don't you open your doors, invite your neighbours in, go to see them, and stop your father from saying such dreadful things?"

"They arc not my doors," she said, "and could you keep your father from saying anything he chooses?"

I stood and blinked at her. Of course I wouldn't even dare try that.

"I'm so sorry," was all I could think to say.

I couldn't ask her to come to our house. I knew no one wanted her. But if I couldn't speak for the others, surely I might for myself. I let go the willows and went to the door. The Princess arose and sat on the seat Laddie had made for the Queen's daughter. It was an awful pity to tell her she shouldn't sit there, for I had my doubts if the real, true Princess would be half as lovely when she came—if she ever did. Some way the Princess, who was not a Princess, appeared so real, I couldn't keep from becoming confused and forgetting that she was only just Pamela Pryor. Already the lovely lights had gone from her face until it made me so sad I wanted to cry, and I was no easy cry-baby either. If I couldn't offer friendship for my family I would for myself.

"You may call me Little Sister, if you like," I said. "I won't be a stranger."

"Why how lovely!" cried the Princess.

You should have seen the dancing lights fly back to her eyes. Probably you won't believe this, but the first thing I knew I was beside her on the throne, her arm was around me, and it's the gospel truth that she hugged me tight. I just had sense enough to reach over and pick Laddie's letter from her fingers, and then I was on her side. I don't know what she did to me, but all at once I knew that she was dreadfully lonely; that she hated being a stranger; that she was sorry enough to cry because their house was one of mystery, and that she would open the door if she could.

"I like you," I said, reaching up to touch her curls.

I never had seen her that I did not want to. They were like I thought they would be. Father and Laddie and some of us had wavy hair, but hers was crisp—and it clung to your fingers, and wrapped around them and seemed to tug at your heart like it does when a baby grips you. I drew away my hand, and the hair stretched out until it was long as any of ours, and then curled up again, and you could see that no tins had stabbed into her head to make those curls. I began trying to single out one hair.

"What are you doing?" she asked.

"I want to know if only one hair is strong enough to draw a drowning man from the water or strangle an unhappy one," I said.

"Believe me, no!" cried the Princess. "It would take all I have, woven into a rope, to do that."

"Laddie knows curls that just one hair of them is strong enough," I boasted.

"I wonder now!" said the Princess. "I think he must have been making poetry or telling Fairy tales."

"He was telling the truth," I assured her. "Father doesn't believe in Fairies, and mother laughs, but Laddie and I know. Do you believe in Fairies?"

"Of course I do!" she said.

"Then you know that this *could* be an Enchanted Wood?"

"I have found it so," said the Princess.

"And *maybe* this is a Magic Carpet?"

"It surely is a Magic Carpet."

"And you *might* be the daughter of the Queen? Your eyes are 'moonlit pools of darkness.' If only your hair were stronger, and you knew about making sunshine!"

"Maybe it is stronger than I think. It never has been tested. Perhaps I do know about making sunshine. Possibly I am as true as the wood and the carpet."

I drew away and stared at her. The longer I looked the more uncertain I became. Maybe her mother was the Queen. Perhaps that was the mystery. It might be the reason she didn't want the people to see her. Maybe she was so busy making sunshine for the Princess to bring to Laddie that she had no time to sew carpet rags, and to go to quiltings, and funerals, and make visits. It was hard to know what to think.

"I wish you'd tell me plain out if you are the Queen's daughter," I said. "It's most important. You can't have this letter unless I *know*. It's the very first time Laddie ever trusted me with a letter, and I just can't give it to the wrong person."

"Then why don't you leave it where he told you?"

"But you have gone and found the place. You started to take it once; you would again, soon as I left."

"Look me straight in the eyes, Little Sister," said the Princess softly. "Am I like a person who would take anything that didn't belong to her?"

"No!" I said instantly.

"How do you think I happened to come to this place?"

"Maybe our woods are prettier than yours."

"How do you think I knew where the letter was?"

I shook my head.

"If I show you some others exactly like the one you have there, then will you believe that is for me?"

"Yes," I answered.

I believed it anyway. It just *seemed* so, the better you knew her. The Princess slipped her hand among the folds of the trailing pale green skirt, and from a hidden pocket drew other letters exactly like the one I held. She opened one and ran her finger along the top line and I read, "To the Princess," and then she pointed to the ending and it was merely signed, "Laddie," but all the words written between were his writing. Slowly I handed her the letter.

"You don't want me to have it?" she asked.

"Yes," I said. "I want you to have it if Laddie wrote it for you—but mother and father won't, not at all."

"What makes you think so?" she asked gently.

"Don't you know what people say about you?"

"Some of it, perhaps."

"Well?"

"Do you think it is true?"

"Not that you're stuck up, and hateful and proud, not that you don't want to be neighbourly with other people, no, I don't think that. But your father said in our home that there was no God, and you wouldn't let my mother in when she put on her best dress and went in the carriage, and wanted to be friends. I have to believe that."

"Yes, you can't help believing that," said the Princess.

"Then can't you see why you'll be likely to show Laddie the way to find trouble, instead of sunshine?"

"I can see," said the Princess.

"Oh Princess, you won't do it, will you?" I cried.

"Don't you think such a big man as Laddie can take care of himself?" she asked, and the dancing lights that had begun to fade came back. "Over there," she pointed through our woods toward the southwest, "lives a man you know. What do his neighbours call him?"

"Stiff-necked Johnny," I answered promptly.

"And the man who lives next him?"

"Pinch-fist Williams."

Her finger veered to another neighbour's.

"The girls of that house?"

"Giggle-head Smithsons."

"What about the man who lives over there?"

"He beats his wife."

"And the house beyond?"

"Mother whispers about them. I don't know."

"And the woman on the hill?"

"She doesn't do anything but gossip and make every one trouble."

"Exactly!" said the Princess. "Yet most of these people come to your house, and your family goes to theirs. Do you suppose people they know nothing about are so much worse than these others?"

"If your father will take it back about God, and your mother will let people in—my mother and father both wanted to be friends, you know."

"That I can't possibly do," she said, "but maybe I could change their feelings toward me."

"Do it!" I cried. "Oh, I'd just love you to do it! I wish you would come to our house and be friends. Sally is pretty as you are, only a different way, and I know she'd like you, and so would Shelley. If Laddie writes you letters and comes here about sunshine, of course he'd be delighted if mother knew you; because she loves him best of any of us. She depends on him most as much as father."

"Then will you keep the secret until I have time to try—say until this time next year?"

"I'll keep it just as long as Laddie wants me to."

"Good!" said the Princess. "No wonder Laddie thinks you the finest Little Sister any one ever had."

"Does Laddie think that?" I asked.

"He does indeed!" said the Princess.

"Then I'm not afraid to go home," I said. "And I'll bring his letter the next time he can't come."

"Were you scared this time?"

I told her about that Something in the dry bed, the wolves, wildcats, Paddy Ryan, and the Gypsies.

"You little goosie," said the Princess. "I am afraid that brother Leon of yours is the biggest rogue loose in this part of the country. Didn't it ever occur to you that people named Wolfe live over there, and they call that crowd next us 'wildcats,' because they just went on some land and took it, and began living there without any more permission than real wildcats ask to enter the woods? Do you suppose I would be here, and everywhere else I want to go, if there were any danger? Did anything really harm you coming?"

"You're harmed when you're scared until you can't breathe," I said. "Anyway, nothing could get me coming, because I held the letter tight in my hand, like Laddie said. If you'd write me one to take back, I'd be safe going home."

"I see," said the Princess. "But I've no pencil, and no paper, unless I use the back of one of Laddie's letters, and that wouldn't be polite."

"You can make new fashions," I said, "but you don't know much about the woods, do you? I could fix fifty ways to send a message to Laddie."

"How would you?" asked the Princess.

Running to the pawpaw bushes I pulled some big tender leaves. Then I took the bark from the box and laid a leaf on it.

"Press with one of your rings," I said, "and print what you want to say. I write to the Fairies every day that way, only I use an old knife handle."

She tried. She spoiled two or three by bearing down so hard she cut the leaves. She didn't even know enough to write on the frosty side, until she was told. But pretty soon she got along so well she printed all over two big ones. Then I took a stick and punched little holes and stuck a piece of foxfire bloom through.

"What makes you do that?" she asked.

"That's the stamp," I explained.

"But it's my letter, and I didn't put it there."

"Has to be there or the Fairies won't like it," I said.

"Well then, let it go," said the Princess.

I put back the bark and replaced the stone, gathered up the scattered leaves, and put the two with writing on between fresh ones.

"Now I must run," I said, "or Laddie will think the Gypsies have got me sure."

"I'll go with you past the dry creek," she offered.

"You better not," I said. "I'd love to have you, but it would be best for you to change their opinion, before father or mother sees you on their land."

"Perhaps it would," said the Princess. "I'll wait here until you reach the fence and then you call and I'll know you are in the open and feel comfortable."

"I am most all over being afraid now," I told her.

Just to show her, I walked to the creek, climbed the gate and went down the lane. Almost to the road I began wondering what I could do with the letter, when looking ahead I saw Laddie coming.

"I was just starting to find you. You've been an age, child," he said.

I held up the letter.

"No one is looking," I said, "and this won't go in your pocket."

You should have seen his face.

"Where did you get it?" he asked.

I told him all about it. I told him everything—about the hair that maybe was stronger than she thought, and that she was going to change father's and mother's opinions, and that I put the red flower on, but she left it; and when I was done Laddie almost hugged the life out of me. I never did see him so happy.

"If you be very, very careful never to breathe a whisper, I'll take you with me some day," he promised.

CHAPTER II

Our Angel Boy

"I had a brother once—a gracious boy,
   Full of all gentleness, of calmest hope,
   Of sweet and quiet joy,—there was the look
Of heaven upon his face."

IT WAS supper time when we reached home, and Bobby was at the front gate to meet me. He always hunted me all over the place when the big bell in the yard rang at meal time, because if he crowed nicely when he was told, he was allowed to stand on the back of my chair and every little while I held up my plate and shared bites with him. I have seen many white bantams, but never another like Bobby. My big brothers bought him for me in Fort Wayne, and sent him in a box, alone on the cars. Father and I drove to Groveville to meet him. The minute father pried off the lid, Bobby hopped on the edge of the box and crowed— the biggest crow you ever heard from such a mite of a body; he wasn't in the least afraid of us and we were pleased about it. You scarcely could see his beady black eyes for his bushy topknot, his wing tips touched the ground, his tail had two beautiful plumy feathers much longer than the others, his feet were covered with feathers, and his knee tufts dragged. He was the sauciest, spunkiest little fellow, and white as muslin. We went to supper together, but no one asked where I had been, and because I was so bursting full of importance, I talked only to Bobby, in order to be safe.

After supper I finished Hezekiah's trousers, and May cut his coat for me. School would begin in September and our clothes were being made, so I used the scraps to dress him. His suit was done by the next forenoon, and father never laughed harder than when Hezekiah hopped down the walk to meet him dressed in pink trousers and coat. The coat had flowing sleeves like the Princess wore, so Hezekiah could fly, and he seemed to like them. His suit was such a success I began a sunbonnet, and when that was tied on him, the folks almost had spasms. They said he wouldn't like being dressed; that he would fly away to punish me, but he did no such thing. He stayed around the house and was tame as ever.

When I became tired sewing that afternoon, I went down the lane leading to our meadow, where Leon was killing thistles with a grubbing hoe. I thought he would be glad to see me, and he was. Every one had been busy in the house, so I went to the cellar the outside way and ate all I wanted from the cupboard. Then I spread two big slices of bread the best I could with my fingers, putting apple butter on one, and mashed potatoes on the other. Leon leaned on the hoe and watched me coming. He was a hungry boy, and lonesome too, but he couldn't be forced to say so.

"Laddie is at work in the barn," he said.

"I'm going to play in the creek," I answered.

Crossing our meadow there was a stream that had grassy banks, big trees, willows, bushes and vines for shade, a solid pebbly bed; it was all turns and bends so that the water hurried until it bubbled and sang as it went; in it lived tiny fish coloured brightly as flowers, beside it ran killdeer, plover and solemn blue herons almost as tall as I was came from the river to fish; for a place to play on an August afternoon, it couldn't be beaten. The sheep had been put in the lower pasture; so the cross old Shropshire ram was not there to bother us.

"Come to the shade," I said to Leon, and when we were comfortably seated under a big maple weighted down with trailing grapevines, I offered the bread. Leon took a piece in each hand and began to eat as if he were starving. Laddie would have kissed me and said: "What a fine treat! Thank you, Little Sister."

Leon was different. He ate so greedily you had to know he was glad to get it, but he wouldn't say so, not if he never got any more. When you knew him, you understood he wouldn't forget it, and he'd be certain to do something nice for you before the day was over to pay back. We sat there talking about everything we saw, and at last Leon said with a grin: "Shelley isn't getting much grape sap is she?"

"I didn't know she wanted grape sap."

"She read about it in a paper. It said to cut the vine of a wild grape, catch the drippings and moisten your hair. This would make it glossy and grow faster."

"What on earth does Shelley want with more hair than she has?"

"Oh, she has heard it bragged on so much she thinks people would say more if she could improve it."

I looked and there was the vine, dry as could be, and a milk crock beneath it.

"Didn't the silly know she had to cut the vine in the spring when the sap was running?"

"Bear witness, O vine! that she did not," said Leon, "and speak, ye voiceless pottery, and testify that she expected to find you overflowing."

"Too bad that she's going to be disappointed."

"She isn't! She's going to find ample liquid to bathe her streaming tresses. Keep quiet and watch me."

He picked up the crock, carried it to the creek and dipped it full of water.

"That's too much," I objected. "She'll know she never got a crock full from a dry vine."

"She'll think the vine bled itself dry for her sake."

"She isn't that silly."

"Well then, how silly is she?" asked Leon, spilling out half. "About so?"

"Not so bad as that. Less yet!"

"Anything to please the ladies," said Leon, pouring out more. Then we sat and giggled a while.

"What are you going to do now?" asked Leon.

"Play in the creek," I answered.

"All right! I'll work near you."

He rolled his trousers above his knees and took the hoe, but he was in the water most of the time. We had to climb on the bank when we came to the deep curve, under the stump of the old oak that father cut because Pete Billings would climb it and yowl like a wildcat on cold winter nights. Pete was wrong in his head like Paddy Ryan, only worse. As we passed we heard the faintest sounds, so we lay and looked, and there in the dark place under the roots, where the water was deepest, huddled some of the cunningest little downy wild ducks you ever saw. We looked at each other and never said a word. Leon chased them out with the hoe and they swam down stream faster than old ones. I stood in the shallow water behind them and kept them from going back to the deep place, while Leon worked to catch them. Every time he got one he brought it to me, and I made a bag of my apron front to put them in. The supper bell rang before we caught all of them. We were dripping wet with creek water and perspiration, but we had the ducks, every one of them, and proudly started home. I'll wager Leon was sorry he didn't wear aprons so he could carry them. He did keep the last one in his hands, and held its little fluffy body against his cheeks every few minutes.

"Couldn't anything be prettier than a young duck."

"Except a little guinea," I said.

"That's so!" said Leon. "They are most as pretty as quail. I guess all young things that have down are about as cunning as they can be. I don't believe I know which I like best, myself."

"Baby killdeers."

"I mean tame. Things we raise."

"I'll take guineas."

"I'll say white turkeys. They seem so innocent. Nothing of ours is pretty as these."

"But these are wild."

"So they are," said Leon. "Twelve of them. Won't mother be pleased?"

She was not in the least. She said we were a sight to behold; that she was ashamed to be the mother of two children who didn't know tame ducks from wild ones. She remembered instantly that Amanda Deam had set a speckled Dorking hen on Mallard duck eggs, where she got the eggs, and what she paid for them. She said the ducks had found the creek that flowed beside Deams' barnyard before it entered our land, and they had swum away from the hen, and both the hen and Amanda would be frantic. She put the ducks into a basket and said to take them back soon as ever we got our suppers, and we must hurry because we had to bathe and learn our texts for Sunday-school in the morning.

We went through the orchard, down the hill and across the meadow until we came to the creek. By that time we were tired of the basket. It was one father had woven himself of shaved and soaked hickory strips, and it was heavy. The sight of water suggested the proper place for ducks, anyway. We talked it over and decided that they would be much more comfortable swimming than in the basket, and it was more fun to wade than to walk, so we went above the deep place, I stood in the creek to to keep them from going down, and Leon poured them on the water. Pigs couldn't have acted more contrary. Those ducks *liked* us. They wouldn't go to Deams'. They just fought to swim back to us. Anyway, we had the worst time you ever saw. Leon cut long switches to herd them with, and both of us waded and tried to drive them, but they would dart under embankments and roots, and dive and hide.

Before we reached the Deams' I wished that we had carried them as mother told us, for we had lost three, and if we stopped to hunt them, more would hide. By the time we drove them under the floodgate crossing the creek between our land and the Deams' four were gone. Leon left me on the gate with both switches to keep them from going back and he ran to call Mrs. Deam. She had red hair and a hot temper, and we were not very anxious to see her, but we had to do it. While Leon was gone I was thinking pretty fast and I knew exactly how things would happen. First time mother saw Mrs. Deam she would ask her if the ducks were all right, and she would tell that four were gone. Mother would ask how many she had, and she would say twelve, then mother

would remember that she started us with twelve in the basket
—Oh what's the use! Something had to be done. It had to be
done quickly too, for I could hear Amanda Deam, her boy Sammy
and Leon coming across the barnyard. I looked around in despair,
but when things are the very worst, there is almost always some
way out.

On the dry straw worked between and pushing against the
panels of the floodgate, not far from me, I saw a big black water
snake. I took one good look at it: no coppery head, no geometry
patterns, no rattlebox, so I knew it wasn't poisonous and wouldn't
bite until it was hurt, and if it did, all you had to do was to suck
the place, and it wouldn't amount to more than two little pricks
as if pins had stuck you; but a big snake was a good excuse. I
rolled from the floodgate among the ducks, and cried, "Snake!"
They scattered everywhere. The snake lazily uncoiled and slid
across the straw so slowly that—thank goodness! Amanda Deam
got a fair look at it. She immediately began to jump up and down
and scream. Leon grabbed a stick and came running to the water.
I cried so he had to help me out first.

"Don't let her count them!" I whispered.

Leon gave me one swift look and all the mischief in his blue
eyes peeped out. He was the funniest boy you ever knew, anyway.
Mostly he looked scowly and abused. He had a grievance against
everybody and everything. He said none of us liked him, and we
imposed on him. Father said that if he tanned Leon's jacket for
anything, and set him down to think it over, he would pout a
while, then he would look thoughtful, suddenly his face would
light up and he would go away sparkling; and you could depend
upon it he would do the same thing over, or something worse,
inside an hour. When he wanted to, he could smile the most winning smile, and he could coax you into anything. Mother said she
dreaded to have to borrow a dime from him, if a peddler caught
her without change, because she knew she'd be kept paying it
back for the next six months. Right now he was the busiest kind
of a boy.

"Where is it? Let me get a good lick at it! Don't scare the ducks!" he would cry, and chase them from one bank to the other, while Amanda danced and fought imaginary snakes. For a woman who had seen as many as she must have in her life, it was too funny. I don't think I could laugh harder, or Leon and Sammy. We enjoyed ourselves so much that at last she began to be angry. She quit dancing, and commenced hunting ducks, for sure. She held her skirts high, poked along the banks, jumped the creek and didn't always get clear across. Her hair shook down, she lost a sidecomb, and she couldn't find half the ducks.

"You younguns pack right out of here," she said. "Me and Sammy can get them better ourselves, and if we don't find all of them, we'll know where they are."

"We haven't got any of your ducks," I said angrily, but Leon smiled his most angelic smile, and it seemed as if he were going to cry.

"Of course, if you want to accuse mother of stealing your ducks, you can," he said plaintively, "but I should think you'd be ashamed to do it, after all the trouble we took to catch them before they swam to the river, where you never would have found one of them. Come on, Little Sister, let's go home."

He started and I followed. As soon as we got around the bend we sat on the bank, hung our feet in the water, leaned against each other and laughed. We just laughed ourselves almost sick. When Amanda's face got fire red, and her hair came down, and she jumped and didn't go quite over, she looked a perfect fright.

"Will she ever find all of them?" I asked at last.

"Of course," said Leon. "She will comb the grass and strain the water until she gets every one."

"Hoo-hoo!"

I looked at Leon. He was so intently watching an old turkey buzzard hanging in the air, he never heard the call that meant it was time for us to be home and cleaning up for Sunday. It was difficult to hurry, for after we had been soaped and scoured, we had to sit on the back steps and commit to memory verses from the Bible. At last we waded toward home. Two of the ducks we had lost swam before us all the way, so we knew they were alive, and all they needed was finding.

"If she hadn't accused mother of stealing her old ducks, I'd catch those and carry them back to her," said Leon. "But since she thinks we are so mean, I'll just let her and little Sammy find them."

Then we heard their voices as they came down the creek, so Leon reached me his hand and we scampered across the water and meadow, never stopping until we sat on the top rail of our back orchard fence. There we heard another call, but that was only two. We sat there, rested and looked at the green apples above our heads, wishing they were ripe, and talking about the ducks. We could see Mrs. Deam and Sammy coming down the creek, one on each side. We slid from the fence and ran into a queer hollow that was cut into the hill between the never-fail and the Baldwin apple trees. That hollow was overgrown with weeds, and full of trimmings from trees, stumps, everything that no one wanted any place else in the orchard. It was the only unkept spot on our land, and I always wondered why father didn't clean it out and make it look respectable. I said so to Leon as we crouched there watching down the hill where Mrs. Deam and Sammy hunted ducks with not such very grand success. They seemed to have so many they couldn't decide whether to go back or go on, so they must have found most of them.

"You know I've always had my suspicions about this place," said Leon. "There is somewhere on our land that people can be hidden for a long time. I can remember well enough before the war ever so long, and while it was going worst, we would find the wagon covered with more mud in the morning than had been on it at night; and the horses would be splashed and tired. Once I was awake in the night and heard voices. It made me want a drink, so I went downstairs for it, and ran right into the biggest, blackest man who ever grew. If father and mother hadn't been there I'd have been scared into fits. Next morning he was gone and there wasn't a whisper. Father said I'd had bad dreams. That night the horses made another mysterious trip. Now where did they keep the black man all that day?"

"What did they have a black man for?"

"They were helping him run away from slavery to be free in Canada. It was all right. I'd have done the same thing. They helped a lot. Father was a friend of the Governor. There were letters from him, and there was some good reason why father stayed at home, when he was crazy about the war. I think this farm was what they called an Underground Station. What I want to know is where the station was."

"Maybe it's here. Let's hunt," I said. "If the black men were here some time, they would have to be fed, and this is not far from the house."

So we took long sticks and began poking into the weeds. Then we moved the brush, and sure as you live, we found an old door with a big stone against it. I looked at Leon and he looked at me.

"Hoo-hoo!" came mother's voice, and that was the third call.

"Hum! Must be for us," said Leon. "We better go as soon as we get a little dryer."

He slid down the bank on one side, and I on the other, and we pushed at the stone. I thought we never would get it rolled away so we could open the door a crack, but when we did what we saw was most surprising. There was a little room, dreadfully small, but a room. There was straw scattered over the floor, very deep on one side, where an old blanket showed that it had been a bed. Across the end there was a shelf. On it was a candlestick, with a half-burned candle in it, a pie pan with some mouldy crumbs, crusts, bones in it, and a tin can. Leon picked up the can and looked in. I could see too.

It had been used for water or coffee, as the plate had for food, once, but now it was stuffed full of money. I saw Leon pull some out and then shove it back, and he came to the door white as could be, shut it behind him and began to push at the stone. When we got it in place we put the brush over it, and fixed everything like it had been.

At last Leon said: "That's the time we got into something not intended for us, and if father finds it out, we are in for a good thrashing. Are you just a blubbering baby, or are you big enough to keep still?"

"I am old enough that I could have gone to school two years ago, and I won't tell!" I said stoutly.

"All right! Come on then," said Leon. "I don't know but mother has been calling us."

We started up the orchard path at the fourth call.

"Hoo-hoo!" answered Leon in a sick little voice to make it sound far away. Must have made mother think we were on Deams' hill. Then we went on side by side.

"Say Leon, you found the Station, didn't you?"

"Don't talk about it!" snapped Leon.

I changed the subject.

"Whose money do you suppose that is?"

"Oh crackey! You can depend on a girl to see everything," groaned Leon. "Do you think you'll be able to stand the switching that job will bring you, without getting sick in bed?"

Now I never had been sick in bed, and from what I had seen of other people who were, I never wanted to be. The idea of being switched until it made me sick was too much for me. I shut my mouth tight and I never opened it about the Station place. As we reached the maiden's-blush apple tree came another call, and it sounded pretty cross, I can tell you. Leon reached his hand.

"Now, it's time to run. Let me do the talking."

We were out of breath when we reached the back door. There stood the tub on the kitchen floor, the boiler on the stove, soap, towels, and clean clothing on chairs. Leon had his turn at having his ears washed first, because he could bathe himself while mother did my hair.

"Was Mrs. Deam glad to get her ducks back?" she asked as she fine-combed Leon.

"Aw, you never can tell whether she's glad about anything or not," growled Leon. "You'd have thought from the way she acted, that we'd been trying to steal her ducks. She said if she missed any she'd know where to find them."

"Well as I live!" cried mother. "Why I wouldn't have believed that of Amanda Deam. You told her you thought they were wild, of course."

"I didn't have a chance to tell her anything. The minute the ducks struck the water they started right back down stream, and there was a big snake, and we had an awful time. We got wet trying to head them back, and then we didn't find all of them."

"They are like little eels. You should have helped Amanda."

"Well, you called so cross we thought you would come after us, so we had to run."

"One never knows," sighed mother. "I thought you were loitering. Of course if I had known you were having trouble with the ducks! I think you had better go back and help them."

"Didn't I do enough to take them home? Can't Sammy Deam catch ducks as fast as I can?"

"I suppose so," said mother. "And I must get your bathing out of the way of supper. You use the tub while I do Little Sister's hair."

I almost hated Sunday, because of what had to be done to my hair on Saturday, to get ready for it. All week it hung in two long braids that were brushed and arranged each morning. But on Saturday it had to be combed with a fine comb, oiled and rolled around strips of tin until Sunday morning. Mother did everything thoroughly. She raked that fine comb over our scalps until she almost raised the blood. She hadn't time to fool with tangles, and we had so much hair she didn't know what to do with all of it, anyway. When she was busy talking she reached around too far and combed across our foreheads or raked the tip of an ear.

But on Sunday morning we forgot all that, when we walked down the aisle with shining curls hanging below our waists. Mother was using the fine comb, when she looked up, and there stood Mrs. Freshett. We could see at a glance that she was out of breath.

"Have I beat them?" she cried.

"Whom are you trying to beat?" asked mother as she told May to set a chair for Mrs. Freshett and bring her a drink.

"The grave-kiver men," she said. "I wanted to get to you first."

"Well, you have," said mother. "Rest a while and then tell me."

But Mrs. Freshett was so excited she couldn't rest.

"I thought they were coming straight on down," she said, "but they must have turned off at the cross roads. I want to do what's right by my children here or there," panted Mrs. Freshett, "and these men seemed to think the contrivance they was sellin' perfectly grand, an' like to be an aid to the soul's salvation. Nice as it seemed, an' convincin' as they talked, I couldn't get the consent of my mind to order, until I knowed if you was goin' to kiver your dead with the contraption. None of the rest of the neighbours seem over friendly to me, an' I've told Josiah many's the time, that I didn't care a rap if they wa'n't, so long as I had you. Says I, 'Josiah, to my way of thinkin', she is top crust in this neighbourhood, and I'm on the safe side apin' her ways clost as possible.' "

"I'll gladly help you all I can," said my mother.

"Thanky!" said Mrs. Freshett. "I knowed you would. Josiah he says to me, 'Don't you be apin' nobody.' 'Josiah,' says I, 'it takes a pretty smart woman in this world to realize what she doesn't know. Now I know what I know, well enough, but all I know is like to keep me an' my children in a log cabin an' on log cabin ways to the end of our time. You ain't even got the remains of the cabin you started in for a cow shed.' Says I, 'Josiah, Miss Stanton knows how to get out of a cabin an' into a grand big palace, fit fur a queen woman. She's a ridin' in a shinin' kerridge, 'stid of a spring wagon. She goes abroad dressed so's you men all stand starin' like cabbage heads. All hern go to church, an' Sunday-school, an' college, an' come out on the top of the heap. She does jest what I'd like to if I knowed how. An' she ain't come-uppety one morsel.' If I was to strike acrost fields to them stuck-up Pryors, I'd get the door slammed in my face if 'twas the missus, a sneer if 'twas the man, an' at best a nod cold as an iceberg if 'twas the girl. Them as want to call her kind

'Princess,' and encourage her in being more stuck up 'an she was born to be, can, but to my mind a Princess is a person who thinks of some one besides herself once in a while."

"I don't find the Pryors easy to become acquainted with," said mother. "I have never met the woman; I know the man very slightly; he has been here on business once or twice, but the girl seems as if she would be nice, if one knew her."

"Well, I wouldn't have s'posed she was your kind," said Mrs. Freshett. "If she is, I won't open my head against her any more. Anyway, it was the grave-kivers I come about."

"Just what is it, Mrs. Freshett?" asked mother.

"It's two men sellin' a patent iron kiver for to protect the graves of your dead from the sun an' the rain."

"Who wants the graves of their dead protected from the sun and the rain?" demanded my mother sharply.

"I said to Josiah, 'I don't know how she'll feel about it, but I can't do more than ask.' "

"Do they carry a sample? What is it like?"

"Jest the len'th an' width of a grave. They got from baby to six-footer sizes. They are cast iron like the bottom of a cook stove on the under side, but atop they are polished so they shine somethin' beautiful. You can get them in a solid piece, or with a hole in the centre about the size of a milk crock to set flowers through. They come ten to the grave, an' they are mighty stylish lookin' things. I have been savin' all I could skimp from butter, an' eggs, to get Samantha a organ; but says I to her: 'You are gettin' all I can do for you every day; there lays your poor brother 'at ain't had a finger lifted for him since he was took so sudden he was gone before I knowed he was goin'.' I never can get over Henry bein' took the way he was, so I says: 'If this would be a nice thing to have for Henry's grave, and the neighbours are goin' to have them for theirn, looks to me like some of the organ money will have to go, an' we'll make it up later.' I don't 'low for Henry to be slighted bekase he rid himself to death trying to make a president out of his pa's gin'ral."

"You never told me how you lost your son," said mother, feeling so badly she wiped one of my eyes full of oil.

"Law now, didn't I?" inquired Mrs. Freshett. "Well mebby that is bekase I ain't had a chance to tell you much of anythin', your bein' always so busy like, an' me not wantin' to wear out my welcome. It was like this: All endurin' the war Henry an' me did the best we could without pa at home, but by the time it was over, Henry was most a man. Seemed as if when he got home, his pa was all tired out and glad to set down an' rest, but Henry was afire to be up an' goin'. His pa filled him so full o' Grant, it was runnin' out of his ears. Come the second run the Gin'ral made, peered like Henry set out to 'lect him all by hisself. He wore every horse on the place out, ridin' to rallies. Sometimes he was gone three days at a stretch. He'd git one place an' hear of a rally on ten miles or so furder, an' blest if he didn't ride plum acrost the state 'fore he got through with one trip. He set out in July, and he rid right straight through to November, nigh onto every day of his life. He got white, an' thin, an' narvous, from loss of sleep an' lack of food, an' his pa got restless, said Henry was takin' the 'lection more serious 'an he ever took the war. Last few days before votin' was cold an' raw an' Henry rid constant. 'Lection day he couldn't vote, for he lacked a year of bein' o' age, an' he rid in with a hard chill, an' white as a ghost, an' he says: 'Ma,' says he, 'I've 'lected Grant, but I'm all tuckered out. Put me to bed an' kiver me warm.' "

I forgot the sting in my eyes watching Mrs. Freshett. She was the largest woman I knew, and strong as most men. Her hair was black and glisteny, her eyes black, her cheeks red, her skin a clear, even dark tint. She was handsome, she was honest, and she was in earnest over everything. There was something about her, or her family, that had to be told in whispers, and some of the neighbours would have nothing to do with her. But mother said Mrs. Freshett was doing the very best she knew, and for the sake of that, and of her children, anyone who wouldn't help her was not a Christian, and not to be a Christian was the very worst thing that could happen to you. I stared at her steadily. She talked straight along, so rapidly you scarcely could keep up with the words; you couldn't if you wanted to think about them any between. There was not a quiver in her voice, but from her eyes there rolled, steadily, the biggest, roundest tears I ever saw. They ran down her cheeks, formed a stream in the first groove of her double chin, overflowed it, and dripped drop, drop, a drop at a time, on the breast of her stiffly starched calico dress, and from there shot to her knees.

" 'Twa'n't no time at all 'til he was chokin' an' burnin' red with fever, an' his pa and me, stout as we be, couldn't hold him down nor keep him kivered. He was speechifyin' to beat anythin' you ever heard. His pa said he was repeatin' what he'd heard said by every big stump speaker from Greeley to Logan. When he got so hoarse we couldn't tell what he said any more, he jest mouthed it, an' at last he dropped back and laid like he was pinned to the sheets, an' I thought he was restin', but 'twa'n't an hour 'til he was gone."

Suddenly Mrs. Freshett lifted her apron, covered her face and sobbed until her broad shoulders shook.

"Oh you poor soul!" said my mother. "I'm so sorry for you!"

"I never knowed he was a-goin' until he was gone," she said. "He was the only one of mine I ever lost, an' I thought it would jest lay me out. I couldn't 'a' stood it at all if I hadn't 'a' knowed he was saved. I well know my Henry went straight to Heaven. Why Miss Stanton, he riz right up in bed at the last, and clear and strong he jest yelled it: 'Hurrah fur Grant!'"

My mother's fingers tightened in my hair until I thought she would pull out a lot, and I could feel her knees stiffen. Leon just whooped. Mother sprang up and ran to the door.

"Leon!" she cried. Then there was a slam. "What in the world is the matter?" she asked.

"Stepped out of the tub right on the soap, and it threw me down," explained Leon.

"For mercy sake, be careful!" said my mother, and shut the door.

It wasn't a minute before the knob turned and it opened again a little.

I never saw mother's face look so queer, but at last she said softly: "You were thinking of the grave cover for him?"

"Yes, but I wanted to ask you before I bound myself. I heard you lost two when the scarlet fever was ragin' an' I'm goin' to do jest what you do. If you have kivers, I will. If you don't like them when you see how bright and shiny they are, I won't get any either."

"I can tell you without seeing them, Mrs. Freshett," said my mother, wrapping a strand of hair around the tin so tight I slipped up my fingers to feel whether my neck wasn't like a buckeye hull looks, and it was. "I don't want any cover for the graves of my dead but grass and flowers, and sky and clouds. I like the rain to fall on them, and the sun to shine, so that the grass and flowers will grow. If you are satisfied that the soul of Henry is safe in Heaven, that is all that is necessary. Laying a slab of iron on top of earth six feet above his body will make no difference to him. If he is singing with the angels, by all means save your money for the organ."

"I don't know about the singin', but I'd stake my last red cent he's still hollerin' fur Grant. I was kind o' took with the idea; the things was so shiny and scilloped at the edges, peered like it was payin' considerable respect to the dead to kiver them that-a-way."

"What good would it do?" asked mother. "The sun shining on the iron would make it so hot it would burn any flower you tried to plant in the opening; the water couldn't reach the roots, and all that fell on the slab would run off and make it that much wetter at the edges. The iron would soon rust and grow dreadfully ugly lying under winter snow. There is nothing at all in it, save a method to work on the feelings of the living, and get them to pay their money for something that wouldn't affect their dead a particle."

" 'Twould be a poor idea for me," said Mrs. Freshett. "I said to the men that I wanted to honour Henry all I could, but with

my bulk, I'd hev all I could do, come Jedgment Day, to bust my
box, an' heave up the clods, without havin' to hist up a piece of
iron an' klim from under it."

Mother stiffened and Leon slipped again. He could have more
accidents than any boy I ever knew. But it was only a few minutes until he came to mother and gave her a Bible to mark the
verses he had to learn to recite at Sunday-school next day.
Mother couldn't take the time when she had company, so she
asked if he weren't big enough to pick out ten proper verses and
learn them by himself, and he said of course he was. He took his
Bible and he and May and I sat on the back steps and studied
our verses. He and May were so big they had ten; but I had only
two, and mine were not very long. Leon giggled half the time he
was studying. I haven't found anything so very funny in the
Bible. Every few minutes he would whisper to himself: "That's a
good one!"

He took the book and heard May do hers until she had them
perfectly, then he went and sat on the back fence with his book
and studied as I never before had seen him. Mrs. Freshett stayed
so long mother had no time to hear him, but he told her he had
them all learned so he could repeat them without a mistake.

Next morning mother was busy, so she had no time then.
Father, Shelley, and I rode on the front seat, mother, May, and
Sally on the back, while the boys started early and walked.

When we reached the top of the hill, the road was lined with
carriages, wagons, spring wagons, and saddle horses. Father
found a place for our team and we went down the walk between
the hitching rack and the cemetery fence. Mother opened the
gate and knelt beside two small graves covered with grass,
shaded by yellow rose bushes, and marked with little white
stones. She laid some flowers on each and wiped the dust from
the carved letters with her handkerchief. The little sisters who
had scarlet fever and whooping cough lay there. Mother was still
a minute and then she said softly: " 'The Lord has given and the
Lord has taken away. Blessed be the name of the Lord.' "

She was very pale when she came to us, but her eyes were

bright and she smiled as she put her arms around as many of us as she could reach.

"What a beautiful horse!" said Sally. "Look at that saddle and bridle! The Pryor girl is here."

"Why should she come?" asked Shelley.

"To show her fine clothes and queen it over us!"

"Children, children!" said mother. " 'Judge not!' This is a house of worship. The Lord may be drawing her in His own way. It is for us to help Him by being kind and making her welcome."

At the church door we parted and sat with our teachers, but for the first time as I went down the aisle I was not thinking of my linen dress, my patent leather slippers, and my pretty curls. It suddenly seemed cheap to me to twist my hair when it was straight as a shingle, and cut my head on tin. If the Lord had wanted me to have curls, my hair would have been like Sally's. Seemed to me hers tried to see into what big soft curls it could roll. May said ours was so straight it bent back the other way. Anyway, I made up my mind to talk it over with father and always wear braids after that, if I could get him to coax mother to let me.

Our church was quite new and it was beautiful. All the casings were oiled wood, and the walls had just a little yellow in the last skin coating used to make them smooth, so they were a creamy colour, and the blinds were yellow. The windows were wide open and the wind drifted through, while the birds sang as much as they ever do in August, among the trees and bushes of the cemetery. Every one had planted so many flowers of all kinds on the graves you could scent sweet odours. Often a big, black-striped, brown butterfly came sailing in through one of the windows, followed the draft across the room, and out of another. I was thinking something funny: it was about what the Princess had said of other people, and whether hers were worse. I looked at my father sitting in calm dignity in his Sunday suit and thought him quite as fine and handsome as mother did. Every Sabbath he wore the same suit, he sat in the same spot, he worshipped the Lord in his calm, earnest way. The ministers changed, but father was as much a part of the service as the Bible on the desk or the communion table. I wondered if people said things about him, and if they did, what they were. I never had heard. Twisting in my seat, one by one I studied the faces on the men's side, and then the women. It was a mighty good-looking crowd. Some had finer clothes than others—that is always the way—but as a rule every one was clean, neat, and good to see. From some you scarcely could turn away. There was Widow Fall. She was French, from Virginia, and she talked like little tinkly notes of music. I just loved to hear her, and she walked like high-up royalty. Her dress was always black, with white bands at the neck and sleeves, black rustly silk, and her eyes and hair were like the dress. There was a little red on her cheeks and lips, and her face was always grave until she saw you directly before her, and then she smiled the sweetest smile.

Maybe Sarah Hood was not pretty, but there was something about her lean face and shining eyes that made you look twice before you were sure of it, and by that time you had got so used to her, you liked her better as she was, and wouldn't have changed her for anything. Mrs. Fritz had a pretty face and dresses and manners, and so did Hannah Dover, only she talked too much. So I studied them and remembered what the Princess had said, and I wondered if she heard some one say that Peter Justice beat his wife, or if she showed it in her face and manner. She reminded me of a scared cowslip that had been cut and laid in the sun an hour. I don't know as that expresses it. Perhaps a flower couldn't look scared, but it could be wilted and faded. I wondered if she ever had bright hair, laughing eyes, and red in her lips and cheeks. She must have been pretty if she had.

At last I reached my mother. There was nothing scared or faded about her, and she was dreadfully sick too, once in a while since she had the fever. She was a little bit of a woman, coloured like a wild rose petal, face and body—a piece of pink porcelain Dutch, father said. She had brown eyes, hair like silk, and she always had three best dresses. There was one of alpaca or woollen, of black, gray or brown, and two silks. Always there was a fine rustly black one with a bonnet and mantle to match, and then a softer, finer one of either gold brown, like her hair, or dainty gray, like a dove's wing. When these grew too old for fine use, she wore them to Sunday-school and had a fresh one for best. There was a new gray in her closet at home, so she put on the old brown to-day, and she was lovely in it.

Usually the minister didn't come for church services until Sunday-school was half over, so the superintendent read a chapter, Daddy Debs prayed, and all of us stood up and sang: "Ring Out the Joy Bells." Then the superintendent read the lesson over as impressively as he could. The secretary made his report, we sang another song, gathered the pennies, and each teacher took a class and talked over the lesson a few minutes. Then we repeated the verses we had committed to memory to our teachers; the member of each class who had learned the nicest texts, and knew them best, was selected to recite before the school. Beginning with the littlest people, we came to the big folks. Each one recited two texts until they reached the class above mine. We walked to the front, stood inside the altar, made a little bow, and the superintendent kept score. I could see that mother appeared worried when Leon's name was called for his class, for she hadn't heard him, and she was afraid he would forget.

Among the funny things about Leon was this: while you had to drive other boys of his age to recite, you almost had to hold him to keep him from it. Father said he was born for a politician or a preacher, if he would be good, and grow into the right kind of a man to do such responsible work.

"I forgot several last Sabbath, so I have thirteen to-day," he said politely.

Of course no one expected anything like that. You never knew what might happen when Leon did anything. He must have been about sixteen. He was a slender lad, having almost sandy hair, like his English grandfather. He wore a white ruffled shirt with a broad collar, and cuffs turning back over his black jacket, and his trousers fitted his slight legs closely. The wind whipped his soft black tie a little and ruffled the light hair where it was longest and wavy above his forehead. Such a perfect picture of innocence you never saw. There was one part of him that couldn't be described any better than the way Mr. Rienzi told about his brother in his "Address to the Romans," in McGuffey's Sixth. "The look of heaven on his face" stayed most of the time; again, there was a dealish twinkle that sparkled and flashed while he was thinking up something mischievous to do. When he was fighting angry, and going to thrash Absalom Saunders or die trying, he was plain white and his eyes were like steel. Mother called him "Weiscope," half the time. I can only spell the way that sounds, but it means "white-head," and she always used that name when she loved him most. "The look of heaven" was strong on his face now.

"One," said the recording secretary.

"Jesus wept," answered Leon promptly.

There was not a sound in the church. You could almost hear the butterflies pass. Father looked down and laid his lower lip in folds with his fingers, like he did sometimes when it wouldn't behave to suit him.

"Two," said the secretary after just a breath of pause.

Leon looked over the congregation easily and then fastened his eyes on Abram Saunders, the father of Absalom, and said reprovingly: "Give not sleep to thine eyes nor slumber to thine eyelids."

Abram straightened up suddenly and blinked in astonishment, while father held fast to his lip.

"Three," called the secretary hurriedly.

Leon shifted his gaze to Betsy Alton, who hadn't spoken to her next door neighbour in five years.

"Hatred stirreth up strife," he told her softly, "but love covereth all sins."

Things were so quiet it seemed as if the air would snap.

"Four."

The mild blue eyes travelled back to the men's side and settled on Isaac Thomas, a man too lazy to plow and sow land his father had left him. They were not so mild, and the voice was touched with command: "Go to the ant, thou sluggard, consider her ways and be wise."

Still that silence.

"Five," said the secretary hurriedly, as if he wished it were over. Back came the eyes to the women's side and past all question looked straight at Hannah Dover.

"As a jewel of gold in a swine's snout, so is a fair woman without discretion."

"Six," said the secretary and looked appealingly at father, whose face was filled with dismay.

Again Leon's eyes crossed the aisle and he looked directly at the man whom everybody in the community called "Stiff-necked Johnny." I think he was rather proud of it, he worked so hard to keep them doing it.

"Lift not up your horn on high: speak not with a stiff neck," Leon commanded him.

Toward the door some one tittered.

"Seven," called the secretary hastily.

Leon glanced around the room.

"But how good and how pleasant it is for brethren to dwell together in unity," he announced in delighted tones as if he had found it out by himself.

"Eight," called the secretary with something like a breath of relief.

Our angel boy never had looked so angelic, and he was beaming on the Princess.

"Thou art all fair, my love; there is no spot in thee," he told her.

Laddie would thrash him for that.

Instantly after, "Nine," he recited straight at Laddie: "I made a covenant with mine eyes; why then should I think upon a maid?"

More than one giggled that time.

"Ten!" came almost sharply.

Leon looked scared for the first time. He actually seemed to shiver. Maybe he realized at last that it was a pretty serious thing he was doing. When he spoke he said these words in the most surprised voice you ever heard: "I was almost in all evil in the midst of the congregation and assembly."

"Eleven."

Perhaps these words are in the Bible. They are not there to read the way Leon repeated them, for he put a short pause after the first name, and he glanced toward our father: "Jesus Christ, the *same*, yesterday, and to-day, and forever!"

Sure as you live my mother's shoulders shook.

"Twelve."

Suddenly Leon seemed to be forsaken. He surely shrank in size and appeared abused.

"When my father and my mother forsake me, then the Lord will take me up," he announced, and looked as happy over the ending as he had seemed forlorn at the beginning.

"Thirteen."

"The Lord is on my side; I will not fear; what can man do unto me?" inquired Leon of every one in the church. Then he soberly made a bow and walked to his seat.

Father's voice broke that silence. "Let us kneel in prayer," he said.

He took a step forward, knelt, laid his hands on the altar, closed his eyes and turned his face upward.

"Our Heavenly Father, we come before Thee in a trying situation," he said. "Thy word of truth has been spoken to us by a thoughtless boy, whether in a spirit of helpfulness or of jest, Thou knowest. Since we are reasoning creatures, it little matters in what form Thy truth comes to us; the essential thing is that we soften our hearts for its entrance, and grow in grace by its application. Tears of compassion such as our dear Saviour wept are in our eyes this morning as we plead with Thee to help us to apply these words to the betterment of this community."

Then father began to pray. If the Lord had been standing six feet in front of him, and his life had depended on what he said, he could have prayed no harder. Goodness knows how fathers remember. He began at "Jesus wept" and told about this sinful world and why He wept over it; then one at a time he took those other twelve verses and hammered them down where they belonged much harder than Leon ever could by merely looking at people. After that he prayed all around each one so fervently that those who had been hit the very worst cried aloud and said: "Amen!" You wouldn't think any one could do a thing like that; but I heard and saw my father do it.

When he arose the tears were running down his cheeks, and before him stood Leon. He was white as could be, but he spoke out loudly and clearly.

"Please forgive me, sir; I didn't intend to hurt your feelings. Please every one forgive me. I didn't mean to offend any one. It happened through hunting short verses. All the short ones seemed to be like that, and they made me think——"

He got no farther. Father must have been afraid of what he might say next. He threw his arms around Leon's shoulders, drew him to the seat, and with the tears still rolling, he laughed as happily as you ever heard, and he cried: " 'Sweeping through the Gates!' All join in!"

You never heard such singing in your life. That was another wonderful thing. My father didn't know the notes. He couldn't sing; he said so himself. Neither could half the people there, yet all of them were singing at the tops of their voices, and I don't believe the angels in Heaven could make grander music. My father was leading:

"These, these are they, who in the conflict dire——"

You could tell Emanuel Ripley had been in the war from the way he roared:

"Boldly have stood amidst the hottest fire——"

The Widow Fall soared above all of them on the next line; her man was there, and maybe she was lonely and would have been glad to go to him:

"Jesus now says, 'Come up higher——'"

Then my little mother:

"Washed in the blood of the Lamb——"

Like thunder all of them rolled into the chorus:

"Sweeping through the gates to the New Jerusalem——"

You wouldn't have been left out of that company for anything in all this world, and nothing else ever could make you want to go so badly as to hear every one sing, straight from the heart, a grand old song like that. It is no right way to have to sit and keep still, and pay other people money to sing about Heaven to you. No matter if you can't sing by note, if your heart and soul are full, until they are running over, so that you are forced to sing as those people did, whether you can or not, you are sure to be straight on the way to the Gates.

Before three lines were finished my father was keeping time like a choirmaster, his face all beaming with shining light; mother was rocking on her toes like a wood robin on a twig at twilight, and at the end of the chorus she cried "Glory!" right out loud, and turned and started down the aisle, shaking hands with every one, singing as she went. When she reached Betsy Alton she held her hand and led her down the aisle straight toward Rachel Brown. When Rachel saw them coming she hurried to meet them, and they shook hands and were glad to make up as any two people you ever saw. It must have been perfectly dreadful to see a woman every day for five years, and not to give her a pie, when you felt sure yours were better than she could make, or loan her a new pattern, or tell her first who had a baby, or was married, or dead, or anything like that. It was no wonder they felt glad. Mother came on, and as she passed me the verses were all finished and every one began talking and moving. Johnny Dover forgot his neck and shook hands too, and father pronounced the benediction. He always had to when the minister wasn't there, because he was ordained himself, and you didn't dare pronounce the benediction unless you were.

Every one began talking again, and wondering if the minister wouldn't come soon, and some one went out to see. There was mother standing only a few feet from the Princess, and I thought of something. I had seen it done often enough, but I never had tried it myself, yet I wanted to so badly, there was no time to think how scared I would be. I took mother's hand and led her a few steps farther and said: "Mother, this is my friend, Pamela Pryor."

I believe I did it fairly well. Mother must have been surprised, but she put out her hand.

"I didn't know Miss Pryor and you were acquainted."

"It's only been a little while," I told her. "I met her when I was on some business with the Fairies. They know everything and they told me her father was busy"—I thought she wouldn't want me to tell that he was plain *cross,* where every one could hear, so I said "busy" for politeness—"and her mother not very strong, and that she was a good girl, and dreadfully lonesome. Can't you do something, mother?"

"Well, I should think so!" said mother, for her heart was soft as rose leaves. Maybe you won't believe this, but it's quite true. My mother took the Princess' arm and led her to Sally and Shelley, and introduced her to all the girls. By the time the minister came and mother went back to her seat, she had forgotten all about the "indisposed" word she disliked, and as you live! she invited the Princess to go home with us to dinner. She stood tall and straight, her eyes very bright, and her cheeks a little redder than usual, as she shook hands and said a few pleasant words that were like from a book, they fitted and were so right. When mother asked her to dinner she said: "Thank you kindly. I should be glad to go, but my people expect me at home and they would be uneasy. Perhaps you would allow me to ride over some week day and become acquainted?"

Mother said she would be happy to have her, and Shelley said so too, but Sally was none too cordial. She had dark curls and pink cheeks herself, and every one had said she was the prettiest girl in the county before Shelley began to blossom out and show what she was going to be. Sally never minded that, but when the

Princess came she was a little taller, and her hair was a trifle longer, and heavier, and blacker, and her eyes were a little larger and darker, and where Sally had pink skin and red lips, the Princess was dark as olive, and her lips and cheeks were like red velvet. Anyway, the Princess had said she would come over; mother and Shelley had been decent to her, and Sally hadn't been exactly insulting. It would be a little more than you could expect for her to be wild about the Princess. I believe she was pleased over having been invited to dinner, and as she was a stranger she couldn't know that mother had what we called the "invitation habit."

I have seen her ask from fifteen to twenty in one trip down the aisle on Sunday morning. She wanted them to come too; the more who came, the better she liked it. If the hitching rack and barnyard were full on Sunday she just beamed. If the sermon pleased her, she invited more. That morning she was feeling so good she asked seventeen; and as she only had dressed six chickens—third table, backs and ham, for me as usual; but when the prospects were as now, I always managed to coax a few gizzards from Candace; she didn't dare give me livers—they were counted. Almost everyone in the church was the happiest that morning they had been in years. When the preacher came, he breathed it from the air, and it worked on him so he preached the best sermon he ever had, and never knew that Leon made him do it. Maybe after all it's a good thing to tell people about their meanness and give them a stirring up once in a while.

CHAPTER III

Mr. Pryor's Door

"Grief will be joy if on its edge
Fall soft that holiest ray,
Joy will be grief if no faint pledge
Be there of heavenly day."

HAVE Sally and Peter said anything about getting married yet?" asked my big sister Lucy of mother. Lucy was home on a visit. She was bathing her baby and mother was sewing.

"Not a word!"

"Are they engaged?"

"Sally hasn't mentioned it."

"Well, can't you find out?"

"How could I?" asked mother.

"Why, watch them a little and see how they act when they are together. If he kisses her when he leaves, of course they are engaged."

"It would be best to wait until Sally tells me," laughed mother.

I heard this from the back steps. Neither mother nor Lucy knew I was there. I went in to see if they would let me take the baby. Of course they wouldn't! Mother took it herself. She was rocking, and softly singing my Dutch song that I loved best; I can't spell it, but it sounds like this:

"Trus, trus, trill;
Der power rid der fill,
Fill sphring aveck,
Plodschlicter power in der dreck."

Once I asked mother to sing it in English, and she couldn't because it didn't rhyme that way and the words wouldn't fit the notes; it was just, "Trot, trot, trot, a boy rode a colt. The colt sprang aside; down went the boy in the dirt."

"Aw, don't sing my song to that little red, pug-nosed baldhead!" I said.

Really, it was a very nice baby; I only said that because I wanted to hold it, and mother wouldn't give it up. I tried to coax May to the dam snake hunting, but she couldn't go, so I had to amuse myself. I had a doll, but I never played with it except when I was dressed up on Sunday. Anyway, what's the use of a doll when there's a live baby in the house? I didn't care much for my playhouse since I had seen one so much finer that Laddie had made for the Princess. Of course I knew moss wouldn't take root in our orchard as it did in the woods, neither would willow cuttings or the red flowers. Finally, I decided to go hunting. I went into the garden and gathered every ripe touch-me-not pod I could find, and all the portulaca. Then I stripped the tiger lilies of each little black ball at the bases of the leaves, and took all the four o'clock seed there was. Then I got my biggest alder popgun and started up the road toward Sarah Hood's.

I was going along singing a little verse; it wasn't Dutch cither; the old baby could have that if it wanted it. Soon as I got from sight of the house I made a powderhorn of a curled leaf, loaded my gun with portulaca powder, rammed in a tiger lily bullet, laid the weapon across my shoulder, and stepped high and lightly as Laddie does when he's in the Big Woods hunting for squirrel. It must have been my own singing—I am rather good at hearing things, but I never noticed a sound that time, until a voice like a rusty saw said: "Good morning, Nimrod!"

I sprang from the soft dust and landed among the dog fennel of a fence corner, in a flying leap. Then I looked. It was the Princess' father, tall, and gray, and grim, riding a big black horse that seemed as if it had been curried with the fine comb and brushed with the grease rag.

"Good morning!" I said when I could speak.

"Am I correct in the surmise that you are on the chase with a popgun?" he asked politely.

"Yes sir," I answered, getting my breath the best I could.

It came easier after I noticed he didn't seem to be angry about anything.

"Where is your hunting ground, and what game are you after?" he asked gravely.

"You can see the great African jungle over there. I am going to hunt for lions and tigers."

You always must answer politely any one who speaks to you; and you get soundly thrashed, at least at our house, if you don't be politest of all to an older person especially with white hair. Father is extremely particular about white hair. It is a "crown of glory," when it is found in the way of the Lord. Mahlon Pryor had enough crown of glory for three men, but maybe his wasn't exactly glory, because he wasn't in the way of the Lord. He was in a way of his own. He must have had much confidence in himself. At our house we would rather trust in the Lord. I only told him about the lions and tigers because he asked me, and that was the way I played. But you should have heard him laugh. You wouldn't have supposed to see him that he could.

"Umph!" he said at last. "I am a little curious about your ammunition. Just how do you bring down your prey?"

"I use portulaca powder and tiger lily bullets on the tigers, and four o'clocks on the lions," I said.

You could have heard him a mile, dried up as he was.

"I used to wear a red coat and ride to the hounds fox hunting," he said. "It's great sport. Won't you take me with you to the jungle?"

I didn't want him in the least, but if any one older asks right out to go with you, what can you do? I am going to tell several things you won't believe, and this is one of them: He got off his horse, tied it to the fence, and climbed over after me. He went on asking questions and of course I had to tell him. Most of what he wanted to know, his people should have taught him before he was

ten years old, but father says they do things differently in
England.

"There doesn't seem to be many trees in the jungle."

"Well, there's one, and it's about the most important on our
land," I told him. "Father wouldn't cut it down for a farm. You
see that little dark bag nearly as big as your fist, swinging out
there on that limb? Well, every spring one of these birds, yellow
as orange peel, with velvet black wings, weaves a nest like that,
and over on that big branch, high up, one just as bright red as
the other is yellow, and the same black wings, builds a cradle for
his babies. Father says a red bird and a yellow one keeping house
in the same tree is the biggest thing that ever happened in our
family. They come every year and that is their tree. I believe
father would shoot any one who drove them away."

"Your father is a gunner also?" he asked, and I thought he
was laughing to himself.

"He's enough of a gunner to bring mother in a wagon from
Pennsylvania all the way here, and he kept wolves, bears, Indians,
and Gypsies from her, and shot things for food. Yes sir, my father can shoot if he wants to, better than any of our family except
Laddie."

"And does Laddie shoot well?"

"Laddie does everything well," I answered proudly. "He won't
try to do anything at all, until he practises so he can do it well."

"Score one for Laddie," he said in a queer voice.

"Are you in a hurry about the lions and tigers?"

"Not at all," he answered.

"Well, here I always stop and let Governor Oglesby go swimming," I said.

Mr. Mahlon Pryor sat on the bank of our Little Creek, took off
his hat and shook back his hair as if the wind felt good on his
forehead. I fished Dick Oglesby from the ammunition in my
apron pocket, and held him toward the cross old man, and he
wasn't cross at all. It's funny how you come to get such wrong
ideas about people.

"My big married sister who lives in Westchester sent him to me last Christmas," I explained. "I have another doll, great big, with a Scotch plaid dress made from pieces of mine, but I only play with her on Sunday when I dare not do much else. I like Dick the best because he fits my apron pocket. Father wanted me to change his name and call him Oliver P. Morton, after a friend of his, but I told him this doll had to be called by the name he came with, and if he wanted me to have one named for his friend, to get it, and I'd play with it."

"What did he do?"

"He didn't want one named Morton that much."

Mr. Pryor took Dick Oglesby in his fingers and looked at his curly black hair and blue eyes, his chubby outstretched arms, like a baby when it wants you to take it, and his plump little feet and the white shirt with red stripes all a piece of him as he was made, and said: "The honourable governor of our sister state seems a little weighty; I am at a loss to understand how he swims."

"It's a new way," I said. "He just stands still and the water swims around him. It's very easy for him."

Then I carried Dick to the water, waded in and stood him against a stone. Something funny happened instantly. It always did. I found it out one day when I got some apple butter on the governor giving him a bite of my bread, and put him in the wash bowl to soak. He was two and a half inches tall; but the minute you stood him in water he went down to about half that height and spread out to twice his size around. You should have heard Mr. Pryor.

"If you will lie on the bank and watch you'll have more to laugh at than that," I promised.

He lay down and never paid the least attention to his clothes. Pretty soon a little chub fish came swimming around to make friends with Governor Oglesby, and then a shiner and some more chub. They nibbled at his hands and toes, and then went flashing away, and from under the stone came backing a big crayfish and seized the governor by the leg and started dragging him, so I had to jump in and stop it. I took a shot at the crayfish with the tiger ammunition and then loaded for lions.

We went on until the marsh became a thicket of cattails, bul-
rushes, willow bushes, and blue flags; then I found a path where
the lions left the jungle, hid Mr. Pryor and told him he must be
very still or they wouldn't come. At last I heard one. I touched
Mr. Pryor's sleeve to warn him to keep his eyes on the trail. Pretty
soon the lion came in sight. Really it was only a little gray rabbit
hopping along, but when it was opposite us, I pinged it in the
side, it jumped up and turned a somersault with surprise, and
squealed a funny little squeal,—well, I wondered if Mr. Pryor's
people didn't hear him, and think he had gone crazy as Paddy
Ryan. I never did hear any one laugh so. I thought if he enjoyed
it like that, I'd let him shoot one. I do May sometimes; so we
went to another place I knew where there was a tiger's den, and
I loaded with tiger lily bullets, gave him the gun and showed him
where to aim. After we had waited a long time out came a muskrat, and started for the river. I looked to see why Mr. Pryor didn't
shoot, and there he was gazing at it as if a snake had charmed
him; his hands shaking a little, his cheeks almost red, his eyes
very bright.

"Shoot!" I whispered. "It won't stay all day!"

He forgot how to push the ramrod like I showed him, so he
reached out and tried to hit it with the gun.

"Don't do that!" I said.

"But it's getting away! It's getting away!" he cried.

"Well, what if it is?" I asked, half provoked. "Do you suppose
I really would hurt a poor little muskrat? Maybe it has six hungry
babies in its home."

"Oh *that* way," he said, but he kept looking at it, so he made
me think if I hadn't been there, he would have thrown a stone or
hit it with a stick. It is perfectly wonderful about how some men
can't get along without killing things, such little bits of helpless
creatures too. I thought he'd better be got from the jungle, so I
invited him to see the place at the foot of the hill below our
orchard where some men thought they had discovered gold before
the war. They had been to California in '49, and although they
didn't come home with millions, or anything else except sick and

tired, they thought they had learned enough about gold to know it when they saw it.

I told him about it and he was interested and anxious to see the place. If there had been a shovel, I am quite sure he would have gone to digging. He kept poking around with his boot toe, and he said maybe the yokels didn't look good.

He said our meadow was a beautiful place, and when he praised the creek I told him about the wild ducks, and he laughed again. He didn't seem to be the same man when we went back to the road. I pulled some sweet marsh grass and gave his horse bites, so Mr. Pryor asked if I liked animals. I said I loved horses, Laddie's best of all. He asked about it and I told him.

"Hasn't your father but one thoroughbred?"

"Father hasn't any," I said. "Flos really belongs to Laddie, and we are mighty glad he has her."

"You should have one soon, yourself," he said.

"Well, if the rest of them will hurry up and marry off, so the expenses won't be so heavy, maybe I can."

"How many of you are there?" he asked.

"Only twelve," I said.

He looked down the road at our house.

"Do you mean to tell me you have twelve children there?" he inquired.

"Oh no!" I answered. "Some of the big boys have gone into business in the cities around, and some of the girls are married. Mother says she has only to show her girls in the cities to have them snapped up like hot cakes."

"I fancy that is the truth," he said. "I've passed the one who rides the little black pony and she is a picture. A fine, healthy, sensible-appearing young woman!"

"I don't think she's as pretty as your girl," I said.

"Perhaps I don't either," he replied, smiling at me.

Then he mounted his horse.

"I don't remember that I ever have passed that house," he said, "without hearing some one singing. Does it go on all the time?"

"Yes, unless mother is sick."

"And what is it all about?"

"Oh just joy! Gladness that we are alive, that we have things to do that we like, and praising the Lord."

"Umph!" said Mr. Pryor.

"It's just letting out what our hearts are full of," I told him. "Don't you know that song:

> " 'Tis the old time religion
> And you cannot keep it still?' "

He shook his head.

"It's an awful nice song," I explained. "After it sings about all the other things religion is good for, there is one line that says: 'It's good for those in trouble.' "

I looked at him straight and hard, but he only turned white and seemed sick.

"So?" said Mr. Pryor. "Well, thank you for the most interesting morning I've had this side England. I should be delighted if you would come and hunt lions in my woods with me some time."

"Oh, do you open the door to children?"

"Certainly we open the door to children," he said, and as I live, he looked so sad I couldn't help thinking he was sorry to close it against any one. A mystery is the dreadfulest thing.

"Then if children don't matter, maybe I can come lion-hunting some time with the Princess, after she has made the visit at our house she said she would."

"Indeed! I hadn't been informed that my daughter contemplated visiting your house," he said. "When was it arranged?"

"My mother invited her last Sunday."

I didn't like the way he said: "O-o-o-h!" Some way it seemed insulting to my mother.

"She did it to please me," I said. "There was a Fairy Princess told me the other day that your girl felt like a stranger, and that to be a stranger was the hardest thing in all the world. She sat a little way from the others, and she looked so lonely. I pulled my mother's sleeve and led her to your girl and made them shake hands, and then mother *had* to ask her to come to dinner with us. She always invites every one she meets coming down the aisle; she couldn't help asking your girl, too. She said she was expected at home, but she'd come some day and get acquainted. She needn't if you object. My mother only asked her because she thought she was lonely, and maybe she wanted to come."

He sat there staring straight ahead and he seemed to grow whiter, and older, and colder every minute.

"Possibly she is lonely," he said at last. "This isn't much like the life she left. Perhaps she does feel herself a stranger. It was very kind of your mother to invite her. If she wants to come, I shall make no objections."

"No, but my father will," I said.

He straightened up as if something had hit him.

"Why will he object?"

"On account of what you said about God at our house," I told him. "And then, too, father's people were from England, and he says real Englishmen have their doors wide open, and welcome people who offer friendliness."

Mr. Pryor hit his horse an awful blow. It reared and went racing up the road until I thought it was running away. I could see I had made him angry enough to burst. Mother always tells me not to repeat things; but I'm not smart enough to know what to say, so I don't see what is left but to tell what mother, or father, or Laddie says when grown people ask me questions.

I went home, but every one was too busy even to look at me, so I took Bobby under my arm, hunted father, and told him all about the morning. I wondered what he would think. I never found out. He wouldn't say anything, so Bobby and I went across the lane, and climbed the gate into the orchard to see if Hezekiah were there and wanted to fight. He hadn't time to fight Bobby because he was busy chasing every wild jay from our orchard. By the time he got that done, he was tired, so he came hopping along on branches above us as Bobby and I went down the west fence beside the lane.

If I had been compelled to choose the side of our orchard I liked best, I don't know which I would have selected. The west side—that is, the one behind the dooryard—was running over with interesting things. Two gates opened into it, one from near each corner of the yard. Between these there was quite a wide level space, where mother fed the big chickens and kept the hens in coops with little ones. She had to have them close enough that the big hawks were afraid to come to earth, or they would take more chickens than they could pay for, by cleaning rabbits, snakes, and mice from the fields. Then came a double row of prize peach trees; rare fruit that mother canned to take to county fairs. One bore big, white freestones, and around the seed they were pink as a rose. One was a white cling, and one was yellow. There was a yellow freestone as big as a young sun, and as golden, and the queerest of all was a cling purple as a beet.

Sometimes father read about the hairs of the head being numbered, because we were so precious in the sight of the Almighty. Mother was just as particular with her purple tree; every peach on it was counted, and if we found one on the ground, we had to carry it to her, because it *might* be sound enough to can or spice for a fair, or she had promised the seed to some one halfway across the state. At each end of the peach row was an enormous big pear tree; not far from one the chicken house stood on the path to the barn, and beside the other the smoke house with the dog kennel a yard away. Father said there was a distinct relationship between a smoke house and a dog kennel, and bulldogs were best. Just at present we were out of bulldogs, but Jones, Jenkins and Co. could make as much noise as any dog you ever heard. On the left grew the plum trees all the way to the south fence, and I think there was one of every kind in the fruit catalogues. Father spent hours pruning, grafting, and fertilizing them. He said they required twice as much work as peaches.

Around the other sides of the orchard were two rows of peach trees of every variety; but one cling on the north was just a little the best of any, and we might eat all we wanted from any tree we liked, after father tested them and said: "Peaches are ripe!" In the middle were the apple; selected trees, planted, trimmed, and cultivated like human beings. The apples were so big and fine they were picked by hand, wrapped in paper, packed in barrels, and all we could not use at home went to J. B. White in Fort Wayne for the biggest fruit house in the state. My! but father was proud! He always packed especially fine ones for Mr. White's family. He said he liked him, because he was a real sandy Scotchman, who knew when an apple was right, and wasn't afraid to say so.

On the south side of the orchard there was the earliest June apple tree. The apples were small, bright red with yellow stripes, crisp, juicy and sweet enough to be just right. The tree was very large, and so heavy it leaned far to the northeast. This sounds like make-believe, but it's gospel truth. Almost two feet from the ground there was a big round growth, the size of a hash bowl. The tree must have been hurt when very small and the place enlarged with the trunk. Now it made a grand step. If you understood that no one could keep from running the last few rods from the tree, then figured on the help to be had from this step, you could see how we went up it like squirrels. All the bark on the south side was worn away and the trunk was smooth and shiny. The birds loved to nest among the branches, and under the peach tree in the fence corner opposite was a big bed of my mother's favourite wild flowers, blue-eyed Marys. They had dainty stems from six to eight inches high and delicate heads of bloom made up of little flowers, two petals up, blue, two turning down, white. Perhaps you don't know about anything prettier than that. There were maiden-hair ferns among them too! and the biggest lichens you ever saw on the fence, while in the hollow of a rotten rail a little chippy bird always built a hair nest. She got the hairs at our barn, for most of them were gray from our carriage horses, Ned and Jo. All down that side of the orchard the fence corners were filled with long grass and wild flowers, a few alder bushes left to furnish berries for the birds, and wild roses for us, to keep their beauty impressed on us, father said.

The east end ran along the brow of a hill so steep we coasted down it on the big meat board all winter. The board was six inches thick, two and a half feet wide, and six long. Father said slipping over ice and snow gave it the good scouring it needed, and it was thick enough to last all our lives, so we might play with it as we pleased. At least seven of us could go skimming down that hill and halfway across the meadow on it. In the very place we slid across, in summer lay the cowslip bed. The world is full of beautiful spots, but I doubt if any of them ever were prettier than that. Father called it swale. We didn't sink deep, but all summer there was water standing there. The grass was long and very sweet, there were ferns and a few calamus flowers, and there must have been an acre of cowslips—cowslips with big-veined, heartshaped, green leaves, and large pale gold flowers. I used to sit on the top rail of that orchard fence and look down at them, and try to figure out what God was thinking when He created them, and I wished that I might have been where I could watch His face as He worked.

Halfway across the east side was a gully where Leon and I found the Underground Station, and from any place along the north you looked, you saw the Little Creek and the marsh. At the same time the cowslips were most golden, the marsh was blue with flags, pink with smart weed, white and yellow with dodder, yellow with marsh buttercups having ragged frosty leaves, while the yellow and the red birds flashed above it, the red crying, "Chip," "Chip," in short, sharp notes, the yellow spilling music all over the marsh while on wing.

It would take a whole book to describe the butterflies; once in a while you scared up a big, wonderful moth, large as a sparrow; and the orchard was alive with doves, thrushes, catbirds, blue-birds, vireos, and orioles. When you climbed the fence, or a tree, and kept quiet, and heard the music and studied the pictures, it made you feel as if you had to put it into words. I often had meeting all by myself, unless Bobby and Hezekiah were along, and I tried to tell God what I thought about things. Probably He was so busy making more birds and flowers for other worlds, He never heard me; but I didn't say anything disrespectful at all, so it made no difference if He did listen. It just seemed as if I must tell what I thought, and I felt better, not so full and restless after I had finished.

All of us were alike about that. At that minute I knew mother was humming, as she did a dozen times a day:

> *"I think when I read that sweet story of old,*
> *When Jesus was here among men*
> *How He called little children as lambs to His fold,*
> *I should like to have been with Him then."*

Lucy would be rocking her baby and singing, "Hush, my dear, lie still and slumber." Candace's favourite she made up about her man who had been killed in the war, when they had been married only six weeks, which hadn't given her time to grow tired of him if he hadn't been "all her fancy painted." She arranged the words like "Ben Battle was a soldier bold," and she sang them to suit herself, and cried every single minute:

> *"They wrapped him in his uniform,*
> *They laid him in the tomb,*
> *My aching heart I thought 'twould break,*
> *But such was my sad doom."*

Candace just loved that song. She sang it all the time. Leon said our pie always tasted salty from her tears, and he'd take a bite and smile at her sweetly and say: "How *uniform* you get your pie, Candace!"

May's favourite was "Joy Bells." Father would be whispering over to himself the speech he was preparing to make at the next prayer-meeting. We never could learn his speeches, because he read and studied so much it kept his head so full, he made a new one every time. You could hear Laddie's deep bass booming the "Bedouin Love Song" for a mile; this minute it came rolling across the corn:

> *"Open the door of thy heart,*
> *And open thy chamber door,*

And my kisses shall teach thy lips
The love that shall fade no more
Till the sun grows cold,
And the stars are old,
And the leaves of the Judgment
Book unfold!"

I don't know how the Princess stood it. If he had been singing that song where I could hear it and I had known it was about me, as she must have known he meant her, I couldn't have kept my arms from around his neck. Over in the barn Leon was singing:

"A life on the ocean wave,
A home on the rolling deep,
Where codfish waggle their tails
'Mid tadpoles two feet deep."

The minute he finished, he would begin reciting "Marco Boz-zaris," and you could be sure that he would reach the last line, only to commence on the speech of "Logan, Chief of the Min-goes," or any one of the fifty others. He could make your hair stand a little straighter than any one else; the best teachers we ever had, or even Laddie, couldn't make you shivery and creepy as he could. Because all of us kept going like that every day, people couldn't pass without hearing, so *that* was what Mr. Pryor meant.

I had a pulpit in the southeast corner of the orchard. I liked that place best of all because from it you could see two sides at once. The very first little, old log cabin that had been on our land, the one my father and mother moved into, had stood in that corner. It was all gone now; but a flowerbed of tiny, purple iris, not so tall as the grass, spread there, and some striped grass in the shadiest places, and among the flowers a lark brooded every spring. In the fence corner mother's big white turkey hen always nested. To protect her from rain and too hot sun, father had slipped some boards between the rails about three feet from the ground. After the turkey left, that was my pulpit. I stood there and used the top of the fence for my railing.

The little flags and all the orchard and birds were behind me; on one hand was the broad, grassy meadow with the creek running so swiftly, I could hear it, and the breath of the cowslips came up the hill. Straight in front was the lane running down from the barn, crossing the creek and spreading into the woods pasture, where the water ran wider and yet swifter, big forest trees grew, and bushes of berries, pawpaws, willow, everything ever found in an Indiana thicket; grass under foot, and many wild flowers and ferns wherever the cattle and horses didn't trample them, and bigger, wilder birds, many having names I didn't know. On the left, across the lane, was a large cornfield, with trees here and there, and down the valley I could see the Big Creek coming from the west, the Big Hill with the church on top, and always the white gravestones around it. Always too there was the sky overhead, often with clouds banked until you felt if you only could reach them, you could climb straight to the gates that father was so fond of singing about sweeping through. Mostly there was a big hawk or a turkey buzzard hanging among them, just to show us that we were not so much, and that we couldn't shoot them, unless they chose to come down and give us a chance.

I set Bobby and Hezekiah on the fence and stood between them. "We will open service this morning by singing the thirty-fifth hymn," I said. "Sister Dover, will you pitch the tune?"

Then I made my voice high and squeally like hers and sang:

> *"Come ye that love the Lord,*
> *And let your joys be known,*
> *Join in a song of sweet accord,*
> *And thus surround the throne."*

I sang all of it and then said: "Brother Hastings, will you lead us in prayer?"

Then I knelt down, and prayed Brother Hastings' prayer. I could have repeated any one of a dozen of the prayers the men of our church prayed, but I liked Brother Hastings' best, because it had the biggest words in it. I loved words that filled your mouth, and sounded as if you were used to books. It began sort of sing-songy and measured in stops, like a poetry piece:

"Our Heavenly Father: We come before Thee this morning,
Humble worms of the dust, imploring thy blessing.
We beseech Thee to forgive our transgressions,
Heal our backsliding, and love us freely."

Sometimes from there on it changed a little, but it always began and ended exactly the same way. Father said Brother Hastings was powerful in prayer, but he did wish he'd leave out the "worms of the dust." He said we were not "worms of the dust"; we were reasoning, progressive, inventive men and women. He said a worm would never be anything except a worm, but we could study and improve ourselves, help others, make great machines, paint pictures, write books, and go to an extent that must almost amaze the Almighty Himself. He said that if Brother Hastings had done more plowing in his time, and had a little closer acquaintance with worms, he wouldn't be so ready to call himself and every one else a worm. Now if you are talking about cutworms or fishworms, father is right. But there is that place where—"Charles his heel had raised, upon the humble worm to tread," and the worm lifted up its voice and spake thus to Charles:

"I know I'm now among the things
Uncomely to your sight,
But, by and by, on splendid wings,
You'll see me high and bright."

Now I'll bet a cent *that* is the kind of worm Brother Hastings said we were. I must speak to father about it. I don't want him to be mistaken; and I really think he is about worms. Of course he knows the kind that have wings and fly. Brother Hastings mixed him up by saying "worms of the dust" when he should have said worms of the leaves. Those that go into little round cases in earth or spin cocoons on trees always live on leaves, and many of them rear the head, having large horns, and wave it in a manner far from humble. So father and Brother Hastings were both partly right, and partly wrong.

When the prayer came to a close, where every one always said "Amen," I punched Bobby and whispered, "Crow, Bobby, crow!" and he stood up and brought it out strong, like he always did when I told him. I had to stop the service to feed him a little wheat, to pay him for crowing; but as no one was there except us, that didn't matter. Then Hezekiah crowded over for some, so I had to pretend I was Mrs. Daniels feeding her children caraway cake, like she always did in meeting. If I had been the mother of children who couldn't have gone without things to eat in church I'd have kept them at home. Mrs. Daniels always had the carpet greasy with cake crumbs wherever she sat, and mother didn't think the Lord liked a dirty church any more than we would have wanted a mussy house. When I had Bobby and Hezekiah settled I took my text from my head, because I didn't know the meeting feeling was coming on me when I started, and I had brought no Bible along.

"Blessed are all men, but most blessed are they who hold their tempers." I had to stroke Bobby a little and pat Hezekiah once in a while, to keep them from flying down and fighting, but mostly I could give my attention to my sermon.

"We have only to look around us this morning to see that all men are blessed," I said. "The sky is big enough to cover every one. If the sun gets too hot, there are trees for shade or the clouds come up for a while. If the earth becomes too dry, it always rains before it is everlastingly too late. There are birds enough to sing for every one, butterflies enough to go around, and so many flowers we can't always keep the cattle and horses from tramping down and even devouring beautiful ones, like Daniel thought the lions would devour him—but they didn't. Wouldn't it be a good idea, O Lord, for You to shut the cows' mouths and save the cowslips also; they may not be worth as much as a man, but they are lots better looking, and they make fine greens. It doesn't seem right for cows to eat flowers; but maybe it is as right for them as it is for us. The best way would be for our cattle to do like that piece about the cow in the meadow exactly the same as ours:

> *" 'And through it ran a little brook,*
> *Where oft the cows would drink,*
> *And then lie down among the flowers,*
> *That grew upon the brink.'*

"You notice, O Lord, the cows did not eat the flowers in this instance; they merely rested among them, and goodness knows, that's enough for any cow. They had better done like the next verse, where it says:

> *" 'They like to lie beneath the trees,*
> *All shaded by the boughs,*
> *Whene'er the noontide heat came on:*
> *Sure, they were happy cows!'*

"Now, O Lord, this plainly teaches that if cows are happy, men should be much more so, for like the cows, they have all Thou canst do for them, and all they can do for themselves, besides. So every man is blessed, because Thy bounty has provided all these things for him, without money and without price. If some men are not so blessed as others, it is their own fault, and not Yours. You made the earth, and all that is therein, and You made the men. Of course You had to make men different, so each woman can tell which one belongs to her; but I believe it would have been a good idea while You were at it, if You would have made all of them enough alike that they would all work. Perhaps it isn't polite of me to ask more of You than You saw fit to do; and then, again, it may be that there are some things impossible, even to You. If there is anything at all, seems as if making Isaac Thomas work would be it. Father says that man would rather starve and see his wife and children hungry than to take off his coat, roll up his sleeves, and plow corn; so it was good enough for him when Leon said, 'Go to the ant, thou sluggard,' right at him. So, of course, Isaac is not so blessed as some men, because he won't work, and thus he never knows whether he's going to have a big dinner on Sunday, until after some one asks him, because he looks so empty. Mother thinks it isn't fair to feed Isaac and send him home with his stomach full, while Mandy and the babies are sick and hungry. But Isaac is some blessed, because he has religion and gets real happy, and sings, and shouts, and he's going to Heaven when he dies. He must wish he'd go soon, especially in winter.

"There are men who do not have even this blessing, and to make things worse, O Lord, they get mad as fire and hit their horses, and look like all possessed. The words of my text this morning apply especially to a man who has all the blessings Thou hast showered and flowered upon men who work, or whose people worked and left them so much money they don't need to, and yet a sadder face I never saw, or a crosser one. He looks like he was going to hit people, and he does hit his horse an awful crack. It's no way to hit a horse, not even if it balks, because it can't hit back, and it's a cowardly thing to do. If you rub their ears and talk to them, they come quicker, O our Heavenly Father, and if you hit them just because you are mad, it's a bigger sin yet.

"No man is nearly so blessed as he might be who goes around looking killed with grief when he should cheer up, no matter what ails him; and who shuts up his door and says his wife is sick when she isn't, and who scowls at every one, when he can be real pleasant if he likes, as some in Divine Presence can testify. So we are going to beseech Thee, O Lord, to lay Thy mighty hand upon the man who got mad this beautiful morning and make him feel Thy might, until he will know for himself and not another, that You are not a myth. Teach him to have a pleasant countenance, an open door, and to hold his temper. Help him to come over to our house and be friendly with all his neighbours, and get all the blessings You have provided for every one; but please don't make him have any more trouble than he has now, for if You do, You'll surely kill him. Have patience with him, and have mercy on him, O Lord! Let us pray."

That time I prayed myself. I looked into the sky just as straight and as far as I could see, and if I had any influence at all, I used it then. Right out loud, I just begged the Lord to get after Mr.

Pryor and make him behave like other people, and let the Princess come to our house, and for him to come too; because I liked him heaps when he was lion hunting, and I wanted to go with him again the worst way. I had seen him sail right over the fences on his big black horse, and when he did it in England, wearing a red coat, and the dogs flew over thick around him, it must have looked grand, but it was mighty hard on the fox. I do hope it got away. Anyway, I prayed as hard as I could, and every time I said the strongest thing I knew, I punched Bobby to crow, and he never came out stronger. Then I was Sister Dover and started: "Oh come let us gather at the fountain, the fountain that never goes dry."

Just as I was going to pronounce the benediction like father, I heard something, so I looked around, and there went he and Dr. Fenner. They were going toward the house, and yet, they hadn't passed me. I was not scared, because I knew no one was sick. Dr. Fenner always stopped when he passed, if he had a minute, and if he hadn't, mother sent some one to the gate with buttermilk and slices of bread and butter, and jelly an inch thick. When a meal was almost cooked she heaped some on a plate and he ate as he drove and left the plate next time he passed. Often he was so dead tired, he was asleep in his buggy, and his old gray horse always stopped at our gate.

I ended with "Amen," because I wanted to know if they had been listening; so I climbed the fence, ran down the lane behind the bushes, and hid a minute. Sure enough they had! I suppose I had been so in earnest I hadn't heard a sound, but it's a wonder Hezekiah hadn't told me. He was always seeing something to make danger signals about. He never let me run on a snake, or a hawk get one of the chickens, or Paddy Ryan come too close. I only wanted to know if they had gone and listened, and then I intended to run straight back to Bobby and Hezekiah; but they stopped under the greening apple tree, and what they said was so interesting I waited longer than I should, because it's about the worst thing you can do to listen when older people don't know. They were talking about me.

"I can't account for her," said father.

"I can!" said Dr. Fenner. "She is the only child I ever have had in my practice who managed to reach earth as all children should. During the impressionable stage, no one expected her, so there was no time spent in worrying, fretting, and discontent. I don't mean that these things were customary with Ruth. No woman ever accepted motherhood in a more beautiful spirit; but if she would have protested at any time, it would have been then. Instead, she lived happily, naturally, and enjoyed herself as she never had before. She was in the fields, the woods, and the garden constantly, which accounts for this child's outdoor tendencies. Then you must remember that both of you were at top notch intellectually, and physically, fully matured. She had the benefit of ripened minds, and at a time when every faculty recently had been stirred by the excitement and suffering of the war. Oh, you can account for her easily enough, but I don't know what on earth you are going to do with her. You'll have to go careful, Paul. I warn you she will not be like the others."

"We realize that. Mother says she doubts if she can ever teach her to sew and become a housewife."

"She isn't cut out for a seamstress or a housewife, Paul. Tell Ruth not to try to force those things on her. Turn her loose out of doors; give her good books, and leave her alone. You won't be disappointed in the woman who evolves."

Right there I realized what I was doing, and I turned and ran for the pulpit with all my might. I could always repeat things, but I couldn't see much sense to the first part of that; the last was as plain as the nose on your face. Dr. Fenner said they mustn't force me to sew, and do housework; and mother didn't mind the Almighty any better than she did the doctor. There was nothing in this world I disliked so much as being kept indoors, and made to hem cap and apron strings so particularly that I had to count the number of threads between every stitch, and in each stitch, so that I got all of them just exactly even. I liked carpet rags a little better, because I didn't have to be so particular about stitches, and I always picked out all the bright, pretty colours. Mother said she could follow my work all over the floor by the bright spots. Perhaps if I were not to be kept in the house I wouldn't have to sew any more. That made me so happy I wondered if I couldn't stretch out my arms and wave them and fly. I sat on the pulpit wishing I had feathers. It made me pretty blue to have to stay on the ground all the time, when I wanted to be sailing up among the clouds with the turkey buzzards. It called to my mind that place in McGuffey's Fifth where it says:

> *"Sweet bird, thy bower is ever green,*
> *Thy sky is ever clear;*
> *Thou hast no sorrow in thy song,*
> *No winter in thy year."*

Of course, I never heard a turkey buzzard sing. Laddie said they couldn't; but that didn't prove it. He said half the members of our church couldn't sing, but they *did;* and when all of them were going at the tops of their voices, it was just grand. So maybe the turkey buzzard could sing if it wanted to; seemed as if it should, if Isaac Thomas could; and anyway, it was the next verse I was thinking most about:

> *"Oh, could I fly, I'd fly with thee!*
> *We'd make with joyful wing,*
> *Our annual visit o'er the globe,*
> *Companions of the spring."*

That was so exciting I thought I'd just try it, so I stood on the top rail, spread my arms, waved them, and started. I was bumped in fifty places when I rolled into the cowslip bed at the foot of the steep hill, for stones stuck out all over the side of it, and I felt pretty mean as I climbed back to the pulpit.

The only consolation I had was what Dr. Fenner had said. That would be the greatest possible help in managing father or mother. I was undecided about whether I would go to school, or not. Must be perfectly dreadful to dress like for church, and sit still in a stuffy little room, and do your "abs," and "bes," and "bis," and "bos," all day long. I could spell quite well without looking at a schoolhouse, and read too. I was wondering if I ever would go at all, when I thought of something else. Dr. Fenner had said to give me plenty of good books. I was wild for some that were already promised me. Well, what would they amount to if I couldn't understand them when I got them? *That* seemed to make it sure I would be compelled to go to school until I learned enough to understand what the books contained about birds, flowers, and moths, anyway; and perhaps there would be some having Fairies in them. Of course those would be interesting.

I never hated doing anything so badly, in all my life, but I could see, with no one to tell me, that I had put it off as long as I dared. I would just have to start school when Leon and May went in September. Tilly Baher, who lived across the swamp near Sarah Hood, had gone two winters already, and she was only a year older, and not half my size. I stood on the pulpit and looked a long time in every direction, into the sky the longest of all. It was settled. I must go; I might as well start and have it over. I couldn't look anywhere, right there at home, and not see more things I didn't know about than I did. When mother showed me in the city, I wouldn't be snapped up like hot cakes; I'd be a blockhead no one would have. It made me so vexed to think I had to go, I set Hezekiah on my shoulder, took Bobby under my arm, and went to the house. On the way, I made up my mind that I would ask again, very politely, to hold the little baby, and if the rest of them went and pigged it up straight along, I'd pinch it, if I got a chance.

CHAPTER IV

The Last Day in Eden

" 'Tis the sunset of life gives me mystical lore,
And coming events cast their shadows before."

OF COURSE the baby was asleep and couldn't be touched; but there was some excitement, anyway. Father had come from town with a letter from the new school teacher, that said she would expect him to meet her at the station next Saturday. Mother thought she might as well get the room ready and let her stay at our house, because we were most convenient, and it would be the best place for her. She said that every time, and the teacher always stayed with us. Really it was because father and mother wanted the teacher where they could know as much as possible about what was going on. Sally didn't like having her at all; she said with the wedding coming, the teacher would be a nuisance. Shelley had finished our school, and the Groveville high school, and instead of attending college she was going to Chicago to study music. She was so anxious over her dresses and getting started, she didn't seem to think much about what was going to happen to us at home; so she didn't care if Miss Amelia stayed at our house. May said it would be best to have the teacher with us, because she could help us with our lessons at home, and we could get ahead of the others. May already had decided that she would be at the head of her class when she finished school, and every time you wanted her and couldn't find her, if you would look across the foot of mother's bed, May would be there with a spelling book. Once she had spelled down our school, when Laddie was not there.

Father had met Peter Dover in town, and he had said that he was coming to see Sally, because he had something of especial importance to tell her.

"Did he say what it was?" asked Sally.

"Only what I have told you," replied father.

Sally wanted to take the broom and sweep the parlour.

"It's clean as a ribbon," said mother.

"If you go in there, you'll wake the baby," said Lucy.

"Will it kill it if I do?" asked Sally.

"No, but it will make it cross as fire, so it will cry all the time Peter is here," said Lucy.

"I'll be surprised if it doesn't scream every minute anyway," said Sally.

"I hope it will," said Lucy. "That will make Peter think a while before he comes so often."

That made Sally so angry she couldn't speak, so she went out and began killing chickens. I helped her catch them. They were so used to me they would come right to my feet when I shelled corn.

"I'm going to kill three," said Sally. "I'm going to be sure we have enough, but don't you tell until their heads are off."

While she was working on them mother came out and asked how many she had, so Sally said three. Mother counted us and said that wasn't enough; there would have to be four at least.

After she was gone Sally looked at me and said: "Well, for land's sake!"

It was so funny she had to laugh, and by the time I caught the fourth one, and began helping pick them, she was over being provoked and we had lots of fun.

The minute I saw Peter Dover he made me think of something. I rode his horse to the barn with Leon leading it. There we saw Laddie.

"Guess what!" I cried.

"Never could!" laughed Laddie, giving Peter Dover's horse a slap as it passed him on the way to a stall.

"Four chickens, ham, biscuit, and cake!" I announced.

"Is it a barbecue?" asked Laddie.

"No, the extra one is for the baby," said Leon. "Squally little runt, I call it."

"It's a nice baby!" said Laddie.

"What do you know about it?" demanded Leon.

"Well, considering that I started with you, and have brought up two others since, I am schooled in all there is to know," said Laddie.

"Guess what else!" I cried.

"More?" said Laddie. "Out with it! Don't kill me with suspense."

"Father is going to town Saturday to meet the new teacher, and she will stay at our house as usual."

Leon yelled and fell back in a manger, while Laddie held the harness oil to his nose.

"More!" cried Leon, grabbing the bottle.

"Are you sure?" asked Laddie of me earnestly.

"It's decided. Mother said so," I told him.

"Name of a black cat, why?" demanded Laddie.

"Mother said we were most convenient for the teacher."

"Aren't there enough of us?" asked Leon, straightening up and sniffing harness oil as if his life depended on it.

"Any unprejudiced person would probably say so to look in," said Laddie.

"I'll bet she'll be sixty and a cat," said Leon. "Won't I have fun with her?"

"Maybe so, maybe not!" said Laddie. "You can't always tell, for sure. Remember your Alamo! You were going to have fun with the teacher last year, but she had it with you."

Leon threw the oil bottle at him. Laddie caught it and set it on the shelf.

"I don't understand," said Leon.

"I do," said Laddie dryly. "*This* is one reason." He hit Peter Dover's horse another slap.

"Maybe yes," said Leon.

"Shelley to music school, two."

"Yes," said Leon. "Peter Dovers are the greatest expense, and Peter won't happen but once. Shelley will have at least two years in school before it is her turn, and you come next, anyway."

"Shut up!" cried Laddie.

"Thanky! Your orders shall be obeyed gladly."

He laid down the pitchfork, went outside, closed the door, and latched it. Laddie called to him, but he ran to the house. When Laddie and I finished our work, and his, and wanted to go, we had to climb the stairs and leave through the front door on the embankment.

"The monkey!" said Laddie, but he didn't get mad; he just laughed.

The minute I stepped into the house and saw the parlour door closed, I thought of that "something" again. I walked past it, but couldn't hear anything. Of course mother wanted to know; and she would be very thankful to me if I could tell her. I went out the front door, and thought deeply on the situation. The windows were wide open, but I was far below them and I could only hear a sort of murmur. Why can't people speak up loud and plain, anyway? Of course they would sit on the big haircloth sofa. Didn't Leon call it the "sparking bench"? The hemlock tree would be best. I climbed quieter than a cat, for they break bark and make an awful scratching with their claws sometimes; my bare feet were soundless. Up and up I went, slowly, for it was dreadfully rough. They were not on the sofa. I could see plainly through the needles. Then I saw the spruce would have been better, for they were standing in front of the parlour door and Peter had one hand on the knob. His other arm was around my sister Sally. Breathlessly I leaned as far as I could, and watched.

"Father said he'd give me the money to buy a half interest, and furnish a house nicely, if you said 'yes,' Sally," said Peter.

Sally leaned back all pinksome and blushful, and while she laughed at him she

> "*Carelessly tossed off a curl*
> *That played on her delicate brow.*"

exactly like Mary Dow in McGuffey's Third.

"Well, what did I *say?*" she asked.

"Come to think of it, you didn't say anything."

Sally's face was all afire with dancing lights, and she laughed the gayest little laugh.

"Are you so very sure of that, Peter?" she said.

"I'm not sure of anything," said Peter, "except that I am so happy I could fly."

"Try it, fool!" I said to myself, deep in my throat.

Sally laughed again, and Peter took his other hand from the door and put that arm around Sally too, and he drew her to him and kissed her, the longest, hardest kiss I ever saw. I let go and rolled, tumbled, slid, and scratched down the hemlock tree, dropped from the last branch to the ground, and scampered around the house. I reached the dining-room door when every one was gathering for supper.

"Mother!" I cried. "Mother! Yes! They're engaged! He's kissing her, mother! Yes, Lucy, they're engaged!"

I rushed in to tell all of them what they would be glad to know, and if there didn't stand Peter and Sally! How they ever got through that door, and across the sitting-room before me, I don't understand. Sally made a dive at me, and I was so astonished I forgot to run, so she caught me. She started for the wood house with me, and mother followed. Sally turned at the door and she was the whitest of anything you ever saw.

"This is my affair," she said. "I'll attend to this young lady."

"Very well," said mother, and as I live she turned and left me to my sad fate, as it says in a story book we have. I wish when people are going to punish me, they'd take a switch and strike respectably, like mother does. This thing of having some one get all over me, and not having an idea where I'm going to be hit, is the worst punishment that I ever had. I'd been down the hill and up the hemlock that day, anyway. I'd always been told Sally didn't want me. She *proved* it right then. Finally she quit, because she was too tired to strike again, so I crept among the shavings on the work bench and went to sleep. I *thought* they would like to know, and that I was going to please them.

Anyway, they found out, for by the time Sally got back Peter had told them about the store, and the furnished house, and asked father for Sally right before all of them, which father said was pretty brave; but Peter knew it was all right or he couldn't have come like he'd been doing.

After that, you couldn't hear anything at our house but wedding. Sally's share of linen and bedding was all finished long ago. Father took her to Fort Wayne on the cars to buy her wedding, travelling, and working dresses, and her hat, cloak, and linen, like you have when you marry.

It was strange that Sally didn't want mother to go, but she said the trip would tire her too much. Mother said it was because Sally could coax more dresses from father. Anyway, mother told him to set a limit and stick to it. She said she knew he hadn't done it as she got the first glimpse of Sally's face when they came back, but the child looked so beautiful and happy she hadn't the heart to spoil her pleasure.

The next day a sewing woman came; and all of them were shut up in the sitting-room, while the sewing machine just whizzed on the working dresses. Sally said the wedding dress had to be made by hand. She kept the room locked, and every new thing that they made was laid away on the bed in the parlour bedroom, and none of us had a peep until everything was finished. It was awfully exciting, but I wouldn't pretend I cared, because I was huffy at her. I told her I wouldn't kiss her goodbye, and I'd be *glad* when she was gone.

Sally said the school-ma'am simply had to go to Winters', or some place else, but mother said possibly a stranger would have some ideas, and know some new styles, so Sally then thought maybe they had better try it a few days, and she could have her place and be company when she and Shelley left. Shelley was rather silent and blue, and before long I found her crying, because mother had told her she couldn't start for Chicago until after the wedding, and that would make her miss six weeks at the start.

Next day word was sent around that school was to begin the coming Monday; so Saturday afternoon the people who had children large enough to go sent the biggest of them to clean the schoolhouse. May, Leon, and I went to do our share. Just when there were about a bushel of nut shells, and withered apple cores, and inky paper on the floor, the blackboard half cleaned, and ashes trailed deep between the stove and the window Billy Wilson was throwing them from, some one shouted: "There comes Mr. Stanton with Her."

All of us dropped everything and ran to the south windows. I tell you I was proud of our big white team as it came prancing down the hill, and the gleaming patent leather trimmings, and the brass side lamps shining in the sun. Father sat very straight, driving rather fast, as if he would as lief get it over with, and instead of riding on the back seat, where mother always sat, the teacher was in front beside him, and she seemed to be talking constantly. We looked at each other and groaned when father stopped at the hitching post and got out. If we had tried to see what a dreadful muss we could make, things could have looked no worse. I think father told her to wait in the carriage, but we heard her cry: "Oh Mr. Stanton, let me see the dear children I'm to teach, and where I'm to work."

Hopped is the word. She hopped from the carriage and came hopping after father. She was as tall as a clothes prop and scarcely as fat. There were gray hairs coming on her temples. Her face was sallow and wrinkled, and she had faded, pale-blue eyes. Her dress was like my mother had worn several years before, in style, and of stiff gray stuff. She made me feel that no one wanted her at home, and probably that was the reason she had come so far away.

Every one stood dumb. Mother always went to meet people and May was old enough to know it. She went, but she looked exactly as she does when the wafer bursts and the quinine gets in her mouth, and she doesn't dare spit it out, because it costs five dollars a bottle, and it's going to do her good. Father introduced May and some of the older children, and May helped him with the others, and then he told us to "dig in and work like troopers," and he would take Miss Pollard on home.

"Oh do let me remain and help the dear children!" she cried.

"We can finish!" we answered in full chorus.

"How lovely of you!" she chirped.

Chirp makes you think of a bird; and in speech and manner Miss Amelia Pollard was the most birdlike of any human being I ever have seen. She hopped from the step to the walk, turned to us, her head on one side, playfulness in the air around her, and shook her finger at us.

"Be extremely particular that you leave things immaculate at the consummation of your labour," she said. " 'Remember that cleanliness is next to Godliness!' "

"Two terms of that!" gasped Leon, sinking on the stove hearth. "Behold Job mourning as close the ashes as he can."

Billy Wilson had the top lid off, so he reached down and got a big handful of ashes and sifted them over Leon. But it's no fun to do anything like that to him; he only sank in a more dejected heap, and moaned: "Send for Bildad and Zophar to comfort me, and more ashes, please."

"Why does the little feathered dear touch earth at all? Why doesn't she fly?" demanded Silas Shaw.

"I'm going to get a hundred wads ready for Monday," said Jimmy Hood. "We can shoot them when we please."

"Bet ten cents you can't hit her," said Billy Wilson. "There ain't enough of her for a decent mark."

"Let's quit and go home," proposed Leon. "This will look worse than it does now by Monday night."

Then every one began talking at once. Suddenly May seized the poker and began pounding on the top of the stove for order.

"We must clean this up," she said. "We might as well finish. Maybe you'll shoot wads and do what you please, and maybe you won't. Her eyes went around like a cat that smells mice. If she can spell the language she uses, she is the best we've ever had."

That made us blink, and I never forgot it. Many times afterward while listening to people talk, I wondered if they could spell the words they used.

"Well, come on, then!" said Leon. He seized the broom and handed it to Billy Wilson, quoting as he did so, "Work, work, my boy, be not afraid"; and he told Silas Shaw as he gave him the mop, to "Look labour boldly in the face!" but he never did a thing himself, except to keep every one laughing.

So we cleaned up as well as we could, and Leon strutted like Bobby, because he locked the door and carried the key. When we reached home I was sorry I hadn't gone with father, so I could have seen mother, Sally, Candace, and Laddie when first they met the new teacher. The shock showed yet! Miss Amelia had taken off her smothery woollen dress and put on a black calico, but it wasn't any more cheerful. She didn't know what to do, and you could see plainly that no one knew what to do with her, so they united in sending me to show her the place. I asked her what she would like most to see, and she said everything was so charming she couldn't decide. I thought if she had no more choice than that, one place would do as well as another, so I started for the orchard. Quick as we got there, I knew what to do. I led her straight to our best cling peach tree, told her to climb on the fence so she could reach easily, and eat all she chose. We didn't dare shake the tree, because the pigs ran on the other side of the fence, and they chanked up every peach that fell there. Those peaches were too good to feed even father's finest Berkshires.

By the time Miss Amelia had eaten nine or ten, she was so happy to think she was there, she quit tilting her head and using big words. Of course she couldn't know how I loved to hear them, and maybe she thought I wouldn't know what they meant, and that they would be wasted on me. If she had understood how much spelling and defining I'd heard in my life, I guess she might have talked up as big as she could, and still I'd have got most of it. When she reached the place where she ate more slowly, she began to talk. She must have asked me most a hundred questions. What all our names were, how old we were, if our girls had lots of beaus, and if there were many men in the neighbourhood, and dozens of things my mother never asked any one. She always inquired if people were well, if their crops were growing, how much fruit they had, and how near their quilts were finished.

I told her all about Sally and the wedding, because no one cared who knew it, after I had been pounded to mince-meat for telling. She asked if Shelley had any beaus, and I said there wasn't any one who came like Peter, but every man in the neighbourhood wanted to be her beau. Then she asked about Laddie, and I was taking no risks, so I said: "I only see him at home. I don't know where he goes when he's away. You'll have to ask him."

"Oh, I never would dare," she said. "But he must. He is so handsome! The girls would just compel him to go to see them."

"Not if he didn't want to go," I said.

"You must never, never tell him I said so, but I do think he is the handsomest man I ever saw."

"So do I," I said, "and it wouldn't make any difference if I told him."

"Then do you mean you're going to tell him my foolish remark?" she giggled.

"No use," I said. "He knows it now. Every time he parts his hair he sees how good looking he is. He doesn't care. He says the only thing that counts with a man is to be big, strong, manly, and well educated."

"Is he well educated?"

"Yes, I think so, as far as he's gone," I answered. "Of course he will go on being educated every day of his life, same as father. He says it is all rot about 'finishing' your education. You never do. You learn more important things each day, and by the time you are old enough to die, you have almost enough sense to know how to live comfortably. Pity, isn't it?"

"Yes," said Miss Amelia, "it's an awful pity, but it's the truth. Is your mother being educated too?"

"Whole family," I said. "We learn all the time, mother most

of any, because father always looks out for her. You see, it takes so much of her time to manage the house, and sew, and knit, and darn, that she can't study so much as the others; so father reads all the books to her, and tells her about everything he finds out, and so do all of us. Just ask her if you think she doesn't know things."

"I wouldn't know what to ask," said Miss Amelia.

"Ask how long it took to make this world, who invented printing, where English was first spoken, why Greeley changed his politics, how to make bluebell perfumery, cut out a dress, or cure a baby of worms. Just ask her!"

Miss Amelia threw a peach stone through a fence crack and hit a pig. It was a pretty neat shot.

"I don't need ask any of that," she said scornfully. "I know all of it now."

"All right! What is best for worms?" I asked.

"Jayne's vermifuge," said Miss Amelia.

"Wrong!" I cried. "That's a patent medicine. Tea made from male fern root is best, because there's no morphine in it!"

The supper bell rang and I was glad of it. Peaches are not very filling after all, for I couldn't see but that Miss Amelia ate as much as any of us. For a few minutes every one was slow in speaking, then mother asked about cleaning the schoolhouse, Laddie had something to explain to father about corn mould, Sally and the dressmaker talked about pipings—not a bird—a new way to fold goods to make trimmings, and soon everything was going on the same as if the new teacher were not there. I noticed that she kept her head straight, and was not nearly so glib-tongued and birdlike before mother and Sally as she had been at the schoolhouse. Maybe that was why father told mother that night that the new teacher would bear acquaintance.

Sunday was like every other Sabbath, except that I felt so sad all day I could have cried, but I was not going to do it. Seemed as if I never could put on shoes, and so many clothes Monday morning, quite like church, and be shut in a room for hours, to try to learn what was in books, when the world was running over with things to find out where you could have your feet in water, leaves in your hair, and little living creatures in your hands. In the afternoon Miss Amelia asked Laddie to take her for a walk to see the creek, and the barn, and he couldn't escape.

I suppose our barn was exactly like hundreds of others. It was built against an embankment so that on one side you could drive right on the threshing floor with big loads of grain. On the sunny side in the lower part were the sheep pens, cattle stalls, and horse mangers. It was always half bursting with overflowing grain bins and haylofts in the fall; the swallows twittered under the roof until time to go south for winter, as they sailed from the ventilators to their nests plastered against the rafters or eaves. The big swinging doors front and back could be opened to let the wind blow through in a strong draft. From the east doors you could see for miles across the country.

I said our barn was like others, but it was not. There was not another like it in the whole world. Father, the boys, and the hired men always kept it cleaned and in proper shape every day. The upper floor was as neat as some women's houses. It was swept, the sun shone in, the winds drifted through, the odours of drying hay and grain were heavy, and from the top of the natural little hill against which it stood you could see for miles in all directions.

The barn was our great playhouse on Sundays. It was clean there, we were where we could be called when wanted, and we liked to climb the ladders to the top of the haymows, walk the beams to the granaries, and jump to the hay. One day May came down on a snake that had been brought in with a load. I can hear her yell now, and it made her so frantic she's been killing them ever since. It was only a harmless little garter snake, but she was so surprised.

Miss Amelia held her head very much on one side all the time she walked with Laddie, and she was so birdlike Leon slipped him a brick and told him to have her hold it to keep her down. Seemed as if she might fly any minute. She thought our barn was the nicest she ever had seen and the cleanest. When Laddie opened the doors on the east side, and she could see the big, red, yellow, and green apples thick as leaves on the trees in the orchard, the lane, the woods pasture, and the meadow with scattering trees, two running springs, and the meeting of the creeks, she said it was the loveliest sight she ever saw—I mean beheld. Laddie liked that, so he told her about the beautiful town, and the lake, and the Wabash River, that our creek emptied into, and how people came from other states and big cities and stayed all summer to fish, row, swim, and have good times.

She asked him to take her to the meadow, but he excused himself, because he had an engagement. So she stood in the door, and watched him saddle Flos and start to the house to dress in his riding clothes. After that she didn't care a thing about the meadow, so we went back.

Our house looked as if we had a party. We were all dressed in our best, and every one was out in the yard, garden, or orchard. Peter and Sally were under the big pearmain apple tree at the foot of the orchard, Shelley and a half dozen beaus were everywhere. May had her spelling book in one hand and was in my big catalpa talking to Billy Stevens, who was going to be her beau as soon as mother said she was old enough. Father was reading a wonderful new book to mother and some of the neighbours. Leon was perfectly happy because no one wanted him, so he could tease all of them by saying things they didn't like to hear. When Laddie came out and mounted, Leon asked him where he was going, and Laddie said he hadn't fully decided: he might ride to Elizabeth's, and not come back until Monday morning.

"You think you're pretty slick," said Leon. "But if we could see north to the cross road we could watch you turn west, and go past Pryors to show yourself off, or try to find the Princess on the road walking or riding. I know something I'm saving to tell next time you get smart, Mr. Laddie."

Laddie seemed annoyed and no one was quicker to see it than Leon. Instantly he jumped on the horse block, pulled down his face long as he could, stretched his hands toward Laddie, and

making his voice all wavery and tremulous, he began reciting
from "Lochiel's Warning," in tones of agonizing pleading:

> *"Laddie, Laddie, beware of the day!*
> *For, dark and despairing, my sight, I may seal,*
> *But man cannot cover what God would reveal;*
> *'Tis the sunset of life gives me mystical lore,*
> *And coming events cast their shadows before."*

That scared me. I begged Leon to tell, but he wouldn't say
a word more. He went and talked to Miss Amelia as friendly as
you please, and asked her to take a walk in the orchard and get
some peaches, and she went flying. He got her all she could carry
and guided her to Peter and Sally, introduced her to Peter, and
then slipped away and left her. Then he and Sally couldn't talk
about their wedding, and Peter couldn't squeeze her hand, and
she couldn't fix his tie, and it was awful. Shelley and her boys
almost laughed themselves sick over it, and then she cried, "To
the rescue!" and started, so they followed. They captured Miss
Amelia and brought her back, and left her with father and the
wonderful book, but I'm sure she liked the orchard better.

I took Grace Greenwood under my arm, Hezekiah on my
shoulder, and with Bobby at my heels went away. I didn't want
my hair pulled, or to be teased that day. There was such a hard-
ness around my heart, and such a lump in my throat, that I
didn't care what happened to me one minute, and the next I
knew I'd slap any one who teased me, if I were sent to bed for
it. As I went down the lane Peter called to me to come and see
him, but I knew exactly how he looked, and didn't propose to
make up. There was not any sense in Sally clawing me all over,
when I only tried to help mother and Lucy find out what they
wanted to know so badly. I went down the hill, crossed the creek
on the stepping-stones, and followed the cowpath into the woods
pasture. It ran beside the creek bank through the spice thicket
and blackberry patches, under pawpaw groves, and beneath
giant oaks and elms. Just where the creek turned at the open
pasture, below the church and cemetery, right at the deep bend,

stood the biggest white oak father owned. It was about a tree exactly like this that an Englishman wrote a beautiful poem in McGuffey's Sixth, that begins:

> *"A song to the oak, the brave old oak,*
> *Who hath ruled in the greenwood long;*
> *Here's health and renown to his broad green crown,*
> *And his fifty arms so strong."*

I knew it was the same, because I counted the arms time and again, and there were exactly fifty. There was a pawpaw and spice hedge around three sides of this one, and water on the other. Wild grapes climbed from the bushes to the lower branches and trailed back to earth again. Here, I had two secrets I didn't propose to tell. One was that in the crotch of some tiptop branches the biggest chicken hawks you ever saw had their nest, and if they took too many chickens father said they'd have to be frightened a little with a gun. I can't begin to tell how I loved those hawks. They did the one thing I wanted to most, and never could. When I saw them serenely soar above the lowest of the soft fleecy September clouds, I was wild with envy. I would have gone without chicken myself rather than have seen one of those splendid big brown birds dropped from the skies. I was so careful to shield them, that I selected this for my especial retreat when I wanted most to be alone, and I carefully gathered up any offal from the nest that might point out their location, and threw it into the water where it ran the swiftest.

I parted the vines and crept where the roots of the big oak stretched like bony fingers over the water, that was slowly eating under it and baring its roots. I sat on them above the water and thought. I had decided the day before about my going to school, and the day before that, and many, many times before that, and here I was having to settle it all over again. Doubled on the oak roots, a troubled little soul, I settled it once more. No books or teachers were needed to tell me about flowing water and fish, how hawks raised their broods and kept house, about the softly cooing doves of the spice thickets, the cuckoos slipping snakelike

in and out of the wild crab-apple bushes, or the brown thrush's
weird call from the thorn bush. I knew what they said and did,
but their names, where they came from, where they went when
the wind blew and the snow fell—how was I going to find out
that? Worse yet were the flowers, butterflies, and moths; they
were mysteries past learning alone, and while the names I made
up for them were pretty and suitable, I knew in all reason they
wouldn't be the same in the books. I had to go, but no one will
ever know what it cost. When the supper bell rang, I sat still.
I'd have to wait until at least two tables had been served, anyway, so I sat there and nursed my misery, looked and listened,
and by and by I felt better. I couldn't see or hear a thing that
was standing still. Father said even the rocks grew larger year
by year. The trees were getting bigger, the birds were busy, and
the creek was in a dreadful hurry to reach the river. It was like
that poetry piece that says:

> *"When a playful brook, you gambolled,"*

(Mostly that gambolled word is said about lambs)

> *"And the sunshine o'er you smiled,*
> *On your banks did children loiter,*
> *Looking for the spring flowers wild?"*

The creek was more in earnest and working harder at pushing
steadily ahead without ever stopping than anything else; and like
the poetry piece again, it really did "seem to smile upon us as it
quickly passed us by." I had to quit playing, and go to work some
time; it made me sorry to think how behind I was, because I had
not started two years before, when I should. But that couldn't
be helped now. All there was left was to go this time, for sure.
I got up heavily and slowly as an old person, and then slipped
out and ran down the path to the meadow, because I could hear
Leon whistle as he came to bring the cows.

By fast running I could start them home for him: Rose, Brin-
dle, Bess, and Pidy, Sukey and Muley; they had eaten all day,

but they still snatched bites as they went toward the gate. I wanted to surprise Leon and I did.

"Getting good, ain't you?" he asked. "What do you want?"

"Nothing!" I said. "I just heard you coming and I thought I'd help you."

"Where were you?"

"Playing."

"You don't look as if you'd been having much fun."

"I don't expect ever to have any, after I begin school."

"Oh!" said Leon. "It is kind of tough the first day or two, but you'll soon get over it. You should have behaved yourself, and gone when they started you two years ago."

"Think I don't know it?"

Leon stopped and looked at me sharply.

"I'll help you nights, if you want me to," he offered.

"Can I ever learn?" I asked, almost ready to cry.

"Of course you can," said Leon. "You're smart as the others, I suppose. The sevens and nines of the multiplication table are the stickers, but you ought to do them if other girls can. You needn't feel bad because you are behind a little to start on; you are just that much better prepared to work, and you can soon overtake them. You know a lot none of the rest of us do, and some day it will come your turn to show off. Cheer up, you'll be all right."

Men are such a comfort. I pressed closer for more.

"Do you suppose I will?" I asked.

"Of course," said Leon. "Any minute the woods, or birds, or flowers are mentioned your time will come; and all of us will hear you read and help nights. I'd just as soon as not."

That was the most surprising thing. He never offered to help me before. He never acted as if he cared what became of me. Maybe it was because Laddie always had taken such good care of me, Leon had no chance. He seemed willing enough now. I looked at him closely.

"You'll find out I'll learn things if I try," I boasted. "And you will find out I don't tell secrets either."

"I've been waiting for you to pipe up about——"

"Well, I haven't piped, have I?"

"Not yet."

"I am not going to either."

"I almost believe you. A girl you could trust would be a funny thing to see."

"Tell me what you know about Laddie, and see if I'm funny."

"You'd telltale sure as life!"

"Well, if you know it, he knows it anyway."

"He doesn't know *what* I know."

"Well, be careful and don't worry mother. You know how she is since the fever, and father says all of us must think of her. If it's anything that would bother her, don't tell before her."

"Say, looky here," said Leon, turning on me sharply, "is all this sudden consideration for mother or are you legging for Laddie?"

"For both," I answered stoutly.

"Mostly for Laddie, just the same. You can't fool me, missy. I won't tell you one word."

"You needn't!" I answered, "I don't care!"

"Yes you do," he said. "You'd give anything to find out what I know, and then run to Laddie with it, but you can't fool me. I'm too smart for you."

"All right," I said. "You go and tell anything on Laddie, and I'll watch you, and first trick I catch you at, I'll do some telling myself, Smarty."

"That's a game more than one can play at," said Leon. "Go ahead!"

CHAPTER V

The First Day of School

"Birds in their little nests agree.
And why can't we?"

B-I-R-D-S, birds, i-n, in, t-h-e-i-r, their, l-i-t-t-l-e, little, n-e-s-t-s, nests, a-g-r-e-e, agree."

My feet burned in my new shoes, but most of my body was chilling as I stood beside Miss Amelia on the platform, before the whole school, and followed the point of her pencil, while, a letter at a time, I spelled aloud my first sentence. Nothing ever had happened to me as bad as that. I was not used to so much clothing. It was like taking a colt from the woods pasture and putting it into harness for the first time. That lovely September morning I followed Leon and May down the dusty road, my heart sick with dread.

May was so much smaller that I could have picked her up and carried her. She was a gentle, loving little thing, until some one went too far, and then they got what they deserved, all at once and right away.

Many of the pupils were waiting before the church. Leon climbed the steps, made a deep bow, waved toward the school building across the way, and what he intended to say was, "Still sits the schoolhouse by the road," but he was a little excited and the s's doubled his tongue, so that we heard: "Shill stits the schoolhouse by the road." We just yelled and I forgot a little about myself.

When Miss Amelia came to the door and rang the bell, May

must have remembered something of how her first day felt, for as we reached the steps she waited for me, took me in with her, and found me a seat. If she had not, I'm quite sure I'd have run away and fought until they left me in freedom, as I had two years before. All forenoon I had shivered in my seat, while classes were arranged, and the elder pupils were started on their work; then Miss Amelia called me to her on the platform and tried to find out how much schooling I had. I was ashamed that I knew so little, but there was no sense in her making me spell after a pencil, like a baby. I'd never seen the book she picked up. I could read the line she pointed to, and I told her so, but she said to spell the words; so I thought she had to be obeyed, for one poetry piece I know says:

> *"Quickly speed your steps to school*
> *And there mind your teacher's rule."*

I can see Miss Amelia to-day. Her pale face was lined deeper than ever, her drab hair was dragged back tighter. She wore a black calico dress with white huckleberries, and a white calico apron figured in large black apples, each having a stem and two leaves. In dress she was a fruitful person. She had been a surprise to all of us. Chipper as a sparrow, she had hopped, and chattered, and darted here and there, until the hour of opening. Then in the stress of arranging classes and getting started, all her birdlike ways slipped from her. Stern and bony she stood before us, and with a cold light in her pale eyes, she began business in a manner that made Johnny Hood forget all about his paper wads, and Leon commenced studying like a good boy, and never even tried to have fun with her. Every one was so surprised you could notice it, except May, and she looked, "I told you so!" even in the back. She had a way of doing that very thing as I never saw any one else. From the set of her head, how she carried her shoulders, the stiffness of her spine, and her manner of walking, if you knew her well, you could tell what she thought, the same as if you saw her face.

I followed that pencil point and in a husky voice repeated the letters. I could see Tillie Baher laughing at me from behind her geography, and every one else had stopped what they were doing to watch and listen, so I forgot to be thankful that I even knew my a b c's. I spelled through the sentence, pronounced the words and repeated them without much thought as to the meaning; at that moment it didn't occur to me that she had chosen the lesson because father had told her how I made friends with the birds. The night before he had been putting me through memory tests, and I had recited poem after poem, even long ones in the Sixth Reader, and never made one mistake when the piece was about birds. At our house, we heard next day's lessons for all ages gone over every night so often, that we couldn't help knowing them by heart, if we had any brains at all, and I just loved to get the big folk's readers and learn the bird pieces. Father had been telling her about it, so for that reason she thought she would start me on the birds, but I'm sure she made me spell after a pencil point, like a baby, on purpose to shame me, because I was two years behind the others who were near my age. As I repeated the line Miss Amelia thought she saw her chance. She sprang to her feet, tripped a few steps toward the centre of the platform, and cried: "Classes, attention! Our Youngest Pupil has just completed her first sentence. This sentence contains a Thought. It is a wonderfully beautiful Thought. A Thought that suggests a great moral lesson for each of us. 'Birrrds—in their little nests—agreee.' "

Never have I heard cooing sweetness to equal the melting tones in which Miss Amelia drawled those words. Then she continued, after a good long pause in order to give us time to allow the "Thought" to sink in: "There is a lesson in this for all of us. We are here in our schoolroom, like little birds in their nest. Now how charming it would be if all of us would follow the example of the birds, and at our work, and in our play, agreeee—be kind, loving, and considerate of each other. Let us all remember always this wonderful truth: 'Birrrrds—in their little nests—agreeeee!' "

In three steps I laid hold of her apron. Only last night Leon had said it would come, yet whoever would have thought that I'd get a chance like this, so soon.

"Ho but they don't!" I cried. "They fight like anything! Every day they make the feathers fly!"

In a backward stroke Miss Amelia's fingers, big and bony, struck my cheek a blow that nearly upset me. A red wave crossed her face, and her eyes snapped. I never had been so surprised in all my life. I was only going to tell her the truth. What she had said was altogether false. Ever since I could remember I had watched courting male birds fight all over the farm. After a couple had paired, and were nest building, the father always drove every other bird from his location. In building I had seen him pecked for trying to place a twig. I had seen that happen again for merely offering food to the mother, if she didn't happen to be hungry, or for trying to make love to her when she was brooding. If a young bird failed to get the bite it wanted, it sometimes grabbed one of its nestmates by the bill, or the eye even, and tried to swallow it whole. Always the oldest and strongest climbed on top of the youngest and fooled his mammy into feeding him most by having his head highest, his mouth widest, and begging loudest. There could be no mistake. I was so amazed I forgot the blow, as I stared at the fool woman.

"I don't see why you slap me!" I cried. "It's the truth! Lots of times old birds pull out bunches of feathers fighting, and young ones in the nests bite each other until they squeal."

Miss Amelia caught my shoulders and shook me as hard as she could; and she proved to be stronger than you ever would have thought to look at her.

"Take your seat!" she cried. "You are a rude, untrained child!"

"They do fight!" I insisted, as I held my head high and walked to my desk.

Leon laughed out loud, and that made everyone else. Miss Amelia had so much to do for a few minutes that she forgot me, and I know now why Leon started it, at least partly. He said afterward it was the funniest sight he ever saw. My cheek smarted and burned. I could scarcely keep from feeling to learn whether it were swelling, but I wouldn't have shed a tear or raised my hand for anything you could offer.

Recess was coming and I didn't know what to do. If I went to the playground, all of them would tease me; and if I sat at my desk Miss Amelia would have another chance at me. That was too much to risk, so I followed the others outdoors, and oh joy! there came Laddie down the road. He set me on one of the posts of the hitching rack before the church, and with my arms around his neck, I sobbed out the whole story.

"She didn't understand," said Laddie quietly. "You stay here until I come back. I'll go explain to her about the birds. Perhaps she hasn't watched them as closely as you have."

Recess was over before he returned. He had wet his handkerchief at the water bucket, and now he bathed my face and eyes, straightened my hair with his pocket comb, and began unlacing my shoes.

"What are you going to do?" I asked. "I must wear them. All the girls do. Only the boys are barefoot."

"You are excused," answered Laddie. "Three-fourths of the day is enough to begin on. Miss Amelia says you may come with me."

"Where are you going?"

Laddie was stripping off my stockings as he looked into my eyes, and smiled a peculiar little smile.

"Oh Laddie!" I cried. "Will you take me? Honest!"

He laughed again and then he rubbed my feet.

"Poor abused feet," he said. "Sometimes I wish shoes had never been invented."

"They feel pretty good when there's ice."

"So they do!" said Laddie.

He swung me to the ground, and we crossed the road, climbed the fence, and in a minute our redbird swamp shut the schoolhouse and cross old Miss Amelia from sight. Then we turned and started straight toward our Big Woods. I could scarcely keep on the ground.

"How are the others getting along?" asked Laddie.

"She's cross as two sticks," I told him. "Johnny Hood hasn't shot one paper wad, and Leon hadn't done a thing until he laughed about the birds, and I guess he did that to make her forget me."

"Good!" cried Laddie. "I didn't suppose the boy thought that far."

"Oh, you never can tell by looking at him, how far Leon is thinking," I said.

"That's so, too," said Laddie. "Are your feet comfortable now?"

"Yes, but Laddie, isn't my face marked?"

"I'm afraid it is a little," said Laddie. "We'll bathe it again at the creek. We must get it fixed so mother won't notice."

"What will the Princess think?"

"That you fell, perhaps," said Laddie.

"Do the tears show?"

"Not at all. We washed them all away."

"Did I do wrong, Laddie?"

"Yes, I think you did."

"But it wasn't true, what she said."

"That's not the point."

We had reached the fence of the Big Woods. He lifted me to the top rail and explained, while I combed his waving hair with my fingers.

"She didn't strike you because what you said was not so, for it was. She knew instantly you were right, if she knows anything at all about outdoors. This is what made her angry: it is her first day. She wanted to make a good impression on her pupils, to arouse their interest, and awaken their respect. When you spoke, all of them knew you were right, and she was wrong; that made her ridiculous. Can't you see how it made her look and feel?"

"I didn't notice how she looked, but from the way she hit me, you could tell she felt bad enough."

"She surely did," said Laddie, kissing my cheek softly. "Poor little woman! What a world of things you have to learn!"

"Shouldn't I have told her how mistaken she was?"

"If you had gone to her alone, at recess or noon, or to-night, probably she would have thanked you. Then she could have corrected herself at some convenient time and kept her dignity."

"Must I ask her pardon?"

"What you should do, is to put yourself in Miss Amelia's place and try to understand how she felt. Then if you think you wouldn't have liked any one to do to you what you did to her, you'll know."

I hugged Laddie tight and thought fast—there was no need to think long to see how it was.

"I got to tell her I was wrong," I said. "Now let's go to the Enchanted Wood and see if we can find the Queen's daughter."

"All right!" said Laddie.

He leaped the fence, swung me over, and started toward the pawpaw thicket. He didn't do much going around. He crashed through and over; and soon he began whistling the loveliest little dancy tune. It made your head whirl, and your toes tingle, and you knew it was singing that way in his heart, and he was just letting out the music. That was why it made you want to dance and whirl; it was so alive. But that wasn't the way in an Enchanted Wood. I pulled his hand.

"Laddie!" I cautioned, "keep in the path! You'll step on the Fairies and crush a whole band with one foot. No wonder the Queen makes her daughter grow big when she sends her to you. If you make so much noise, some one will hear you, then this won't be a secret any more."

Laddie laughed, but he stepped carefully in the path after that, and he said: "There are times, Little Sister, when I don't care whether this secret is secret another minute or not. Secrets don't agree with me. I'm too big, and broad, and too much of a man, to go creeping through the woods with a secret. I prefer to print it on a banner and ride up the road waving it."

"Like,—'A youth who bore mid snow and ice, A banner with a strange device,'" I said.

"That would be 'a banner with a strange device,'" laughed Laddie. "But, yes—something like!"

"Have you told the Princess?"

"I have!" Laddie fairly shouted it.

"Does *she* like secrets?"

"No more than I do!"

"Then why——?"

"There you go!" said Laddie. "Zeus, but the woman is beginning to measle out all over you! You know as well as any one that there's something wrong at her house. I don't know what it is; I can't even make a sensible guess as yet, but it's worse than the neighbours think. It's a thing that has driven a family from their home country, under a name that I have doubts about being theirs, and sent them across an ocean, 'strangers in a strange land,' as it says in the Bible. It's something that keeps a cultured gentleman and scholar raging up and down the roads and over the country like a madman. It shuts a white-faced, lovely, little woman from her neighbours, but I have passed her walking the road at night with both hands pressed against her heart. Sometimes it tries the Princess past endurance and control; and it has her so worn and tired struggling with it that she is willing to carry another secret, rather than try to find strength to do anything that would make more trouble for her father and mother."

"Would it trouble them for her to know you, Laddie?"

"So long as they don't and won't become acquainted with me, or any one, of course it would."

"Can't you force them to know you?"

"That I can!" said Laddie. "But you see, I only met the Princess a short time ago, and there would be no use in raising trouble, unless she will make me her Knight!"

"But hasn't she, Laddie?"

"Not in the very littlest least," said Laddie. "For all I know, she is merely using me to help pass a lonely hour. You see, people reared in England have ideas of class, that two or three generations spent here wash out. The Princess and her family are of the unwashed British. Father's people have been here long enough to judge a man on his own merits."

"You mean the Princess' family would think you're not good enough to be her Knight?"

"Exactly!"

"And we know that our family thinks they are infidels, and wicked people; and that if she would have you, mother would be sick in bed over it. Oh Laddie!"

"Precisely!"

"What are you going to do?"

"That I must find out."

"When it will make so much trouble, why not forget her, and go on like you did before she came? Then, all of us were happy. Now, it makes me shiver to think what will happen."

"Me too," said Laddie. "But look here, Little Sister, right in my face. Will you ever forget the Princess?"

"Never!"

"Then how can you ask me to?"

"I didn't mean forget her, exactly. I meant not come here and do things that will make every one unhappy."

"One minute, Chick-a-Biddy," said Laddie. Sometimes he called me that, when he loved me the very most of all. I don't believe any one except me ever heard him do it. "Let me ask you this: does our father love our mother?"

"Love her?" I cried. "Why he just loves her to death! He turns so white, and he suffers so, when her pain is the worst. Love her? And she him? Why, don't you remember the other day when he tipped her head against him and kissed her throat as he left the table; that he asked her if she 'loved him yet,' and she said right before all of us, 'Why Paul, I love you, until I scarcely can keep my fingers off you!' Laddie, is it like that with you and the Princess?"

"It is with me," said Laddie. "Not with the Princess! Now, can I forget her? Can I keep away from even the chance to pass her on the road?"

"No," I said. "No, you can't, Laddie. But can you ever make her love you?"

"It takes time to find that out," said Laddie. "I have got to try; so you be a woman and keep my secret a little while longer, until I find a way out, but don't bother your head about it!"

"I can't help bothering my head, Laddie. Can't you make her understand that God is not a myth?"

"I'm none too sure what I believe myself," said Laddie. "Not that there is no God—I don't mean that—but I surely don't believe all father's teachings."

"If you believe God, do other little things matter, Laddie?"

"I think not," said Laddie, "else Heaven would be all Methodists. As for the Princess, all she has heard in her life has been against there being a God. Now, she is learning something on the other side. After a while she can judge for herself. It is for us, who profess to be a Christian family, to prove to her why we believe in God, and what He does for us."

"Well, she would think He could do a good deal, if she knew how mother hated asking her to come to our house; and yet she did it, beautifully too, just to give her a chance to see that very thing. But I almost made her do it. I don't believe she ever would alone, Laddie, or at least not for a long time yet."

"I saw that, and understood it perfectly," said Laddie. "Thank you, Little Sister." He picked me up and hugged me tight. "If I could only make you see!"

"But Laddie, I do! I'm not a baby! I know how people love and make homes for themselves, like Sally and Peter are going to. If it is with you about the Princess as it is with father and mother, why I do know."

"All right! Here we are!" said Laddie.

He parted the willows and we stepped on the Magic Carpet, and that minute the Magic worked. I forgot every awful, solemn, troublous thing we had been talking about, and looked around while Laddie knelt and hunted for a letter, and there was none. That meant the Princess was coming, so we sat on the throne to wait. We hadn't remembered to bathe my cheek, we had been so busy when we passed the water, and I doubt if we were thinking much then. We just waited. The willow walls waved gently, the moss carpet was spotted with little gold patches of sunlight, in the shade a few of the red flowers still bloomed, and big, lazy bumblebees hummed around them, or a hummingbird stood on air before them. A sort of golden throbbing filled the woods, and my heart began to leap, why, I don't know; but I'm sure Laddie's did too, for I looked at him and his eyes were shining as I never had seen them before, while his cheeks were a little red, and he was breathing like when you've been running; then suddenly his body grew tense against mine, and that meant she was coming.

Like that first day, she came slowly through the woods, stopping here and there to touch the trunk of a tree, put back a branch, or bend over a flower face. Brown as the wood floor was her dress, and cardinal flowers blazed on her breast, and the same colour showed on her cheeks and lips. Her eyes were like Laddie's for brightness, and she was breathing the same way. I thought sure there was going to be something to remember a lifetime—I was so excited I couldn't stand still. Before it could happen Laddie went and said it was a "beautiful day," and she said "it didn't show in the woods, but the pastures needed rain." Then she kissed me. Well if I ever! I sank on the throne and sat there. They went on talking like that, until it was too dull to bear, so I slipped out and wandered away to see what I could find. When I grew tired and went back, Laddie was sitting on the Magic Carpet with his back against the beech, and the Princess was on the throne reading from a little book, reading such interesting things that I decided to listen. After a while she came to this:

"Thou are mated with a clown,
And the grossness of his nature, will have weight to bear thee down."

Laddie threw back his head, and how he laughed! The Princess put down the book and looked at him so surprised.

"Are you reading that to me because you think it appropriate?" asked Laddie.

"I am reading it because it is conceded to be one of the most beautiful poems ever written," said the Princess.

"You knew when you began that you would come to those lines."

"I never even thought of such a thing."

"But you knew that is how your father would regard any relationship, friendly or deeper, with me!"

"I cannot possibly be held responsible for what my father thinks."

"It is natural that you should think alike."

"Not necessarily! You told me recently that you didn't agree with your father on many subjects."

"Kindly answer me this," said Laddie: "Do you feel that I'm a 'clown' because I'm not schooled to the point on all questions of good manners? Do you find me gross because I plow and sow?"

"You surprise me," said the Princess. "My consenting to know and to spend a friendly hour with you here is sufficient answer. I have not found the slightest fault with your manners. I have seen no suspicion of 'grossness' about you."

"Will you tell me, frankly, exactly what you do think of me?"

"Surely! I think you are a clean, decent man, who occasionally kindly consents to put a touch of human interest into an hour, for a very lonely girl. What has happened, Laddie? This is not like you."

Laddie sat straight and studied the beech branches. Father said beech trees didn't amount to much; but I first learned all about them from that one, and what it taught me made me almost worship them always. There were the big trunk with great rough spreading roots, the bark in little ridges in places, smooth purple gray between, big lichens for ornament, the low flat branches, the waxy, wavy-edged leaves, with clear veins, and the delicious nuts in their little brown burrs. The Princess and I both stared at the branches and waited while a little breath of air stirred the leaves, the sunshine flickered, and a cricket sang a sort of lonesome song. Laddie leaned against the tree again, and he was thinking so hard, to look at him made me begin to repeat to myself the beech part of that beautiful churchyard poem our big folks recite:

"There, at the foot of yonder nodding beech,
That wreathes its old fantastic roots so high,
His listless length at noontide he would stretch,
And pore upon the brook that babbles by."

Only he was studying so deeply you could almost feel what was in his mind, and it was not about the brook at all, even if one ran close. Soon he began talking.

"Not so bad!" he said. "You might think worse. I admit the cleanliness, I strive for decency, I delight in being humanely interesting, even for an hour; you might think worse, much worse! You might consider me a 'clown.' 'A country clod.' Rather a lowdown, common thing, a 'clod,' don't you think? And a 'clown'! And 'gross' on top of that!"

"What can you mean?" asked the Princess.

"Since you don't seem to share the estimate of me, I believe I'll tell you," said Laddie. "The other day I was driving from the gravel pit with a very heavy load. The road was wide and level on either side. A man came toward me on horseback. Now the law of the road is to give half to a vehicle similar to the one you are driving, but to keep all of it when you are heavily loaded, if you are passing people afoot or horseback. The man took half the road, and kept it until the nose of his horse touched one of the team I was driving. I stopped and said: 'Good morning, sir! Do you wish to speak with me?' He called angrily: 'Get out of my way, you clod!' 'Sorry sir, but I can't,' I said. 'The law gives me this road when I am heavily loaded, and you are on foot or horseback.' "

"What did he do?" asked the Princess.

And from the way she looked I just knew she guessed the man was the same one I thought of.

"He raised his whip to strike my horse," said Laddie.

"Ah, surely!" said the Princess. "Always an arm raised to strike. And you, Man? What did you do?" she cried eagerly.

"I stood on my load, suddenly," said Laddie, "and I called: 'Hold one minute!' "

"And he?" breathed the Princess.

"Something made him pause with his arm still raised. I said to him: 'You must not strike my horse. It never has been struck, and it can't defend itself. If you want to come a few steps farther and tackle me, come ahead! I can take it or return it, as I choose.' "

"Go on!" said the Princess.

"That's all," said Laddie, "or at least almost all."

"Did he strike?"

"He did not. He stared at me a second, and then he rode around me; but he was making forceful remarks as he passed about 'country clods,' and there was an interesting one about a 'gross clown.' What you read made me think of it, that is all."

The Princess stared into the beech branches for a time and then she said: "I will ask your pardon for him. He always had a domineering temper, and trouble he had lately has almost driven him mad; he is scarcely responsible at times. I hesitate about making him angry."

"I think perhaps," said Laddie, "I would have done myself credit if I had recognized that, and given him the road, when he made a point of claiming it."

"Indeed no!" cried the Princess. "To be beaten at the game he started was exactly what he needed. If you had turned from his way, he would have considered you a clod all his life. Since you made him go around, it may possibly dawn on him that you are a man. You did the very best thing."

Then she began to laugh, and how she did laugh.

"I would give my allowance for a quarter to have seen it," she cried. "I must hurry home and tell mother."

"Does your mother know about me?" he demanded. "Does she know that you come here?"

The Princess arose and stood very tall and straight.

"You may beg my pardon or cease to know me," she said. "Whatever led you to suppose that I would know or meet you without my mother's knowledge?"

Then she started toward the entrance.

"One minute!" cried Laddie.

A leap carried him to her side. He caught her hands and held them tight, and looked straight into her eyes. Then he kissed her hands over and over. I thought from the look on her face he might have kissed her cheek if he had dared risk it; but he didn't seem to notice. Then she stooped and kissed me, and turned toward home, while Laddie and I crossed the woods to the west road, and went back past the schoolhouse. I was so tired Laddie tied the strings together and hung my shoes across his shoulders and took me by the arm the last mile.

All of them were at home when we got there, and Miss Amelia came to the gate to meet us. She was mealy-mouthed and good as pie, not at all as I had supposed she would be. I wonder what Laddie said to her. But then he always could manage things for every one. That set me to wondering if by any possible means he could fix them for himself. I climbed to the catalpa to think, and the more I thought, the more I feared he couldn't; but still mother always says one never can tell until they try, and I knew he would try with every ounce of brain and muscle in him. I sat there until the supper bell rang, and then I washed and reached the table last. The very first thing, mother asked how I bruised my face, and before I could think what to tell her, Leon said just as careless like: "Oh she must have run against something hard, playing tag at recess." Laddie began talking about Peter coming that night, and every one forgot me, but pretty soon I slipped a glance at Miss Amelia, and saw that her face was redder than mine.

CHAPTER VI

The Wedding Gown

"The gay belles of fashion may boast of excelling
  In waltz or cotillon, at whist or quadrille;
And seek admiration by vauntingly telling
  Of drawing and painting, and musical skill;
But give me the fair one, in country or city,
  Whose home and its duties are dear to her heart,
Who cheerfully warbles some rustical ditty,
  While plying the needle with exquisite art:
The bright little needle, the swift-flying needle,
  The needle directed by beauty and art."

THE next morning Miss Amelia finished the chapter—that made two for our family. Father always read one before breakfast—no wonder I knew the Bible quite well—then we sang a song, and she made a stiff, little prayer. I had my doubts about her prayers; she was on no such terms with the Lord as my father. He got right at Him and talked like a doctor, and you felt he had some influence, and there was at least a possibility that he might get what he asked for; but Miss Amelia prayed as if the Lord were ten million miles away, and she would be surprised to pieces if she got anything she wanted. When she asked the Almighty to make us good, obedient children, there was not a word she said that showed she trusted either the Lord or us, or thought there was anything between us and heaven that might make us good because we wanted to be. You couldn't keep your eyes from the big gad and ruler on her desk; she often fingered them as she prayed, and you knew from her stiff, little, sawed-out petition that her faith was in implements, and she'd hit you a crack the minute she was the least angry, same as she had me the day before. I didn't feel any too good toward her, but when the blood of the Crusaders was in the veins, right must be done even if it took a struggle. I had to live up to those little gold shells on the trinket. Father said they knew I was coming down the line, so they put on a bird for me; but I told him I would be worthy of the shells too. This took about as hard a fight for me as any Crusade would for a big, trained soldier. I had been wrong, Laddie had made me see that. So I held up my hand, and Miss Amelia saw me as she picked up Ray's arithmetic.

"What is it?"

I held to the desk to brace myself, and tried twice before I could raise my voice so that she heard.

"Please, Miss Amelia," I said, "I was wrong about the birds yesterday. Not that they don't fight—they do! But I was wrong to contradict you before every one, and on your first day, and if you'll only excuse me, the next time you make a mistake, I'll tell you after school or at recess."

The room was so still you could hear the others breathing. Miss Amelia picked up the ruler and started toward me. Possibly I raised my hands. That would be no Crusader way, but you might do it before you had time to think, when the ruler was big and your head was the only place that would be hit. The last glimpse I had of her in the midst of all my trouble made me think of Sabethany Perkins.

Sabethany died, and they buried her at the foot of the hill in our graveyard before I could remember. But her people thought heaps of her, and spent much money on the biggest tombstone in the cemetery, and planted pinies and purple phlox on her, and went every Sunday to visit her. When they moved away, they missed her so, they decided to come back and take her along. The men were at work, and Leon and I went to see what was going on. They told us, and said we had better go away, because possibly things might happen that children would sleep better not to see. Strange how a thing like that makes you bound you will see. We went and sat on the fence and waited. Soon they reached

Sabethany, but they could not seem to get her out. They tried, and tried, and at last they sent for more men. It took nine of them to bring her to the surface. What little wood was left, they laid back to see what made her so fearfully heavy, and there she was turned to solid stone. They couldn't chip a piece off her with the shovel. Mother always said, "For goodness sake, don't let your mouth hang open," and as a rule we kept ours shut; but you should have seen Leon's when he saw Sabethany wouldn't chip off, and no doubt mine was as bad.

"When Gabriel blows his trumpet, and the dead arise and come forth, what on earth will they do with Sabethany?" I gasped. "Why, she couldn't fly to Heaven with wings a mile wide, and what use could they make of her if she got there?"

"I can't see a thing she'd be good for except a hitching post," said Leon, "and I guess they don't let horses in. Let's go home."

He acted sick and I felt that way; so we went, but the last glimpse of Sabethany remained with me.

As my head went down that day, I saw that Miss Amelia looked exactly like her. You would have needed a pick-ax or a crowbar to flake off even a tiny speck of her. When I had waited for my head to be cracked, until I had time to remember that a Crusader didn't dodge and hide, I looked up, and there she stood with the ruler lifted; but now she had turned just the shade of the wattles on our fightingest turkey gobbler.

"Won't you please forgive me?"

I never knew I had said it until I heard it, and then the only way to be sure was because no one else would have been likely to speak at that time.

Miss Amelia's arm dropped and she glared at me. I wondered whether I ever would understand grown people; I doubted if they understood themselves, for after turning to stone in a second —father said it had taken Sabethany seven years—and changing to gobbler red, Miss Amelia suddenly began to laugh. To laugh, of all things! And then, of course, every one else just yelled. I was so mortified I dropped my head again and began to cry as I never would if she'd hit me.

"Don't feel badly!" said Miss Amelia. "Certainly, I'll forgive you. I see you had no intention of giving offense, so none is taken. Get out your book and study hard on another lesson."

That was surprising. I supposed I'd have to do the same one over, but I might take a new one. I was either getting along fast, or Miss Amelia had her fill of birds. I wiped my eyes as straight in front of me as I could slip up my handkerchief, and began studying the first lesson in my reader: "Pretty bee, pray tell me why, thus from flower to flower you fly, culling sweets the livelong day, never leaving off to play?" That was a poetry piece, and it was quite cheery, although it was all strung together like prose, but you couldn't fool me on poetry; I knew it every time. As I studied I felt better, and when Miss Amelia came to hear me she was good as gold. She asked if I liked honey, and I started to tell her about the queen bee, but she had no time to listen, so she said I should wait until after school. Then we both forgot it, for when we reached home, the Princess' horse was hitched to our rack, and I fairly ran in, I was so anxious to know what was happening.

I was just perfectly amazed at grown people! After all the things our folks had said! You'd have supposed that Laddie would have been locked in the barn; father reading the thirty-second Psalm to the Princess, and mother on her knees asking God to open her eyes like Saul's when he tried to kick against the pricks, and make her to see, as he did, that God was not a myth. Well, there was no one in the sitting-room or the parlour, but there were voices farther on; so I slipped in. I really had to slip, for there was no other place they could be except the parlour bedroom, and Sally's wedding things were locked up there, and we were not to see until everything was finished, like I told you.

Well, this was what I saw: our bedroom had been a porch once, and when we had been crowded on account of all of us coming, father enclosed it and made a room. But he never had taken out the window in the wall. So all I had to do when I wanted to know how fast the dresses were being made, was to shove up the window above my bed, push back the blind, and look in. I didn't care what she had. I just wanted to get ahead of her and see before she was ready, to pay her for beating me. I knew what she had, and I meant to tell her, and walk away with my nose in the air when she offered to show me; but this was different. I was wild to see what was going on because the Princess was there. The room was small, and the big cherry four-poster was very large, and all of them were talking, so no one paid the slightest attention to me.

Mother sat in the big rocking chair, with Sally on one of its arms, leaning against her shoulder. Shelley and May and the sewing woman were crowded between the wall and the foot-board, and the others lined against the wall. The bed was heaped in a tumble of everything a woman ever wore. Seemed to me there was more stuff there than all the rest of us had, put to-gether. The working dresses and aprons had been made on the machine, but there were heaps and stacks of hand-made under-clothes. I could see the lovely chemise mother embroidered lying on top of a pile of bedding, and over and over Sally had said that every stitch in the wedding gown must be taken by hand. The Princess stood beside the bed. A funny little tight hat like a man's and a riding whip lay on a chair close by. I couldn't see what she wore—her usual riding clothes probably—for she had a nip in each shoulder of a dress she was holding to her chin and looking down at. After all, I hadn't seen everything! Never before or since have I seen a lovelier dress than that. It was what always had been wrapped in the sheet on the foot of the bed and I hadn't got a peep at it. The pale green silk with tiny pink moss roses in it, that I had been thinking was the wedding dress, looked about right to wash the dishes in, compared with this.

This was a wedding dress. You didn't need any one to tell you. The Princess had as much red as I ever had seen in her cheeks, her eyes were bright, and she was half-laughing and half-crying.

"Oh you lucky, lucky girl!" she was saying. "What a perfectly beautiful bride you will be! Never have I seen a more wonderful dress! Where did you get the material?"

Now we had been trained always to wait for mother to answer

a visitor as she thought suitable, or at least to speak one at a time and not interrupt; but about six of those grown people told the Princess all at the same time how our oldest sister Elizabeth was married to a merchant who had a store at Westchester and how he got the dress in New York, and gave it to Sally for her wedding present, or she never could have had it.

The Princess lifted it and set it down softly. "Oh look!" she cried. "Look! It will stand alone!"

There it stood! Silk stiff enough to stand by itself, made into a little round waist, cut with a round neck and sleeves elbow length and flowing almost to where Sally's knees would come. It was a pale pearl-gray silk crossed in bars four inches square, made up of a dim yellow line almost as wide as a wheat straw, with a thread of black on each side of it, and all over, very wide apart, were little faint splashes of black as if they had been lightly painted on. The skirt was so wide it almost filled the room. Every inch of that dress was lined with soft, white silk. There was exquisite lace made into a flat collar around the neck, and ruffled from sight up the inside of the wide sleeves. That was the beginning. The finish was something you never saw anything like before. It was a trimming made of white and yellow beads. There was a little heading of white beads sewed into a pattern, then a lacy fringe that was pale yellow beads, white inside, each an inch long, that dangled, and every bead ended with three tiny white ones. That went around the neck, the outside of the sleeves, and in a pattern like a big letter V all the way around the skirt. And there it stood—alone!

The Princess, graceful as a bird and glowing like fire, danced around it, and touched it, and lifted the sleeves, and made the bead fringe swing, and laughed, and talked every second. Sally, and mother, and all of them had smiled such wide smiles for so long, their faces looked almost as set as Sabethany's, but of course far different. Being dead was one thing, getting ready for a wedding another.

And it looked too as if God might be a myth, for all they cared, so long as the Princess could make the wedding dress stand alone, and talk a blue streak of things that pleased them. It was not put on either, for there stood the dress, shimmering like the inside of a pearl-lined shell, white as a lily, and the tinkly gold fringe. No one *could* have said enough about it, so no matter what the Princess said, it had to be all right. She kept straight on showing all of them how lovely it was, exactly as if they hadn't seen it before, and she had to make them understand about it, as if she felt afraid they might have missed some elegant touch she had seen.

"Do look how the lace falls when I raise this sleeve! Oh how will you wear this and think of a man enough to say the right words in the right place?"

Mother laughed, and so did all of them.

"Do please show me the rest," begged the Princess. "I know there are slippers and a bonnet!"

Sally just oozed pride. She untied the strings and pushed the prettiest striped bag from a lovely pink bandbox and took out a dear little gray bonnet with white ribbons, and the yellow bead fringe, and a bunch of white roses with a few green leaves. These she touched softly, "I'm not quite sure about the leaves," she said.

The Princess had the bonnet, turning and tilting it.

"Perfect!" she cried. "Quite perfect! You need that touch of colour, and it blends with everything. How I envy you! Oh why doesn't some one ask me, so I can have things like these? I think your brother is a genius. I'm going to ride to Westchester to-morrow and give him an order to fill for me the next time he goes to the city. No one shows me such fabrics when I go, and Aunt Beatrice sends nothing from London I like nearly so well. Oh! Oh!"

She was on her knees now, lifting the skirt to set under little white satin slippers with gold buckles, and white bead buttons. When she had them arranged to suit her, she sat on the floor and kept straight on saying the things my mother and sisters seemed crazy to hear. When Sally showed her the long white silk mitts that went with the bonnet, the Princess cried: "Oh do ride home with me and let me give you a handkerchief Aunt Beatrice sent me, to carry in your hand!"

Then her face flushed and she added without giving Sally time to say what she would do: "Or I can bring it the next time I come past. It belongs with these things and I have no use for it. May I?"

"Please do! I'll use it for the thing I borrow."

"But I mean it to be a gift," said the Princess. "It was made to go with these lace mitts and satin slippers. You must take it!"

"Thank you very much," said Sally. "If you really want me to have it, of course I'd love to."

"I'll bring it to-morrow," promised the Princess. "And I wish you'd let me try a way I know to dress hair for a wedding. Yours is so beautiful."

"You're kind, I'm sure," said Sally. "I had intended to wear it as I always do, so I would appear perfectly natural to the folks; but if you know a more becoming way, I could begin it now, and they would be familiar with it by that time."

"I shan't touch it," said the Princess, studying Sally's face. "Your idea is right. You don't want to commence any new, unfamiliar style that would make you seem different, just at a time when every one should see how lovely you are, as you always have been. But don't forget to wear something blue, and something borrowed for luck, and oh do please put on one of my garters!"

"Well for mercy sake!" cried my mother. "Why?"

"So some one will propose to me before the year is out," laughed the Princess. "I think it must be the most fun of all, to make beautiful things for your very own home, and lovely dresses, and be surrounded by friends all eager to help you, and to arrange a house and live with a man you love well enough to marry, and fix for little people who might come———"

"You know perfectly there isn't a single man in the county who wouldn't propose to you, if you'd let him come within a mile of you," said Shelley.

"When the right man comes I'll go half the mile to meet him, you may be sure of that; won't I, Mrs. Stanton?" the Princess turned to mother.

"I have known girls who went even farther," said my mother rather dryly.

"I draw the line at half," laughed the Princess. "Now I must go; I have been so long my people will be wondering what I'm doing."

Standing in the middle of the room she put on her hat, picked up her whip and gloves, and led the way to the hitching rack, while all of us followed. At the gate stood Laddie as he had come from the field. His old hat was on the back of his head, his face flushed, his collar loosened so that his strong white neck showed, and his sleeves were rolled to the elbow, as they had been all summer, and his arms were burned almost to blisters. When he heard us coming he opened the gate, went to the rack, untied the Princess' horse and led it beside the mounting block. As she came toward him, he took off his hat and pitched it over the fence on the grass.

"Miss Pryor, allow me to make you acquainted with my son," said mother.

I felt as if I would blow up. I couldn't keep my eyes from turning toward the Princess. Gee! I could have saved my feelings. She made mother the prettiest little courtsey I ever set eyes on, and then turned and made a deeper one to Laddie.

"I met your son in one of the village stores some time ago," she said. "Back her one step farther, please!"

Laddie backed the horse, and quicker than you could see how it was done, she flashed up the steps and sat the saddle; but as she leaned over the horse's neck to take the rein from Laddie, he got one level look straight in the eyes that I was sure none of the others saw, because they were not watching for it, and I was. Laddie bowed from the waist, and put the reins in her fingers all in one movement. He caught the glance she gave him too; I could almost feel it like a band passing between them. Then she called a laughing good-bye to all of us at once, and showed us how to ride right, as she flashed toward the Little Hill. That was riding, you may believe, and mother sighed as she watched her.

"If I were a girl again," she said, "I would ride as well as that, or I'd never mount a horse."

"She's been trained from her cradle, and her father deals in horses. Half the battle in riding is a thoroughbred," said Laddie. "No such horse as that ever stepped these roads before."

"And no such girl ever travelled them," said my mother, folding her hands one over the other on top of a post of the hitching rack. "I must say I don't know how this is coming out, and it troubles me."

"Why, what's up?" asked Laddie, covering her hands with his and looking her in the eyes.

"Just this," said my mother. "She's more beautiful of face and form than God ought to allow any woman to be, in mercy to the men who will be forced to meet her. Her speech is highly cultured. Her manners are perfect, and that is a big and unusual thing in a girl of her age. Every word she said, every move she made to-day, was exactly as I would have been proud to hear, and to see a daughter of mine speak and move. If I had only myself to consider, I would make her my friend, because I'm seasoned in the ways of the world, and she could influence me only as I chose to allow her. With you youngsters it is different. You'll find her captivating, and you may let her ways sway you without even knowing it. All these outward things are not essential; they are pleasing, I grant, but they have nothing to do with the one big, elemental fact that a Godless life is not even half a life. I never yet have known any man or woman who attempted it who did not waste life's grandest opportunities, and then come crawling and defeated to the foot of the cross in the end, asking God's mercy where none was deserved or earned. It seems to me a craven way. I know all about the forgiveness on the cross! I know God is big enough and merciful enough to accept even death-bed repentance, but what is that to compare with laying out your course and running it a lifetime without swerving? I detest and distrust this infidel business. I want no child of mine under its influence, or in contact with it."

"But when your time comes, if you said just those things to her, and won her, what a triumph, little mother!"

" 'If!' " answered mother. "That's always the trouble! One can't be sure! 'If' I knew I could accomplish that, I would get on my knees and wrestle with the Lord for the salvation of the soul of a girl like that, not to mention her poor, housebound mother, and that man with the unhappiest face I ever have seen, her father. It's worth trying, but suppose I try and fail, and at the same time find that in bringing her among us she has influenced some of mine to the loss of their immortal souls—*then,* what will I have done?"

"Mother," said Laddie; "mother, have you such a poor opinion of the things you and father have taught us, and the lives you've lived before us, that you're really afraid of a slip of a girl, almost a stranger?"

"The most attractive girl I ever have seen, and mighty willing to be no longer a stranger, Lad."

"Well, I can't promise for the others," said Laddie, "but for myself I will give you my word of honour that I won't be influenced the breadth of one hair by her, in a doctrinal way."

"Humph!" said my mother. "And it is for you I fear. If a young man is given the slightest encouragement by a girl like that, even his God can't always hold him; and you never have made a confession of faith, Laddie. It is you she will be most likely to captivate."

"If you think I have any chance, I'll go straight over and ask her father for her this very evening," said Laddie, and even mother laughed; then all of us started to the house, for it was almost supper time. I got ready and thought I'd take one more peep at the dress before Sally pinned it in the sheet again, and when I went back, there all huddled in a bunch before it stood Miss Amelia, the tears running down her cheeks.

"Did Sally say you might come here?" I asked.

"No," said Miss Amelia, "but I've been so crazy to see I just slipped in to take a peep when I noticed the open door. I'll go this minute. Please don't tell her."

I didn't say what I would do, but I didn't intend to.

"What are you crying about?" I inquired.

"Ah, I too have known love," sobbed Miss Amelia. "Once I made a wedding dress, and expected to be a happy bride."

"Well, wasn't you?" I asked, and knew at once it was a silly question, for of course she would not be a miss, if she had not missed marrying.

"He died!" sobbed Miss Amelia.

If he could have seen her then, I believe he'd have been glad of it; but maybe he looked as bony and dejected as she did before he went; and he may have turned to stone afterward, as sometimes happens. Right then I heard Sally coming, so I grabbed Miss Amelia and dragged her under the fourposter, where I always hid when caught doing something I shouldn't. But Sally had so much stuff she couldn't keep all of it on the bed, and when she stooped and lifted the ruffle to shove a box under, she pushed it right against us, and knelt to look, and there we were.

"Well upon my soul!" she cried, and sat flat on the floor, holding the ruffle, peering in. "Miss Amelia! And in tears! Whatever is the trouble?"

Miss Amelia's face was redder than any crying ever made it, and I saw she wanted to kill me for getting her into such a fix, and if she became too angry probably she'd take it out on me in school the next day, so I thought I'd better keep her at work shedding tears.

" 'He died!' " I told Sally as pathetically as ever I could.

Sally dropped the ruffle instantly, but I saw her knees shake against the floor. After a while she lifted the curtain and offered Miss Amelia her hand.

"I was leaving my dress to show you before putting it away," she said.

I didn't believe it; but that was what she said. Maybe it was an impulse. Mother always said Sally was a creature of impulse. When she took off her flannel petticoat and gave it to poor little half-frozen Annie Hasty, that was a good impulse, but it sent Sally to bed for a week. And when she threw a shovel of coals on Bill Ramsdell's dog, because Bill was a shiftless lout, and the dog was so starved it all the time came over and sucked our eggs, that was a bad impulse, because it didn't do Bill a particle of good, and it hurt the dog, which would have been glad to suck eggs at home, no doubt, if Bill hadn't been too worthless to keep hens.

That was a good impulse she had then, for she asked Miss Amelia to help her straighten the room, and of course that meant to fold and put away wedding things. Any woman would have been wild to do that. Then she told Miss Amelia that she was going to ask father to dismiss school for half a day, and allow her to see the wedding, and she asked her if she would help serve the breakfast. Miss Amelia wiped her eyes, and soon laughed and was just beaming. I would have been willing to bet my three cents for lead pencils the next time the huckster came, that Sally never thought of wanting her until that minute; and then she arranged for her to wait on table to keep her from trying to eat with the wedding party, because Miss Amelia had no pretty clothes for one thing, and for another, you shouldn't act as if you were hungry out in company, and she ate every meal as if she were breaking a forty days' fast. I wondered what her folks cooked at home.

After supper Peter came, and the instant I saw him I thought of something, and it was such a teasing thought I followed around and watched him harder every minute . At last he noticed me, and put his arms around me.

"Well, what is it, Little Sister?" he asked.

I did wish he would quit that. No one really had a right to call me that, except Laddie. Maybe I had to put up with Peter doing it when I was his sister by law, but before, the old name the preacher baptized on me was good enough for Peter. I was thinking about that so hard, I didn't answer, and he asked again.

"I have seen Sally's wedding dress," I told him.

"But that's no reason why you should stare at me."

"That's just exactly the reason," I answered. "I was trying to see what in the world there is about you to be worth a dress like that."

Peter laughed and laughed. At last he said that he was not really worth even a calico dress; and he was so little worthy of Sally that he would button her shoes, if she would let him. He got that mixed. The buttons were on her slippers: her shoes laced. But it showed a humble spirit in Peter. Not that I care for humble spirits. I am sure the Crusaders didn't have them. I don't believe Laddie would lace even the Princess' shoes, at least not to make a steady business of it. But maybe Peter and Sally had an agreement to help each other. She was always fixing his tie, and straightening his hair. Maybe that was an impulse, though, and mother said Sally would get over being so impulsive when she cut her eye teeth.

CHAPTER VII

When Sally Married Peter

"Mid pleasures and palaces though we may roam,
 Be it ever so humble there's no place like home!
 A charm from the skies seems to hallow us there,
 Which, seek through the world, is ne'er met with elsewhere."

WHEN they began arranging the house for the wedding, it could be seen that they had been expecting it, and getting ready for a long time. From all the closets, shelves and chests poured heaps of new things. First, the walls were cleaned and some of them freshly papered, then the windows were all washed long before regular housecleaning time, the floors were scrubbed and new carpet put down. Mother had some window blinds that Winfield had brought her from New York in the spring, and she had laid them away; no one knew why, then. We all knew now. When mother was ready to put them up, father had a busy day and couldn't help her, and she was really provoked. She almost cried about it, when Leon rode in bringing the mail, and said Hannah Dover had some exactly like ours at her windows, that her son had sent from Illinois. Father felt badly enough then, for he always did everything he could to help mother to be first with everything; but so she wouldn't blame him, he said crosslike that if she had let him put them up when they came, as he wanted to, she'd have been six months ahead.

When they finally got ready to hang the blinds no one knew how they went. They were a beautiful shiny green, plain on one side, and on the other there was a silver border across the bottom and one pink rose as big as a pie plate. Mother had neglected to ask Winfield on which side the rose belonged. Father said from

the way the roll ran, it went inside. Mother said they were rolled
that way to protect the roses, and that didn't prove anything.
Laddie said he would jump on a horse and ride round the section,
and see how Hannah Dover had hers, and exactly opposite would
be right. Everyone laughed, but no one thought he meant it.
Mother had father hold one against the window, and she stepped
outside to see if she could tell from there. When she came in she
said the flower looked mighty pretty, and she guessed that was
the way, so father started hanging them. He had only two up
when Laddie came racing down the Big Hill bareback, calling
for him to stop.

"I tell you that's not right, mother!" he said as he hurried in.

"But I went outside and father held one, and it looked real
pretty," said mother.

"One! Yes!" said Laddie. "But have you stopped to consider
how two rows across the house are going to look? Nine big pink
roses, with the sun shining on them! Anything funnier than
Dovers' front I never saw. And look here!"

Laddie picked up a blind. "See this plain back? It's double
coated like a glaze. That is so the sun shining through glass won't
fade it. The flowers would be gone in a week. They belong inside,
mother, sure as you live."

"Then when the blinds are rolled to the middle sash in the
daytime no one can see them," wailed mother, who was wild
about pink roses.

"But at night, when they are down, you can put the curtains
back enough to let the roses show, and think how pretty they will
look then."

"Laddie is right!" said father, climbing on the barrel to take
down the ones he had fixed.

"What do you think, girls?" asked mother.

"I think the Princess is coming down the Little Hill," said
Shelley. "Hurry, father! Take them down before she sees! I'm
sure they're wrong."

Father got one all right, but tore the corner of the other.
Mother scolded him dreadfully cross, and he was so flustered he

forgot about being on the barrel, so he stepped back the same as on the floor, and fell crashing. He might have broken some of his bones, if Laddie hadn't seen and caught him.

"If you are *sure* the flowers go inside, fix one before she comes!" cried mother.

Father stepped too close the edge of the chair, and by that time he didn't know how to hang anything, so Laddie climbed up and had one nailed before the Princess stopped. She came to bring Sally the handkerchief, and it was the loveliest one any of us ever had seen. There was a little patch in the middle about four inches square, and around it a wide ruffle of dainty lace. It was made to carry in a hand covered with white lace mitts, when you were wearing a wedding gown of silver silk, lined with white. Of course it wouldn't have been the slightest use for a funeral or with a cold in your head. And it had come from across the sea! From the minute she took it by a pinch in the middle, Sally carried her head so much higher than she ever had before, that you could notice the difference.

Laddie went straight on nailing up the blinds, and every one he fixed he let down full length so the Princess could see the roses were inside; he was so sure he was right. After she had talked a few minutes she noticed the blinds going up. Laddie, in a front window, waved to her from the barrel. She laughed and answered with her whip, and then she laughed again.

"Do you know," she said, "there is the funniest thing at Dovers'. I rode past on the way to Groveville this morning and they have some blinds like those you are putting up."

"Indeed?" inquired my mother. "Winfield sent us these from New York in the spring, but I thought the hot summer sun would fade them, so I saved them until the fall cleaning. The wedding coming on makes us a little early but——"

"Well, they may not be exactly the same," said the Princess. "I only saw from the highway." She meant road; there were many things she said differently. "Have yours big pink roses and silver scrolls inside?"

"Yes," said mother.

The Princess bubbled until it made you think one of those yellow oriole birds had perched on her saddle. "That poor woman has gone and put hers up wrong side out. The effect of all those big pink roses on her white house front is most amusing. It looks as if the house were covered with a particularly gaudy piece of comfort calico. Only fancy!"

She laughed again and rode away. Mother came in just gasping.

"Well, for all His mercies, large and small, the Lord be praised!" she cried piously, as she dropped into the big rocking chair. "*That* is what I consider escaping by the skin of your teeth!"

Then father and Laddie laughed, and said they thought so too. When the blinds were up, the outside looked well, and you should have seen the inside! The woodwork was enamelled white, and the wall paper was striped in white and silver. Every so far on the silver there was a little pink moss rose having green leaves. The carpet was plum red and green in wide stripes, and the lace curtains were freshly washed, snowy, and touched the floor. The big rocker, the straight-backed chairs, and the sofa were beautiful red mahogany wood, and the seats shining haircloth. If no one happened to be looking, you could sit on a sofa arm, stick your feet out and shoot off like riding down a haystack; the landing was much better. On the sofa you bounced two feet high the first time; one, the second; and a little way the third. On the haystack, maybe you hit a soft spot, and maybe you struck a rock. Sometimes if you got smart, and tried a new place, and your feet caught in a tangle of weeds and stuck, you came up straight, pitched over, and landed on your head. *Then* if you struck a rock, you were still, quite a while. I was once. But you never dared let mother see you—on the sofa, I mean; she didn't care about the haystack.

There were pictures in oval black frames having fancy edges, and a whatnot where all our Christmas and birthday gifts, almost too dainty to handle, were kept. You fairly held your breath when you looked at the nest of spun green glass, with the white dove in it, that George Washington Mitchell gave to Shelley. Of course a dove's nest was never deep, and round, and green, and the bird didn't have red eyes and a black bill. I thought whoever could blow glass as beautifully as that, might just as easy have made it right while he was at it; but anyway, it was pretty. There were pitchers, mugs, and vases, almost too delicate to touch, and the cloth-covered box with braids of hair coiled in wreaths from the heads of the little fever and whooping cough sisters.

Laddie asked Sally if she and Peter were going to have the ceremony performed while they sat on the sofa. Seemed the right place. They had done all their courting there, even on hot summer days; but I supposed that was because Sally didn't want to be seen fixing Peter's tie until she was ready. She made no bones about it then. She fixed it whenever she pleased; likewise he held her hand. Shelley said that was disgusting, and you wouldn't catch her. Leon said he bet a dollar he would; and I said if he knew he'd get beaten as I did, I bet two dollars he wouldn't tell what he saw. The mantel was white, with vases of the lovely grasses that grew beside the stream at the foot of the Big Hill. Mother gathered the fanciest every fall, dried them, and dipped them in melted alum coloured with copperas, aniline, and indigo. Then she took bunches of the colours that went together best and made bouquets for the big vases. They were pretty in the daytime, but at night you could watch them sparkle and shimmer forever.

I always thought the sitting-room was nicer than the parlour. The woodwork was white enamel there too, but the bureau and chairs were just cherry and not too precious to use. They were every bit as pretty. The mantel was much larger. I could stand up in the fireplace, and it took two men to put on an everyday log, four the Christmas one. On each side were the book shelves above, and the linen closets below. The mantel set between these, and mother always used the biggest, most gorgeous bouquets there, because she had so much room. The hearth was a slab of stone that came far into the room. We could sit on it and crack nuts, roast apples, chestnuts, and warm our cider, then sweep all the muss we made into the fire. The wall paper was white and pale pink in stripes, and on the pink were little handled baskets filled with tiny flowers of different colours. We sewed the rags for the carpet ourselves, and it was the prettiest thing. One stripe was wide, all gray, brown, and dull colours, and the other was pink. There were green blinds and lace curtains here also, and nice braided rugs that all of us worked on of winter evenings. Everything got spicker and spanner each day.

Mother said there was no use in putting down a carpet in a dining-room where you constantly fed a host, and the boys didn't clean their feet as carefully as they should in winter; but there were useful rags where they belonged, and in our bedroom opening from it also. The dining-room wall paper had a broad stripe of rich cream with pink cabbage roses scattered over it and a narrow pink stripe, while the woodwork was something perfectly marvellous. I didn't know what kind of wood it was, but a man who could turn his hand to anything, painted it. First, he put on a pale yellow coat and let it dry. Then he added wood brown, and while it was wet, with a coarse toothed comb, a rag, and his fingers, he imitated the grain, the even wood, and knotholes of dressed lumber, until many a time I found myself staring steadily at a knot to see if a worm wouldn't really come working out. You have to see a thing like that to understand how wonderful it is. You couldn't see why they washed the bedding, and took the feathers from the pillows and steamed them in mosquito netting bags and dried them in the shade, when Sally's was to be a morning wedding, but they did. I even had to take a bucket and gather from around the walls all the little heaps of rocks and shells that Uncle Abraham had sent mother from California, take them out and wash and wipe them, and stack them back, with the fanciest ones on top. He sent her a ring made of gold he dug himself. She always kept the ring in a bottle in her bureau, and she meant to wear it at the wedding, with her new silk dress. I had a new dress too. I don't know how they got everything done. All of them worked, until the last few days they were perfect cross patches.

When they couldn't find another thing indoors to scour, they began on the yard, orchard, barn and road. Mother even had

Leon stack the wood pile straighter. She said when corded wood
leaned at an angle, it made people seem shiftless; and she never
passed a place where it looked that way that her fingers didn't
just itch to get at it. He had to pull every ragweed on each side
of the road as far as our land reached, and lay every rail straight
in the fences. Father had to take spikes and our biggest maul
and go to the bridges at the foot of the Big and the Little Hill,
and see that every plank was fast, so none of them would rattle
when important guests drove across. She said she just simply
wouldn't have them in such a condition that Judge Pettis couldn't
hear himself think when he crossed; for you could tell from his
looks that it was very important that none of the things he
thought should be lost. There wasn't a single spot about the place
inside or out that wasn't gone over; and to lots of it you never
would have known anything had been done if you hadn't seen,
because the place was always in proper shape anyway; but father
said mother acted just like that, even when her sons were married
at other people's houses; and if she kept on getting worse, every
girl she married off, by the time she reached me, we'd all be
scoured threadbare and she'd be on the verge of the grave. May
and I weeded the flowerbeds, picked all the ripe seed, and pulled
up and burned all the stalks that were done blooming. Father
and Laddie went over the garden carefully; they scraped the
walks and even shook the palings to see if one were going to come
loose right at the last minute, when every one would be so flus-
trated there would be no time to fix it.

Then they began to talk about arrangements for the ceremony,
whether we should have our regular minister, or Presiding Elder
Lemon, and what people they were going to invite. Just when we
had planned to ask every one, have the wedding in the church,
and the breakfast at the house, and all drive in a joyous procession to Groveville to give them a good send-off in walked Sally.
She had been visiting Peter's people, and we planned a lot while
she was away.

"What's going on here?" she asked, standing in the doorway,
dangling her bonnet by the ties.

She never looked prettier. Her hair had blown out in little curls around her face from riding, her cheeks were so pink, and her eyes so bright.

"We were talking about having the ceremony in the church, so every one can be comfortably seated, and see and hear well," answered mother.

Sally straightened up and began jerking the roses on her bonnet far too roughly for artificial flowers. Perhaps I surprised you with that artificial word, but I can spell and define it; it's easy divided into syllables. Goodness knows, I have seen enough flowers made from the hair of the dead, wax, and paper, where you get the shape, but the colour never is right. These of Sally's were much too bright, but they were better than the ones made at our house. Hers were of cloth and bought at a store. You couldn't tell why, but Sally jerked her roses; I wished she wouldn't, because I very well knew they would be used to trim my hat the next summer, and she said: "Well, people don't have to be comfortable during a wedding ceremony; they can stand up if I can, and as for seeing and hearing, I'm asking a good many that I don't intend to have see or hear either one!"

"My soul!" cried mother, and she dropped her hands and her mouth fell open, like she always told us we never should let ours, while she stared at Sally.

"I don't care!" said Sally, straightening taller yet; her eyes began to shine and her lips to quiver, as if she would cry in a minute; "I don't care——!"

"Which means, my child, that you *do* care, very much," said father. "Suppose you cease such reckless talk, and explain to us exactly what it is that you do want."

Sally gave her bonnet an awful jerk. Those roses would look like sin before my turn to wear them came, and she said: "Well then, I do care! I care with all my might! The church is all right, of course; but I want to be married in my very own home! Every one can think whatever they please about their home, and so can I, and what I think is, that this is the nicest and the prettiest place in all the world, and I belong here——"

Father lifted his head, his face began to shine, and his eyes to grow teary; while mother started toward Sally. She put out her hand and held mother from her at arm's length, and she turned and looked behind her through the sitting-room and parlour, and then at us, and she talked so fast you never could have understood what she said if you hadn't known all of it anyway, and thought exactly the same thing yourself.

"I have just loved this house ever since it was built," she said, "and I've had as good times here as any girl ever had. If any one thinks I'm so very anxious to leave it, and you, and mother, and all the others, why it's a big mistake. Seems as if a girl is expected to marry and go to a home of her own; it's drummed into her and things fixed for her from the day of her birth; and of course I do like Peter, but no home in the world, not even the one he provides for me, will ever be any dearer to me than my own home; and as I've always lived in it, I want to be married in it, and I want to stay here until the very last second——"

"You shall, my child, you shall!" sobbed mother.

"And as for having a crowd of men that father is planning to ask, staring at me, because he changes harvest help and wood chopping with them, or being criticised and clawed over by some women simply because they'll be angry if they don't get the chance, I just won't—so there! Not if I have to stand the minister against the wall, and turn our backs to every one. I think——"

"That will do!" said father, wiping his eyes. "That will do, Sally! Your mother and I have got a pretty clear understanding of how you feel, now. Don't excite yourself! Your wedding shan't be used to pay off our scores. You may ask exactly whom you please, want, and feel quite comfortable to have around you——"

Then Sally fell on mother's neck and every one cried a while; then we wiped up, Leon gave Sally his slate, and she came and sat beside the table and began to make out a list of those she really wanted to invite. First she put down all of our family, even many away in Ohio, and all of Peter's, and then his friends, and hers. Once in the list of girls she stopped and said: "If I take that beautiful imported handkerchief from Pamela Pryor, I have just got to invite her——"

"And she will outdress and outshine you at your own wedding," put in Shelley.

"Let her, if she can!" said Sally calmly. "She'll have to hump herself if she beats that dress of mine; and as for looks, I know lots of people who think gray eyes, pink cheeks, and brown curls far daintier and prettier than red cheeks and black eyes and curls. If she really is better looking than I am, it isn't her fault; God made her that way, and He wouldn't like us to punish her for it; and it would, because any one can see she wants to be friends; don't you think, mother?"—mother nodded—"and besides, I think she's better looking than I am, myself!"

Sally said that, and wrote down the Princess' name in big letters, and no one cheeped.

Then she began on our neighbourhood, thinking out loud and writing what she thought. So all of us were as still, and held our breath in softly and waited, and Sally said slow and musing like, "Of course we couldn't have anything at *this* house without Sarah Hood. She dressed most of us when we were born, nursed us when we were sick, helped with threshing, company, and parties, and she's just splendid anyway; we better ask all the Hoods"; so she wrote them down. "And it will be lonely for Widow Willis and the girls to see every one else here—we must have them; and of course Deams—Amanda is always such splendid help; and the Widow Fall is so perfectly lovely, we want her for decorative purposes; and we could scarcely leave out Shaws; they always have all of us everything they do; and Dr. Fenner of course; and we'll want Flo and Agnes Kuntz to wait on table, so their folks might as well come too——"

So she went on taking up each family we knew, and telling what they had done for us, or what we had done for them; and she found some good reason for inviting them, and pretty soon father settled back in his chair and never took his eyes from Sally's shining head as she bent over the slate, and then he began pulling his lower lip, like when it won't behave, and his eyes danced exactly as I've seen Leon's. I never had noticed that before.

Sally went straight on and at last she came to Freshetts. "I am going to have all of them, too," she said. "The children are good children, and it will help them along to see how things are done when they are right; and I don't care what any one says, I *like* Mrs. Freshett. I'll ask her to help work, and that will keep her from talking, and give the other women a chance to see that she's clean, and human, and would be a good neighbour if they'd be friendly. If we ask her, then the others will."

When she finished—as you live—there wasn't a soul she had left out except Bill Ramsdell, who starved his dog until it sucked our eggs, and Isaac Thomas, who was so lazy he wouldn't work enough to keep his wife and children dressed so they ever could go anywhere, but he always went, even with rags flying, and got his stomach full just by talking about how he loved the Lord. To save me I couldn't see Isaac Thomas without beginning to myself:

> " 'Tis the voice of the sluggard; I hear him complain,
> You have waked me too soon, I must slumber again.
> I passed by his garden, I saw the wild brier,
> The thorn, and the thistle, grow broader and higher;
> The clothes that hang on him are turning to rags;
> And his money he wastes, till he starves or he begs."

That described Isaac to the last tatter, only he couldn't waste money; he never had any. Once I asked father what he thought Isaac would do with it, if by some unforeseen working of Divine Providence, he got ten dollars. Father said he could tell me exactly, because Isaac once sold some timber and had a hundred all at once. He went straight to town and bought Mandy a red silk dress and a brass breastpin, when she had no shoes. He got the children an organ, when they were hungry; and himself a plug hat. Mandy and the children cried because he forgot candy and oranges until the last cent was gone. Father said the only time Isaac ever worked since he knew him was when he saw how the hat looked with his rags. He actually helped the men fell the trees until he got enough to buy a suit, the remains of which he still wore on Sunday. I asked father why he didn't wear the hat too, and father said the loss of that hat was a blow, from which Isaac never had recovered. Once at camp-meeting he laid it aside to pray his longest, most impressive prayer, and an affectionate cow strayed up and licked the nap all off before Isaac finished, so he never could wear it again.

Sally said: "I'll be switched if I'll have that disgusting creature around stuffing himself on my wedding day; but if you're not in bed, when it's all over, mother, I do wish you'd send Mandy and the children a basket."

Mother promised, and father sat and looked on and pulled his lower lip until his ears almost wiggled. Then Sally said she wanted Laddie and Shelley to stand at the parlour door and keep it tight shut, and seat every one in the sitting-room except a special list she had made out to send in there. She wanted all our family and Peter's, and only a few very close friends, but it was enough to fill the room. She said when she and Peter came downstairs every one could see how they looked when they crossed the sitting-room, and for all the difference the door would make, it could be left open then; she would be walled in by people she wanted around her, and the others could have the fun of being there, seeing what they could, and getting all they wanted to eat. Father and mother said that was all right, only to say nothing about the plan to shut the door; but when the time came just to close it and everything would be satisfactory.

Then Sally took the slate upstairs to copy the list with ink, so every one went about something, while mother crossed to father and he took her on his lap, and they looked at each other the longest and the hardest, and neither of them said a word. After a while they cried and laughed, and cried some more, and it was about as sensible as what a flock of geese say when they are let out of the barn and start for the meadow in the morning. Then father, all laughy and criey, said: "Thank God! Oh, thank God, the girl loves the home we have made for her!"

Just said it over and over, and mother kept putting in: "It pays, Paul! It pays!"

Next day Sally put on her riding habit and fixed herself as pretty as ever she could, and went around to have a last little visit with every one, and invited them herself, and then she wrote letters to people away. Elizabeth and Lucy came home, and every one began to work. Father and mother went to the village in the carriage and brought home the bed full of things to eat, and all we had was added, and mother began to pack butter, and save eggs for cakes, and the day before, I thought there wouldn't be a chicken left on the place. They killed and killed, and Sarah Hood, Amanda Deam, and Mrs. Freshett picked and picked.

"I'll bet a dollar we get something this time besides ribs and neck," said Leon. "How do you suppose thigh and breast would taste?"

"I was always crazy to try the tail," I said.

"Much chance you got," sniggered Leon. " 'Member the time that father asked the Presiding Elder, 'Brother Lemon, what piece of the fowl do you prefer?' and he up and said: 'I'm partial to the rump, Brother Stanton.' There sat father bound he wouldn't give him mother's piece, so he pretended he couldn't find it, and forked all over the platter and then gave him the ribs and the thigh. Gee, how mother scolded him after the preacher had gone! You notice father hasn't asked that since. Now, he always says: 'Do you prefer light or dark meat?' Much chance you have of ever tasting a tail, if father won't even give one to the Presiding Elder!"

"But as many as they are killing——"

"Oh *this* time," said Leon with a flourish, "this time we are going to have livers, and breast, and thighs, *and* tails, if you are beholden to tail."

"I'd like to know how we are?"

"Well, since you have proved that you can keep your mouth shut, for a little while, anyway, I'm going to take you in on this," said Leon. "You keep your eyes on me. When the wedding gets going good, you watch me, and slip out. That's all! I'll be fixed to do the rest. But mind this, get out when I do."

"All right," I promised.

They must have wakened about four o'clock on the wedding day; it wasn't really light when I got up. I had some breakfast in my night dress, and then I was all fixed up in my new clothes, and made to sit on a chair, and never move for fear I would soil my dress, for no one had time to do me over, and there was only one dress anyway. There was so much to see you could keep interested just watching, and I was as anxious to look nice before the boys and girls, and the big people, as any one.

Every mantel and table and bureau was covered with flowers, and you could have smelled the kitchen a mile away, I know. The dining table was set for the wedding party, our father and mother, and Peter's, and the others had to wait. You couldn't have laid the flat of your hand on that table anywhere, it was so covered with things to eat. Miss Amelia, in a dress none of us ever had seen before, a real nice white dress, pranced around it and smirked at every one, and waved the peacock feather brush to keep the flies from the jelly, preserves, jam, butter, and things that were not cooked.

For hours Mrs. Freshett had stood in the kitchen on one side of the stove frying chicken and heaping it in baking pans in the oven, and Amanda Deam on the other, frying ham, while Sarah Hood cooked other things, and made a wash boiler of coffee. Everything was ready by the time it should have been. I had watched them until I was tired, when Sally came through the room where I was, and she said I might come along upstairs and see her dressed. When we reached the door I wondered where she would put me, but she pushed clothing together on a bed, and helped me up, and that was great fun.

She had been bathed and had on her beautiful new linen underclothing that mother punched full of holes and embroidered in flowers and vines, and Shelley was brushing her hair, when some one called out: "The Princess is coming!"

I jumped for the window, and all of them, even Sally, crowded behind. Well, talk about carriages! No one ever had seen *that* one before. It *was* a carriage. And such horses! The funny " 'orse, 'ouse" man who made the Pryor garden was driving. He stopped at the gate, got out and opened a door, and the Princess' father stepped down, tall and straight, all in shiny black. He turned around and held out his hand, bowing double, and the Princess laid her hand in his and stepped out too. He walked with her to the gate, made another bow, kissed her hand, and stepped back, and she came down the walk alone. He got in the carriage, the man closed the door, and they drove away.

Sally must have arranged before that the Princess was to come early, for she came straight upstairs. She wore a soft white silk dress with big faded pink roses in it, and her hair was fastened at each ear with a bunch of little pink roses. She was lovely, but she didn't "outdress or outshine" Sally one bit, and she never even glanced at the mirror to see how she looked; she began helping with Sally's hair, and to dress her. When Bess Kuntz prinked so long she made every one disgusted, the Princess said: "Oh save your trouble. No one will look at you when there's a bride in the house."

There was a roll almost as thick as your arm of garters that all the other girls wanted Sally to wear for them so they would get a chance to marry that year, and Agnes Kuntz's was so large it went twice around, and they just laughed about it. They put a blue ribbon on Sally's stays for luck, and she borrowed Peter's sister Mary's comb to hold her back hair. They had the most fun, and when she was all ready except her dress they went away, and Sally stood in the middle of the room trembling a little. Outside you could hear carriage wheels rolling, the beat of horses' hoofs, and voices crying greetings. "There was a sound of revelry," by day. Mother came in hurriedly. She wore her new brown silk, with a lace collar pinned at the throat with the pin that had a brown goldstone setting in it, and her precious ring was on her finger. She was dainty and pretty enough to have been a bride herself. She turned Sally around slowly, touching her hair a little and her skirts; then she went to the closet, took out the wedding dress, put the skirt over Sally's head, and she came up through the whiteness, pink and glowing. She slipped her arms into the sleeves, and mother fastened it, shook out the skirt, saw that the bead fringe hung right, and the lace collar lay flat, then she took Sally in her arms, held her tight and said: "God bless you, dear, and keep you always. Amen."

Then she stepped to the door, and Peter, all shining and new, came in. He hugged Sally and kissed her like it didn't make the least difference whether she had on calico or a wedding dress, and he just stared, and stared at her, and never said a word, so at last she asked: "Well Peter, do you like my dress?"

And the idiot said: "Why Sally, I hadn't even seen it!"

Then both of them laughed, and the Presiding Elder came.

I never liked to look at him very well because something had happened, and he had only one eye. I always wondered if he had "plucked it out" because it had "offended" him; but if you could forget his eye, and just listen to his voice, it was like the sweetest music. He married those two people right there in the bedroom, all but about three words at the end. I heard and saw every bit of it. Then Sally said it was time for me to go to mother, but she followed me into the boys' room and shut the door. Then she knelt in her beautiful silver dress, and put her arms around me and said: "Honest, Little Sister, aren't you going to kiss me good-bye?"

"Oh I can if you want me to," I said, but I didn't look at her; I looked out of the window.

She laughed a breathless little catchy sort of laugh and said: "That's exactly what I do want."

"You didn't even want me, to begin with," I reminded her.

"There isn't a doubt but whoever told you that, could have been in better business," said Sally, angry-like. "I was much younger then, and there were many things I didn't understand, and it wasn't *you* I didn't want; it was just no baby at all. I wouldn't have wanted a boy, or any other girl a bit more. I foolishly thought we had children enough in this house. I see now very plainly that we didn't, for this family never could get along

without you, and I'm sorry I ever thought so, and I'd give anything if I hadn't struck you and——"

"Oh be still, and go on and get married!" I said. I could just
feel a regular beller coming in my throat. "I was only fooling to
pay you up. I meant all the time to kiss you good-bye when the
others did. I'll nearly die being lonesome when you're gone——"

Then I ran for downstairs, and when I reached the door,
where the steps went into the sitting-room, I stopped, scared at
all the people. It was like camp-meeting. You could see the yard
full through the windows. Just as I was thinking I'd go back to
the boys' room, and from there into the garret, and down the
back stairway, Laddie went and saw me. He came over, led me
to the parlour door, put me inside, and there mother took my
hand and held me tight, and I couldn't see Leon anywhere.

I was caught, but they didn't have him. Mother never hung
on as she did that day. I tried and tried to pull away, and she
held tight. It was only a minute until the door opened, people
crowded back, and the Presiding Elder, followed by Sally and
Peter, came into the room, and they began being married all over
again.

If it hadn't grown so solemn my mother sprung a tear, I never
would have made it. She just had to let me go to sop her face,
because tears are salty, and they would turn her new brown silk
front yellow. The minute my hand was free, I slipped between
the people and looked at the parlour door. It was wedged full
and more standing on chairs behind them. No one could get out
there. I thought I would fail Leon sure, and then I remembered
the parlour bedroom. I got through that door easy as anything,
and it was no trick at all to slip behind the blind, raise the window, and drop into mother's room from the sill. From there I
reached the back dining-room door easy enough, went around
to the kitchen, and called Leon softly. He opened the door at
once and I slipped in. He had just got there. We looked all
around and couldn't see where to begin at first. There was
enough cooked food there to load two wagons.

An old pillow-case that had dried sage in it was lying across a chair and Leon picked it up and poured the sage into the wood-box, and handed the case to me. He went over and knelt before the oven, while I followed and held open the case. Leon rolled his eyes to the ceiling and said so exactly like father when he is serving company that not one of us could have told the difference: "Which part of the fowl do you prefer, Brother Lemon?"

It was so funny it made me snigger, but I straightened up and answered as well as I could: "I'm especially fond of the rump, Brother Stanton."

Leon stirred the heap and piled four or five tails in the case. I thought that was all I could manage before they would spoil, so I said: "Do you prefer light or dark meat, Sister Abigail?"

"I wish to choose breast," said Leon, simpering just like that silly Abigail Webster. He put in six breasts. Then we found them hidden away back in the oven in a pie pan, for the bride's table, I bet, and we took two livers apiece; we didn't dare take more for fear they had been counted. Then he threw in whatever he came to that was a first choice big piece, until I was really scared, and begged him to stop; but he repeated what the fox said in the story of the "Quarrelsome Cocks"—"Poco was very good, but I have not had enough yet," so he piled in pieces until I ran away with the pillow-case; then he slid in a whole plateful of bread, another of cake, and put the plates in a tub of dishes under the table. Then we took some of everything that wasn't too runny. Just then the silence broke in the front part of the house, and we scooted from the back door, closing it behind us, ran to the wood house and climbed the ladder to the loft over the front part. There we were safe as could be, we could see to the road, hear almost everything said in the kitchen, and "eat our bites in peace," like Peter Justice told the Presiding Elder at the church trial that he wanted his wife to, the time he slapped her. Before very long, they began calling us, and called, and called. We hadn't an idea what they wanted, so we ate away. We heard them first while I was holding over a back to let Leon taste kidney, and it made him blink when he got it good.

"Well my soul!" he said. "No wonder father didn't want to

feed that to another man when mother isn't very well, and likes it! No wonder!"

Then he gave me a big bite of breast. It was sort of dry and tasteless; I didn't like it.

"Why, I think neck or back beats that all to pieces!" I said in surprise.

"Fact is, they do!" said Leon. "I guess the people who 'wish to choose breast,' do it to get the biggest piece."

I never had thought of it before, but of course that would be the reason.

"Allow me, Sister Stanton," said Leon, holding out a piece of thigh.

That was really chicken! Then we went over the backs and picked out all the kidneys, and ate the little crusty places, and all the cake we could swallow; then Leon fixed up the bag the best he could, and set it inside an old cracked churn and put on the lid. He said that would do almost as well as the cellar, and the food would keep until to-morrow. I wanted to slip down and put it in the Underground Station; but Leon said father must be spending a lot of money right now, and he might go there to get some, so that wouldn't be safe. Then he cleaned my face, and I told him when he got his right, and we slipped from the back door, crossed the Lawton blackberry patch, and went to the house from the orchard. Leon took an apple and broke it in two, and we went in eating as if we were starving. When father asked us where in this world we had been, Leon told him we thought it would be so awful long before the fourth or fifth table, and we hadn't had much breakfast, and we were so hungry we went and hunted something to eat.

"If you'd only held your horses a minute," said father; "they were calling you to take places at the bride's table."

Well for land's sake! Our mouths dropped open until it's a wonder the cake and chicken didn't show, and we never said a word. There didn't seem to be anything to say, for Leon loved to be with grown folks, and to have eaten at the bride's table would have been the biggest thing that ever happened to me.

At last, when I could speak, I asked who had taken our places, and bless your heart if it wasn't that mealy-faced little sister of Peter's, and one of the aunts from Ohio. They had finished, and Sally was upstairs putting on her travelling dress, while the guests were eating, when I heard Laddie ask the Princess to ride with him and Sally's other friends, who were going to escort her to the depot.

"You'll want all your horses. What could I ride?"

"If I find you a good horse and saddle will you go?"

"I will. I think it would be fine sport."

Laddie turned and went from sight that minute. The Princess laughed and kept on making friends with every one, helping wait on people, thinking of nice things to do, and just as the carriage was at the gate for father and mother, and Sally and Peter, and every one else was untying their horses to ride in the procession to the village, from where I was standing on the mounting block I saw something coming down the Little Hill. I took one look, ran to the Princess, and almost dragged her.

Up raced Laddie, his face bright, his eyes snapping with fun. He rode Flos, was leading the Princess' horse Maud, and carrying a big bundle under his arm. He leaped from the saddle and fastened both horses.

"Gracious Heaven! What have you done?" gasped the Princess.

"Brought your mount," said Laddie, quite as if he were used to going to Pryors' after the sausage grinder or the grain sacks. But the Princess was pale and trembling. She stepped so close she touched him, and he immediately got a little closer. You couldn't get ahead of Laddie, and he didn't seem to care who saw, and neither did she.

"Tell me exactly what occurred," she said, just as father does when he means to whale us completely.

"I rapped at the front door," said Laddie.

"And who opened it?" cried the Princess.

"Your father!"

"My father?"

"Yes, your father!" said Laddie. "And because I was in such a hurry, I didn't wait for him to speak. I said: 'Good morning, Mr. Pryor. I'm one of the Stanton boys, and I came for Miss Pryor's mount and habit. All the young people who are on horseback are going to ride an escort to the village, around my sister's bridal carriage, and Miss Pryor thinks she would enjoy going. Please excuse such haste, but we only this minute made the plan, and the train won't wait.' "

"And he?"

"He said: 'Surely! Hold one minute.' I stood on the step and waited, and I could hear him give the order to some one to get your riding habit quickly, and then he blew a shrill whistle, and your horse was at the gate the fastest of anything I ever saw."

"Did he do or say——"

"Nothing about 'clods, and clowns, and grossness!' Every other word he spoke was when I said, 'Thank you, and good morning,' and was turning away. He asked: 'Did Miss Pryor say whether she preferred to ride home, or shall I escort her in the carriage?' "

" 'She did not,' I answered. 'The plan was so sudden she had no time to think that far. But since she will have her horse and habit, why not allow my father to escort her?' So you see, I'm going to take you home," exulted Laddie.

"But you told him your *father*," said the Princess.

"And thereby created the urgent necessity," said Laddie with a flourish, "for speaking to him again, and telling him that my father had visitors from Ohio, and couldn't leave them. We will get all the fun from the day that we can; but before dusk, too early for them to have any cause for cavil, 'the gross country clod' is going to take you home!"

One at a time, Laddie pounded those last words into the hitching post, with his doubled fist.

"Suppose he sets the dogs on you! You know he keeps two dreadful ones."

Laddie just roared. He leaned closer.

"Beaucheous Lady," he said, "I have fed those same dogs and

rubbed their ears so many nights lately, he'll get the surprise of his life if he tries that."

The Princess drew away and stared at Laddie the funniest. "On my life!" she said at last. "Well for a country clod——!"

Then she turned with the habit bundle, and ran into the house. Father and mother came from the front door arm in arm and walked to the carriage, and Sally and Peter followed. My, but they looked fine! The Princess had gone to the garden and gathered flowers and lined all the children in rows down each side of the walk. They were loaded with blooms to throw at Sally; but when she came out, in her beautiful gray poplin travelling dress, trimmed in brown ribbon, the same shade as her curls, her face all pink, her eyes shining, and the ties of her little brown bonnet waving to her waist, she was so perfectly beautiful, every single child watched her open mouthed, gripped its flowers, and forgot to throw them at all.

And this you scarcely will believe after what she had said the day she made her list, and when all of us knew her heart was all torn up, Sally just swept along smiling at every one and calling "good-bye" to those who had no way to ride to the village, as if leaving didn't amount to much. At the carriage, a little white, but still smiling, she turned and took one long look at everything, and then she got in and called for me, right out loud before every one, so I got to hold up my head as high as it would go, and step in too, and ride all the way to Groveville between her and Peter, and instead of holding his hand, she held mine, just gripped it tight. She gripped so hard she squeezed all the soreness at her from my heart, and when she kissed me good-bye the very last of all, I whispered in her ear that I wouldn't ever be angry any more, and I wasn't, because after she had explained I saw how it had been. It wasn't *me* she didn't want; it was just no baby.

After our carriage came Peter's people, then one father borrowed for the Ohio relatives, then the other children, and all the neighbours followed, and when we reached the high hill where you turn beside the woods, I saw father gather up the lines and brace himself, for Ned and Jo were what he called "mettlesome." "Then came a burst of thunder sound," as it says in "Casabianca," and the horseback riders came sweeping around us, Laddie and the Princess leading. These two rode ahead of us, and the others lined three deep on either side, and the next carriage dropped back and let them close in behind, so Sally and Peter were "in the midst thereof." Instead of throwing old shoes, as always had been done, the Princess coaxed them to throw rice and roses, and every other flower pulled from the bouquets at home, and from the gardens we had passed. Every one was out watching us go by, and when William Justus rode beside the fences crying, "Flowers for the bride! Give us flowers for the bride!" some of the women were so excited they pulled things up by the roots and gave him armloads, and he rode ahead and supplied Laddie and the Princess, and they kept scattering them in the road until every foot of the way to Groveville was covered with flowers, "the fair young flowers that lately sprang and stood." He even made side-cuts into swampy places and gathered armloads of those perfectly lovely, fringy blue gentians, caught up, and filled the carriage and scattered them in a wicked way, because you should only take a few of those rare, late flowers that only grow from seed.

Sally looked just as if she had come into her own and was made for it; I never did see her look so pretty, but Peter sweated and acted awful silly. Father had a time with the team. Ned and Jo became excited and just ranted. They simply danced. Laddie had braided their manes and tails, and they waved like silken floss in the sunshine, and the carriage was freshly washed and the patent leather and brass shone, and we rode flower-covered. Ahead, Laddie and the Princess fairly tried themselves. She hadn't put on her hat or habit after all. When Laddie told her they were going to lead, she said: "Very well! Then I shall go as I am. The dress makes no difference. It's the first time I've had a chance to spoil one since I left England."

When the other girls saw what she was going to do, nearly every one of them left off their hats and riding skirts. Every family had saddle horses those days, and when the riders came racing up they looked like flying flowers, they were all laughing, bloom ladened, singing and calling jokes. Ahead, Laddie and the Princess just plain showed off. Her horse came from England with them, and Laddie said it had Arab blood in it, like the one in the Fourth Reader poem, "Fret not to roam the desert now, With all thy winged speed," and the Princess loved her horse more than that man did his. She said she'd starve before she'd sell it, and if her family were starving, she'd go to work and earn food for them, and keep her horse. Laddie's was a Kentucky thoroughbred he'd saved money for years to buy; and he took a young one and trained it himself, almost like a circus horse. Both of them *could* ride; so that day they did. They ran those horses neck and neck, right up the hill approaching Groveville, until they were almost from sight, then they whirled and came sweeping back fast as the wind. The Princess' eyes were like dead coals, and her black curls streamed, the thin silk dress wrapped tight around her and waved back like a gossamer web such as spiders spin in October. Laddie's hair was blowing, his cheeks and eyes were bright, and with one eye on the Princess—she didn't need it— and one on the road, he cut curves, turned, wheeled, and raced, and as he rode, so did she.

"Will they break their foolish necks?" wailed mother.

"They are the handsomest couple I ever have seen in my life!" said father.

"Yes, and you two watch out, or you'll strike trouble right there," said Sally, leaning forward.

I gave her an awful nudge. It made me so happy I could have screamed to see them flying away together like that.

"Well, if that girl represents trouble," said father, "God knows it never before came in such charming guise."

"You can trust a man to forget his God and his immortal soul if a sufficiently beautiful woman comes along," said my mother dryly, and all of them laughed.

She didn't mean that to be funny, though. You could always tell by the set of her lips and the light in her eyes.

Just this side of Groveville we passed a man on horseback. He took off his hat and drew his horse to one side when Laddie and the Princess rode toward him. He had a big roll of papers under his arm, to show that he had been for his mail. But I knew, so did Laddie and the Princess, that he had been compelled to saddle and ride like mad, to reach town and come that far back in time to watch us pass; for it was the Princess' father, and *watch* was exactly what he was doing; he wanted to see for himself. Laddie and the Princess rode straight at him, neck and neck, and then both of them made their horses drop on their knees and they waved a salute, and then they were up and away. Of course father and mother saw, so mother bowed, and father waved his whip as we passed. He sat there like he'd turned the same on horseback as Sabethany had in her coffin; but he had to see almost a mile of us driving our best horses and carriages, wearing our wedding garments and fine raiment, and all that "cavalcade," father called it, of young, reckless riders. You'd have thought if there were a hint of a smile in his whole being it would have shown when Sally leaned from the carriage to let him see that her face and clothes were as good as need be and smiled a lovely smile on him, and threw him a rose. He did leave his hat off and bow low, and then Shelley, always the very dickens for daring, rode right up to him and laughed in his face, and she leaned and thrust a flower into his bony hands; you would have thought he would have been simply forced to smile then, but he looked far more as if he would tumble over and roll from the saddle. My heart ached for a man in trouble like that. I asked the Lord to preserve us from secrets we couldn't tell the neighbours!

At the station there wasn't a thing those young people didn't do. They tied flowers and ribbons all over Sally's satchel and trunk. They sowed rice as if it were seeding time in a wheatfield. They formed a circle around Sally and Peter and as mushy as ever they could they sang, "As sure as the grass grows around the stump, You are my darling sugar lump," while they danced. They just smiled all the time no matter what was done to them.

Some of it made me angry, but I suppose to be pleasant was the right way. Sally was strong on always doing the right thing, so she just laughed, and so did all of us. Going home it was wilder yet, for all of them raced and showed how they could ride. At the house people were hungry again, so the table was set and they ate up every scrap in sight, and Leon and I ate with them that time and saved ours. Then one by one the carriages, spring wagons, and horseback riders went away, all the people saying Sally was the loveliest bride, and hers had been the prettiest wedding they'd ever seen, and the most good things to eat, and Laddie and the Princess went with them. When the last one was gone, and only the relatives from Ohio were left, mother pitched on the bed, gripped her hands and cried as if she'd go to pieces, and father cried too, and all of us, even Mrs. Freshett, who stayed to wash up the dishes. She was so tickled to be there, and see, and help, that mother had hard work to keep her from washing the linen that same night. She did finish the last dish, scrub the kitchen floor, black the stove, and pack all the borrowed china in tubs, ready to be taken home, and things like that. Mother said it was a burning shame for any neighbourhood to let a woman get so starved out and lonesome she'd act that way. She said enough was enough, and when Mrs. Freshett had cooked all day, and washed dishes until the last skillet was in place, she had done as much as any neighbour ought to do, and the other things she went on and did were a rebuke to us.

I felt sore, weepy, and tired out. It made me sick to think of the sage bag in the cracked churn, so I climbed my very own catalpa tree in the corner, watched up the road for Laddie, and thought things over. If I ever get married I want a dress, and a wedding exactly like that, but I would like a man quite different from Peter; like Laddie would suit me better. When he rode under the tree, I dropped from a limb into his arms, and went with him to the barn. He asked me what was going on at the house, and I told him about Mrs. Freshett being a rebuke to us; and Laddie said she was, and he didn't believe one word against her. When I told him mother was in bed crying like anything, he said: "I knew that had to come when she kept up so bravely at the station. Thank the Lord, she showed her breeding by holding in until she got where she had a right to cry if she pleased."

Then I whispered for fear Leon might be around: "Did he set the dogs on you?"

"He did not," said Laddie, laughing softly.

"Did he call you names again?"

"He did!" said Laddie, "but I started it. You see, when we get there, Thomas was raking the grass and he came to take the Princess' horse. Her father was reading on a bench under a tree. I helped her down, and walked with her to the door and said good-bye, and thanked her for the pleasure she had added to the day for us, loudly enough that he could hear; then I went over to him and said: 'Good evening, Mr. Pryor. If my father knew anything about it, he would very much regret that company from Ohio detained him and compelled me to escort your daughter home. He would greatly have enjoyed the privilege, but I honestly believe that I appreciated it far more than he could.' "

"Oh Laddie, what did he say?"

"He arose and glared at me, and choked on it, and he tried several times, until I thought the clods were going to fly again, but at last he just spluttered: 'You blathering rascal, you!' That was such a compliment compared with what I thought he was going to say that I had to laugh. He tried, but he couldn't keep from smiling himself, and then I said: 'Please think it over, Mr. Pryor, and if you find that Miss Pryor has had an agreeable, entertaining day, won't you give your consent for her to come among us again? Won't you allow me to come here, if it can be arranged in such a way that I intrude on no one?' "

"Oh Laddie!"

"He exploded in a kind of a snarl that meant, I'll see you in the Bad Place first. So I said to him: 'Thank you very much for to-day, anyway. I'm sure Miss Pryor has enjoyed this day, and it has been the happiest of my life—one to be remembered always. Of course I won't come here if I am unwelcome, but I am in honour bound to tell you that I intend to meet your daughter elsewhere, whenever I possibly can. I thought it would be a better way for you to know and have us where you could see what was going on, if you chose, than for us to meet without your knowledge."

"Oh Laddie," I wailed, "now you've gone and ruined everything!"

"Not so bad as that, Little Sister," laughed Laddie. "Not half so bad! He exploded in another growl, and he shook his walking stick at me, and he said—guess what he said."

"That he would kill you," I panted, clinging to him.

"Right!" said Laddie. "You have it exactly. He said: 'Young man, I'll brain you with my walking stick if ever I meet you anywhere with my daughter, when you have not come to her home and taken her with my permission.' "

"What!" I stammered. "What! Oh Laddie, say it over! Does it mean——?"

"It means," said Laddie, squeezing me until I was near losing my breath, "it means, Little Sister, that I shall march to his door and ask him squarely, and if it is anywhere the Princess wants to go, I shall take her."

"Like, 'See the conquering hero comes?' "

"Exactly!" laughed Laddie.

"What will mother say?"

"She hasn't made up her mind yet," answered Laddie.

"Do you mean——?" I gasped again.

"Of course!" said Laddie. "I wasn't going to let a girl get far ahead of me. The minute I knew she had told her mother, I told mine the very first chance."

"Mother knows that you feel about the Princess as father does about her?"

"Mother knows," answered Laddie, "and so does father. I told both of them."

Both of them knew! And it hadn't made enough difference that any one living right with them every day could have told it. Time and work will be needed to understand grown people.

CHAPTER VIII

The Shropshire and the Crusader

"For, among the rich and gay,
   Fine, and grand, and decked in laces,
None appear more glad then they,
   With happier hearts, or happier faces."

EVERY one told mother for a week before the wedding that she would be sick when it was over, and sure enough she was. She had been on her feet too much, and had so many things to think about, and there had been such a dreadful amount of work for her and Candace, even after all the neighbours helped, that she was sick in bed and we couldn't find a thing she could eat, until she was almost wild with hunger and father seemed as if he couldn't possibly bear it a day longer.

After Candace had tried everything she could think of, I went up and talked it over with Sarah Hood, and she came down, pretending she happened in, and she tried thickened milk, toast and mulled buttermilk; she kept trying for two days before she gave up. Candace thought of new things, and Mrs. Freshett came and made all the sick dishes she knew, but mother couldn't even taste them; so we were pretty blue, and we nearly starved ourselves, for how could we sit and eat everything you could mention, and mother lying there, almost crying with hunger?

Saturday morning I was hanging around her room hoping maybe she could think of some least little thing I could do for her, even if no more than to bring a glass of water, or a late rose to lay on her pillow; it would be better than not being able to do anything at all. After a while she opened her eyes and looked at me, and I scarcely knew her. She smiled the bravest she could and said: "Sorry for mother, dear?"

I nodded. I couldn't say much, and she tried harder than ever to be cheerful and asked: "What are you planning to do to-day?"

"If you can't think of one thing I can do for you, guess I'll go fishing," I said.

Her eyes grew brighter and she seemed half interested.

"Why, Little Sister," she said, "if you can catch some of those fish like you do sometimes, I believe I could eat one of them."

I never had such a be-hanged time getting started. I slipped from the room, and never told a soul even where I was going. I fell over the shovel and couldn't find anything quick enough but my pocket to put the worms in, and I forgot my stringer. At last, when I raced down the hill to the creek and climbed over the water of the deep place, on the roots of the Pete Billings yowling tree, I had only six worms, my apple sucker pole, my cotton cord line, and bent pin hook. I put the first worm on carefully, and if ever I prayed! Sometimes it was hard to understand about this praying business. My mother was the best and most beautiful woman who ever lived. She was clean, and good, and always helped "the poor and needy who cluster round your door," like it says in the poetry piece, and there never could have been a reason why God would want a woman to suffer herself, when she went flying on horseback even dark nights through rain or snow, to doctor other people's pain, and when she gave away things like she did—why, I've seen her take a big piece of meat from the barrel, and a sack of meal, and heaps of apples and potatoes to carry to Mandy Thomas—when she gave away food by the wagonload at a time, God couldn't have *wanted* her to be hungry, and yet she *was* that very minute almost crying for food; and I prayed, oh how I did pray! and a sneaking old back-ended crayfish took my very first worm. I just looked at the sky and said: "Well, when it's for a sick woman, can't You do any better than that?"

I suppose I shouldn't have said it, but if it had been your mother, how would you have felt? I pinched the next worm in two, so if a crayfish took that, it wouldn't get but half. I lay

down across the roots and pulled my bonnet far over my face
and tried to see to the bottom. I read in school the other day:

> *"And by those little rings on the water I know*
> *The fishes are merrily swimming below."*

There were no rings on the water, but after a while I saw
some fish darting around, only they didn't seem to be hungry;
for they would come right up and nibble a tiny bit at my worm,
but they wouldn't swallow it. Then one did, so I jerked with all
my might, jerked so hard the fish and worm both flew off, and
I had only the hook left. I put on the other half and tried again.
I prayed straight along, but the tears would come that time, and
the prayer was no powerful effort like Brother Hastings would
have made; it was little torn up pieces mostly: "O Lord, please
do make only one fish bite!" At last one did bite good, so I swung
carefully that time, and landed it on the grass, but it was so little
and it hit a stone and was killed. I had no stringer to put it back
in the water to keep cool, and the sun was hot that day, like times
in the fall. Stretched on the roots, with it shining on my back, and
striking the water and coming up from below, I dripped with
heat and excitement.

I threw that one away, put on another worm, and a big turtle
took it, the hook, and broke my line, and almost pulled me in.
I wouldn't have let go if it had, for I just had to have a fish.
There was no help from the Lord in that, so I quit praying,
only what I said when I didn't know it. Father said man was
born a praying animal, and no matter how wicked he was, if
he had an accident, or saw he had just got to die, he cried aloud
to the Lord for help and mercy before he knew what he was
doing.

I could hear the roosters in the barnyard, the turkey gobbler,
and the old ganders screamed once in a while, and sometimes a
bird sang a skimpy little fall song; nothing like spring, except the
killdeers and larks; they were always good to hear—and then the
dinner bell rang. I wished I had been where I couldn't have
heard that, because I didn't intend going home until I had a fish

that would do for mother if I stayed until night. If the best one in the family had to starve, we might as well all go together; but I wouldn't have known how hungry I was, if the bell hadn't rung and told me the others were eating. So I bent another pin and tried again. I lost the next worm without knowing how, and then I turned baby and cried right out loud. I was so thirsty, the salty tears running down my cheeks tasted good, and doing something besides fishing sort of rested me; so I looked around and up at the sky, wiped my face on the skirt of my sunbonnet, and put on another worm. I had only one more left, and I began to wonder if I could wade in and catch a fish by hand; I did teeny ones sometimes, but I knew the water there was far above my head, for I had measured it often with the pole; it wouldn't do to try that; instead of helping mother any, a funeral would kill her, too, so I fell back on the Crusaders, and tried again.

Strange how thinking about them helped. I pretended I was fighting my way to the Holy City, and this was the Jordan just where it met the sea, and I had to catch enough fish to last me during the pilgrimage west or I'd never reach Jerusalem to bring home a shell for the Stanton crest. I pretended so hard, that I got braver and stronger, and asked the Lord more like there was some chance of being heard. All at once there was a jerk that almost pulled me in, so I jerked too, and a big fish flew over my head and hit the bank behind me with a thump. Of course by a big fish I don't mean a red horse so long as my arm, like the boys bring from the river; I mean the biggest fish I ever caught with a pin in our creek. It looked like the whale that swallowed Jonah, as it went over my head. I laid the pole across the roots, jumped up and turned, and I had to grab the stump to keep from falling in the water and dying. There lay the fish, the biggest one I ever had seen, but it was flopping wildly, and it wasn't a foot from a hole in the grass where a muskrat had burrowed through. If it gave one flop that way, it would slide down the hole straight back into the water; and between me and the fish stood our cross old Shropshire ram. I always looked to see if the sheep were in the meadow before I went to the creek, but that morning I had been so crazy to get something for mother to eat, I never once thought of them—and there it stood!

That ram hadn't been cross at first, and father said it never would be if treated right, and not teased, and if it were, there would be trouble for all of us. I was having more than my share that minute, and it bothered me a lot almost every day. I never dared enter a field any more if it were there, and now it was stamping up and down the bank, shaking its head, and trying to get me; with one flop the fish went *almost* in the hole, and the next a little away from it. Everything put together, I thought I couldn't stand it. I never wanted anything as I wanted that fish, and I never hated anything as I hated that sheep. It wasn't the sheep's fault either; Leon teased it on purpose, just to see it chase Polly Martin; but that was more her doings than his.

She was a widow and she crossed our front meadow going to her sister's. She had two boys big as Laddie, and three girls, and father said they lived like "the lilies of the field; they toiled not, neither did they spin." They never looked really hungry or freezing, but they never plowed, or planted, they had no cattle or pigs or chickens, only a little corn for meal, and some cabbage, and wild things they shot for meat, and coons to trade the skins for more powder and lead—bet they ate the coons—never any new clothes, never clean, they or their house. Once when father and mother were driving past, they saw Polly at the well and they stopped for politeness sake to ask how she was, like they always did with every one. Polly had a tin cup of water and was sopping at her neck with a carpet rag, and when mother asked, "How are you, Mrs. Martin?" she answered: "Oh I ain't very well this spring; I gest I got the go-backs!"

Mother said Polly looked as if she'd been born with the "go-backs," and had given them to all her children, her home, garden, fields, and even the *fences*. We hadn't a particle of patience with such people. When you are lazy like that it is very probable that you'll live to see the day when your children will peep through the fence cracks and cry for bread. I have seen those Martin children come mighty near doing it when the rest of us opened our dinner baskets at school; and if mother hadn't always put in enough so that we could divide, I bet they would. If Polly Martin had walked up as if she were alive, and had been washed and neat, and going somewhere to do some one good, Leon never would have dreamed of such a thing as training the Shropshire to bunt her. She was so long and skinny, always wore a ragged shawl over her head, a floppy old dress that the wind whipped out behind, and when she came to the creek, she sat astride the foot log, and hunched along with her hands; that tickled the boys so, Leon began teasing the sheep on purpose to make it get her. But inasmuch as she saw fit to go abroad looking so funny, that any one could see she'd be a perfect circus if she were chased, I didn't feel that it was Leon's fault. If, like the little busy bee, she had "improved each shining hour," he never would have done it. Seems to me, she brought the trouble on her own head.

First, Leon ran at the Shropshire and then jumped aside; but soon it grew so strong and quick he couldn't manage that, so he put his hat on a stick and poked it back and forth through a fence crack, and that made the ram raving mad. At last it would butt the fence until it would knock itself down, and if he dangled the hat again, get right up and do it over. Father never caught Leon, so he couldn't understand what made the sheep so dreadfully cross, because he had thought it was quite peaceable when he bought it. The first time it got after Polly, she threw her shawl over its head, pulled up her skirts, and Leon said she hit just eleven high places crossing an eighty-acre field; she came to the house crying, and father had to go after her shawl, and mother gave her a roll of butter and a cherry pie to comfort her. The Shropshire never really got Polly, but any one could easily see what it would do to me if I dared step around that stump, and it was dancing and panting to begin. If whoever wrote that "Gentle Sheep, pray tell me why," piece ever had seen a sheep acting like that, it wouldn't have been in the books; at least I think it wouldn't, but one can't be sure. He proved that he didn't know much about anything outdoors or he wouldn't have said that sheep were "eating grass and daisies white, from the morning till the night," when daisies are bitter as gall.

Flop! went the fish, and its tail touched the edge of the hole. Then I turned around and picked up the pole. I put my sunbonnet over the big end of it, and poked it at the ram, and drew it back as Leon did his hat. One more jump and mother's fish would be gone. I stood on the roots and waved my bonnet. The sheep lowered its head and came at it with a rush. I drew back the pole, and the sheep's forefeet slid over the edge, and it braced and began to work to keep from going in. The fish gave a big flop and went down the hole. Then I turned Crusader and began to fight, and I didn't care if I were whipped black and blue, I meant to finish that old black-faced Shropshire. I set the pole on the back of its neck and pushed with all my might, and I got it in, too. My, but it made a splash! It wasn't much good at swimming either, and it had no chance, for I stood on the roots and pushed it down, and hit it over the nose with all my might, and I didn't care how far it came on the cars, or how much money it cost, it never would chase me, and make me lose my fish again.

I didn't hear him until he splashed under the roots and then I was so mad I didn't see that it was Laddie; I only knew that it was someone who was going to help out that miserable ram, so I struck with all my might, the sheep when I could hit it, if not, the man.

"You little demon, stop!" cried Laddie.

I got in a good one right on the ram's nose. Then Laddie dropped the sheep and twisted the fish pole from my fingers, and I pushed him as hard as I could, but he was too strong. He lifted the sheep, pulled it to the bank, and rolled it, worked its jaws, and squeezed water from it, and worked and worked.

"I guess you've killed it!" he said at last.

"Goody!" I shouted. "Goody! Oh but I am glad it's dead!"

"What on earth has turned you to a fiend?" asked Laddie, beginning work on the sheep again.

"That ram!" I said. "Ever since Leon made it cross so it would chase Polly Martin, it's got me oftener than her. I can't go anywhere for it, and to-day it made me lose a big fish, and mother is waiting. She thought maybe she could eat some."

Then I roared; bet I sounded like Bashan's bull.

"Dear Lord!" said Laddie dropping the sheep and taking me in his wet arms. "Tell me, Biddy! Tell me how it is."

Then I forgot I was a Crusader, and told him all about it as well as I could for choking, and when I finished he bathed my hot face, and helped me from the roots. Then he went and looked down the hole I showed him and he cried out quicklike, and threw himself on the grass, and in a second up came the fish. Some one had rolled a big stone in the hole, so the fish was all right, not even dead yet, and Laddie said it was the biggest one he ever had seen taken from the creek. Then he said if I'd forgive him and all our family, for spoiling the kind of a life I had a perfect right to lead, and if I'd run to the house and get a big bottle from the medicine case quick, he would see to it that some place was fixed for that sheep where it would never bother me again. So I took the fish and ran as fast as I could, but I sent May back with the bottle, and did the scaling myself. No one at our house could do it better, for Laddie taught me the right way long ago, when I was small, and I'd done it hundreds of times.

Then I went to Candace and she put a little bit of butter and a speck of lard in a skillet, and cooked the fish brown. She made a slice of toast and boiled a cup of water and carried it to the door; then she went in and set the table beside the bed, and I took in the tray, and didn't spill a drop. Mother never said a word; she just reached out and broke off a tiny speck and nibbled it, and it stayed; she tried a little bigger piece, and another, and she said: "Take out the bones, Candace!" She ate every scrap of that fish like the hungriest traveller who ever came to our door, and the toast, and drank the hot water. Then she went into a long sleep and all of us walked tiptoe, and when she waked up she was better, and in a few days she could sit in her chair again, and she began getting Shelley ready to go to music school.

I have to tell you the rest, too. Laddie made the ram come alive, and father sold it the next day for more than he paid for it. He said he hoped I'd forgive him for not having seen how it had been bothering me, and that he never would have had it on the place a day if he'd known. The next time he went to town he bought me a truly little cane rod, a real fishing line, several hooks, and a red bobber too lovely to put into the water. I thought I was a great person from the fuss all of them made over me, until I noticed Laddie shrug his shoulders, and reach back and rub one, and then I remembered.

I went flying, and thank goodness! he held out his arms.

"Oh Laddie! I never did it!" I cried. "I never, never did! I couldn't! Laddie, I love you best of any one; you know I do!"

"Of course you didn't!" said Laddie. "My Little Sister wasn't anywhere around when that happened. That was a poor little girl I never saw before, and she was in such trouble she didn't know *what* she was doing. And I hope I'll never see her again," he ended, twisting his shoulder. But he kissed me and made it all right, and really I didn't do that; I just simply couldn't have struck Laddie.

Marrying off Sally was little worse than getting Shelley ready for school. She had to have three suits of everything, and a new dress of each kind, and three hats; her trunk wouldn't hold all there was to put in it; and father said he never could pay the bills. He had promised her to go, and he didn't know what in this world to do; because he never had borrowed money in his life, and he couldn't begin; for if he died suddenly, that would leave mother in debt, and they might take the land from her. That meant he'd spent what he had in the bank on Sally's wedding, and all that was in the Underground Station, or maybe the Station money wasn't his.

Just when he was awfully bothered, mother said to never mind, she believed she could fix it. She sent all of us into the orchard to pick the fine apples that didn't keep well, and father made three trips to town to sell them. She had big jars of lard she wouldn't need before butchering time came again, and she sold dried apples, peaches, and raspberries from last year. She got lots of money for barrels of feathers she'd saved to improve her feather beds and pillows; she said she would see to that later. Father was so tickled to get the money to help him out that he said he'd get her a pair of those wonderful new blue geese like Pryors had, that every one stopped to look at. When there was not quite enough yet, from somewhere mother brought out money that she'd saved for a long time, from butter and eggs, and chickens, and turkeys, and fruit and lard, and things that belonged to her. Father hated to use it the worst way, but she said she'd saved it for an emergency, and now seemed to be the time.

She said if the child really had talent, she should be about developing it, and while there would be many who would have far finer things than Shelley, still she meant her to have enough that she wouldn't be the worst looking one, and so ashamed she couldn't keep her mind on her work. Father said, with her face it didn't make any difference what she wore, and mother said that was just like a man; it made all the difference in the world what a girl wore. Father said maybe it did to the girl, and other women; what he meant was that it made none to a man. Mother said the chief aim and end of a girl's life was not wrapped up in a man; and father said maybe not with some girls, but it would be with Shelley: she was too pretty to escape. I do wonder if I'm going to be too pretty to escape, when I put on long dresses. Sometimes I look in the glass to see if it's coming, but I don't suppose it's any use. Mother says you can't tell a thing at the growing age about how a girl is going to look at eighteen.

When everything was almost ready, Leon came in one day and said: "Shelley, what about improving your hair? Have you tried your wild grape sap yet?"

Shelley said: "Why, goodness me! We've been so busy getting Sally married, and my clothes made, I forgot all about that. Have you noticed the crock in passing? Is there anything in it?"

"It was about half full, once when I went by," said Leon. "I haven't seen it lately."

"Do please be a dear and look, when you go after the cows this evening," said Shelley. "If there's anything in it, bring it up."

> *"Do it yourself for want of me,*
> *The boy replied quite manfully,"*

quoted Leon from "The Little Lord and the Farmer." He was always teasing.

"I think you're mean as dirt if you don't bring it," said Shelley.

Leon grinned, and you should have heard the nasty, teasing way he said more of that same piece:

> *"Anger and pride are both unwise,*
> *Vinegar never catches flies——"*

I wondered she didn't slap him. You could see she wanted to.

"I can get it myself," she said angrily.

"What will you give me to bring it?" asked Leon, who never missed a chance to make a bargain.

"My grateful thanks. Are they not a proper reward?" asked Shelley.

"Thanks your foot!" said Leon. "Will you bring something pretty from Chicago for Susie Fall's Christmas present?"

Every one laughed, but Leon never cared. He liked Susie best of any of the girls, and he wanted every one to know it. He went straight to her whenever he had a chance, and he'd already told her mother to keep all the other boys away, because he meant to marry her when he grew up, and Widow Fall said that was fair enough, and she'd save her for him. So Shelley said she would get him something for Susie, and Leon brought the crock. Shelley looked at it sort of dubious-like, tipped it, and stared at the dirt settled in the bottom, and then stuck in her finger and tasted it. She looked at Leon with a queer grin and said: "Smarty, smarty, think you're smart!" She threw the creek water into the swill bucket. No one said a word, but Leon looked much sillier than she did. After he was gone I asked her if she would bring him a Christmas present for Susie *now,* and she said she ought to bring him a pretty glass bottle labelled perfume, with hartshorn in it, and she would, if she thought he'd smell it first.

Shelley felt badly about leaving mother when she wasn't very well; but mother said it was all right, she had Candace to keep house, and May and me, and father, and all of us to take care of her, and it would be best for Shelley to go now and work hard as she could, while she had the chance. So one afternoon father took her trunk to the depot and bought the tickets and got the checks, and the next day Laddie drove to Groveville with father and Shelley, and she was gone. Right at the last, she didn't seem to want to leave so badly, but all of them said she must. Peter's cousin, who had gone last year, was to meet her, and have a room ready where she boarded if she could, and if she couldn't right away, then the first one who left, Shelley was to have the place, so they'd be together.

There were eight of us left, counting Candace and Miss Amelia, and you wouldn't think a house with eight people living in it would be empty, but ours was. Everything seemed to wilt. The roses on the window blinds didn't look so bright as they had; mother said the only way she could get along was to keep right on working. She helped Candace all she could, but she couldn't be on her feet very much, so she sat all day long and peeled peaches to dry, showed Candace how to jelly, preserve, and spice them, and peeled apples for butter and to dry, quantities more than we could use, but she said she always could sell such things, and with the bunch of us to educate yet, we'd need the money.

When it grew cold enough to shut the doors, and have fire at night, first thing after supper all of us helped clear the table, then we took our slates and books and learned our lessons for the next day, and then father lined us against the wall, all in a row from Laddie down, and he pronounced words—easy ones that divided into syllables nicely, for me, harder for May, and so up until I might sit down. For Laddie, May and Leon he used the geography, the Bible, Roland's history, the *Christian Advocate,* and the *Agriculturist.* My, but he had them so they could spell! After that, as memory tests, all of us recited our reading lesson for the next day, especially the poetry pieces. I knew most of them, from hearing the big folks repeat them so often and prac- tise the proper way to read them. I could do "Rienzi's Address to the Romans," "Casabianca," "Gray's Elegy," or "Mark Antony's Speech," but best of all, I liked "Lines to a Water-fowl." When he was tired, if it were not bedtime yet, all of us, boys too, sewed rags for carpet and rugs. Laddie braided corn husks for the kitchen and outside door mats, and they were pretty, and "very useful too," like the dog that got his head patted in McGuffey's Second.

Then they picked the apples. These had to be picked by hand, wrapped in soft paper, packed in barrels, and shipped to Fort Wayne. Where they couldn't reach by hand, they stood on barrels or ladders, and used a long handled picker, so as not to bruise the fruit. Laddie helped with everything through the day, worked at his books at night, and whenever he stepped outside he looked in the direction of Pryors'. He climbed to the topmost limbs of the trees with a big basket, picked it full and let it down with a long piece of clothesline. I loved to be in the orchard when they were working; there were plenty of summer apples to eat yet; it was fun to watch the men, and sometimes I could be useful by handing baskets or heaping up apples to be buried for us.

One night father read about a man who had been hanged for killing another man, and they cut him down too soon, so he came alive, and they had to hang him over; and father got all worked up about it. He said the man had suffered death the first time to "all intents and purposes," so that fulfilled the requirements of the law, and they were wrong when they hanged him again. Laddie said it was a piece of bungling sure enough, but the law said a man must be "hanged by his neck until he was dead," and if he weren't dead, why, it was plain he hadn't fulfilled the requirements of the law, so they were forced to hang him again. Father said that law was wrong; the man never should have been hanged in the first place. They talked and argued until we were all excited about it, and the next evening after school Leon and I were helping pick apples, and when father and Laddie went to the barn with a load we sat down to rest and we thought about what they said.

"Gee, that was tough on the man!" said Leon, "but I guess the law is all right. Of course he wouldn't want to die, and twice over at that, but I don't suppose the man he killed liked to die either. I think if you take a life, it's all right to give your own to pay for it."

"Leon," I said, "some time when you are fighting Absalom Saunders or Lou Wicks, just awful, if you hit them too hard on some tender spot and kill them, would you want to die to pay for it?"

"I wouldn't want to, but I guess I'd have to," said Leon. "That's the law, and it's as good a way to make it as any. But I'm not going to kill any one. I've studied my physiology hard to find all the spots that will kill. I never hit them behind the ear, or in the pit of the stomach; I just black their eyes, bloody their snoots, and swat them on the chin to finish off with."

"Well, suppose they don't study their physiologies like you do, and hit *you* in the wrong place, and kill you, would you want *them* hanged by the neck until they were dead, to pay for it?"

"I don't think I'd want anything if I were dead," he said. "I wonder how it feels to die. Now *that* man knew. I'd like to be hanged enough to find out how it goes, and then come back, and brag about it. I don't think it hurts much; I believe I'll try it."

So Leon took the rope Laddie lowered the baskets with, and threw it over a big limb. Then he rolled up a barrel and stood on it and put my sunbonnet on with the crown over his face, for a black cap, and made the rope into a slip noose over his head, and told me to stand back by the apple tree and hold the rope tight, until he said he was hanged enough. Then he stepped from the barrel. It jerked me toward him about a yard, as he came down smash! on his feet. I held with all my might, but he was too heavy —and falling that way. So he went to trying to fix some other plan, and I told him the sensible thing to do would be for him to hang me, because he'd be strong enough to hold me and I could tell him how it felt just as well. So we fixed me up like we had him, and when Leon got the rope stretched, he wrapped it twice around the apple tree so it wouldn't jerk him as it had me, and when he said "Ready," I stepped from the barrel. The last thing I heard was Leon telling me to say when I was hanged enough. I was so heavy, the rope stretched, and I went down until it almost tore off my head, and I couldn't get a single breath, so of course I didn't tell him, and I couldn't get on the barrel, and my tongue went out, and my chest swelled up, and my ears roared, and I kicked and struggled, and all the time I could hear Leon laughing, and shouting to keep it up, that I was dying fine; only he didn't know that I really was, and at last I didn't feel or know anything more.

When I came to, I was lying on the grass, while father was pumping my arms, and Laddie was pouring creek water on my face from his hat, and Leon was running around in circles, clear crazy. I heard father tell him he'd give him a scutching he'd remember to the day of his death; but inasmuch as I had told Leon to do it, I had to grab father and hold to him tight as I could, until I got breath enough to explain how it happened. Even then I wasn't sure what he was going to do.

After all that, when I tried to tell Leon how it felt, he just cried like a baby, and he wouldn't listen to a word, even when he'd wanted to know so badly. He said if I hadn't come back, he'd have gone to the barn and used the swing rope on himself, so it was a good thing I did, for one funeral would have cost enough, when we needed money so badly, not to mention how mother would have felt to have two of us go at once, like she had before. And anyway, it didn't amount to so awful much. It was pretty bad at first, but it didn't last long, and the next day my neck was only a little blue and stiff, and in three days it was all over, only a rough place where the rope grained the skin as I went down; but I never got to tell Leon how it felt; I just couldn't talk him into hearing, and it was quite interesting too; but still I easily saw why the man in the paper would object to dying twice, to pay for killing another man once.

When the apples were picked and the cabbage, beets, turnips, and potatoes were buried, some corn dried in the garret for new meal, pumpkins put in the cellar, the field corn all husked, and the butchering done, father said the work was in such fine shape, with Laddie to help, and there was so much more corn than he needed for us, and the price was so high, and the turkeys did so well, and everything, that he could pay back what mother helped him, and have quite a sum over.

It was Thanksgiving by that time, and all of Winfield's, Lucy's, Sally and Peter, and our boys came home. We had a big time, all but Shelley; it was too expensive for her to come so far for one day, but mother sent her a box with a whole turkey for herself and her friends; and cake, popcorn, nuts, and just everything that wasn't too drippy. Shelley wrote such lovely letters that mother saved them and after we had eaten as much dinner as we could, she read them before we left the table.

I had heard most of them, but I liked to listen again, because they sounded so happy. You could hear Shelley laugh on every page. She told about how Peter's cousin was waiting when the train stopped. They couldn't room together right away, but they were going to the first chance they had. Shelley felt badly because they were so far apart, but she was in a nice place, where she could go with other girls of the school until she learned the way. She told about her room and the woman she boarded with and what she had to eat; she wrote mother not to worry about clothes, because most of the others were from the country, or small towns, and getting ready to teach, and lots of them didn't have *nearly* as many or as pretty dresses as she did. She told about the big building, the classes, the professors, and of going to public recitals where some of the pupils who knew enough played; and she was working her fingers almost to the bone, so she could next year. She told of people she met, and how one of the teachers took a number of girls in his class to see a great picture gallery. She wrote pages about a young Chicago lawyer she met there, and only a few lines about the pictures, so father said as that was the best collection of art work in Chicago, it was easy enough to see that Shelley had been far more impressed with the man than she had been with the pictures. Mother said she didn't see how he could say a thing like that about the child. Of course she couldn't tell in a letter about hundreds of pictures, but it was easy enough to tell all about a man.

Father got sort of spunky at that, and he said it was mighty little that mattered most, that could be told about a Chicago lawyer; and mother had better caution Shelley to think more about her work, and write less of the man. Mother said that would stop the child's confidences completely and she'd think all the time about the man, and never mention him again, so she wouldn't know what *was* going on. She said she was glad Shelley had found pleasing, refined friends, and she'd encourage her all she could in cultivating them; but of course she'd caution her to be careful, and she'd tell her what the danger was, and after that Shelley wrote and wrote. Mother didn't always read the letters to us, but she answered every one she got that same night. Sometimes she pushed the pen so she jabbed the paper, and often she smiled or laughed softly.

I liked Thanksgiving. We always had a house full of company, and they didn't stay until we were tired of them, as they did at Christmas, and there was as much to eat; the only difference was that there were no presents. It wasn't nearly so much work to fix for one day as it was for a week; so it wasn't so hard on mother and Candace, and father didn't have to spend much money. We were wearing all our clothes from last fall that we could, and our coats from last winter to help out, but we didn't care. We had a lot of fun, and we wanted Sally and Shelley to have fine dresses, because they were in big cities where they needed them, and in due season, no doubt, we would have much more than they, because, as May figured it, there would be only a few of us by that time, so we could have more to spend. That looked sensible, and I thought it would be that way, too. We were talking it over coming from school one evening, and when we had settled it, we began to play "Dip and Fade." That was a game we made up from being at church, and fall and spring were the only times we could play it, because then the rains filled all the ditches beside the road where the dirt was plowed up to make the bed higher, and we had to have the water to dip in and fade over.

We played it like that, because it was as near as we could come to working out a song Isaac Thomas sang every time he got happy. He had a lot of children at home, and more who had died, from being half-fed and frozen, mother thought; and he was always talking about meeting the "pore innocents" in Heaven, and singing that one song. Every time he made exactly the same speech in meeting. It began like reciting poetry, only it didn't rhyme, but it sort of cut off in lines, and Isaac waved back and forth on his feet, and half sung it, and the rags waved too, but you just couldn't feel any thrills of earnestness about what he said, because he needed washing, and to go to work and get him some clothes and food to fill out his frame. He only looked funny, and made you want to laugh. It took Emanuel Ripley to raise your hair. I don't know why men like my father, and the minister, and John Dover stood it; they talked over asking Isaac to keep quiet numbers of times, but the minister said there were people like that in every church, they always came among the Lord's anointed, and it was better to pluck out your right eye than to offend one of them, and he was doubtful about doing it. So we children all knew that the grown people scarcely could stand Isaac's speech, and prayer, and song, and that they were afraid to tell him plain out that he did more harm than good. Every meeting about the third man up was Isaac, and we had to watch him wave, and rant, and go sing-songy:

"Oh brethering and sistering—ah,
It delights my heart—ah to gather with you,
In this holy house of worship—ah.
In his sacred word—ah,
The Lord—ah tells us,
That we are all his childring—ah.
And now, lemme exhort you to-night—ah,
As one that loves you—ah,
To choose that good part, that Mary chose—ah,
That the worrrr-uld kin neither give ner take away—ah."

That went on until he was hoarse, then he prayed, and arose and sang his song. Other men spoke where they stood. Isaac always walked to the altar, faced the people, and he was tired out when he finished, but so proud of himself, so happy, and he felt

so sure that his efforts were worth a warm bed, sausage, pan-
cakes, maple syrup, and coffee for breakfast, that it was mighty
seldom he failed to fool some one else into thinking so too, and
if he could, he wouldn't have to walk four miles home on cold
nights, with no overcoat. In summer, mostly, they let him go.
Isaac always was fattest in winter, especially during revivals, but
at any time mother said he looked like a sheep's carcass after the
buzzards had picked it. It could be seen that he was perfectly
strong, and could have fed and clothed himself, and Mandy and
the children, quite as well as our father did us, if he had wanted
to work, for we had the biggest family of the neighbourhood. So
we children made fun of him and we had to hold our mouths
shut when he got up all tired and teary-like, and began to
quaver:

> *"Many dear childurn we know dew stan',*
> *Un toon ther harps in the better lan',*
> *Ther little hans frum each soundin' string,*
> *Bring music sweet, wile the Anguls sing,*
> *Bring music sweet, wile the Anguls sing,—*
> > *We shell meet them agin on that shore,*
> > *We shell meet them agin on that shore,*
> > *With fairer face, un angel grace,*
> > *Each loved un ull welcome us ther.*

> *"They uster mourn when the childurn died,*
> *Un said goo-bye at the river side,*
> *They dipped ther feet in the glidin' stream,*
> *Un faded away, like a loveli dream,*
> *Un faded away like a loveli dream."*

Then the chorus again, and then Isaac dropped on the front
seat exhausted, and stayed there until some good-hearted woman,
mostly my mother, felt so sorry about his shiftlessness she asked
him to go home with us and warmed and fed him, and put him
in the traveller's bed to sleep. The way we played it was this: we
stood together at the edge of a roadside puddle and sang the first
verse and the chorus exactly as Isaac did. Then I sang the second

verse, and May was one of the "many dear childurn," and as I came to the lines she dipped her feet in the "glidin' stream," and for "fading away," she jumped across.

Now May was a careful little soul, and always watched what she was doing, so she walked up a short way, chose a good place, and when I sang the line, she was almost birdlike, she dipped and faded so gracefully. Then we laughed like dunces, and then May began to sway and swing, and drone through her nose for me, and I was so excited I never looked. I just dipped and faded on the spot. I faded all right too, for I couldn't jump nearly across, and when I landed in pure clay that had been covered with water for three weeks, I went down to my knees in mud, to my waist in water, and lost my balance and fell backward.

A man passing on horseback pried me out with a rail and helped me home. Of course he didn't know how I happened to fall in, and I was too chilled to talk. I noticed May only said I fell, so I went to bed scorched inside with red pepper tea, and never told a word about dipping and fading. Leon whispered and said he bet it was the last time I would play that, so as soon as my coat and dress were washed and dried, and I could go back to school, I did it again, just to show him I was no cowardy-calf; but I had learned from May to choose a puddle I could manage before I faded.

CHAPTER IX

"Even So"

"All things whatsoever ye would
That men should do to you,
Do ye even so to them."

OUR big girls and boys always made a dreadful fuss and said we
would catch every disease you could mention, but mother and
father were set about it, just like the big rocks in the hills. They
said they, themselves, once had been at the mercy of the people,
and they knew how it felt. Mother said when they were coming
here in a wagon, and she had ridden until she had to walk to rest
her feet, and held a big baby until her arms became so tired she
drove while father took it, and when at last they saw a house and
stopped, she said if the woman hadn't invited her in, and let her
cook on the stove, given her milk and eggs, and furnished her a
bed to sleep in once in a while, she couldn't have reached here at
all; and she never had been refused once. Then she always
quoted: "All things whatsoever ye would that men should do to
you, do ye *even so* to them."

Father said there were men who made a business of splitting
hairs, and of finding different meanings in almost everything in
the Bible. I would like to have seen any one split hairs about that,
or it made to mean something else. Of all the things in the Bible
that you had to do because it said to, whether you liked it or not,
that was the one you struck oftenest in life and it took the hardest
pull to obey. It was just the hatefulest text of any, and made you
squirm most. There was no possible way to get around it. It
meant, that if you liked a splinter new slate, and a sharp pencil

all covered with gold paper, to make pictures and write your lessons, when Clarissa Polk sat next you and sang so low the teacher
couldn't hear until she put herself to sleep on it, "I *wisht* I had a
slate! I wisht I *had* a slate! I wisht I had a *slate!* Oh I *wisht I
had a slate!"*—it meant that you just had to wash up yours and
stop making pictures yourself, and pass it over; you even had to
smile when you offered it, if you did it right. I seldom got through
it as the Lord would, for any one who loaned Clarissa a slate
knew that it would come back with greasy, sweaty finger marks
on it you almost had to dig a hole to wash off, and your pencil
would be wet. And if there were the least flaw of crystal in the
pencil, she found it, and bore down so hard that what she wrote
never would come off.

The Lord always seemed bigger and more majestic to me, than
at any other time, when I remembered that He could have known
all that, and yet smiled as He loaned Clarissa His slate. And that
old Bible thing meant, too, that if you would like it if you were
travelling a long way, say to California to hunt gold, or even just
to Indiana, to find a farm fit to live on—it meant that if you were
tired, hungry, and sore, and would want to be taken in and fed
and rested, you had to let in other people when they reached your
house. Father and mother had been through it themselves, and
they must have been tired as could be, before they reached Sarah
Hood's and she took them in, and rested and fed them, even
when they were only a short way from the top of the Little Hill,
where next morning they looked down and stopped the wagon,
until they chose the place to build their house. Sarah Hood came
along, and helped mother all day, so by night she was settled in
the old cabin that was on the land, and ready to go to work
making money to build a new one, and then a big house, and fix
the farm all beautiful like it was then. They knew so well how it
felt, that they kept one bed in the boys' room, and any man who
came at dusk got his supper, to sleep there, and his breakfast, and
there never was anything to pay. The girls always scolded dreadfully about the extra washing, but mother said she slept on sheets
when she came out, and some one washed them.

One time Sally said: "Mother, have you ever figured out how many hundred sheets you've washed since, to pay for that?"

Mother said: "No, but I just hope it will make a stack high enough for me to climb from into Heaven."

Sally said: "The talk at the church always led me to think that you flew to Heaven."

Mother answered: "So I get there, I don't mind if I creep."

Then Sally knew it was time to stop. We always knew. And we stopped, too!

We had heard that "All things" quotation, until the first two words were as much as mother ever needed repeat of it any more, and we had cooked, washed for, and waited on people travelling, until Leon got so when he saw any one coming—of course we knew all the neighbours, and their horses and wagons and carriages—he always said: "Here comes another 'Even So!' " He said we had done "even so" to people until it was about our share, but mother said our share was going to last until the Lord said, "Well done, good and faithful servant," and took us home. She had much more about the stranger at the gate and entertaining angels unawares; why, she knew every single thing in the Bible that meant it was her duty to feed and give a bed to any one, no matter how dirty or miserable looking he was! So when Leon came in one evening at dusk and said, "There's another 'Even So' coming down the Little Hill!" all of us knew that we'd have company for the night, and we had.

I didn't like that man, but some of the others seemed to find him amusing. Maybe it was because I had nothing to do but sit and watch him, and so I saw more of him than the ones who came and went all the time. As long as there was any one in the room, he complained dreadfully about his sore foot, and then cheered up and talked, and he could tell interesting things. He was young, but he must have been most everywhere and seen everything. He was very brave and could stand off three men who were going to take from him the money he was carrying to buy a piece of land in Illinois. The minute the grown folks left the room to milk, do the night feeding, and begin supper, he twisted

in his chair and looked at every door, and went and stood at the
back dining-room window, where he could see the barn and what
was out there, and coming back he took a peep into father's and
mother's room, and although he limped dreadfully when he came,
he walked like any one when he went over and picked up father's
gun and looked to see if it were loaded, and seemed mighty glad
when he found it wasn't. Father said he could load in a flash
when it was necessary, but he was dubious about a loaded gun in
a house full of children. Not one of us ever touched it, until the
boys were big enough to have permission, like Laddie and Leon
had. He said a gun was such a great "moral persuader," that the
sight of one was mostly all that was needed, and nobody could
tell by looking at it whether it was loaded or not. This man could,
for he examined the lock and smiled in a pleased way over it, and
he never limped a step going back to his chair. He kept on com-
plaining, until father told him before bedtime that he had better
rest a day or two, and mother said that would be a good idea.

He talked so much we couldn't do our lessons or spell very well,
but it was Friday and we'd have another chance Saturday, so it
didn't make so much difference. Father said the traveller must be
tired and sleepy and Leon should take a light and show him to
bed. He stayed so long father went to the foot of the stairway,
and asked him why he didn't come down and he said he was in
bed too. The next morning he was sleepy at breakfast and Laddie
said it was no wonder, because Leon and the traveller were talking when he went upstairs. The man turned to father and said:
"That's a mighty smart boy, Mr. Stanton." Father frowned and
said: "Praise to the face is open disgrace. I hope he will be smart
enough not to disgrace us, anyway."

The traveller said he was sure he would be, and we could see
that he had taken a liking to Leon, for he went with him to the
barn to help do the morning feeding. They stayed so long mother
sent me to call them, and when I got there, the man was telling
Leon how foolish it was for boys to live on a farm; how they
never would amount to anything unless they went to cities, and
about all the fun there was there, and how nice it was to travel,

even along the roads, because every one fed you, and gave you a good bed. He forgot that walking had made his foot lame, and I couldn't see, to save me, why he was going to spend his money to buy a farm, if he thought a town the only place where it was fit to live.

He stayed all Saturday, and father said Sunday was no suitable time to start on a journey again, and the man's foot was bad when father was around, so it would be better to wait until Monday. The traveller tagged Leon and told him what a fine fellow he was, how smart he was, and to prove it, Leon boasted about everything he knew, and showed the man all over the farm.

I even saw them pass the Station in the orchard, and heard Leon brag how father had been an agent for the Governor; but of course he didn't really show him the place, and probably it would have made no difference if he had, for all the money must have been spent on Sally's wedding. Of course father might have put some there he had got since, or that money might never have been his at all, but it seemed as if it would be, because it was on his land.

Sunday evening all of us attended church, but the traveller was too tired, so when Leon said he'd stay with him, father thought it was all right. I could see no one wanted to leave the man alone in the house. He said they'd go to bed early, and we came in quite late. The lamp was turned low, the door unlocked, and everything in place. Laddie went to bed without a candle, and said he'd undress and slip in easy so as not to waken them.

In the morning when he got up the traveller's bed hadn't been slept in, and neither had Leon's. The gun was gone, and father stared at mother, and mother stared at Laddie, and he turned and ran straight toward the Station, and in a minute he was back, whiter than a plate. He just said: "All gone!" Father and mother both sat down suddenly and hard. Then Laddie ran to the barn and came back and said none of the horses had been taken. Soon they went into the parlour and shut the door, and when they came out father staggered and mother looked exactly like Sabethany. Laddie ran to the barn, saddled Flos and rode away.

Father wanted to ring an alarm on the dinner bell, like he had a call arranged to get all the neighbours there quickly if we had sickness or trouble, and mother said: "Paul, you shall not! He's so young! We've got to keep this as long as we can, and maybe the Lord will help us find him, and we can give him another chance."

Father started to say something, and mother held up her hand and just said, "Paul!" and he sank back in the chair and kept still. Mother always had spoken of him as "the Head of the Family," and here he wasn't at all! He minded her quickly as I would.

When Miss Amelia came downstairs they let her start to school and never told her a word, but mother said May and I were not to go. So I slipped out and ran through the orchard to look at the Station, and sure enough! the stone was rolled back, the door open and the can lying on the floor. I slid down and picked it up, and there was one sheet of paper money left in it stuck to the sides. It was all plain as a pikestaff. Leon must have thought the money had been spent, and showed the traveller the Station, just to brag, and he guessed there might be something there, and had gone while we were at church and taken it. He had all night the start of us, and he might have a horse waiting somewhere, and be almost to Illinois by this time, and if the money belonged to father, there would be no Christmas; and if it happened to be the money the county gave him to pay the men who worked the roads every fall, and Miss Amelia, or collections from the church, he'd have to pay it back, even if it put him in debt; and if he died, they might take the land, like he said; and where on earth was Leon? Knew what he'd done and hiding, I bet! He needed the thrashing he would get that time, and I started out to hunt him and have it over with, so mother wouldn't be uneasy about him yet; and then I remembered Laddie had said Leon hadn't been in bed all night. He was gone too!

Maybe he wanted to try life in a city, where the traveller had said everything was so grand; but he must have known that he'd kill his mother if he went, and while he didn't kiss her so often, and talk so much as some of us, I never could see that he didn't run quite as fast to get her a chair or save her a step. He was so slim and light he could race for the doctor faster than Laddie or father, either one. Of course he loved his mother, just as all of us did; he never, never could go away and not let her know about it. If he had gone, that watchful-eyed man, who was lame only part of the time, had taken the gun and made him go. I thought I might as well save the money he'd overlooked, so I gripped it tight in my hand, and put it in my apron pocket, the same as I had Laddie's note to the Princess, and started to the barn, on the chance that Leon might be hiding. I knew precious well I would, if I were in his place. So I hunted the granaries, the haymow, the stalls, then I stood on the threshing floor and cried: "Leon! If you're hiding come quick! Mother will be sick with worrying and father will be so glad to see you, he won't do anything much. Do please hurry!"

Then I listened, and all I could hear was a rat gnawing at a corner of the granary under the hay. Might as well have saved its teeth, it would strike a strip of tin when it got through, but of course it couldn't know that. Then I went to every hole around the haystack, where the cattle had eaten; none were deep yet, like they would be later in the season, and all the way I begged of Leon to come out. Once a rooster screamed, flew in my face and scared me good, but no Leon; so I tried the corn crib, the implement shed, and the wood house, climbing the ladder with the money still gripped in one hand. Then I slipped in the front door, up the stairs, and searched the garret, even away back where I didn't like to very well. At last I went to the dining-room, and I don't think either father or mother had moved, while Sabethany turned to stone looked good compared with them. Seemed as if it would have been better if they'd cried, or scolded, or anything but just sit there as they did, when you could see by their moving once in a while that they were alive. In the kitchen Candace and May finished the morning work, and both of them cried steadily. I slipped to May, "Whose money was it?" I whispered. "Father's, or the county's, or the church's?"

"All three," said May.

"The traveller took it."

"How would he find it? None of us knew there was such a place before."

"Laddie seemed to know!"

"Oh Laddie! Father trusts him about everything."

"They don't think *he* told?"

"Of course not, silly. It's Leon who is gone!"

"Leon may have told about the Station!" I cried. "He didn't touch the money. He never touched it!"

Then I went straight to father. Keeping a secret was one thing; seeing the only father you had look like that, was another. I held out the money.

"There's one piece old Even So didn't get, anyway," I said. "Found it on the floor of the Station, where it was stuck to the can. And I thought Leon must be hiding for fear he'd be whipped for telling, but I've hunted where we usually hide, and promised him everything under the sun if he'd come out; but he didn't, so I guess that traveller man must have used the gun to make him go along."

Father sat and stared at me. He never offered to touch the money, not even when I held it against his hand. So I saw that money wasn't the trouble, else he'd have looked quick enough to see how much I had. They were thinking about Leon being gone, at least father was. Mother called me to her and asked: "You knew about the Station?"

I nodded.

"When?"

"On the way back from taking Amanda Deam her ducks this summer."

"Leon was with you?"

"He found it."

"What were you doing?"

"Sitting on the fence eating apples. We were wondering why that ravine place wasn't cleaned up, when everywhere else was, and then Leon said there might be a reason. He told about having seen a black man, and that he was hidden some place, and we hunted there and found it. We rolled back the stone, and opened the door, and Leon went in, and both of us saw a can full of money."

"Go on."

"We didn't touch it, mother! Truly we didn't! Leon said we'd found something not intended for children, and we'd be whipped sick if we ever went near or told, and we never did, not even once, unless Leon wanted to boast to the traveller man, but if he showed him the place, he thought sure the money had all been spent on the wedding and sending Shelley away."

Father's arms shot out, and his head pitched on the table. Mother got up and began to walk the floor, and never went near or even touched him. I couldn't bear it. I went and pulled his arm and put the bill under his hand.

"Leon didn't take your money! He didn't! He didn't! I just know he didn't! He does tricks because they are so funny, or he thinks they'll be, but he doesn't steal! He doesn't touch a single thing that is not his, only melons, or chicken out of the skillet, or bread from the cellar; but not money and things. I take gizzards and bread myself, but I don't steal, and Leon or none of us do! Oh father, we don't! Not one of us do! Don't you remember about 'Thou shalt not,' and the Crusaders? Leon's the best fighter of any of us. I'm not sure that he couldn't even whip Laddie, if he got mad enough! Maybe he can't whip the traveller if he has the gun, but, father, Leon simply couldn't take the money. Laddie will stay home and work, and all of us. We can help get it back. We can sell a lot of things. Laddie will sell Flos before he'll see you suffer so; and all of us will give up Christmas, and we'll work! We'll work as hard as ever we can, and maybe you could spare the little piece Joe Risdell wants to build his cabin on. We can manage about the money, father, indeed we can. But you don't dare think Leon took it! He never did! Why, he's yours! Yours and mother's!"

Father lifted his head and reached out his arms.

"You blessing!" he said. "You blessing from the Lord!"

Then he gave me a cold, stiff kiss on the forehead, went to mother, took her arm, and said: "Come, mommy, let's go and tell the Lord about it, and then we'll try to make some plan. Perhaps Laddie will be back with word soon."

But he almost had to carry her. Then we could hear him praying, and he was so anxious, and he made it so earnest it sounded exactly like the Lord was in our room and father was talking right to His face. I tried to think, and this is what I thought: as father left the room, he looked exactly as I had seen Mr. Pryor more than once, and my mother had both hands gripped over her heart, and she said we must not let any one know. Now if something could happen to us to make my father look like the Princess' and my mother hold her heart with both hands, and if no one were to know about it like they had said, how were we any different from Pryors? We might be of the Lord's anointed, but we could get into the same kind of trouble the infidels could, and have secrets ourselves, or at least it seemed as if it might be very nearly the same, when it made father and mother look and act the way they did. I wondered if we'd have to leave our lovely, lovely home, cross a sea and be strangers in a strange land, as Laddie said; and if people would talk about us, and make us feel that being a stranger was the loneliest, hardest thing in all the world. Well, if mysteries are like this, and we have to live with one days and years, the Lord have mercy on us! Then I saw the money lying on the table, so I took it and put it in the Bible. Then I went out and climbed the catalpa tree to watch for Laddie.

Soon I saw a funny thing, such as I never before had seen. Coming across the fields, straight toward our house, sailing over the fences like a bird, came the Princess on one of her horses. Its legs stretched out so far its body almost touched the ground, and it lifted up and swept over the rails. She took our meadow fence lengthwiselike, and at the hitching rack she threw the bridle over the post, dismounted, and then I saw she had been riding astride, like a man. I ran before her and opened the sitting-room door, but no one was there, so I went on to the dining-room. Father had come in, and mother was sitting in her chair. Both of them looked at the Princess and never said a word.

She stopped inside the dining-room door and spoke breathlessly, as if she as well as the horse had raced.

"I hope I'm not intruding," she said, "but a man north of us told our Thomas in the village that robbers had taken quite a large sum of hidden money you held for the county, and church, and of your own, and your gun, and got away while you were at church last night. Is it true?"

"Practically," said my father.

Then my mother motioned toward a chair.

"You are kind to come," she said. "Won't you be seated?"

The Princess stepped to the chair, but she gripped the back in both hands and stood straight, breathing fast, her eyes shining with excitement, her lips and cheeks red, so lovely you just had to look, and look.

"No," she said. "I'll tell you why I came, and then if there is nothing I can do here, and no errand I can ride for you, I'll go. Mother has heart trouble, the worst in all the world, the kind no doctor can ever hope to cure, and sometimes, mostly at night, she is driven to have outside air. Last night she was unusually ill, and I heard her leave the house, after I'd gone to my room. I watched from my window and saw her take a seat on a bench under the nearest tree. I was moving around and often I looked to see if she were still there. Then the dogs began to rave, and I hurried down. They used to run free, but lately, on account of her going out, father has been forced to tie them at night. They were straining at their chains, and barking dreadfully. I met her at the door, but she would only say some one passed and gave her a fright. When Thomas came in and told what he had heard, she said instantly that she had seen the man.

"She said he was about the size of Thomas, that he came from your direction, that he ran when our dogs barked, but he kept beside the fences, and climbed over where there were trees. He crossed our barnyard and went toward the northwest. Mother saw him distinctly as he reached the road, and she said he was not a large man, he stooped when he ran, and she thought he moved like a slinking, city thief. She is sure he's the man who took your money; she says he acted exactly as if he were trying to escape pursuit; but I was to be *sure* to tell you that he didn't carry a gun. If your gun is gone, there must have been two, and the other man took that and went a different way. Did two men stop here?"

"No," said father. "Only one."

The Princess looked at him thoughtfully.

"Do you think, Mr. Stanton," she said, "that the man who took the money would burden himself with a gun? Isn't a rifle heavy for one in flight to carry?"

"It is," said father. "Your mother saw nothing of two men?"

"Only one, and she knows he didn't carry a gun. Except the man you took in, no stranger has been noticed around here lately?"

"No one. We are quite careful. Even the gun was not loaded as it stood; whoever took it carried the ammunition also, but he couldn't fire until he loaded."

Father turned to the corner where the gun always stood and then he stooped and picked up two little white squares from the floor. They were bits of unbleached muslin in which he wrapped the bullets he made.

"The rifle was loaded before starting, and in a hurry," he said, as he held up the squares of muslin. Then he scratched a match, bent, and ran it back and forth over the floor, and at one place there was a flash, and the flame went around in funny little fizzes as it caught a grain of powder here and there. "You see the measure was overrun."

"Wouldn't the man naturally think the gun was loaded, and take it as it stood?"

"That would be a reasonable conclusion," said father.

"But he looked!" I cried. "That first night when you and the boys went to the barn, and the girls were getting supper, he looked at the gun, and he *liked* it when he saw it wasn't loaded. He smiled. And he didn't limp a mite when I was the only one in the room. He and Leon knew it wasn't loaded, and I guess he didn't load it, for he liked having it empty so well."

"Ummmm!" said father. "What it would save in this world if a child only knew when to talk and when to keep still. Little Sister, the next time you see a stranger examine my gun when I'm not in the room, suppose you take father out alone and whisper to him about it."

"Yes, sir," I said.

The way I wished I had told that at the right time made me dizzy, but then there were several good switchings I'd had for telling things, besides what Sally did to me about her and Peter. I would have enjoyed knowing how one could be sure. Hereafter, it will be all right about the gun, anyway.

"Could I take my horse and carry a message anywhere for you? Are both your sons riding to tell the neighbours?"

Father hesitated, but it seemed as if he stopped to think, so I just told her: "Laddie is riding. Leon didn't take a horse."

Father said there was nothing she could do, so she took my hand and we started for the gate.

"I do hope they will find him, and get back the money, and give him what he deserves!" she cried.

"Yes, father and mother are praying that they'll find him," I said. "It doesn't seem to make the least difference to them about the money. Father didn't even look at a big paper piece I found where it was hidden. But they are anxious about the man. Mother says he is so young, we just must find him, and keep this a secret, and give him another chance. You won't tell, will you?"

The Princess stood still on our walk, and then of all things! if she didn't begin to go Sabethany-like. The colour left her cheeks and lips and she shivered and shook and never said one word. I caught her arm. "Say, what ails you?" I cried. "You haven't gone and got heart trouble too, have you?"

She stood there trembling, and then, wheeling suddenly, ran back into the house, and went to my mother. On her knees, the Princess buried her face in mother's breast and said: "Oh Mrs. Stanton! Oh, if I only could help you!"

She began to cry as if something inside her had broken, and she'd shake to pieces.

Mother stared above her head at father, with her eyebrows raised high, and he waved his hand toward me. Mother turned to me, but already she had put her arms around the Princess, and was trying to hold her together.

"What did you tell her that made her come back?" she asked sternlike.

"You forgot to explain that the man was so young, and you wanted to keep it a secret and give him another chance," I said. "I just asked her not to tell."

Mother looked at father and all the colour went from her face, and she began to shake. He stared at her, then he opened her door and lifted the Princess with one arm, and mother with the other, and helped them into mother's room, stepped back and closed the door. After a while it opened and they came out together, with both mother's arms around the Princess, and she had cried until she staggered. Mother lifted her face and kissed her, when they reached the door and said: "Tell your mother I understand enough to sympathize. Carry her my love. I do wish she would give herself the comfort of asking God to help her."

"She does! Oh, I'm sure she does!" said the Princess. "It's father who has lost all judgment and reason."

Father went with her to the gate, and this time she needed help to mount her horse, and she left it to choose its way and go where it pleased on the road. When father came in he looked at mother, and she said: "I haven't the details, but she understands too well. The Pryor mystery isn't much of a mystery any more. God help their poor souls, and save us from suffering like that!"

She said so little and meant so much, I couldn't figure out exactly what she did mean, but father seemed to understand.

"I've often wondered," he said, but he didn't say what he wondered, and he hurried to the barn and saddled our best horse and came in and began getting ready to ride, and we knew he would go northwest. I went back to the catalpa tree and wondered myself; but it was too much for me to straighten out: just why my mother wanting to give the traveller man another chance would make the Princess feel like that. If she had known my mother as I did, she'd have known that she *always* wanted to give every man a second chance, no matter whether he was young or old.

Then I saw Laddie coming down the Big Hill beside the church, but he was riding so fast I thought he wouldn't want to bother with me, so I slid from the tree, and ran to tell mother. She went to the door and watched as he rode up, but you could see by his face he had not heard of them.

"Nothing, but I have some men out. I am going east now," he said. "I wish, father, you would rub Flos down, blanket her, and if you can, walk her slowly an hour while she cools off. I am afraid I've ruined her. How much had you there?"

"I haven't stopped to figure," said father. "I think I'd better take the horse I have ready and go on one of the northwest roads. The Pryor girl was here a few moments ago, and her mother saw a man cross their place about the right time last evening. He ran and acted suspiciously when the dogs barked. But he was alone and he didn't have a gun."

"Was she sure?"

"Positive."

"Then it couldn't have been our man, but I'll ride in that direction and start a search. They would keep to the woods, I think! You'd better stay with mother. I'll ask Jacob Hood to take your place."

So Laddie rode away again without even going into the house, and mother said to father: "What can he be saying to people, that the neighbours don't come?"

Father answered: "I don't know, but if any one can save the situation, Laddie will."

Mother went to bed, while father sat beside her reading aloud little scraps from the Bible, and they took turns praying. From the way they talked to the Lord, you could plainly see that they were reminding Him of all the promises He had made to take care of people, comfort those in trouble, and heal the broken-hearted. One thing was so curious, I asked May if she noticed, and she had. When they had made such a fuss about money only a short while before, and worked so hard to get our share together, and when they would have to pay back all that belonged to the county and church, neither of them ever even mentioned money then. Every minute I expected father to ask where I'd put the piece I found, and when he opened right at it, in the Bible, he turned on past, exactly as if it were an obituary, or a piece of Sally's wedding dress, or baby hair from some of our heads. He went on hunting places where the Lord said sure and strong that He'd help people who loved Him. When either of them prayed, they asked the Lord to help those near them who were in trouble, as often and earnestly as they begged Him to help them. There were no people near us who were in trouble that we knew of, excepting Pryors. Hard as father and mother worked, you'd have thought the Lord wouldn't have minded if they asked only once to get the money back, or if they forgot the neighbours, but they did neither one. May said because they were big like that was why all of us loved them so.

I would almost freeze in the catalpa, but as I could see far in all directions there, I went back, and watched the roads, and when I remembered what Laddie had said, I kept an eye on the fields too. At almost dusk, and frozen so stiff I could scarcely hang to the limb, I heard the bulldogs at Pryors' begin to rave. They kept on steadily, and I thought Gypsies must be passing. Then from the woods came a queer party that started across the cornfield toward the Big Meadow in front of the house, and I thought they were hunters. I stood in the tree and watched until they climbed the meadow fence, and by that time I could see plainly.

The traveller man got over first, then Leon and the dogs, and then Mr. Pryor handed Leon the gun, leaped over, and took it. I looked again, and then fell from the tree and almost bursted. As soon as I could get up, and breathe, I ran to the front door, screaming: "Father! Father! Come open the Big Gate. Leon's got him, but he's so tired Mr. Pryor is carrying the gun, and helping him walk!"

Just like one, all of us ran; father crossed the road, and opened the gate. The traveller man wouldn't look up, he just slouched along. But Leon's chin was up and his head high. He was scratched, torn, and dirty. He was wheezing every breath most from his knees, and Mr. Pryor half carried him and the gun. When they met us, Leon reached in his trousers pocket and drew out a big roll of money that he held toward father. "My fault!" he gasped. "But I got it back for you."

Then he fell over and father caught him in his arms and carried him into the house, and laid him on the couch in the dining-room. Mr. Pryor got down and gathered up the money from the road. He followed into the house and set the gun in the corner.

"Don't be frightened," he said to mother. "The boy has walked all night, and all day, with no sleep or food, and the gun was a heavy load for him. I gathered from what he said, when the dogs let us know they were coming, that this hound took your money. Your dog barked and awakened the boy and he loaded the gun and followed. The fellow had a good start and he didn't get him until near daybreak. It's been a stiff pull for the youngster and he seems to feel it was his fault that this cowardly cur you sheltered learned where you kept your money. If that is true, I hope you won't be hard on him!"

Father was unfastening Leon's neckband, mother was rubbing his hands, Candace was taking off his shoes, and May was spilling water father had called for, all over the carpet, she shook so. When Leon drew a deep breath and his head rolled on the pillow, father looked at Mr. Pryor. I don't think he heard all of it, but he caught the last words.

"'Hard on him! Hard on him!'" he said, the tears rolling down his cheeks. "'This my son, who was lost, is found!'"

"Oh!" shouted Mr. Pryor, slamming the money on the table. "Poor drivel to fit the circumstances. If I stood in your boots, sir, I would rise up in the mighty strength of my pride and pull out foundation stones until I shook the nation! I never envied mortal man as I envy you to-day!"

Candace cried out: "Oh look, his poor feet! They are blistered and bleeding!"

Mother moved down a little, gathered them in her arms, and began kissing them. Father wet Leon's lips and arose. He held out his hand, and Mr. Pryor took it.

"I will pray God," he said, "that it may happen 'even so' to you."

Leon opened his eyes and caught only the last words.

"You had better look out for the 'Even So's,' father," he said.

And father had to laugh, but Mr. Pryor went out, and slammed the door, until I looked to see if it had cracked from top to bottom; but we didn't care if it had, we were so happy over having Leon back.

I went and picked up the money and carried it to father to put away, and that time he took it. But even then he didn't stop to see if he had all of it.

"You see!" I said, "I told you——"

"You did indeed!" said father. "And you almost saved our reason. There are times when things we have come to feel we can't live without, so press us, that money seems of the greatest importance. This is our lesson. Hereafter, I and all my family, who have been through this, will know that money is not even worth thinking about when the life and honour of one you love hangs in the balance. When he can understand, your brother shall know of the wondrous faith his Little Sister had in him."

"Maybe he won't like what you and mother thought. Maybe we better not tell him. I can keep secrets real well. I have several big ones I've never told, and I didn't say a word about the Station when Leon said I shouldn't."

"After this there will be no money kept on the place," said father. "It's saving time at too great cost. All we have goes into the bank, and some of us will cheerfully ride for what we want, when we need it. As for not telling Leon, that is as your mother decides. For myself, I believe I'd feel better to make a clean breast of it."

Mother heard, for she sobbed as she bathed Leon's feet, and when his eyes came open so they'd stay a little while, he kept looking at her so funny, between sips of hot milk.

"Don't *cry,* mammy!" he said. "*I'm* all right. Sorry such a rumpus! Let him fool me. Be smart as the next fellow, after this! Know how glad you are to get the money!"

Mother sat back on her heels and roared as I do when I step in a bumblebee's nest, and they get me. Leon was growing better every minute, and he stared at her, and then his dealish, funny old grin began to twist his lips and he cried: "Oh golly! You thought *I* helped take it and went with him, didn't you?"

"Oh my son, my son!" wailed mother until she made me think of Absalom under the oak.

"Well, I be ding-busted!" said Leon, sort of slow and wondering-like, and father never opened his head to tell him that was no way to talk.

Mother cried more than ever, and between sobs she tried to explain that I heard what the traveller man had said about how bad it was to live in the country; and how Leon was now at an age where she'd known boys to get wrong ideas, and how things looked, and in the middle of it he raised on his elbow and took her in his arms and said: "Well of all the geese! And I 'spose father was in it too! But since it's the first time, and since it is you——! Go to bed now, and let me sleep—— But see that you don't ever let this happen again."

Then he kissed her over and over and clung to her tight and at last dropped back and groaned:

> "*My reputation, O my reputation!*
> *I've lost my reputation!*"

She had to laugh while the tears were still running, and father and Laddie looked at each other and shouted. I guess they thought Leon was about right after that. Laddie went and bent over him and took his hand.

"Don't be in quite such a hurry, old man," he said. "Before you wink out I have got to tell you how proud I am of having a brother who is a real Crusader. The Lord knows this took nerve! You're great, boy, simply great!"

Leon grabbed Laddie's hand with both of his and held tight and laughed. You could see the big tears squeeze out, although he fought to wink them back. He held to Laddie and said low-like, only for him to hear: "It's all right if you stay by a while, old man."

He began to talk slowly.

"It was a long time before I caught up, and then I had to hide, and follow until day, and he wasn't so very easy to handle. Once I thought he had me sure! It was an awful load, but if it hadn't been for the good old gun, I'd never have got him. When we mixed up, I had fine luck getting that chin punch on him; good thing I worked it out so slick on Absalom Saunders, and while old Even So was groggy I got the money away from him, took the gun, and stood back some distance, before he came out of it. Once we had it settled who walked ahead, and who carried the money and gun, we got along better, but I had to keep an eye on him every minute. To come through the woods was the shortest, but I'm tired out, and so is he. Getting close I most felt sorry for him, he was so forlorn, and so scared about what would be done to him. He stopped and pulled out another roll, and offered me all of it, if I'd let him go. I didn't know whether it was really his, or part of father's, so I told him he could just drop it until I found out. Made him sweat blood, but I had the gun, and he had to mind. I was master then. So there may be more in the roll I gave father than Even So took. Father can figure up and keep what belongs to him. Even So had gone away past Flannigans' before I tackled him, and I was sleepy, cold, and hungry; you'd have thought there'd have been a man out hunting, or passing on the road, but not a soul did we see 'til Pryors'! Say, the old man was bully! He helped me so, I almost thought I belonged to him! My! he's fine, when you know him! After he came on the job, you bet old Even So walked up. Say, where is he? Have you fed him?"

Laddie looked at father, who was listening, and we all rushed to the door, but it must have been an hour, and Even So hadn't waited. Father said it was a great pity, because a man like that shouldn't be left to prey on the community; but mother said she didn't want to be mixed up with a trial, or to be responsible for taking the liberty of a fellow creature, and father said that was exactly like a woman. Leon went to sleep, but none of us thought of going to bed; we just stood around and looked at him, and smiled over him, and cried about him, until you would have thought he had been shipped to us in a glass case, and cost, maybe, a hundred dollars.

Father got out his books and figured up his own and the road money, and Miss Amelia's, and the church's. Laddie didn't want her around, so he stopped at the schoolhouse and told her to stay at Justices' that night, we'd need all our rooms; but she didn't like being sent away when there was such excitement, but every one minded Laddie when he said so for sure.

When father had everything counted there was more than his, quite a lot of it, stolen from other people who sheltered the traveller no doubt, father said. We thought he wouldn't be likely to come back for it, and father said he was at loss what to do with it, but Laddie said he wasn't—it was Leon's—he had earned it; so father said he would try to find out if anything else had been stolen, and he'd keep it a year, and then if no one claimed it, he would put it on interest until Leon decided what he wanted to do with it.

When you watched Leon sleep you could tell a lot more about what had happened to him than he could. He moaned, and muttered constantly, and panted, and felt around for the gun, and breathed like he was running again, and fought until Laddie had to hold him on the couch, and finally awakened him. But it did no good; he went right off to sleep again, and it happened all over. Then father began getting his Crusader blood up, although he always said he was a man of peace. But it was a lucky thing Even So got away; for after father had watched Leon a while, he said if that man had been on the premises, his fingers itched so to get at him, he was positive he'd have vented a little righteous indignation on him that would have cost him within an inch of his life. And he'd have done it too! He was like that. It took a lot, and it was slow coming, but when he became angry enough, and felt justified in it, why you'd be much safer to be some one else than the man who provoked him.

After ten o'clock the dog barked, some one tapped, and father went; he always would open the door; you couldn't make him pretend he was asleep, or not at home when he was, and there stood Mr. Pryor. He said they could see the lights and they were afraid the boy was ill, and could any of them help. Father said there was nothing they could do; Leon was asleep. Then Mr. Pryor said: "If he is off sound, so it won't disturb him, I would like to see him again."

Father told him Leon was restless, but so exhausted a railroad train wouldn't waken him, so Mr. Pryor came in and went to the couch. He took off his hat, like you do beside a grave, while his face slowly grew whiter than his hair, and that would be snow-white; then he turned at last and stumbled toward the door. Laddie held it for him, but he didn't seem to remember he was there. He muttered over and over: "Why? Why? In the name of God, why?" Laddie followed to the gate to help him on his horse, because he thought he was almost out of his head, but he had walked across the fields, so Laddie kept far behind and watched until he saw him go safely inside his own door.

I think father and Laddie sat beside Leon all night. The others went to sleep. A little after daybreak, just as Laddie was starting to feed, there was an awful clamour, and here came a lot of neighbours with Even So. Mr. Freshett had found him asleep in a cattle hole in the straw stack, and searched him, and he had more money, and that made Mr. Freshett sure; and as he was very strong, and had been for years a soldier, and really loved to fight, he marched poor Even So back to our house. Every few rods they met more men out searching who came with them, until there were so many, our front yard and the road were crowded. Of all the sights you ever saw, Even So looked the worst. You could see that he'd drop over at much more. Those men kept crying they were going to hang him; but mother went out and talked to them, and said they mustn't kill a man for taking only money. She told them how little it was worth compared with other things; she had Candace bring Even So a cup of hot coffee, lots of bread, and sausage from the skillet, and she said it was our money, and our lad, and we wanted nothing done about it. The men didn't like it, but the traveller did. He grabbed and gobbled like a beast at the hot food and cried, and mother said she forgave him, and to let him go.

Then Mr. Freshett looked awful disappointed, and he came up to father, with his back toward mother, and asked: "That's your say too, Mr. Stanton?" Father grinned sort of rueful-like, but he said to give Even So his money and let him go. He told all about getting ours back, and having had him at the house once before. He brought the money Leon took from him, but the men said no doubt he had stolen that, and Leon had earned it bringing him back, so the traveller shouldn't have it. They took him away on a horse and said they'd let him go, but that they'd escort him from the county. Father told Mr. Freshett that he was a little suspicious of them, and he would hold him responsible for the man's life. Mr. Freshett said that he'd give his word that the man would be safe; they only wanted to make sure he wouldn't come back, and that he'd be careful in the future how he abused hospitality, so they went, and all of us were glad of it.

I don't know what Mr. Freshett calls safe, for they took Even So to Groveville and locked him up until night. Then they led him to the railroad, and made him crawl back and forth through an old engine beside the track, until he was blacker than any negro ever born; and then they had him swallow a big dose of croton oil for his health. That was the only *kind* thing they did, for afterward they started him down the track and told him to run, and all of them shot at his feet as he went. Hannah Freshett told me at school the next day. Her father said Even So just howled, and flew up in the air, and ducked, and dodged and ran like he'd never walked a step, or was a bit tired. We made a game of it, and after that one of the boys was Even So, and the others were the mob, and the one who could howl nicest, jump highest, and go fastest, could be "It" oftenest.

Leon grew all right faster than you would think. He went to school day after next, and the boys were sick with envy. They asked and asked, but Leon wouldn't tell much. He didn't seem to like to talk about it, and he wouldn't play the game or even watch us. He talked a blue streak about the money. Father was going to write to every sheriff of the counties along the way the man said he had come, and if he could find no one before spring who had been robbed, he said Leon might do what he liked with the money. I used to pretend it was coming to me, and each day I thought of a new way to spend it. Leon was so sure he'd get it he marched right over and asked Mr. Pryor about a nice young thoroughbred horse, from his stables, and when he came back he could get a coltlike one so very cheap that father and Laddie looked at each other and gasped, and never said a word. They figured up, and if Leon got the money, he could have the horse, and save some for college, and from the start he never changed a mite about those two things he wanted to do with it. He had the horse picked out and went to the field to feed and pet it and make it gentle, so he could ride bareback, and mother said he would be almost sick if the owner of the money turned up.

Pulling his boots one night, father said so too, and that the thoughts of it worried him. He said Mr. Pryor had shaded his price so that if the money had to go, he would be tempted to see if we couldn't manage it ourselves. I don't know how shading the price of a horse would make her feel better, but it did, and maybe Leon is going to get it.

CHAPTER X

Laddie Takes the Plunge

"This is the state of man: to-day he puts forth
The tender leaves of hopes; to-morrow blossoms,
And bears his blushing honors thick upon him;
The third day comes a frost, a killing frost,
And, when he thinks, good, easy man, full surely
His greatness is a-ripening, nips his root,
And then he falls, as I do."

WATCH me take the plunge!" said Laddie.

" 'Mad frenzy fires him now,' " quoted Leon.

It was Sunday after dinner. We had been to church and Sun-day-school in the forenoon, and we had a houseful of company for dinner. All of them remained to spend the afternoon, because in our home it was perfectly lovely. We had a big dinner with everything good to start on, and then we talked and visited and told all the news. The women exchanged new recipes for cook-ing, advised each other about how to get more work done with less worry, to doctor their sick folks, and to make their dresses. At last, when every thing was talked over, and there began to be a quiet time, father would reach across the table, pick up a paper and read all the interesting things that had happened in the country during the past week; the jokes too, and they made peo-ple think of funny stories to tell, and we just laughed. In the *Agriculturist* there were new ways to farm easier, to make land bear more crops; so he divided that with the neighbours, also how to make gardens, and prune trees. Before he finished, he always managed to work in a lot about being honest, kind, and loving God.

He and mother felt so good over Leon, and by this time they were beginning to see that they were mighty glad about the money too. It wouldn't have been so easy to work, and earn, and pay back all that for our school, roads, and the church; and every day you could see plainer how happy they felt that they didn't have to do it. Because they were so glad about these things, they invited every one they met that day; but we knew Saturday mother felt that probably she would ask a crowd, from the chickens, pie, and cake she got ready. When the reading part was over, and the women were beginning to look at the clock, and you knew they felt they should go home, and didn't want to, Laddie arose and said that, and Leon piped up like he always does and made every one laugh. Of course they looked at Laddie, and no one knew what he meant, so all the women and a few of the men asked him.

"Watch me, I said," laughed Laddie as he left the room.

Soon Mrs. Dover, sitting beside the front window, cried: "Here he is at the gate!"

He was on his horse, but he hitched it and went around the house and up the back way. Before long the stair door of the sitting-room opened, and there he stood. We stared at him. Of course he was bathed, and in clean clothing to start with, but he had washed and brushed some more, until he shone. His cheeks were as smooth and as clear pink as any girl's, his eyes blue-gray and big, with long lashes and heavy brows. His hair was bright brown and wavy, and he was so big and broad. He never had been sick a day in his life, and he didn't look as if he ever would be.

And clothes *do* make a difference. He would have had exactly the same hair, face, and body, wearing a hickory shirt and denim trousers; but he wouldn't have looked as he did in the clothes he wore at college, when it was Sunday there, or he was invited to a party at the President's. I don't see how any man could possibly be handsomer or look finer. His shirt, collar, and cuffs were snow-white, like everything had to be before mother got through with it; his big loose tie almost reached his shoulders; and our men could do a thing no other man in the neighbourhood did: they could appear easier in the finest suit they could put on than in their working clothes.

Mother used to say one thing she dreaded about Sunday was the evident tortures of the poor men squirming in boots she knew pinched them, coats too tight, and collars too high. She said they acted like half-broken colts fretting over restriction. Always she said to father and the boys when they went to buy their new clothes: "Now, *don't* join the harness fighters! Get your clothing big enough to set your bodies with comfort and ease."

I suppose those other men would have looked like ours if their mothers had told them. You can always see that a man needs a woman to help him out awful bad.

Of course Laddie knew he was handsome; he had to know all of them were looking at him curiously, but he stood there buttoning his glove and laughing to himself until Sarah Hood asked: "Now what are you up to?"

He took a step toward her, ran one hand under her lantern-jawed chin, pulled her head against his side and turned up her face.

"Sarah," he said. " 'member the day we spoiled the washing?"

Every one laughed. They had made jokes about it until our friends knew what they meant.

"What are you going to spoil now?" asked Sarah.

"The Egyptians! The 'furriners.' I'm going right after them!"

"Well, you could be in better business," said Sarah Hood sharply.

Laddie laughed and squeezed her chin, and hugged her head against him.

"Listen to that, now!" he cried. "My best friend going back on me. Sarah, I thought you, of all people, would wish me luck."

"I do!" she said instantly. "And that's the very reason I don't want you mixed up with that mysterious, offish, stuck-up mess."

"Bless your dear heart!" said Laddie, giving her a harder squeeze than ever. "You got that all wrong, Sarah. You'll live to see the day, very shortly, when you'll change every word of it."

"I haven't done anything but get surer about it every day for two years, anyway," said Sarah Hood.

"Exactly!" said Laddie, "but wait until I have taken the plunge! Let me tell you how the Pryor family strikes me. I think he is a high-tempered, domineering man, proud as Lucifer! For some cause, just or not, he is ruining his life and that of his family because he so firmly believes it just; he is hiding here from his home country, his relatives, and friends. I think she is, barring you and mother, the handsomest woman of her age I ever saw——"

All of them laughed, because Sarah Hood was nearly as homely as a woman could grow, and maybe other people didn't find our mother so lovely as we thought her. I once heard one of her best friends say she was "distinctly plain." I didn't see how she could; but she said that.

"—and the most pitiful," Laddie went on. "Sarah, what do you suppose sends a frail little woman pacing the yard, and up and down the road, sometimes in storm and rain, gripping both hands over her heart?"

"I suppose it's some shameful thing I don't want you mixed up with!" said Sarah Hood promptly, and people just shouted.

"Sarah," said Laddie, "I've seen her closely, watched her move, and studied her expression. There's not one grain of possibility that you, or mother, or Mrs. Fall, or any woman here, could be any closer connected with *shame*. Shame there is," said Laddie, "and what a word! How it stings, burns, withers, and causes heart trouble and hiding; but shame in connection with that woman, more than shame thrust upon her, which might come to any of us, at any time, shame that is her error, in the life of a woman having a face like hers, Sarah, I am ashamed of you! Your only excuse is that you haven't persisted as I have until you got to see for yourself."

"I am not much on persistence in the face of a locked door, a cast-iron man with a big cane, and two raving bulldogs," said Mrs. Hood. "Wait, young man! Just wait until he sets them on you."

Laddie's head went back and how he laughed.

"Hist! A word with you, Sarah!" he said. " 'Member I have a sort of knack with animals. I never yet have failed with one I undertook to win. Now those bulldogs of Pryors' are as mild as kittens with a man who knows the right word. Reason I know, Sarah, I've said the word to them, separately and collectively, and it worked. There is a contrast, Sarah, between what I say and do to those dogs, and the kicks and curses they get from their owner. I'll wager you two to one that if you can get Mr. Pryor to go into a 'sic-ing' contest with me, I can have his own dogs at his throat, when he can't make them do more than to lick my hands."

They laughed as if that were funny.

"Well, I didn't know about this," said Sarah. "How long have you lived at Pryors'?"

You couldn't have heard what Laddie said if he'd spoken; so he waited until he could be heard, and it never worried him a speck. He only stood and laughed too; then, "Long enough," he said, "to know that all of us are making a big and cruel mistake in taking them at their word, and leaving them penned up there weltering in misery. What we should do, is to go over there, one at a time, or in a body, and batter at the door of their hearts, until we break down the wall of pride they have built around them, ease their pain, and bring them with us socially, if they are going to live among us. You people who talk loudly and often about loving God, and 'doing unto others,' should have gone long ago, for Jesus' sake; I'm going for the sake of a girl, with a face as sweet, and a heart as pure, as any accepted angel at the foot of the throne. Mother, I want a cup of peach jelly, and some of that exceptionally fine cake you served at dinner, to take to our sick neighbour."

Mother left the room.

"Father, I want permission to cut and carry a generous chestnut branch, burred, and full fruited, to the young woman. There is none save ours in this part of the country, and she may never have seen any, and be interested. And I want that article about foot disease in horses, for Mr. Pryor. I'll bring it back when he finishes."

Father folded the paper and handed it to Laddie, who slipped it in his pocket.

"Take the finest branch you can select," father said, and I almost fell over.

He had carried those trees from Ohio, before I had been born, and mother said for years he wrapped them in her shawl in winter and held an umbrella over them in summer, and father always went red and grinned when she told it. He was wild about trees, and bushes, so he made up his mind he'd have chestnuts. He planted them one place, and if they didn't like it, he dug them up and set them another where he thought they could have what they needed and hadn't got the last place. Finally, he put them, on the fourth move, on a little sandy ridge across the road from the wood yard, and that was the spot. They shot up, branched, spread, and one was a male and two were females, so the pollen flew, the burrs filled right, and we had a bag of chestnuts to send each child away from home, every Christmas. The brown leaves and burrs were so lovely, mother cut one of the finest branches she could select and hung it above the steel engraving of "Lincoln Freeing the Slaves," in the boys' room, and nothing in the house was looked at oftener, or thought prettier. That must have been what was in the back of Laddie's head when he wanted a branch for the Princess.

Mother came in with the cake and jelly in a little fancy basket, and Laddie said: "Thank you! Now every one wish me luck! I'm going to ride to Pryors', knock at the door, and present these offerings with my compliments. If I'm invited in, I'm going to make the effort of my life at driving the entering wedge toward social intercourse between Pryors and their neighbours. If I'm not, I'll be back in thirty minutes and tell you what happened to me. If they refuse my gifts, you shall have the jelly, Sarah; I'll give Mrs. Fall the olive branch, bring back the paper, and eat the cake to console my wounded spirits."

Of course every one laughed; they couldn't help it. I watched
father and he laughed hardest of the men, but mother was more
stiff-lipped about it; she couldn't help a little, though. And I
noticed some of those women acted as if they had lost something.
Maybe it was a chance to gossip about Laddie, for he hadn't
left them a thing to guess at, and mother says the reason gossip
is so dreadful is because it is always *guesswork*. Well, that was all
fair and plain. He had told those people, our very best friends,
what he thought about everything, the way they acted included.
He was carrying something to each member of the Pryor family,
and he'd left a way to return joking and unashamed, if they
wouldn't let him in. He had fixed things so no one had anything
to guess at, and it would look much worse for the Pryors than
it would for him, if he did come back.

I wondered if he had been born that smart, or if he learned it
in college. If he did, no wonder Leon was bound to go. Come to
think of it, though, mother said Laddie was always like that. She
said he never bit her when he nursed; he never mauled her as if
she couldn't be hurt when he was little, he never tore his clothes
and made extra work as he grew, and never in his life gave her
an hour's uneasiness. But I guess she couldn't have said that about
uneasiness lately, for she couldn't keep from looking troubled
as all of us followed to the gate to see him start.

How they joked, and tried to tease him! But they couldn't
get a breath ahead. He shot back answers as fast as they could
ask questions, while he cut the branch and untied the horse. He
gave the limb and basket to mother to hold, kissed her good-bye,
and me too, before he mounted. With my arms around his neck
—I never missed a chance to try to squeeze into him how I loved
him—I whispered: "Laddie, is it a secret any more?"

He threw back his head and laughed the happiest.

"Not the ghost of a secret!" he said. "But you let me do the
talking, until I tell you." Then he went on right out loud: "I'm
riding up the road waving the banner of peace. If I suffer repulse,
the same thing has happened to better men before, so I'll get a
different banner and try again."

Laddie mounted, swept a circle in the road, dropped Flos on her knees in a bow, and waved the branch. Leon began to sing at the top of his voice, "Nothing but leaves, nothing but leaves," while Laddie went flashing up the road.

The women went back to the house; the men stood around the gate, watched him from sight, talked about his horse, how he rode, and made wagers that he'd get shut out, like every one did, but they said if that happened he wouldn't come back. Father was annoyed.

"You heard Laddie say he'd return immediately if they wouldn't let him in," he said. "He's a man of his word. He will either enter or come home at once."

It was pitch dark and we had supper before some of them left; they never stayed so late. After we came from church, father read the chapter and we were ready for bed; still Laddie hadn't come back. And father liked it! He just plain liked it! He chuckled behind the *Advocate* until you could see it shake; but mother had very little to say, and her lips closed tight.

At bedtime he said to mother: "Well, they don't seem in a hurry about sending the boy back."

"Did you really think he *would* be sent back?" asked mother.

"Not ordinarily," said father, "no! If he had no brain, no wit, no culture, on an animal basis, a woman would look twice before she'd send him away; but with such fanatics as Pryors, one can't always tell what will happen."

"In a case like this, one can be reasonably certain," said mother.

"You don't know what social position they occupied at home. Their earmarks are all good. We've no such notions here as they have."

"Thank God for so much, at any rate," said mother. "How old England would rise up and exult if she had a man in line with Laddie's body, blood and brain, to set on her throne. This talk about class and social position makes me sick. Men are men, and Laddie is as much above the customary timber found in kings and princes, physically and mentally, as the sky is above the earth. Talk me no talk about class! If I catch it coming from any of mine, save you, I will beat it out of them. He has admitted he's in love with the girl; the real question is, whether she's fit to be his wife."

"I should say she appears so," said father.

"Drat appearances!" cried mother. "When it's a question of lifetime misery, and the soul's salvation of my son, if things go wrong, I've no time for appearances. I want to know!"

He might have known he would make her angry when he laughed. She punched the pillow, and wouldn't say another word; so I went to sleep, and didn't miss anything that time.

Next morning at breakfast Laddie was beaming, and father hardly waited to ask the blessing before he inquired: "Well, how did you make it, son?"

Laddie laughed and answered: "Altogether, it might have been much worse."

That was all he would say until Miss Amelia started to school, then he took me on his lap and talked as he buttoned my coat.

"Thomas met me at the gate," he said, "and held my horse while I went to the door. One of their women opened it, and I inquired for Mr. Pryor. She said he was in the field looking at the horses, so I asked for Miss Pryor. She came in a minute, so I gave her the branch, told her about it, and offered the jelly and cake for her mother. The Princess invited me to enter. I told her I couldn't without her father's permission, so I went to the field to see him. The dogs were with him and he had the surprise of his life when his man-eaters rolled at my feet, and licked my hands."

"What did he say?" chuckled father.

"Told Thomas they'd been overfed and didn't amount to a brass farthing; to take them to the woods and shoot them. Thomas said he'd see to it the very first thing in the morning, and then Mr. Pryor told him he would shoot him if he did."

"Charming man to work for," said mother.

"Then I told him I'd been at the house to carry a little gift to his wife and daughter, and to inquire if I might visit an hour, and as he was not there, I had come to the field to ask him. Then I looked him in the eye and said: 'May I?'

" 'I'll warrant the women asked you to come in,' he said.

" 'Miss Pryor was so kind,' I answered, 'but I enter no man's house without his permission. May I talk with your daughter an hour, and your wife, if she cares to see me?'

" 'It makes no earthly difference to me,' he said, which was not gracious, but might have been worse, so I thanked him, and went back to the house. When I knocked the second time, the Princess came, and I told her the word was that it made 'no difference to her father' if I came in, so she opened the door widely, took my hat and offered me a seat. Then she went to the next room and said: 'Mother, father has given Mr. Stanton permission to pay us a call. Do you feel able to meet him?' She came at once, offering her hand and saying: 'I have already met Mr. Stanton so often, really, we should have the privilege of speaking.' "

"What did she mean by that?" asked mother.

"She meant that I have haunted the road passing their place for two years, and she'd seen me so frequently that she came to recognize me."

"Umph!" said mother.

"Laddie tell on!" I begged.

"Well, I sharpened all the wits I had and went to work. I never tried so hard in my life to be entertaining. Of course I had to feel my way. I'd no idea what would interest a delicate, high-bred lady"—mother sniffed again—"so I had to search and probe, and go by guess until I saw a shade of interest, then I worked in more of the same. It was easy enough to talk to the Princess—all young folks have a lot in common, we could get along on fifty topics; it was different with the housebound mother. I did my best, and after a while Mr. Pryor came in. I asked him if any of his horses had been attacked with the trouble some of the neighbours were having, and told him what it was. He had the grace to thank me. He said he would tell Thomas not to tie his horse at the public hitching rack when he went to town,

and once he got started, he was wild to talk with a man, and I'd
no chance to say a word to the women. He was interested in our
colleges, state, and national laws, in land development, and everything that all live men are. When a maid announced dinner I
apologized for having stayed so long, and excused myself, because
I had been so interested, but Mrs. Pryor merely said: 'I'm waiting to be offered your arm.'

"Well, you should have seen me drop my hat and step up. I
did my best, and while I talked to him a little, I made it most
to the women. Any one could see they were starved for company,
so I took the job of entertaining them. I told some college jokes,
funny things that had happened in the neighbourhood, and everything of interest I could think up. I know we were at the table
for two hours with things coming and going on silver platters."

Mother sat straight suddenly.

"Just what did they have to eat, and how did they serve it?"
she asked.

"Couldn't tell if I were to be shot for it, mummy," said Laddie. "Forgive me! Next time I'll take notes for you. This first
plunge, I had to use all my brains, not to be a bore to them; and
to handle food and cutlery as the women did. It's quite a process,
but as they were served first, I could do right by waiting. I never
was where things were done quite so elaborately before."

"And they didn't know they would have company until you
went to the table?"

"Well, they must have thought likely, there was a place for
me."

"Umph!" said mother. "Fine idea! Then any one who drops
in can be served, and see that they are not a mite of trouble.
Candace, always an extra place after this!"

Father just shouted.

"I thought you'd get something out of it!" he said.

"Happy to have justified your faith!" replied mother calmly.
"Go on, son!"

"That's all!" said Laddie. "We left the table and talked an
hour more. The women asked me to come again; he didn't say

anything on that subject; but when he ordered my horse, he asked the Princess if she would enjoy a little exercise, and she said she would, so he told Thomas to bring their horses, and we rode around the section, the Princess and I ahead, Mr. Pryor following. Where the road was good and the light fine enough that there was no danger of laming a horse, we dropped back, one on either side of him, so we could talk. Mrs. Pryor ate the cake and said it was fine; and the 'conserve,' she called it, delicious as she ever had tasted. She said all our fruits here had much more flavour than at home; she thought it was the dryer climate and more sunshine. She sent her grateful thanks, and she wants your recipe before next preserving time."

Mother just beamed. My! but she did love to have the things she cooked, bragged on.

"Possibly she'd like my strawberries?" she said.

"There isn't a doubt about it," said Laddie. "I've yet to see the first person who doesn't."

"Is that all?" asked mother.

"I can think of nothing more at this minute," answered Laddie. "If anything comes to my mind later, I won't forget to tell you. Oh yes, there was one thing: You couldn't keep Mr. Pryor from talking about Leon. He must have taken a great fancy to him. He talked until he worried the Princess, and she tried to keep him away from the subject, but his mind seemed to run on it constantly. When we were riding she talked quite as much as he, and it will hustle us to think what the little scamp did, any bigger than they do. Of course, father, you understood the price Mr. Pryor made on one of his very finest colts was a joke. There's a strain of Arab in the father—he showed me the record—and the mother is bluegrass. There you get gentleness and endurance combined with speed and nerve. I'd trade Flos for that colt as it stands to-day. There's nothing better on earth in the way of horse. His offer is practically giving it away. I know, with the records to prove its pedigree, what that colt would bring him in any city market."

"I don't like it," said mother. "I want Leon to have a horse, but a boy in a first experience, and reckless as he is, doesn't need a horse like that, for one thing, and what is more important, I refuse to be put under any obligations to Pryors."

"That's the reason Mr. Pryor asked anything at all for the horse. It is my opinion that he would be greatly pleased to give it to Leon, if he could do what he liked."

"Well, that's precisely the thing he can't do in this family," said mother sternly.

"What do you think, father?" asked Laddie.

"I think Amen! to that proposition," said father; "but I would have to take time to thresh it out completely. It appeals to me that Leon is old enough to recognize the value of the animal; and that the care of it would develop and strengthen his character. It would be a responsibility that would steady him. You could teach him to tend and break it."

"Break it!" cried Laddie. "Break it! Why father, he's riding it bareback all over the Pryor meadow now, and jumping it over logs. Whenever he leaves, it follows him to the fence, and the Princess says almost any hour of the day you look out you can see it pacing up and down watching this way and whinnying for him to come."

"And your best judgment is——?"

Laddie laughed as he tied my hood strings. "Well I don't feel about the Pryors as the rest of you do," he said. "If the money isn't claimed inside the time you specified, I would let Leon and Mr. Pryor make their own bargain. The boy won't know for years that it is practically a gift, and it would please Mr. Pryor immensely. Now run, or you'll be late!"

I had to go, so I didn't know how they settled it, but if they wouldn't let Leon have that horse, it was downright mean. What if we were under obligations to Mr. Pryor? We were to Sarah Hood, and half the people we knew, and what was more, we *liked* to be.

When I came from school that night father had been to town. He had an ax and was opening a big crate, containing two of the largest, bluest geese you ever saw. Laddie said being boxed that way and seeing them so close made them look so big; really, they were no finer than Pryors', where he had got the address of the place that sold them. Mother was so pleased. She said she had needed a new strain, for a long time, to improve her feathers; now she would have pillows worth while, in a few years. They put them in the barn where our geese stayed over night, and how they did scream. That is, one of them did; the other acted queerly and father said to Laddie that he was afraid the trip was hard on it. Laddie said it might have been hurt, and mother was worried too. Before she had them an hour, she had sold all our ganders; spring had come, she had saved the blue goose eggs, set them under a hen, raised the goslings with the little chickens, never lost one, picked them and made a new pair of pillows too fine for any one less important than a bishop, or a judge, or Dr. Fenner to sleep on. Then she began saving for a featherbed. And still the goose didn't act as spry or feel as good as the gander. He stuck up his head, screamed, spread his wings and waved them, and the butts looked so big and hard, I was not right certain whether it would be safe to tease him or not.

The first person who came to see them was Sarah Hood, and she left with the promise of a pair as soon as mother could raise them. Father said the only reason mother didn't divide her hair with Sarah Hood was because it was fast, and she couldn't. Mother said gracious goodness! she'd be glad to get rid of some of it if she could, and of course Sarah should have first chance at it. Hadn't she kept her over night so she could see her new home when she was rested, and didn't she come with her, and help her get settled, and had she ever failed when we had a baby, or sickness, or trouble, or thrashers, or a party? Of course she'd gladly divide, even the hair of her head, with Sarah Hood. And father said, "Yes, he guessed she would, and come to think of it, he'd just as soon spare Sarah part of his," and then they both laughed, when it was nothing so very funny that I could see.

The next caller the geese had was Mrs. Freshett. My! she thought they were big and fine. Mother promised her a couple of eggs to set under a hen. Father said she was gradually coming down the scale of her feelings, and before two weeks she'd give Isaac Thomas, at least, a quill for a pen. Almost no one wrote with them any more, but often father made a few, and showed us how to use them. He said they were gone with candles, sand boxes, and snuff. Mother said she had no use for snuff, but candles were not gone, she'd make and use them to the day of her death, as they were the nicest light ever invented to carry from room to room, or when you only wanted to sit and think. Father said there was really no good pen except the quill you sharpened yourself; and while he often used steel ones like we children had at school to write to the brothers and sisters away, and his family, he always kept a few choice quills in the till of his chest, and when he wrote a deed, or any valuable paper, where there was a deal with money, he used them. He said it lent the dignity of a past day to an important occasion.

After mother and Mrs. Freshett had talked over every single thing about the geese, and that they were like Pryors' had been settled, Mrs. Freshett said: "Since he told about it before all of us, and started out the way he did, would it be amiss to ask how Laddie got on at Pryors'?"

"Just the way I thought he would," said mother. "He stayed until all of us were in bed, and I'd never have known when he came in, if it were not a habit of his always to come to my door to see if I'm sleeping. Sometimes I'm wakeful, and if he pommels my pillow good, brings me a drink, and rubs my head a few strokes with his strong, cool hands, I can settle down and have a good night's rest. I was awake when he came, or I'd never have known. It was almost midnight; but they sat two hours at the table, and then all of them rode."

"Not the Missus?"

"Oh no! She's not strong enough. She really has incurable heart trouble, the worst kind there is; her daughter told me so."

"Then they better look out," said Mrs. Freshett. "She is likely to keel over at a breath."

"They must know it. That's why she keeps so quiet."

"And they had him to supper?"

"It was a dinner served at night. Yes. He took Mrs. Pryor in on his arm, and it was like a grand party, just as they fixed for themselves, alone. Waiters, and silver trays, and things carried in and out in courses."

"My land! Well, I s'pose he had enough schoolin' to get him through it all right!"

My mother's face grew red. She never left any one in doubt as to what she meant. Father said that "was the Dutch of it." And mother always answered that if any one living could put things plainer than the English, she would like to hear them do it.

"He certainly had," said mother, "or they wouldn't have invited him to come again. And all mine, Mrs. Freshett, knew how to sit properly at the table, and manage a knife, fork and napkin, before they ever took a meal away from home."

"No 'fence," laughed Mrs. Freshett. "I meant that maybe his years of college schoolin' had give him ways more like theirs than most of us have. For all the money it takes to send a boy to college, he ought to get somethin' out of it more than jest fillin' his head with figgers, an' stars, an' oratin'; an' most always you can see that he does."

"It is contact with cultivated people," said mother. "You are always influenced by it, without knowing it often."

"Maybe you are, bein' so fine yourself," said Mrs. Freshett. "An' me too, I never get among my betters that I don't carry home a lot I put right into daily use, an' nobody knows it plainer. I come here expectin' to learn things that help me, an' when I go home I know I have."

"Why, thank you," said mother. "I'm sure that is a very nice compliment, and I wish I really could feel that it is well deserved."

"Oh I guess you do!" said Mrs. Freshett laughing. "I often noticed you makin' a special effort to teach puddin' heads like me somethin', an' I always thank you for it. There's a world in right teachin'. I never had any. So all I can pick up an' hammer into mine is a gain for me an' them. If my Henry had lived, an' come out anything like that boy o' yourn an' the show he made last Sunday, I'd do well if I didn't swell up an' bust with pride. An' the little tow-haired strip, takin' the gun an' startin' out alone after a robber, even if he wa'n't much of a man, that was downright spunky. If my boys will come out anywhere near like yourn, I'll be glad."

"I don't know how my boys will come out," said mother. "But I work, pray, hope, and hang to them; that's all I know to do."

"Well, if they don't come out right, they ought to be bumped!" said Mrs. Freshett. "After all the chances they've had! I don' know jest how Freshett was brung up, but I'd no chance at all. My folks—well, I guess the less said—little pitchers, you know! I can't see as I was to blame. I was the youngest, an' I knew things was wrong. I fought to go to school, an' pap let me enough that I saw how other people lived. Come night I'd go to the garret, an' bar the trapdoor; but there would be times when I couldn't help seein' what was goin' on. How'd you like chances such as that for a girl of yourn?"

"Dreadful!" said mother. "Mrs. Freshett, please do be careful!"

"Sure!" laughed Mrs. Freshett. "I was jest goin' to tell you about me an' Josiah. He come to our house one night, a stranger off the road. He said he was sick, an' tired, an' could he have a bed. Mother said, 'No, for him to move on.' He tried an' he couldn't. They was somethin' about him—well, you know how them things go! I wa'n't only sixteen, but I felt so sorry for him, all fever burned and mumblin', I helped pap put him to bed, an' doctored him all I could. Come mornin' he was a sick man. Pap went for the county doctor, an' he took jest one look an' says: 'Small pox! All of ye git!'

"I was bound I wouldn't go, but pap made me, an' the doctor said he'd send a man who'd had it; so I started, but I felt so bad, come a chanct when they got to Groveville, I slipped out an' went back. The man hadn't come, so I set to work the best I knowed. 'Fore long Josiah was a little better an' he asked who I was, an' where my folks went, an' I told him, an' he asked *why* I came back, an' I didn't know what to say, so I jest hung my head an' couldn't face him. After a while he says, 'All right! I guess I got this sized up. If you'll stay an' nuss me through, I'll be well enough to pull you out, by the time you get it, an' soon as you're able we'll splice, if you say so.' "'Marry me, you mean?' says I. They wa'n't ever any talk about marryin' at our house. 'Sure!' says he. 'You're a mighty likely lookin' girl! I'll do fair by ye.' An' he always has, too! But I didn't feel right to let him go it blind, so I jest up and says, 'You wouldn't if you knowed my folks!' 'You look as decent as I do,' says he; 'I'll chance it!' Then I tole him I was as good as I was born, an' he believed me, an' he always has, an' I was too! So I nussed him, but I didn't make the job of it he did. You 'member he is pitted considerable. He was so strong I jest couldn't keep him from disfigerin' himself, but he tied me. I begged to be loose, an' he wouldn't listen, so I got a clean face, only three little scars, an' they ain't deep to speak of. He says he looks like a piece of side meat, but say! they ain't nothin' the matter with his looks to me!

"The nuss man never did come, but the county doctor passed things in the winder, till I was over the worst, an' Josiah sent for a preacher an' he married us through the winder—I got the writin's to show, all framed an' proper. Josiah said he'd see I got all they was in it long that line, anyway. When I was well, hanged if he didn't perdooce a wad from his clothes before they burnt 'em, an' he got us new things to wear, an' a horse, an' wagon, an' we driv away here where we thought we could start right, an' after we had the land, an' built the cabin, an' jest as happy as heart could wish, long come a man I'd made mad once, an' he tole everythin' up and down. Josiah was good about it. He offered to sell the land, an' pull up an' go furder. 'What's the use?' says I. 'Hundreds know it. We can't go so far it won't be like to follow us; le's stay here an' fight it.' 'All right,' says Josiah, but time an' ag'in he has offered to go, if I couldn't make it. 'Hang on a little longer,' says I, every time he knew I was snubbed an' slighted. I never tole what he didn't notice. I tried church, when my children began to git a size I wanted 'em to have right teachin', an' you come an' welcomed me an' you been my friend, an' now the others is comin' over at last, an' visitin' me, an' they ain't a thing more I want in life."

"I am so glad!" said mother. "Oh my dear, I am so glad!"

"Goin' right home an' tell that to Josiah," said Mrs. Freshett, jumping up laughing and crying like, "an' mebby I'll jest spread wings and fly! I never was so happy in all my life as I was Sunday, when you ast me before all of them, so cordial like, an' says I to Josiah, 'We'll go an' try it once,' an' we come an' nobody turned a cold shoulder on us, an' I wa'n't wearin' specks to see if they did, for I never knowed him so happy in all his days. Orter heard him whistle goin' home, an' he's tryin' all them things he learned, on our place, an' you can see it looks a heap better a'ready, an' now he's talkin' about buildin' in the spring. I knowed he had money, but he never mentioned buildin' before, an' I always thought it was bekase he 'sposed likely we'd have to move on, some time. 'Pears now as if we can settle, an' live like other folks, after all these years. I knowed ye didn't want me to talk, but I had to tell you! When you ast us to the weddin', and others began comin' round, says I to Josiah, 'Won't she be glad to know that my skirts is clear, an' I did as well as I could?' An' he says, 'That she will! An' more am I,' says he. 'I mighty proud of you,' says he. Proud! Think of that! Miss Stanton, I'd jest wade fire and blood for you!"

"Oh my dear!" said mother. "What a dreadful thing to say!"

"Gimme the chanct, an' watch if I don't," said Mrs. Freshett. "Now, Josiah is proud I stuck it out! Now, I can have a house! Now, my children can have all the show we can raise to give 'em! I'm done cringin' an' dodgin'! I've always done my best; henceforth I mean to hold up my head an' say so. I sure can't be held for what was done 'fore I was on earth, or since neither. You've given me my show, I'm goin' to take it, but if you want to know what's in my heart about you, gimme any kind of a chanct to prove, an' see if I don't pony right up to it!"

Mother laughed until the tears rolled, she couldn't help it. She took Mrs. Freshett in her arms and hugged her tight, and kissed her mighty near like she does Sarah Hood. Mrs. Freshett threw her arms around mother, and looked over her shoulder, and said to me, "Sis, when you grow up, always take a chanct on welcomin' the stranger, like your maw does, an' heaven's bound to be your home! My, but your maw is a woman to be proud of!" she said, hugging mother and patting her on the back.

"All of us are proud of her!" I boasted.

"I doubt if you are proud enough!" cried Mrs. Freshett. "I have my doubts! I don't see how people livin' with her, an' seein' her every day, are in a shape to know jest what she can do for a person in the place I was in. I have my doubts!"

That night when I went home from school mother was worrying over the blue goose. When we went to feed, she told Leon that she was afraid it was weak, and not getting enough to eat when it fed with the others. She said after the work was finished, to take it out alone, and give it all it would eat; so when the horses were tended, the cows milked, everything watered, and the barn ready to close for the night, Laddie took the milk to the house, while Leon and I caught the blue goose, carried her to the well, and began to shell corn. She was starved to death, almost. She ate a whole ear in no time and looked for more, so Leon sent me after another. By the time that was most gone she began to eat slower, and stick her bill in the air to help the grains slip down, so I told Leon I thought she had enough.

"No such thing!" said Leon. "You distinctly heard mother tell me to give her 'all she would eat.' She's eating, isn't she? Go bring another ear!"

So she was, but I was doubtful about more.

Leon said I better mind or he would tell mother, so I got it. She didn't begin on it with any enthusiasm. She stuck her bill higher, stretched her neck longer, and she looked so funny when she did it, that we just shrieked. Then Leon reached over, took her by the bill, and stripped her neck to help her swallow, and as soon as he let go, she began to eat again.

"You see!" said Leon, "she's been starved. She can't get enough. I must help her!"

So he did help her every little bit. By that time we were interested in seeing how much she could hold; and she looked so funny that Leon sent me for more corn; but I told him I thought what she needed now was water, so we held her to the trough, and she tried to drink, but she couldn't swallow much. We set her down beside the corn, and she went to eating again.

"Go it, old mill-hopper!" cried Leon.

Right then there was an awful commotion in the barn, and from the squealing we knew one of the horses was loose, and fighting the others. We ran to fix them, and had a time to get Jo back into his stall, and tied. Before we had everything safe, the supper bell rang, and I bet Leon a penny I could reach the house while he shut the door and got there. We forgot every single thing about the goose.

At supper mother asked Leon if he fed the goose all she would eat, and I looked at him guilty-like, for I remembered we hadn't put her back. He frowned at me cross as a bear, and I knew that meant he had remembered, and would slip back and put her inside when he finished his supper, so I didn't say anything.

"I didn't feed her *all* she would eat!" said Leon. "If I had, she'd be at it yet. She was starved sure enough! You never saw anything like the corn she downed."

"Well I declare!" said mother. "Now after this, take her out alone, for a few days, and give her as much as she wants."

"All right!" chuckled Leon, because it was a lot of fun to see her run her bill around, and gobble up the corn, and stick up her head.

The next day was Saturday, so after breakfast I went with Leon to drive the sheep and geese to the creek to water; the trough was so high it was only for the horses and cattle; when we let out the geese, the blue one wasn't there.

"Oh Leon, did you forget to come back and put her in?"

"Yes I did!" he said. "I meant to when I looked at you to keep still, and I started to do it, but Sammy Deam whistled, so I went down in the orchard to see what he wanted, and we got to planning how to get up a fox chase, and I stayed until father called for night, and then I ran and forgot all about the blame old goose."

"Oh Leon! Where is she? What will mother say? 'Spose a fox got her!"

"It wouldn't help me any if it had, after I was to blame for leaving her outside. Blast a girl! If you ever amounted to anything, you could have put her in while I fixed the horses. At least you could have told me to."

I stood there dumblike and stared at him. He has got the awfulest way of telling the truth when he is scared or provoked. Of course I should have thought of the goose when he was having such a hard fight with the horses. If I'd been like he was, I'd have told him that he was older, mother told *him* to do it, and it wasn't my fault; but in my heart I knew he did have his hands full, and if you're your brother's keeper, you ought to *help* your brother remember. So I stood gawking, while Leon slowly turned whiter and whiter.

"We might as well see if we can find her," he said at last, so slow and hopeless like it made my heart ache. So he started around the straw stack one way, and I the other, looking into all the holes, and before I had gone far I had a glimpse of her, and it scared me so I screamed, for her head was down, and she didn't look right. Leon came running and pulled her out. The swelled corn rolled in a little trail after her, and the pigs ran up and began to eat it. Pigs are named righter than anything else I know.

"Busted!" cried Leon in tones of awe; about the worst awe you ever heard, and the worst bust you ever saw.

From bill to breast she was wide open, and the hominy spilling. We just stood staring at her, and then Leon began to kick the pigs; because it would be no use to kick the goose; she would never know. Then he took her up, carried her into the barn, and put her on the floor where the other geese had stayed all night. We stood and looked at her some more, as if looking and hoping would make her get up and be alive again. But there's nothing in all this world so useless as wishing dead things would come alive; we had to do something.

"What are you going to tell mother?"

"Shut up!" said Leon. "I'm trying to think."

"I'll say it was as much my fault as yours. I'll go with you. I'll take half whatever they do to you."

"Little fool!" said Leon. "What good would that do me?"

"Do you know what they cost? Could you get another with some of your horse money?"

I saw it coming and dodged again, before I remembered the Crusaders.

"All right!" I said. "If that's the way you are going to act, Smarty, I'll lay all the blame on you; I won't help you a bit, and I don't care if you are whipped until the blood runs."

Then I went out of the barn and slammed the door. For a minute I felt better; but it was a short time. I *said* that to be mean, but I did care. I cared dreadfully; I was partly to blame, and I knew it. Coming around the barn, I met Laddie, and he saw in a flash I was in trouble, so he stopped and asked: "What now, Chicken?"

"Come into the barn where no one will hear us," I said.

So we went around the outside, entered at the door on the embankment, and he sat in the wheelbarrow on the threshing floor while I told him. I thought I felt badly enough, but after I saw Laddie, it grew worse, for I remembered we were short of money that fall, that the goose was a fine, expensive one, and how proud mother was of her, and how she'd be grieved, and that was trouble for sure.

"Run along and play!" said Laddie, "and don't tell any one else if you can help it. I'll hide the goose, and see if I can get another in time to take the place of this one, so mother won't be worried."

I walked to the house slowly, but I was afraid to enter. When you are all choked up, people are sure to see it, and ask fool questions. So I went around to the gate and stood there looking up and down the road, and over the meadow toward the Big

Woods; and all at once, in one of those high, regular bugle calls, like they mostly scream in spring, one of Pryors' ganders split the echoes for a mile; maybe farther.

I was across the road and slinking down inside the meadow fence before I knew it. There was no thought or plan. I started for Pryors' and went straight ahead, only I kept out of line with our kitchen windows. I tramped through the slush, ice, and crossed fields where I was afraid of horses; but when I got to the top of the Pryor backyard fence, I stuck there, for the bulldogs were loose, and came raving at me. I was going to be eaten alive, for I didn't know the word Laddie did; and those dogs climbed a fence like a person; I saw them the time Leon brought back Even So. I was thinking what a pity it was, after every one had grown accustomed to me, and had begun loving me, that I should be wasted for dog feed, when Mr. Pryor came to the door, and called them; they didn't mind, so he came to the fence, and crossest you ever heard, every bit as bad as the dogs, he cried: "Whose brat are you, and what are you doing here?"

I meant to tell him; but you must have a minute after a thing like that.

"God of my life!" he fairly frothed. "What did anybody send a dumb child here for?"

"Dumb child!" I didn't care if Mr. Pryor did wear a Crown of Glory. It wasn't going to do him one particle of good, unless he was found in the way of the Lord. "Dumb child!" I was no more dumb than he was, until his bulldogs scared me so my heart got all tangled up with my stomach, my lungs, and my liver. That made me mad, and there was nothing that would help me to loosen up and talk fast, like losing my temper. I wondered what kind of a father he had. If he'd been stood against the wall and made to recite, "Speak gently," as often as all of us, perhaps he'd have remembered the verse that says:

> *"Speak gently to the little child;*
> *Its love be sure to gain;*
> *Teach it in accents soft and mild;*
> *It may not long remain."*

I should think not, if it had any chance at all to get away! I was so angry by that time I meant to tell him what I thought. Polite or not polite, I'd take a switching if I had to, but I wasn't going to stand that.

"You haven't got any God in your life," I reminded him, "and no one sent me here. I came to see the Princess, because I'm in awful trouble and I hoped maybe she could fix up a way to help me."

"Ye Gods!" he cried. He would stick to calling on God, whether he believed in Him or not. "If it isn't Nimrod! I didn't recognize you in all that bundling."

Probably he didn't know it, but Nimrod was from the Bible too! By bundling, he meant my hood and coat. He helped me from the fence, sent the bulldogs rolling—sure enough he *did* kick them, and they didn't like it either—took my hand and led me straight into the house, and the Princess was there, and a woman who was her mother no doubt, and he said: "Pamela, here is our little neighbour, and she says she's in trouble, and she thinks you may be of some assistance to her. Of course you will be glad if you can."

"Surely!" said the Princess, and she introduced me to her mother, so I bowed the best I knew, and took off my wet mitten, dirty with climbing fences, to shake hands with her. She was so gracious and lovely I forgot what I went after. The Princess brought a cloth and wiped the wet from my shoes and stockings, and asked me if I wouldn't like a cup of hot tea to keep me from taking a chill.

"I've been much wetter than this," I told her, "and I never have taken a chill, and anyway my throat's too full of trouble to drink."

"Why, you poor child!" said the Princess. "Tell me quickly! Is your mother ill again?"

"Not now, but she's going to be as soon as she finds out," I said, and then I told them.

They all listened without a sound until I got where Leon helped the goose eat, and from that on Mr. Pryor laughed until you could easily see that he had very little feeling for suffering humanity. It was funny enough when we fed her, but now that she was bursted wide open there was nothing amusing about it; and to roar when a visitor plainly told you she was in awful trouble, didn't seem very good manners to me. The Princess and her mother never even smiled; and before I had told nearly all of it, Thomas was called to hitch the Princess' driving cart, and she took me to their barnyard to choose the goose that looked most like mother's, and all of them seemed like hers, so we took the first one Thomas could catch, put it into a bag in the back of the cart, and then we got in and started for our barn. As we reached the road, I said to her: "You'd better go past Dovers', for if we come down our Little Hill they will see us sure; it's baking day."

"All right!" said the Princess, so we went the long way round the section, but goodness me! when she drove no way was far.

When we were opposite our barn she stopped, hitched her horse to the fence, and we climbed over, and slipping behind the barn, carried the goose around to the pen and put it in with ours. She said she wanted the broken one, because her father would enjoy seeing it. I didn't see how he could! We were ready to slip out, when our geese began to run at the new one, hiss and scream, and make such a racket that Laddie and Leon both caught us. They looked at the goose, at me, the Princess, and each other, and neither said a word. She looked back a little bit, and then she laughed as hard as she could. Leon grew red, and he grinned ashamed-like, so she laughed worse than ever. Laddie spoke to me: "You went to Mr. Pryor's and asked for that goose?"

"She did not!" said the Princess before I could answer. "She never asked for anything. She was making a friendly morning call and in the course of her visit she told about the pathetic end of the goose that was expected to lay the golden egg—I mean stuff the Bishop's pillow—and as we have a large flock of blue geese, father gave her one, and he had the best time he's had in years doing it. I wouldn't have had him miss the fun he got from it for any money. He laughed like home again. Now I must slip away before any one sees me, and spoils our secret. Leon, lad, you can go to the house and tell your little mother that the feeding stopped every pain her goose had, and hereafter it looks to you as if she'd be all right."

"Miss Pryor," said Leon, "did you care about what I said at you in church that day?"

" 'Thou art all fair, my love. There is no spot in thee.' Well, it *was* a little pointed, but since you ask a plain question, I have survived it."

"I'm awfully sorry," said Leon. "Of course I never would, if I'd known you could be this nice."

The Princess looked at Laddie and almost gasped, and then both of them laughed. Leon saw that he had told her he was sorry he said she was "fair, and no spot in her."

"Oh I don't mean that!" he said. "What I do mean is that I thank you awful much for the goose, and helping me out like such a brick of a good fellow, and what I wish is, that I was as old as Laddie, and he'd hump himself if he got to be your beau."

The Princess almost ran. Laddie and I followed to the road, where he unhitched the horse and helped her in. Then he stood stroking its neck, as he held the bridle.

"I don't know what to say!" said Laddie.

"In such case, I would counsel silence," advised the Princess.

"I hope you understand how I thank you."

"I fail to see what for. Father gave the goose to Little Sister. Her thanks and Leon's are more than enough for him. We had great sport."

"I insist on adding mine. Deep and fervent!"

"You take everything so serious. Can't you see the fun of this?"

"No," said Laddie. "But if you can, I am glad, and I'm thankful for anything that gives me a glimpse of you."

"Bye, Little Sister," said the Princess, and when she loosened the lines the mud flew a rod high.

CHAPTER XI

Keeping Christmas Our Way

"I remember, I remember
How my childhood fleeted by,—
The mirth of its December,
And the warmth of its July."

WHEN dusk closed in it would be Christmas eve. All day I had three points—a chair beside the kitchen table, a lookout melted through the frost on the front window, and the big sitting-room fireplace.

All the perfumes of Araby floated from our kitchen that day. There was that delicious smell of baking flour from big snowy loaves of bread, light biscuit, golden coffee cake, and cinnamon rolls dripping a waxy mixture of sugar, butter, and spice, much better than the finest butterscotch ever brought from the city. There was the tempting odour of boiling ham and baking pies. The air was filled with the smell of more herbs and spices than I knew the names of, that went into mincemeat, fruit cake, plum pudding, and pies. There was a teasing fragrance in the spiced vinegar heating for pickles, a reminder of winesap and rambo in the boiling cider, while the newly opened bottles of grape juice filled the house with the tang of Concord and muscadine. It seemed to me I never got nicely fixed where I could take a sly dip in the cake dough or snipe a fat raisin from the mincemeat but Candace would say: "Don't you suppose the backlog is half-way down the lane?"

Then I hurried to the front window, where I could see through my melted outlook on the frosted pane, across the west eighty to the woods, where father and Laddie were getting out the Christmas backlog. It was too bitterly cold to keep me there while they worked, but Laddie said that if I would watch, and come to meet them, he would take me up, and I might ride home among the Christmas greens on the log.

So I flattened my nose against the pane and danced and fidgeted until those odours teased me back to the kitchen; and no more did I get nicely located beside a jar of pudding sauce than Candace would object to the place I had hung her stocking. It was my task, my delightful all-day task, to hang the stockings. Father had made me a peg for each one, and I had ten feet of mantel front along which to arrange them. But it was no small job to do this to every one's satisfaction. No matter what happened to any one else, Candace had to be pleased: for did not she so manage that most fowls served on mother's table went gizzardless to the carving? She knew and acknowledged the great importance of trying cookies, pies, and cake while they were hot. She was forever overworked and tired, yet she always found time to make gingerbread women with currant buttons on their frocks, and pudgy doughnut men with clove eyes and cigars of cinnamon. If my own stocking lay on the hearth, Candace's had to go in a place that satisfied her—that was one sure thing. Besides, I had to make up to her for what Leon did, because she was crying into the corner of her apron about that.

He slipped in and stole her stocking, hung it over the broomstick, and marched around the breakfast table singing to the tune of—

> "Ha, ha, ha, who wouldn't go—
>   Up on the housetop click, click, click?
> Down through the chimney,
>   With good Saint Nick——"

words he made up himself. He walked just fast enough that she couldn't catch him, and sang as he went:

> "Ha, ha, ha, good Saint Nick,
>   Come and look at this stocking, quick!

If you undertake its length to fill,
You'll have to bust a ten-dollar bill.
Who does it belong to? Candace Swartz.
Bring extra candy,—seven quarts——"

She got so angry she just roared, so father made Leon stop it, but I couldn't help laughing myself. Then we had to pet her all day, so she'd cheer up, and not salt the Christmas dinner with her tears. I never saw such a monkey as Leon! I trotted out to comfort her, and snipped bites, until I wore a triangle on the carpet between the kitchen and the mantel, the mantel and the window, and the window and the kitchen, while every hour things grew more exciting.

There never had been such a flurry at our house since I could remember; for to-morrow would be Christmas and bring home all the children, and a house full of guests. My big brother, Jerry, who was a lawyer in the city, was coming with his family, and so were Frank, Elizabeth, and Lucy with theirs, and of course Sally and Peter—I wondered if she would still be fixing his tie—and Shelley came yesterday, blushing like a rose, and she laughed if you pointed your finger at her.

Something had happened to her in Chicago. I wasn't so sure as I had been about a city being such a dreadful place of noise, bad air, and wicked people. Nothing had hurt Shelley. She had grown so much that you could see she was larger. Her hair and face—all of Shelley just shone. Her eyes danced, she talked and laughed all the time, and she hugged every one who passed her. She never loved us so before. Leon said she must have been homesick and coming back had given her a spell. I did hope it would be a bad one, and last forever. I would have liked for all our family to have had a spell if it would have made them act and look like Shelley. The Princess was not a speck lovelier, and she didn't act any nicer.

If I could have painted, I'd have made a picture of Shelley with a circle of light above her head like the one of the boy Jesus where He talked with the wise men in the temple. I asked father if he noticed how much prettier and nicer she was, and he said he did. Then I asked him if he thought now, that a city was such a bad place to live in, and he said where she was had nothing to do with it, the same thing would happen here, or anywhere, when life's greatest experience came to a girl. That was all he would say, but figuring it out was easy. The greatest experience that happened to our girls was when they married, like Sally, so it meant that Shelley had gone and fallen in love with that lawyer man, and she liked sitting on the sofa with him, and no doubt she fixed his ties. But if any one thought I would tell anything I saw when he came they were badly mistaken.

All of us rushed around like we were crazy. If father and mother hadn't held steady and kept us down, we might have raised the roof. We were all so glad about getting Leon and the money back; mother hadn't been sick since the fish cured her; the new blue goose was so like the one that had burst, even father never noticed any difference; all the children were either home or coming, and after we had our gifts and the biggest dinner we ever had, Christmas night all of us would go to the schoolhouse to see our school try to spell down three others to whom they had sent saucy invitations to come and be beaten.

Mother sat in the dining-room beside the kitchen door, so that she could watch the baking, brewing, pickling, and spicing. It took four men to handle the backlog, which I noticed father pronounced every year "just a little the finest we ever had," and Laddie strung the house with bittersweet, evergreens, and the most beautiful sprays of myrtle that he raked from under the snow. Father drove to town in the sleigh, and the list of things to be purchased mother gave him as a reminder was almost a yard long.

The minute they finished the outdoor work Laddie and Leon began bringing in baskets of apples, golden bellflowers, green pippins, white winter pearmains, Rhode Island greenings, and striped rambos all covered with hoarfrost, yet not frozen, and so full of juice you had to bite into them carefully or they dripped and offended mother. These they washed and carried to the cellar ready for use.

Then they cracked big dishes of nuts; and popped corn that popped with the most resounding pops in all my experience—popped a tubful, and Laddie melted maple sugar and poured over it and made big balls of fluff and sweetness. He took a pan and filled it with grains, selected one at a time, the very largest and whitest, and made an especial ball, in the middle of which he put a lovely pink candy heart on which was printed in red letters: "How can this heart be mine, yet yours, unless our hearts are one?" He wouldn't let any of them see it except me, and he only let me because he knew I'd be delighted.

It was almost dusk when father came through the kitchen loaded with bundles and found Candace and the girls still cooking.

We were so excited we could scarcely be gathered around the supper table, and mother said we chattered until she couldn't hear herself think. After a while Laddie laid down his fork and looked at our father.

"Have you any objection to my using the sleigh to-morrow night?" he asked.

Father looked at mother.

"Had you planned to use it, mother?"

Mother said: "No. If I go, I'll ride in the big sled with all of us. It is such a little way, and the roads are like glass."

So father said politely, as he always spoke to us: "Then it will give me great pleasure for you to take it, my son."

That made Leon bang his fork loudly as he dared and squirm in his chair, for well he knew that if he had asked, the answer would have been different. If Laddie took the sleigh he would harness carefully, drive fast, but reasonably, blanket his horse, come home at the right time, and put everything exactly where he found it. But Leon would pitch the harness on some way, race every step, never think of his steaming horse, come home when there was no one so wild as he left to play pranks with, and scatter the harness everywhere. He knew our father would love to trust him the same as he did Laddie. He wouldn't always prove himself trustworthy, but he envied Laddie.

"You think you'll take the Princess to the spelling bee, don't you?" he sneered.

"I mean to ask her," replied Laddie.

"Maybe you think she'll ride in our old homemade, hickory cheesebox, when she can sail all over the country like a bird in a velvet-lined cutter with a real buffalo robe."

There was a quick catch in mother's breath and I felt her hand on my chair tremble. Father's lips tightened and a frown settled on his face, while Laddie fairly jumped. He went white to the lips, and one hand dropped on the table, palm up, the fingers closing and unclosing, while his eyes turned first to mother, and then to father, in dumb appeal. We all knew that he was suffering. No one spoke, and Leon having shot his arrow straight home, saw as people so often do in this world that the damage of unkind words could not easily be repaired; so he grew red in the face and squirmed uncomfortably.

At last Laddie drew a deep, quivering breath. "I never thought of that," he said. "She has seemed happy to go with me several times when I asked her, but of course she might not care to ride in ours, when she has such a fine sleigh of her own."

Father's voice fairly boomed down the length of the table.

"Your mother always has found our sleigh suitable," he said.

The fact was, father was rarely proud of it. He had selected the hickory in our woods, cut it and hauled it to the mill, cured the lumber, and used all his spare time for two winters making it. With the exception of having the runners turned at a factory and iron-bound at a smithy, he had completed it alone with great care, even to staining it a beautiful cherry colour, and fitting white sheepskins into the bed. We had all watched him and been so proud of it, and now Leon was sneering at it. He might just as well have undertaken to laugh at father's wedding suit or to make fun of "Clark's Commentaries."

Laddie appealed to mother: "Do you think I'd better not ask her?"

He spoke with an effort.

"Laddie, that is the first time I ever heard you propose to do any one an injustice," she said.

"I don't see how," said Laddie.

"It isn't giving the Princess any chance at all," replied mother "You've just said that she has seemed pleased to accompany you before, now you are proposing to cut her out of what promises to be the most delightful evening of the winter, without even giving her the chance to say whether she'd go with you or not. Has she ever made you feel that anything you offered her or wanted to do for her was not good enough?"

"Never!" exclaimed Laddie fervently.

"Until she does, then, do you think it would be quite manly and honourable to make decisions for her? You say you never thought of anything except a pleasant time with her; possibly she feels the same. Unless she changes, I would scarcely let a boy's foolish tongue disturb her pleasure. Moreover, as to the matter of wealth, your father may be as rich as hers; but they have one, we have many. If what we spend on all our brood could be confined to one child, we could easily duplicate all her luxuries, and I think she has the good sense to realize the fact as quickly as any one. I've no doubt she would gladly exchange half she has for the companionship of a sister or a brother in her lonely life."

Laddie turned to father, and father's smile was happy again. Mother was little but she was mighty. With only a few words she had made Leon feel how unkind and foolish he had been, quieted Laddie's alarm, and soothed the hurt father's pride had felt in that he had not been able to furnish her with so fine a turnout as Pryors had.

Next morning when the excitement of gifts and greetings was over, and Laddie's morning work was all finished, he took a beautiful volume of poems and his popcorn ball and started across the fields due west; all of us knew that he was going to call on and offer them to the Princess, and ask to take her to the spelling bee. I suppose Laddie thought he was taking that trip alone, but really he was surrounded. I watched him from the window, and my heart went with him. Presently father went and sat beside mother's chair, and stroking her hand, whispered softly: "Please don't worry, little mother. It will be all right. Your boy will come home happy."

"I hope so," she answered, "but I can't help feeling dreadfully nervous. If things go wrong with Laddie, it will spoil the day."

"I have much faith in the Princess' good common sense," replied father, "and considering what it means to Laddie, it would hurt me sore to lose it."

Mother sat still, but her lips moved so that I knew she was making soft little whispered prayers for her best loved son. But Laddie, plowing through the drift, never dreamed that all of us were with him. He was always better looking than any other man I ever had seen, but when, two hours later, he stamped into the kitchen he was so much handsomer than usual, that I knew from the flush on his cheek and the light in his eye, that the Princess had been kind, and by the package in his hand, that she had made him a present. He really had two, a beautiful book and a necktie. I wondered to my soul if she gave him that, so she could fix it! I didn't believe she had begun on his ties at that time; but of course when he loved her as he did, he wished she would.

It was the very jolliest Christmas we ever had, but the day seemed long. When night came we were in a precious bustle. The wagon bed on bobs, filled with hay and covers, drawn by Ned and Jo, was brought up for the family, and the sleigh made spick-and-span and drawn by Laddie's thoroughbred, stood beside it. Laddie had filled the kitchen oven with bricks and hung up a comfort at four o'clock to keep the Princess warm.

Because he had to drive out of the way to bring her, Laddie wanted to start early; and when he came down dressed in his college clothes, and looking the manliest of men, some of the folks thought it funny to see him carefully rake his hot bricks from the oven, and pin them in an old red breakfast shawl. I thought it was fine, and I whispered to mother: "Do you suppose that if Laddie ever marries the Princess he will be good to her as he is to you?"

Mother nodded with tear-dimmed eyes, but Shelley said: "I'll wager a strong young girl like the Princess will laugh at you for babying over her."

"Why?" inquired Laddie. "It is a long drive and a bitter night, and if you fancy the Princess will laugh at anything I do, when I am doing the best I know for her comfort, you are mistaken. At least, that is the impression she gave me this morning."

I saw the swift glance mother shot at father, and father laid down his paper and said, while he pretended his glasses needed polishing: "Now there is the right sort of a girl for you. No foolishness about her, when she has every chance. Hurrah for the Princess!"

It was easy to see that she wasn't going to have nearly so hard a time changing father's opinion as she would mother's. It was not nearly a year yet, and here he was changed already. Laddie said good-bye to mother—he never forgot—gathered up his comfort and bricks, and started for Pryors' downright happy. We went to the schoolhouse a little later, all of us scoured, curled, starched, and wearing our very best clothes. My! but it was fine. There were many lights in the room and it was hung with greens. There was a crowd even though it was early. On Miss Amelia's table was a volume of history that was the prize, and every one was looking and acting the very best he knew how, although there were cases where they didn't know so very much.

Our Shelley was the handsomest girl there, until the Princess came, and then they both were. Shelley wore one of her city frocks and a quilted red silk hood that was one of her Christmas gifts, and she looked just like a handsome doll. She made every male creature in that room feel that she was pining for him alone. May had a gay plaid frock and curls nearly a yard long, and so had I, but both our frocks and curls were homemade; mother would have them once in a while; father and I couldn't stop her.

But there was not a soul there who didn't have some sort of gift to rejoice over, and laughter and shouts of "Merry Christmas!" filled the room. It was growing late and there was some talk of choosers, when the door opened and in a rush of frosty air the Princess and Laddie entered. Every one stopped short and stared. There was good reason. The Princess looked as if she had accidentally stepped from a frame. She was always lovely and beautifully dressed, but to-night she was prettier and finer than ever before. You could fairly hear their teeth click as some of the most envious of those girls caught sight of her, for she was wearing a new hat!—a black velvet store hat, fitting closely over her crown, with a rim of twisted velvet, a scarlet bird's wing, and a big silver buckle. Her dress was of scarlet cloth cut in forms, and it fitted as if she had been melted and poured into it. It was edged around the throat, wrists, and skirt with narrow bands of fur, and she wore a loose, long, silk-lined coat of the same material, and worst of all, furs—furs such as we had heard wealthy and stylish city ladies were wearing. A golden brown cape that reached to her elbows, with ends falling to the knees, finished in the tails of some animal, and for her hands a muff as big as a nail keg.

Now, there was not a girl in that room, except the Princess, an she had those clothes, who wouldn't have flirted like a peacock, almost bursting with pride; but because the Princess had them, and they didn't, they sat stolid and sullen, and cast glances at each other as if they were saying: "The stuck-up thing!" "Thinks she's smart, don't she?"

Many of them should have gone to meet her and made her welcome, for she was not of our district and really their guest. Shelley did go, but I noticed she didn't hurry.

The choosers began at once, and Laddie was the first person called for our side, and the Princess for the visitors'. Every one in the room was chosen on one side or the other; even my name was called, but I only sat still and shook my head, for I very well knew that no one except father would remember to pronounce easy ones for me, and besides I was so bitterly disappointed I could scarcely have stood up. They had put me in a seat near the fire; the spellers lined either wall, and a goodly number that refused to spell occupied the middle seats. I couldn't get a glimpse of Laddie or the home folks, or worst of all, of my idolized Princess.

I never could bear to find a fault with Laddie, but I sadly reflected that he might as well have left me at home, if I were to be buried where I could neither hear nor see a thing. I was just wishing it was summer so I could steal out to the cemetery, and have a good visit with the butterflies that always swarmed around Georgiana Jane Titcomb's grave at the corner of the church. I never knew Georgiana Jane, but her people must have been very fond of her, for her grave was scarlet with geraniums, and pink with roses from earliest spring until frost, and the bright colours attracted swarms of butterflies. I had learned that if I stuck a few blossoms in my hair, rubbed some sweet smelling ones over my hands, and knelt and kept so quiet that I fitted into the landscape, the butterflies would think me a flower too, and alight on my hair, dress, and my hands, even. God never made anything more beautiful than those butterflies, with their wings of brightly painted velvet down, their bright eyes, their curious antennæ, and their queer, tickly feet. Laddie had promised me a book telling all about every kind there was, the first time he went to a city, so I was wishing I had it, and was among my pet beauties with it, when I discovered him bending over me.

He took my arm, and marching back to his place, helped me to the deep window seat beside him, where with my head on a level, and within a foot of his, I could see everything in the whole room. I don't know why I ever spent any time pining for the beauties of Georgiana Jane Titcomb's grave, even with its handsome headstone on which was carved a lamb standing on three feet and holding a banner over its shoulder with the fourth, and the geraniums, roses, and the weeping willow that grew over it, thrown in. I might have trusted Laddie. He never had forgotten me; until he did, I should have kept unwavering faith.

Now, I had the best place of any one in the room, and I smoothed my new plaid frock and shook my handmade curls just as near like Shelley as ever I could. But it seems that most of the ointment in this world has a fly in it, like in the Bible, for fine as my location was, I soon knew that I should ask Laddie to put me down, because the window behind me didn't fit its frame, and the night was bitter. Before half an hour I was stiff with cold; but I doubt if I would have given up that location if I had known I would freeze, because this was the most fun I had ever seen.

Miss Amelia began with McGuffey's spelling book, and whenever some poor unfortunate made a bad break the crowd roared with laughter. Peter Justice stood up to spell and before three rounds he was nodding on his feet, so she pronounced "sleepy" to him. Some one nudged Pete and he waked up and spelled it, s-l-e, sle, p-e, pe, and because he really was so sleepy it made every one laugh. James Whittaker spelled compromise with a k, and Isaac Thomas spelled soap, s-o-a-p-e, and it was all the funnier that he couldn't spell it, for from his looks you could tell that he had no acquaintance with it in any shape. Then Miss Amelia gave out "marriage" to the spooniest young man in the district, and "stepfather" to a man who was courting a widow with nine children; and "coquette" to our Shelley, who had been making sheep's eyes at Johnny Myers, so it took her by surprise and she joined the majority, which by that time occupied seats.

There was much laughing and clapping of hands for a time, but when Miss Amelia had let them have their fun and thinned the lines to half a dozen on each side who could really spell, she began business, and pronounced the hardest words she could find in the book, and the spellers caught them up and rattled them off like machines.

"Incompatibility," she gave out, and before the sound of her voice died away the Princess was spelling: "I-n, in, c-o-m, com, incom, p-a-t, pat, incompat, i, incompati, b-i-l, bil, incompatibil, i, incompatibili, t-y, ty, incompatibility."

Then Laddie spelled "incomprehensibility," and they finished up the "bilities" and the "alities" with a rush and changed McGuffey's for Webster, with five on Laddie's side and three on the Princess', and when they quit with it, the Princess was alone, and Laddie and our little May facing her.

From that on you could call it real spelling. They spelled from the grammars, hyperbole, synecdoche, and epizeuxis. They spelled from the physiology, chlorophyll, coccyx, arytenoid, and the names of the bones and nerves, and all the hard words inside you. They tried the diseases and spelled jaundice, neurasthenia, and tongue-tied. They tried all the occupations and professions, and went through the stores and spelled all sorts of hardware, china and dry goods. Each side kept cheering its own and urging them to do their best, and every few minutes some man in the back of the house said something that was too funny. When Miss Amelia pronounced "bombazine" to Laddie our side cried, "Carcful, Laddie, careful! you're out of your element!"

And when she gave "swivel-tree" to the Princess, her side whispered, "Go easy! Do you know what it is? Make her define it."

They branched over the country. May met her Jonah on the mountains. Katahdin was too much for her, and Laddie and the Princess were left to fight it out alone. I didn't think Laddie liked it. I'm sure he never expected it to turn out that way. He must have been certain he could beat her, for after he finished English there were two or three other languages he knew, and every one in the district felt that he could win, and expected him to do it. It was an awful place to put him in, I could see that. He stood a little more erect than usual, with his eyes toward the Princess, and when his side kept crying, "Keep the prize, Laddie! Hold up the glory of the district!" he ground out the words as if he had a spite at them for not being so hard that he would have an excuse for going down.

The Princess was poised lightly on her feet, her thick curls, just touching her shoulders, shining in the light; her eyes like stars, her perfect, dark oval face flushed a rich red, and her deep bosom rising and falling with excitement. Many times in later years I have tried to remember when the Princess was loveliest of all, and that night always stands first.

I was thinking fast. Laddie was a big man. Men were strong on purpose so they could bear things. He loved the Princess so, and he didn't know whether she loved him or not; and every marriageable man in three counties was just aching for the chance to court her, and I didn't feel that he dared risk hurting her feelings.

Laddie said, to be the man who conquered the Princess and to whom she lifted her lips for a first kiss was worth life itself. I

made up my mind that night that he knew just exactly what he
was talking about. I thought so too. And I seemed to understand
why Laddie—Laddie in his youth, strength, and manly beauty,
Laddie, who boasted that there was not a nerve in his body—
trembled before the Princess.

It looked as if she had set herself against him and was working
for the honours, and if she wanted them, I didn't feel that he
should chance beating her, and then, too, it was beginning to be
plain that it was none too sure he could. Laddie didn't seem to
be the only one who had been well drilled in spelling.

I held my jaws set a minute, so that I could speak without
Laddie knowing how I was shivering, and then I whispered:
"Except her eyes are softer, she looks just like a cardinal."

Laddie nodded emphatically and moving a step nearer laid his
elbow across my knees. Heavens, how they spelled! They finished
all the words I ever heard and spelled like lightning through a lot
of others the meaning of which I couldn't imagine. Father never
gave them out at home. They spelled epiphany, gaberdine, ich-
thyology, gewgaw, kaleidoscope, and troubadour. Then Laddie
spelled one word two different ways; and the Princess went him
one better, for she spelled another three.

They spelled from the Bible, Nebuchadnezzar, Potiphar, Peleg,
Belshazzar, Abimelech, and a host of others I never heard the
minister preach about. Then they did the most dreadful thing of
all. "Broom," pronounced the teacher, and I began mentally,
b-r-o-o-m, but Laddie spelled "b-r-o-u-g-h-a-m," and I stared at
him in a daze. A second later Miss Amelia gave out "Beecham"
to the Princess, and again I tried it, b-e-e-c-h, but the Princess
was spelling "B-e-a-u-c-h-a-m-p," and I almost fell from the
window.

They kept that up until I was nearly crazy with nervousness;
I forgot I was half frozen. I pulled Laddie's sleeve and whispered
in his ear: "Do you think she'll cry if you beat her?"

I was half crying myself, the strain had been awful. I was torn
between these dearest loves of mine.

"Seen me have any chance to beat her?" retorted Laddie.

Miss Amelia seemed to have used most of her books, and at last picked up an old geography and began giving out points around the coast, while Laddie and the Princess took turns snatching the words from her mouth and spelling them. Father often did that, so Laddie was safe there. They were just going it when Miss Amelia pronounced, "Terra del Fuego," to the Princess. "T-e-r-r-a, Terra, d-e-l, del, F-i-e-u-g-o," spelled the Princess, and sat down suddenly in the midst of a mighty groan from her side, swelled by a wail from one little home district deserter.

"Next!" called Miss Amelia.

"T-e-r-r-a, Terra, d-e-l, del, F-e-u-g-o," spelled Laddie.

"Wrong!" wailed Miss Amelia, and our side breathed one big groan in concert, and I lifted up my voice in that also. Then every one laughed and pretended they didn't care, and the Princess came over and shook hands with Laddie, and Laddie said to Miss Amelia: "Just let me take that book a minute until I see how the thing really does go." It was well done and satisfied the crowd, which clapped and cheered; but as I had heard him spell it many, many times for father, he didn't fool me.

Laddie and the Princess drew slips for the book and it fell to her. He was so pleased he kissed me as he lifted me down and never noticed I was so stiff I could scarcely stand—and I did fall twice going to the sleigh. My bed was warm and my room was warm, but I chilled the night through and until the next afternoon, when I grew so faint and sleepy I crept to Miss Amelia's desk, half dead with fright—it was my first trip to ask an excuse —and begged: "Oh teacher, I'm so sick. Please let me go home."

I think one glance must have satisfied her that it was true, for she said very kindly that I might, and she would send Leon along to take care of me. But my troubles were only half over when I had her consent. It was very probable I would be called a baby and sent back when I reached home, so I refused company and started alone. It seemed a mile past the cemetery. I was so tired I stopped, and leaning against the fence, peeped through at the white stones and the whiter mounds they covered, and wondered how my mother would feel if she were compelled to lay me beside the two little whooping cough and fever sisters already sleeping there. I decided that it would be so very dreadful, that the tears began to roll down my cheeks and freeze before they fell.

Down the Big Hill slowly I went. How bare it looked then! Only leafless trees and dried seed pods rattling on the bushes, the sand frozen, and not a rush to be seen for the thick blanket of snow. A few rods above the bridge was a footpath, smooth and well worn, that led down to the creek, beaten by the feet of children who raced it every day and took a running slide across the ice. I struck into the path as always; but I was too stiff to run, for I tried. I walked on the ice, and being almost worn out, sat on the bridge and fell to watching the water bubbling under the glassy crust. I was so dull a horse's feet struck the bridge before I heard the bells—for I had bells in my ears that day—and when I looked up it was the Princess—the Princess in her red dress and furs, with a silk hood instead of her hat, her sleigh like a picture, with a buffalo robe, that it was whispered about the country, cost over a hundred dollars, and her thoroughbred mare Maud dancing and prancing. "Bless me! Is it you, Little Sister?" she asked. "Shall I give you a ride home?"

Before I could scarcely realize she was there, I was beside her and she was tucking the fine warm robe over me. I lifted a pair of dull eyes to her face.

"Oh Princess, I am so glad you came," I said. "I don't think I could have gone another step if I had frozen on the bridge."

The Princess bent to look in my face. "Why, you poor child!" she exclaimed, "you're white as death! Where are you ill?"

I leaned on her shoulder, though ordinarily I would not have offered to touch her first, and murmured: "I am not ill, outdoors, only dull, sleepy, and freezing with the cold."

"It was that window!" she exclaimed. "I thought of it, but I trusted Laddie."

That roused me a little.

"Oh Princess," I cried, "you mustn't blame Laddie! I knew it was too cold, but I wouldn't tell him, because if he put me down

I couldn't see you, and we thought, but for your eyes being softer, you looked just like a cardinal."

The Princess hugged me close and laughed merrily. "You darling!" she cried.

Then she shook me up sharply: "Don't you dare go to sleep!" she said. "I must take you home first."

Once there she quieted my mother's alarm, put me to bed, drove three miles for Dr. Fenner and had me started nicely on the road to a month of lung fever, before she left. In my delirium I spelled volumes; and the miracle of it was I never missed a word until I came to "Terra del Fuego," and there I covered my lips and stoutly insisted that it was the Princess' secret.

To keep me from that danger sleep on the road, she shook me up and asked about the spelling bee. I thought it was the grandest thing I had ever seen in my life, and I told her so. She gathered me close and whispered: "Tell me something, Little Sister, please."

The minx! She knew I thought that a far finer title than hers.

"Would Laddie care?" I questioned.

"Not in the least!"

"Well then, I will."

"Can Laddie spell 'Terra del Fuego?' " she whispered.

I nodded.

"Are you sure?"

"I have heard him do it over and over for father."

The Princess forgot I was so sick, forgot her horse, forgot everything. She threw her head back and her hands up, until her horse stopped in answer to the loosened line, and she laughed and laughed. She laughed until peal on peal re-echoed from our Big Woods clear across the west eighty. She laughed until her ringing notes set my slow pulses on fire, and started my numbed brain in one last effort. I stood up and took her lovely face between my palms, turning it until I could see whether the thought that had come to me showed in her eyes, and it did.

"Oh you darling, splendid Princess!" I cried. "You missed it on purpose to let Laddie beat! You can spell it too!"

CHAPTER XII

The Horn of the Hunter

"The dusky night rides down the sky,
  And ushers in the morn:
The hounds all join in glorious cry,
  The huntsman winds his horn."

LEON said our house reminded him of the mourners' bench before
any one had "come through." He said it was so deadly with Sally
and Shelley away, that he had a big notion to marry Susie Fall
and bring her over to liven things up a little. Mother said she
thought that would be a good idea, and Leon started in the direction of Falls', but he only went as far as Deams'. When he came
back he had a great story to tell about dogs chasing their sheep,
and foxes taking their geese. Father said sheep were only safe
behind securely closed doors, especially in winter, and geese also.
Leon said every one hadn't as big a barn as ours, and father said
there was nothing to prevent any man from building the sized
barn he needed to shelter his creatures in safety and comfort, if
he wanted to dig in and earn the money to put it up. There was
no answer to that, and Mr. Leon didn't try to make any. Mostly,
he said something to keep on talking, but sometimes he saw when
he had better quit.

I was having a good time, myself. Of course when the fever
was the worst, and when I never had been sick before, it was
pretty bad, but as soon as I could breathe all right, there was no
pain to speak of, and every one was so good to me. I could have
Bobby on the footboard of my bed as long as I wanted him, and
he would crow whenever I told him to. I kept Grace Greenwood
beside me, and spoiled her dress making her take some of each
dose of medicine I did, but Shelley wrote that she was saving

goods and she would make her another as soon as she came home. I made mother put red flannel on Grace's chest and around her neck, until I could hardly find her mouth when she had to take her medicine, but she swallowed it down all right, or she got her nose held, until she did. She was not nearly so sick as I was, though. We both grew better together, and when Dr. Fenner brought me candy, she had her share.

When I began to get well it was lovely. Such toast, chicken broth, and squirrels, as mother always had. I even got the chicken liver, oranges, and all of them gave me everything they had that I wanted—I must almost have died to make them act like that!

Laddie and father would take me up wrapped in blankets and hold me to rest my back. Father would rock me and sing about "Young Johnny," just as he had when I was little. We always laughed at it, we knew it was a fool song, but we liked it. The tune was smooth and sleepy-like and the words went:

"One day young Johnny, he did go,
Way down in the meadow for to mow.
Li-tu-di-nan-incty, tu-di-nan-incty, noddy O!

He scarce had mowed twice round the field,
When a pesky sarpent bit him on the heel,
Li-tu-di-nan-incty, tu-di-nan-incty, noddy O!

He threw the scythe upon the ground,
An' shut his eyes, and looked all round,
Li-tu-di-nan-incty, tu-di-nan-incty, noddy O!

He took the sarpent in his hand,
And then ran home to Molly Bland,
Li-tu-di-nan-incty, tu-di-nan-incty, noddy O!

O Molly dear, and don't you see,
This pesky sarpent that bit me?
Li-tu-di-nan-incty, tu-di-nan-incty, noddy O!

O Johnny dear, why did you go,
Way down in the meadow for to mow?
Li-tu-di-nan-incty, tu-di-nan-incty, noddy O!

O Molly dear, I thought you knowed
'Twas daddy's grass, and it must be mowed,
Li-tu-di-nan-incty, tu-di-nan-incty, noddy O!

Now all young men a warning take,
And don't get bit by a rattlesnake.
Li-tu-di-nan-incty, tu-di-nan-incty, noddy O!"

All of them told me stories, read to me, and Frank, one of my big gone-away brothers, sent me the prettiest little book. It had a green cover with gold on the back, and it was full of stories and poems, not so very hard, because I could read every one of them, with help on a few words. The piece I liked best was poetry. If it hadn't been for that, I'm afraid, I was having such a good time, I'd have lain there until I forgot how to walk, with all of them trying to see who could be nicest to me. The ones who really could, were Laddie and the Princess, except mother. Laddie lifted me most carefully, the Princess told the best stories, but after all, if the burning and choking grew so bad I could scarcely stand it, mother could lay her hand on my head and say, "Poor child," in a way that made me work to keep on breathing. Maybe I only *thought* I loved Laddie best. I guess if I had been forced to take my choice when I had the fever, I'd have stuck pretty tight to mother. Even Dr. Fenner said if I pulled through she'd have to make me. I might have been lying there yet, if it hadn't been for the book Frank sent me, with the poetry piece in it. It began:

"Somewhere on a sunny bank, buttercups are bright,
Somewhere 'mid the frozen grass, peeps the daisy white."

I read that so often I could repeat it quite as well with the book shut as open, and every time I read it, I wanted outdoors worse. In one place it ran:

"Welcome, yellow buttercups, welcome daisies white,
Ye are in my spirit visioned a delight.
Coming in the springtime of sunny hours to tell,
Speaking to our hearts of Him who doeth all things well."

That piece helped me out of bed, and the blue gander screaming opened the door. It was funny about it too. I don't know *why* it worked on me that way; it just kept singing in my heart all day, and I could shut my eyes and go to sleep seeing buttercups in a gold sheet all over our Big Hill, although there never was a single one there; and meadows full of daisies, which were things father said were a pest he couldn't tolerate, because they spread so, and he grubbed up every one he found. Yet that piece filled our meadow until I imagined I could roll on daisies. They might be a pest to farmers, but sheets of them were pretty good if you were burning with fever. Between the buttercups and the daisies I left the bed with a light head and wobbly legs.

Of course I wasn't an idiot. I knew when I looked from our south window exactly what was to be seen. The person who wrote that piece was the idiot. It sang and sounded pretty, and it pulled you up and pushed you out, but really it was a fool thing, as I very well knew. I couldn't imagine daisies peeping through frozen grass. Any baby should have known they bloomed in July. Skunk cabbage always came first, and hepatica. If I had looked from any of our windows and seen daisies and buttercups in March, I'd have fallen over with the shock. I knew there would be frozen brown earth, last year's dead leaves, caved-in apple and potato holes, the cabbage row almost gone, puddles of water and mud everywhere, and I would hear geese scream and hens sing. And yet that poem kept pulling and pulling, and I was happy as a queen—I wondered if they were for sure; mother had doubts— the day I was wrapped in shawls and might sit an hour in the sun on the top board of the back fence, where I could see the barn, orchard, the creek and the meadow, as you never could in summer because of the leaves. I wasn't looking for buttercups and daisies either. I mighty well knew there wouldn't be any.

But the sun was there. A little taste of willow, oak and maple was in the air. You could see the buds growing fat too, and you could smell them. If you opened your eyes and looked in any direction you could see blue sky, big, ragged white clouds, bare trees, muddy earth with grassy patches, and white spots on the shady sides where unmelted snow made the icy feel in the air, even when the sun shone. You couldn't hear yourself think for the clatter of the turkeys, ganders, roosters, hens, and everything that had a voice. I was so crazy with it I could scarcely hang to the fence; I wanted to get down and scrape my wings like the gobbler, and scream louder than the gander, and crow oftener than the rooster. There was everything all ice and mud. They would have frozen, if they hadn't been put in a house at night, and starved, if they hadn't been fed; they were not at the place where they could hunt and scratch, and not pay any attention to feeding time, because of being so bursting full. They had no nests and babies to rejoice over. But there they were! And so was I! Buttercups and daisies be-hanged! Ice and mud really! But if you breathed that air, and shut your eyes, north, you could see blue flags, scarlet lilies, buttercups, cattails and redbirds sailing over them; east, there would be apple bloom and soft grass, cowslips, and bubbling water, robins, thrushes, and bluebirds; and south, waving corn with wild rose and alder borders, and sparrows, and larks on every fence rider.

Right there I got that daisy thing figured out. It wasn't that there were or ever would be daisies and buttercups among the frozen grass; but it was forever and always that when this *feel* came into the air, you knew they were *coming. That* was what ailed the gander and the gobbler. They hadn't a thing to be thankful for yet, but something inside them was swelling and pushing because of what was coming. I felt exactly as they did, because I wanted to act the same way, but I'd been sick enough to know that I'd better be thankful for the chance to sit on the fence, and think about buttercups and daisies. Really, one old brown and purple skunk cabbage with a half-frozen bee buzzing over it, or a few forlorn little spring beauties, would have set me wild, and when a lark really did go over, away up high, and a dove began to coo in the orchard, if Laddie hadn't come for me, I would have fallen from the fence.

I simply had to get well and quickly too, for the wonderful time was beginning. It was all very well to lie in bed when there was nothing else to do, and every one would pet me and give me things; but here was maple syrup time right at the door, and the sugar camp most fun alive; here was all the neighbourhood crazy mad at the foxes, and planning a great chase covering a circuit of miles before the ground thawed; here was Easter and all the children coming, except Shelley—again, it would cost too much for only one day—and with everything beginning to hum, I found out there would be more amusement outdoors than inside. That was how I came to study out the daisy piece. There was nothing in the silly, untrue lines: the pull and tug was in what they made you think of.

I was still so weak I had to take a nap every day, so I wasn't sleepy as early at night, and I heard father and mother talk over a lot of things before they went to bed. After they mentioned it, I remembered that we hadn't received nearly so many letters from Shelley lately, and mother seldom found time to read them aloud during the day and forgot, or her eyes were tired, at night.

"Are you worrying about Shelley?" asked father one night.

"Yes, I am," answered mother.

"What do you think is the trouble?"

"I'm afraid things are not coming out with Mr. Paget as she hoped."

"If they don't, she is going to be unhappy?"

"That's putting it mildly."

"Well, I was doubtful in the beginning."

"Now hold on," said mother. "So was I; but what are you going to do? I can't go through the world with my girls, and meet men for them. I trained them just as carefully as possible before I started them out; that was all I could do. Shelley knows when a man appears clean, decent and likable. She knows when his calling is respectable. She knows when his speech is proper, his manners correct, and his ways attractive. She found this man all of these things, and she liked him accordingly. At Christmas she told me about it freely."

"Have you any idea how far the thing has gone?"

"She said then that she had seen him twice a week for two

months. He seemed very fond of her. He had told her he cared
more for her than any girl he ever had met, and he had asked her
to come here this summer and pay us a visit, so she wanted to
know if he might."

"Of course you told her yes."

"Certainly I told her yes. I wish now we'd saved money and
you'd gone to visit her and met him when she first wrote of him.
You could have found out who and what he was, and with your
experience you might have pointed out signs that would have
helped her to see, before it was too late."

"What do you think is the trouble?"

"I wish I knew! She simply is failing to mention him in her
letters; all the joy of living has dropped from them, she merely
writes about her work; and now she is beginning to complain of
homesickness and to say that she doesn't know how to endure the
city any longer. There's something wrong."

"Had I better go now?"

"Too late!" said mother, and I could hear her throat go wrong
and the choke come into her voice. "She is deeply in love with
him; he hasn't found in her what he desires; probably he is not
coming any more; what could you do?"

"I could go and see if there is anything I could do?"

"She may not want you. I'll write her to-morrow and suggest
that you or Laddie pay her a visit and learn what she thinks."

"All right," said father.

He kissed her and went to sleep, but mother was awake yet,
and she got up and stood looking down at the church and the two
little white gravestones she could see from her window, until I
thought she would freeze, and she did nearly, for her hands were
cold and the tears falling when she examined my covers, and felt
my face and hands before she went to bed. My, but the mother of
a family like ours is never short of a lot of things to think of! I
had a new one myself. Now what do you suppose there was about
that man?

Of course after having lived all her life with father and Laddie,
Shelley would know how a man should look, and act to be *right;*

and this one must have been right to make her bloom out in winter the way other things do in spring; and now what could be wrong? Maybe city girls were prettier than Shelley. But all women were made alike on the outside, and that was as far as you could see. You couldn't find out whether they had pure blood, true hearts, or clean souls. No girl could be so very much prettier than Shelley; they simply were not made that way. She knew how to behave; she had it beaten into her, like all of us. And she knew her books, what our schools could teach her, and Groveville, and Lucy, who had city chances for years, and there never was a day at our house when books and papers were not read and discussed, and your spelling was hammered into you standing in rows against the wall, and memory tests—what on earth could be the matter with Shelley that a man who could make her look and act as she did at Christmas, would now make her unhappy? Sometimes I wanted to be grown up dreadfully, and again, times like that, I wished my bed could stay in mother's room, and I could creep behind father's paper and go to sleep between his coat and vest, and have him warm my feet in his hands forever.

This world was too much for me. I never worked and worried in all my life as I had over Laddie and the Princess, and Laddie said I, myself, never would know how I had helped him. Of course nothing was settled; he had to try to make her love him by teaching her how lovable he was. We knew, because we always had known him, but she was a stranger and had to learn. It was mighty fine for him that he could force his way past the dogs, Thomas, the other men, her half-crazy father, and through the locked door, and go there to try to make her see, on Sunday nights, and week days, every single chance he could invent, and he could think up more reasons for going to Pryors' than mother could for putting out an extra wash.

Now just as I got settled a little about him, and we could see they really wanted him there, at least the Princess and her mother did, and Mr. Pryor must have been fairly decent or Laddie never would have gone; and the Princess came to our house to bring me things to eat, and ask how mother was, and once to learn how she embroidered Sally's wedding chemise, and social things like that; and when father acted as if he liked her so much he hadn't a word to say, and mother seemed to begin to feel as if Laddie and the Princess could be trusted to fix it up about God; and the old mystery didn't matter after all; why, here Shelley popped up with another mystery, and it belonged to us. But whatever ailed that man I couldn't possibly think. It had got to be him, for Shelley was so all right at Christmas, it made her look that pretty we hardly knew her.

I was thinking about her until I scarcely could study my lessons, so I could recite to Laddie at night, and not fall so far behind at school. Miss Amelia offered to hear me, but I just begged Laddie, and father could see that he taught me fifty things in a lesson that you could tell to look at Miss Amelia, she never knew. Why, he couldn't hear me read:

> *"We charged upon a flock of geese,*
> *And put them all to flight,*
> *Except one sturdy gander*
> *That thought to show us fight,"*—

without teaching me that the oldest picture in all the world was made of a row of geese, some of which were kinds we then had —the earth didn't seem so old when you thought of that—and how a flock of geese once wakened an army and saved a city, and how far wild geese could fly without alighting in migration, and everything you could think of about geese, only he didn't know why eating the same grass made feathers on geese and wool on sheep. Anyway, Miss Amelia never told you a word but what was in the book, and how to read and spell it. May said that father was very much disappointed in her, and he was never going to hire another teacher until he met and talked with her, no matter what kind of letters she could send. He was not going to help her get a summer school, and O my soul! I hope no one does, for if they do, I have to go, and I'd rather die than go to school in the summer.

Leon came in about that time with more fox stories. Been in

Jacob Hood's chicken house and taken his best Dorking rooster, and father said it was time to do something. He never said a word so long as they took Deams', except they should have barn room for their geese, but when anything was the matter at Hoods' father and mother started doing something the instant they heard of it. So father and Laddie rode around the neighbourhood and talked it over, and the next night they had a meeting at our schoolhouse; men for miles came, and they planned a regular old-fashioned foxchase, and every one was wild about it.

Laddie told it at Pryors' and the Princess wanted to go; she asked to go with him, and if you please, Mr. Pryor wanted to go too, and their Thomas. They attended the meeting to tell how people chase foxes in England, where they seem to hunt them most of the time. Father said: "Thank God for even a foxchase, if it will bring Mr. Pryor among his neighbours and help him to act sensibly." They planned to go away fifteen miles or farther, and form a big circle of men from all directions, some walking in a line, and others riding to bring back any foxes that escape, and with dogs, and guns, to rout out every one they could find, and kill them so they wouldn't take the geese, little pigs, lambs, and Hoods' Dorking rooster. Laddie had a horn that Mr. Pryor gave him, when he told him this country was showing signs of becoming civilized at last; but Leon grinned and said he'd beat that.

Then when you wanted him, he was in the wood house loft at work, but father said he couldn't get into mischief there. He should have seen that churn when it was full of wedding breakfast! One night I begged so hard and promised so faithfully he trusted me; he did often, after I didn't tell about the Station; and I went to the loft with him, and watched him work an hour. He had a hollow limb about six inches through and fourteen long. He had cut and burned it to a mere shell, and then he had scraped it with glass inside and out, until it shone like polished horn. He had shaved the wool from a piece of sheepskin, soaked, stretched, and dried it, and then fitted it over one end of the drumlike thing he had made, and tacked and bound it in a little groove at the edge. He put the skin on damp so he could stretch it tight. Then he punched a tiny hole in the middle, and pulled through it, down inside the drum, a sheepskin thong rolled in resin, with a knot big enough to hold it, and not tear the head. Then he took it under his arm and we slipped across the orchard below the Station, and went into the hollow and tried it.

It worked! I almost fell dead with the first frightful sound. It just bellowed and roared. In only a little while he found different ways to make it sound by his manner of working the tongue. A long, steady, even pull got that kind of a roar. A short, quick one made it bark. A pull half the length of the thong, a pause, and another pull, made it sound like a bark and a yelp. To pull hard and quick, made it go louder, and soft and easy made it whine. Before he had tried it ten minutes he could do fifty things with it that would almost scare the livers out of those nasty old foxes that were taking every one's geese, Dorking roosters, and even baby lambs and pigs. Of course people couldn't stand that; something had to be done!

Even in the Bible it says, "Beware of the little foxes that spoil the vines," and geese, especially blue ones, Dorking roosters, lambs, and pigs were much more valuable than mere vines; so Leon made that awful thing to scare the foxes from their holes— that's in the Bible too, about the holes I mean, not the scaring.

I couldn't sleep for excitement, and mother said I might as well, for it would be at least one o'clock before they would round-up in our meadow below the barn. All the neighbours were to shut up their stock, tie their dogs, or lead them with chains, if they took them, so when the foxes were surrounded, they could catch them alive, and save their skins. I wondered how some of those chasing people, even Laddie, Leon, and father—think of that! father was going too—I wondered how they would have liked to have had something as much bigger than they were, as they were bigger than the foxes, chase them with awful noises, guns and dogs, and catch them alive—to save their skins. No wonder I couldn't sleep! If they had been the foxes, maybe they wouldn't have thought it was so funny; but of course, people just couldn't have even their pigs and lambs taken. We had to have wool to spin yarn for our stockings, weave our blankets and coverlids, and our Sunday winter dresses of white flannel with narrow black crossbars were from the backs of our own sheep, and we had to have ham to fry with eggs, and boil for Sunday night suppers, and bacon to cook the greens with—of course it was all right.

Before it was near daylight I heard Laddie making the kitchen fire, so father got right up, Leon came down, and all of them went to the barn to do the feeding. I wanted to get up too, but mother said I should stay in bed until the house was warm, because if I took more cold I'd be sick again. At breakfast May asked father about when to start for Deams' to be ahead of the chase, and he said by ten o'clock at least; because a fox driven mad by pursuit, dogs, and noise, was a very dangerous thing, and a bite might make hy—the same thing as a mad dog. He said our back barn door opening from the threshing floor would afford a fine view of the meet, but Candace, May, and Miss Amelia wanted to be closer. I might go with them, if they would take good care of me, and they promised to; but when the time came to start, there was such a queer feeling inside me, I thought maybe it was more fever, and with mother would be the best place for me, so I said I wanted to watch from the barn. Father thought that was a capital idea, because I would be on the east side, where there would be sun and no wind, and it would be perfectly safe; also, I really could see what was going on better from that height than on the ground.

The sun was going to shine, but it hadn't peeped above Deams' strawstack when father on his best saddle horse, and Laddie on Flos, rode away, their eyes shining, their faces red, their blood pounding so it made their voices sound excited and different. Leon was to go on foot. Father said he would ride a horse to death. He just grinned and never made a word of complaint. Seemed funny for him.

"I was over having a little confidential chat with my horse, last night," he said, "and next year we'll be in the chase, and we'll show you how to take fences, and cut curves; just you wait!"

"Leon, *don't* build so on that horse," wailed mother. "I'm sure that money was stolen like ours, and the owner will claim it! I feel it in my bones!"

"Aw, shucks!" said Leon. "That money is mine. He won't either!"

When they started, father took Leon behind him to ride as far as the county line. He said he would go slowly, and it wouldn't hurt the horse, but Leon slipped off at Hoods', and said he'd go with their boys, so father let him, because light as Leon was, both of them were quite a load for one horse. Laddie went to ride with the Princess. We could see people moving around in Pryors' barn-yard when our men started. Candace washed, Miss Amelia wiped the dishes, May swept, and all of them made the beds, and then they went to Deams' while I stayed with mother. When she thought it was time, she bundled me up warmly, and I went to the barn. Father had the east doors standing open for me, so I could sit in the sun, hang my feet against the warm boards and see every inch of our meadow where the meet was to be. I was really too warm there, and had to take off the scarf, untie my hood, and unbutton my coat.

It was a trifle muddy, but the frost had not left the ground yet, the sparrows were singing fit to burst, so were the hens. I didn't care much for the music of the hen, but I could see she meant well. She liked her nest quite as much as the red velvet bird with black wings, or the bubbly yellow one, and as for baby chickens, from the first peep they beat a little naked, blind, wobbly tree bird, so any hen had a right to sing for joy because she was going to be the mother of a large family of them. A hen had something to sing about all right, and so had we, when we thought of poached eggs and fried chicken. When I remembered them, I saw that it was no wonder the useful hen warbled so proudlike; but that was all nonsense, for I don't suppose a hen ever tasted poached eggs, and surely she wouldn't be happy over the prospect of being fried. Maybe one reason she sang was because she didn't know what was coming; I hardly think she'd be so tuneful if she did.

Sometimes the geese, shut in the barn, raised an awful clatter, and the horses and cattle complained about being kept from the sunshine and fresh air. You couldn't blame them. I didn't care if the fox hunters never came, there was so much to see, hear, and smell. Bud perfume was stronger than last week, many doves and bluebirds were calling, and three days more of such sunshine would make cross-country riding too muddy to be pleasant. I sat there thinking; grown people never know how much children do think, they have so much time, and so many bothersome things to study out. I heard it behind me, a long, wailing, bellowing roar, and my hood raised right up with my hair. I was in the middle of the threshing floor in a second, in another at the little west door, cut into the big one, opening it a tiny crack to take a peep, and see how close they were.

I could see nothing, but I heard a roar of dreadful sound steadily closing in a circle around me. No doubt the mean old foxes wished then they had let the Dorking roosters alone. Closer it came and more dreadful. Never again did I want to hear such sounds coming at me; even when I knew what was making them. And then away off, beyond Pryors', and Hoods', and Dovers', I could see a line of tiny specks coming toward me, and racing flying things that must have been people on horses riding back and forth to give the foxes no chance to find a hiding place. No chance! Laddie and the Princess, Mr. Pryor and father, all of them were after the bad old foxes; and they were going to get them; because they'd have no chance—— Not with a solid line of men with raving dogs surrounding them, and people on horseback racing after them, no! the foxes would wish now that they had left the pigs and lambs alone. In that awful roaring din, they would wish, oh how they would wish, they were birds and could fly! Fly back to their holes like the Bible said they had, where maybe they *liked* to live, and no doubt they had little foxes there, that would starve when their mammies were caught alive, to save their skins.

To save their skins! I could hear myself breathe, and feel my teeth click, and my knees knock together. And then! Oh dear! There they came across our cornfield. Two of them! And they could fly, almost. At least you could scarcely see that they touched the ground. The mean old things were paying up for the pigs and lambs now. Through the fence, across the road, straight toward me they came. Almost red backs, nearly white beneath, long flying tails, beautiful pointed ears, and long tongues, fire red, hanging from their open mouths; their sleek sides pulsing, and that awful din coming through the woods behind them. One second, the first paused to glance toward either side, and threw back its head to listen. What it saw, and heard, showed it. I guess then it was sorry it ever took people's ham, and their greens, and their blankets; and it could see and hear that it had no chance— to save its skin.

"O Lord! Dear Lord! Help me!" I prayed.

It had to be me, there was no one else. I never had opened the big doors; I thought it took a man, but when I pushed with all my might—and maybe if the hairs of our heads were numbered, and the sparrows counted, there would be a little mercy for the foxes—I asked for help; maybe I got it. The doors went back, and I climbed up the ladder to the haymow a few steps and clung there, praying with all my might: "Make them come in! Dear Lord, make them come in! Give them a chance! Help them to save their skins, O Lord!"

With a whizz and a flash one went past me, skimmed the cider press, and rushed across the hay; then the other. I fell to the floor and the next thing I knew the doors were shut, and I was back at my place. I just went down in a heap and leaned against the wall and shook, and then I laughed and said: "Thank you, Lord! Thank you for helping with the door! And the foxes! The beautiful little red and white foxes! They've got their chance! They'll save their skins! They'll get back to their holes and their babies! Praise the Lord!"

I knew when I heard that come out, that it was exactly like my father said it when Amos Hurd was redeemed. I never knew my father to say it so impressively before, because Amos had been so bad, people really were afraid of him, and father said if once he got started right, he would go at it just as hard as he had gone at wrongdoing. I suppose I shouldn't have said it about a fox, but I could hear them pant like run out dogs; and I could hear myself, and I hadn't been driven from my home and babies, maybe— and chased miles and miles, either.

Then I just shook. They came pounding, roaring and braying right around the barn, and down the lane. The little door flew open and a strange man stuck in his head.

"Shut that door!" I screamed. "You'll let them in on me, and they bite! They're poison! They'll kill me!"

I hadn't even thought of it before.

"See any foxes?" cried the man.

"Two crossed our barnyard headed that way!" I cried back, pointing east. "Shut the door!"

The man closed it and ran calling as he went: "It's all right! They crossed the barnyard. We've got them!"

I began to dance and beat my hands, and then I stopped and held my breath. They were passing, and the noise was dreadful. They struck the sides of the barn, poked around the strawstack, and something made me look up, and at the edge of the hay stood a fox ready to spring. If it did, it would go from the door, right into the midst thereof. Nothing but my red hood sailing straight at it, and a yell I gave, drove it back. No one hit the barn again, the line closed up, and went on at a run now, they were so anxious to meet and see what they had. Then came the beat of hoofs and I saw that all the riders had dropped back, and were behind the line of people on foot. I watched Laddie as he flew past waving to me, and I grabbed my scarf to wave at him. The Princess flashed by so swiftly I couldn't see how she looked, and then I heard a voice I knew cry: "Ep! Ep! Over Lad!" And I almost fell dead where I stood. Mr. Pryor sailed right over the barnyard fence into the cornfield, ripping that dumb-bell as he went, and neck and neck, even with him, on one of his finest horses, was our Leon. His feet were in the stirrups, he had the reins tight, he almost stood as he arose, his face was crimson, his head bare, his white hair flying, the grandest sight you ever saw. At the top of my voice I screamed after them, "Ep! Ep! Over Lad!" and then remembered and looked to see if I had to chase back the foxes, but they didn't mind only me, after what they had been through. Then I sat down suddenly again.

Well! What would father think of that! Leon kill a horse of ours, indeed! There he was on one of Mr. Pryor's, worth as much as six of father's no doubt, flying over fences, and the creek was coming, and the bank was steep behind the barn. I was up again straining to see.

"Ep! Ep! Over!" rang the cry.

There they went! Laddie and the Princess too. I'll never spend another cent on paper dolls, candy, raisins, or oranges. I'll give all I have to help Leon buy his horse; then I'm going to begin saving for mine.

The line closed up, a solid wall of men with sticks, clubs and guns; the dogs raged outside, and those on horseback stopped where they could see best; and inside, raced back and forth, and round and round, living creatures. I couldn't count they moved so, but even at that distance I could see that some were poor little cotton tails. The scared things! A whack over the head, a backward toss, and the dogs were mouthing them. The long tailed, sleek, gracefully moving ones, they were the foxes, the foxes driven from their holes, and nothing on earth could save their skins now; those men meant to have them.

I pulled the doors shut suddenly. I was so sick I could scarcely stand. I had to work, but at last I pushed the west doors open again. I don't think the Lord helped me any that time, for I knew what it took—before, they just went. Or maybe He did help me quite as much, but I had harder work to do my share, because I felt so dizzy and ill. Anyway, they opened. Then I climbed the upright ladder to the top beam, walked it to the granary, and there I danced, pounded and yelled so that the foxes jumped from the hay, leaped lightly to the threshing floor, and stood looking and listening. I gave them time to hear where the dreadful racket was, and then I jumped to the hay and threw the pitchfork at them. It came down smash! and both of them sprang from the door. When I got down the ladder and where I could see, they were so rested they were hiking across the cornfield like they never had raced a step before; and as the clamour went up behind me, that probably meant the first fox had lost its beautiful red and white skin, they reached our woods in safety. The doors went shut easier, and I started to the house crying like any blubbering baby; but when mother turned from the east window, and I noticed her face, I forgot the foxes.

"You saw Leon!" I cried.

"That I did!" she exulted, rocking on her toes the same as she does at the Meeting House when she is going to cry, "Glory!" any minute. "That I did! Ah! the brave little chap! Ah! the fine fellow!"

Her cheeks were the loveliest pink, and her eyes blazed. I scarcely knew her.

"What will father say?"

"If his father isn't every particle as proud of him as I am this day, I've a big disappointment coming," she answered. "If Mr. Pryor chose to let him take that fine horse, and taught him how to ride it, father should be glad."

"If he'd gone into the creek, you wouldn't feel so fine."

"Ah! but he didn't! He didn't! He stuck to the saddle and sailed over in one grand, long sweep! It was fine! I hope—to my soul, I hope his father saw it!"

"He did!" I said. "He did! He was about halfway down the lane. He was where he could see fine."

"You didn't notice——?"

"I was watching if Leon went under. What if he had, mother?"

"They'd have taken him out, and brought him to me, and I'd have worked with all the strength and skill God has given me, and if it were possible to us, he would be saved, and if it were not, it would be a proud moment for a woman to offer a boy like that to the God who gave him. One would have nothing to be ashamed of!"

"Could you do it, like you are now, and not cry, mother?" I asked wonderingly.

"Patience no!" said she. "Before long you will find out, child, that the fountain head of tears and laughter lies in the same spot, deep in a woman's heart. Men were made for big things! They must brave the wild animals, the Indians, fight the battles, ride the races, till the fields, build the homes. In the making of a new country men must have the thing in their souls that carried Leon across the creek. If he had checked that horse and gone to the ford, I would have fallen where I stood!"

"Father crossed the ford!"

"True! But that's different. He never had a chance at a horse like that! He never had time for fancy practice, and his nose would have been between the pages of a book if he had. But remember this! Your father's hand has never faltered, and his aim has never failed. All of us are here, safe and comfortable, through him. It was your father who led us across the wilderness, and fended from us the wildcat, wolf, and Indian. He built this house, cleared this land, and gave to all of us the thing we love. Get this in your head straight. Your father rode a plow horse; he never tried flourishes in riding; but no man can stick in the saddle longer, ride harder, and face any danger with calmer front. If you think this is anything, you should have seen his face the day he stood between me and a band of Indians, we had every reason to think, I had angered to the fighting point."

"Tell me! Please tell me!" I begged.

All of us had been brought up on that story, but we were crazy to hear it, and mother loved to tell it, so she dropped on a chair and began:

"We were alone in a cabin in the backwoods of Ohio. Elizabeth was only nine months old, and father always said a mite the prettiest of any baby we ever had. Many of the others have looked quite as well to me, but she was the first, and he was so proud of her he always wanted me to wait in the wagon until he hitched the horses, so he would get to take and to carry her himself. Well, she was in the cradle, cooing and laughing, and I had my work all done, and cabin shining. I was heating a big poker red-hot, and burning holes into the four corners of a board so father could put legs in it to make me a bench. A greasy old squaw came to the door with her papoose on her back. She wanted to trade berries for bread. There were berries everywhere for the picking; I had more dried than I could use in two years. We planted only a little patch of wheat and father had to ride three days to carry to mill what he could take on a horse. I baked in an outoven and when it was done, a loaf of white bread was by far the most precious thing we had to eat. Sometimes I was caught, and forced to let it go. Often I baked during the night and hid the bread in the wheat at the barn. There was none in the cabin that day and I said so. She didn't believe me. She set her papoose on the floor beside the fireplace, and went to the cupboard. There wasn't a crumb there except cornbread, and she didn't want that. She said: 'Brod! Brod!'

"She learned that from the Germans in the settlement. I shook my head. Then she pulled out a big steel hunting knife, such as the whites traded to the Indians so they would have no trouble in scalping us neatly, and walked to the cradle. She took that knife loosely between her thumb and second finger and holding it directly above my baby's face, she swung it lightly back and forth and demanded: 'Brod! Brod!'

"If the knife fell, it would go straight through my baby's head, and Elizabeth was reaching her little hands and laughing. There was only one thing to do, and I did it. I caught that red-hot poker from the fire, and stuck it so close her baby's face, that the papoose drew back and whimpered. I scarcely saw how she snatched it up and left. When your father came, I told him, and we didn't know what to do. We knew she would come back and bring her band. If we were not there, they would burn the cabin, ruin our crops, kill our stock, take everything we had, and we couldn't travel so far, or so fast, that on their ponies they couldn't overtake us. We endangered any one with whom we sought refuge, so we gripped hands, knelt down and told the Lord all about it, and we felt the answer was to stay. Father cleaned the gun, and hours and hours we waited.

"About ten o'clock the next day they came, forty braves in war paint and feathers. I counted until I was too sick to see, then I took the baby in my arms and climbed to the loft, with our big steel knife in one hand. If your father fell, I was to use it, first on Elizabeth, then on myself. The Indians stopped at the woodyard, and the chief of the band came to the door, alone. Your father met him with his gun in reach, and for a whole eternity they stood searching each other's eyes. I was at the trapdoor where I could see both of them.

"To the depths of my soul I enjoyed seeing Leon take the fence and creek: but what was that, child, to compare with the timber that stood your father like a stone wall between me and forty half-naked, paint besmeared, maddened Indians? Don't let any showing the men of to-day can make set you to thinking that father isn't a king among men. Not once, but again and again in earlier days, he fended danger from me like that. I can shut my eyes and see his waving hair, his white brow, his steel blue eyes, his unfaltering hand. I don't remember that I had time or even thought to pray. I gripped the baby, and the knife, and waited for the thing I must do if an arrow or a shot sailed past the chief and felled father. They stood second after second, like two wooden men, and then slowly and deliberately the chief lighted his big pipe, drew a few puffs and handed it to father. He set down his gun, took the pipe and quite as slowly and deliberately he looked at the waiting band, at the chief, and then raised it to his lips.

" 'White squaw brave! Heap much brave!' said the chief.

" 'In the strength of the Lord. Amen!' said father.

"Then he reached his hand and the chief took it, so I came down the ladder and stood beside father, as the Indians began to file in the front door and out the back. As they passed, every man of them made the peace sign and piled in a heap, venison, fish, and game, while each squaw played with the baby and gave me a gift of beads, a metal trinket, or a blanket she had woven. After that they came often, and brought gifts, and if prowling Gypsies were pilfering, I could look to see a big Indian loom up and seat himself at my fireside until any danger was past. I really got so I liked and depended on them, and father left me in their care when he went to mill, and I was safe as with him. You have heard the story over and over, but to-day is the time to impress on you that an exhibition like *this* is the veriest child's play compared with what I have seen your father do repeatedly!"

"But it was you, the chief said was brave!"

Mother laughed.

"I had to be, baby," she said. "Mother had no choice. There's only one way to deal with an Indian. I had lived among them all my life, and I knew what must be done."

"I think both of you were brave," I said, "you, the bravest!"

"Quite the contrary," laughed mother. "I shall have to confess that what I did happened so quickly I'd no time to think. I only realized the coal red iron was menacing the papoose when it drew back and whimpered. Father had all night to face what was coming to him, and it was not one to one, but one to forty, with as many more squaws, as good fighters as the braves, to back them. It was a terror, but I never have been sorry we went through it together. I have rested so securely in your father ever since."

"And he is as safe in you," I insisted.

"As you will," said mother. "This world must have her women quite as much as her men. It is shoulder to shoulder, heart to heart, business."

The door flew open and Leon ran in. He was white with excitement, and trembling.

"Mother, come and see me take a fence on Pryor's Rocket!" he cried.

Mother had him in her arms.

"You little whiffet!" she said. "You little tow-haired whiffet!"

Both of them were laughing and crying at the same time, and so was I.

"I saw you take one fence and the creek, Weiscope!" she said, holding him tight, and stroking his hair. "That will do for to-day. Ride the horse home slowly, rub it down if they will allow you, and be sure to remember your manners when you leave. To trust such a child as you with so valuable a horse, and for Mr. Pryor to personally ride with you and help you, I think that was a big thing for a man like him to do."

"But, mother, he's been showing me for weeks, or I couldn't have done it to-day. It was our secret to surprise you. When I get *my* horse, I'll be able to ride a little, as well as Mr. Laddie."

"Leon, don't," said mother, gripping him tighter. "You must bear in mind, word about that money may come any day."

"Aw, it won't either," said Leon, pulling away. "And say, mother, that dumb-bell was like country boys make in England. He helped me hunt the wood and showed me, and I couldn't ride and manage it, so he had it all day, and you should have heard him make it rip. Say, mother, take my word, he was some pumpkins in England. I bet he ordered the Queen around, when he was there!"

"No doubt!" laughed mother, kissing him and pushing him from the door.

Some people are never satisfied. After that splendid riding and the perfect day, father, Leon, and Laddie came home blaming every one, and finding fault, and trying to explain how it happened, that the people from the east side claimed two foxes, and there was only one left for the west side, when they had seen and knew they had driven three for miles. They said they lost them in our Big Woods.

I didn't care one speck. I would as lief wear a calico dress, and let the little foxes have their mammies to feed them; and I was willing to bet all my money that we would have as much ham, and as many greens next summer as we ever had. And if the foxes took Hoods' Dorkings again, let them build a coop with safe foundations. The way was to use stone and heap up dirt around it in the fall, to be perfectly sure, and make it warmer.

We took care of our chickens because we had to have them. All the year we needed them, but most especially for Easter. Mother said that was ordained chicken time. Turkeys for Thanksgiving, sucking pigs for Christmas, chickens for Easter, goose, she couldn't abide. She thought it was too strong. She said the egg was a symbol of life; of awakening, of birth, and the chickens came from the eggs, first ones about Easter, so that proved it was chicken time.

I am going to quit praying about little things I can manage myself. Father said no prayer would bring an answer unless you took hold and pulled with all your being for what you wanted. I had been intending for days to ask the Lord to help me find where Leon hid his Easter eggs. It had been the law at our house from the very first, that for the last month before Easter, aside from what mother had to have for the house, all of us might gather every egg we could find and keep them until Easter. If we could locate the hiding place of any one else, we might take all theirs. The day before Easter they were brought in, mother put aside what she required, and the one who had the most got to sell all of them and take the money. Sometimes there were two wash-tubs full, and what they brought was worth having, for sure. So we watched all year for safe places, and when the time came we almost ran after the hens with a basket. Because Laddie and Leon were bigger they could outrun us, and lots of hens laid in the barn, so there the boys always had first chance. Often during the month we would find and take each other's eggs a dozen times. We divided them, and hid part in different places, so that if either were found there would still be some left.

Laddie had his in the hopper of the cider press right on the threshing floor, and as he was sure to get more than I had anyway, I usually put mine with his. May had hers some place, and where Leon had his, none of us could find or imagine. I almost lay awake of nights trying to think, and every time I thought of a new place, the next day I would look, and they wouldn't be there. Three days before Easter, mother began to cook and get the big dinner ready, and she ran short of eggs. She told me to go to the barn and tell the boys that each of them must send her a dozen as quickly as they could. Of course that was fair, if she made both give up the same number. So I went to the barn.

The lane was muddy, and as I had been sick, I wore my rubbers that spring. I thought to keep out of the deep mud, where horses and cattle trampled, I'd go up the front embankment, and enter the little door. My feet made no sound, and it so happened that the door didn't either, and as I started to open it, I saw Leon disappearing down the stairway, with a big sack on his back. I thought it was corn for the horses, and followed him, but he went to the cow stable door and started toward the lane, and then I thought it was for the pigs, so I called Laddie and told him about the eggs. He said he'd give me two dozen of his, and Leon could pay him back. We went together to get them, and there was only one there.

Wasn't that exactly like Leon? Leave *one* for a nest egg! If he were dying and saw a joke or a trick, he'd stop to play it before he finished, if he possibly could. If he had no time at all, then he'd go with his eyes twinkling over the thoughts of the fun it would have been if he possibly could have managed it. Of course when we saw that one lonely egg in the cider hopper, just exactly like the "Last Rose of Summer, left to pine on the stem," I thought of the sack Leon carried, and knew what had been in it. We hurried out and tried to find him, but he was swallowed up. You couldn't see him or hear a sound of him anywhere.

Mother was as cross as she ever gets. Right there she made a new rule, and it was that two dozen eggs must be brought to the house each day, whether any were hidden or not. She had to stop baking until she got eggs.

Laddie looked pretty glum when he had to admit he had no eggs; so Leon had to hand over the whole two dozen. Leon didn't mind that, but he said if he must, then all of us should stay in the dining-room until he brought them, because of course he couldn't walk straight and get them in broad daylight with us watching, and not show where they were. Father said that was fair, so Leon went out and before so very long he came back with the eggs.

I thought until my skull almost cracked, about where he *could* have gone, and I was almost to the place where the thing seemed serious enough that I'd ask the Lord to help me find Laddie's eggs, when mother sent me to the garret for red onion skins. She had an hour to rest, and she was going to spend it fixing decorations for our eggs. Of course there were always red and black aniline ones, and yellow and blue, but none of us ever liked them half so well as those mother coloured, herself.

She took the dark red skins and cut boys, girls, dogs, cats, stars, flowers, butterflies, fish, and everything imaginable, and wet the skins a little and laid them on very white eggs that had been soaked in alum water to cut the grease, and then wrapped light yellow skins over, and then darker ones, and at last layer after layer of cloth, and wet that, and roasted them an hour in hot ashes and then let them cool and dry, before unwrapping. When she took them out, rubbed on a little grease and polished them—there they were! They would have our names, flowers, birds, animals, all in pale yellow, deep rich brown, almost red, and perfectly beautiful colours, while you could hunt and hunt before you found everything on one egg. And sometimes the onion skins slipped, and made things of themselves that she never put on.

I was coming from the bin with an apron full of skins and I almost fell over. I couldn't breathe for a long time. I danced on my toes, and held my mouth to keep from screaming. On the garret floor before me lay a little piece of wet mud, and the faintest outline of a boot, a boot about Leon's size. That was all I needed to know. As soon as I could hold steady, I took the skins to mother, slipped back and hunted good; and of course I had to find them—grain sacks half full of them—carried in the front door in the evening, and up the front stairs, where no one went until bedtime, unless there were company. Away back under the eaves, across the joists, behind the old clothing waiting to be ripped, coloured and torn for carpet rags and rugs, Mr. Leon had almost every egg that had been laid on the place for a month. *Now* he'd see what he'd get for taking Laddie's!

Then I stopped short. What I thought most made me sick, but I didn't propose to lie in bed again for a year at least, for it had its bad parts as well as its good; so I went straight and whispered to Laddie. He never looked pleased at all, so I knew I had been right. He kissed me, and thanked me, and then said slowly: "It's mighty good of you, Little Sister, but you see it wouldn't be *fair*. He found mine himself, so he had a right to take them. But I don't dare touch his, when you tell me where they are."

Then I went to father and he laughed. How he did laugh!

"Laddie is right!" he said at last. "He didn't find them, and he mustn't take them. But you may! They're yours! That front door scheme of Leon's was fairly well, but it wasn't quite good enough. If he'd cleaned his feet as he should, before he crossed mother's carpet and climbed the stairs, he'd have made it all right. 'His tracks betrayed him,' as tracks do all of us, if we are careless enough to leave any. The eggs are yours and to-night is the time to produce them. Where do you want to hide them?"

Well of all things! and after I had stumbled on them without pestering the Lord, either! Just as slick as anything! Mine! I never even thought of it. But when I did think, I liked it. The more I thought, the funnier it grew.

"Under mother's bed," I whispered. "But I never can get them. They're in wheat sacks, and full so high, and they'll have to be handled like eggs."

"I'll do the carrying. Come show me!"

So we took the eggs, and put them under mother's bed.

Of course she and Candace saw us, but they didn't hunt eggs and they'd never tell. If ever I thought I'd burst wide open! About dusk I saw Leon coming from the barn carrying his hat at his side—more eggs—so I ran like a streak and locked the front door, and then slipped back in the dining-room and almost screamed, when I could hear him trying it, and he couldn't get in. After a while he came in, fussed around, and finally went into the sitting-room, and the key turned and he went upstairs. I knew I wouldn't dare look at him when he came down, so I got a reader and began on a piece I just love:

"*A nightingale made a mistake;*
She sang a few notes out of tune:
Her heart was ready to break,
And she hid away from the moon."

When I did get a peep, gracious but he was black! Maybe it wasn't going to be much fun after all. But he had the money last year, and the year before, and if he'd cleaned his feet well—I was not hunting his eggs, when I found them. "His tracks betrayed him," as father said. I was thankful supper was ready just then, and while it was going on mother said: "As soon as you finish, all bring in your eggs. I want to wrap the ones to colour to-night, and bury them in the fireplace so they will colour, dry, and be ready to open in the morning."

No one said a word, but neither Laddie nor Leon looked very happy, and I took awful bites to keep my face straight. When all of us finished May brought a lot from the bran barrel in the smoke house, but Laddie and Leon only sat there and looked silly; it really was funny.

"I must have more eggs than this," said mother. "Where are they to come from?"

Father nodded to me and I said: "From under your bed!"

"Oh, it was you! And I never once caught you snooping!" cried Leon.

"Easy son!" said father. "That will do. You lost through your own carelessness. You left wet mud on the garret floor, and she saw it when mother sent her for the onion skins. You robbed Laddie of his last egg this morning; be a good loser yourself!"

"Well, anyway, you didn't get 'em," said Leon to Laddie. "And she only found them by accident!"

Then we had a big time counting all those eggs, and such another heap as there was to sell, after mother filled baskets to cook and colour. When the table was cleared, Laddie and Leon made tallow pencils from a candle and wrote all sorts of things over eggs that had been prepared to colour. Then mother boiled them in copperas water, and aniline, and all the dyes she had, and the boys polished them, and they stood in shining black, red, blue, and yellow heaps. The onion ones would be done in the morning. Leon had a goose egg and mother let him keep it, so he wrote and wrote on it, until Laddie said it would be all writing, and no colour, and he boiled it in red, after mother finished, and polished it himself. It came out real pretty with roses on it and lots of words he wouldn't let any of us read; but of course it was for Susie Fall.

Next morning he slipped it to her at church. When we got home, all of us were there except Shelley, and we had a big din-

ner and a fine time and Laddie stayed until after supper, before
he went to Pryors'.

"How is he making it?" asked Sally.

You could see she was making it all right; she never looked
lovelier, and mother said Peter was letting her spend away too
much money on her clothes. She told him so, but Peter just
laughed and said business was good, and he could afford it, and
she was a fine advertisement for his store when she was dressed
well.

"All I know is," said mother, "that he goes there every whip-
stitch, and the women, at least, seem glad to have him. He says
Mr. Pryor treats him decently, and that is more than he does his
own family and servants. He and the girl and her mother are
divided about something. She treats her father respectfully, but
she's in sympathy with her mother."

"Laddie can't find out what the trouble is?"

"I don't think that he tries."

"Maybe he'd feel better not to know," said Peter.

"Possibly!" said mother.

"Nonsense!" said father.

CHAPTER XIII

The Garden of the Lord

"With what content and merriment,
Their days are spent, whose minds are bent
To follow the useful plow."

THAT spring I decided if school didn't stop pretty soon, I'd run away again, and I didn't in the least care what they did to me. A country road was all right and it was good enough, if it had been heaped up, levelled and plenty of gravel put on; and of course our road would be fine because father was one of the commissioners, and as long as he filled that office, every road in the county would be just as fine as the law would allow him to make it. I have even heard him tell mother that he "stretched it a leetle mite," when he was forced to by people who couldn't seem to be made to understand what was required to upbuild a nation. He said our language was founded on the alphabet, and to master it you had to begin with "a." And he said the nation was like that; it was based on townships, and when a township was clean, had good roads, bridges, schoolhouses, and churches, a county was in fine shape, and when each county was in order, the state was right, and when the state was prosperous, the nation could rejoice in its strength.

He said Atlas in the geography book, carrying the world on his back, was only a symbol, but it was a good one. He said when the county elected him to fill an important office, it used his shoulder as a prop for the nation, so it became his business to stand firmly, and use every ounce of strength and brains he had, first of all to make his own possessions a model, then his township, his county, and his state, and if every one worked together doing that, no nation on earth had our amount of territory and such fine weather, so none of them could beat us.

Our road was like the barn floor, where you drove: on each side was a wide grassy strip, and not a weed the length of our land. All the rails in the fences were laid straight, the gates were solid, sound, and swung firmly on their beams, our fence corners were full of alders, wild roses, sumac, blackberry vines, masses of wild flowers beneath them, and a bird for every bush. Some of the neighbours thought that to drive two rails every so often, lay up the fences straight, and grub out the shrubs was the way, but father said they were vastly mistaken. He said that was such a shortsighted proceeding, he would be ashamed to indulge in it. You did get more land, but if you left no place for the birds, the worms and insects devoured your crops, and you didn't raise half so much as if you furnished the birds shelter and food. So he left mulberries in the fields and fence corners and wild cherries, raspberries, grapes, and every little scrub apple tree from seeds sown by Johnny Appleseed when he crossed our land.

Mother said those apples were so hard a crane couldn't dent them, but she never watched the birds in winter when snow was beginning to come and other things were covered up. They swarmed over those trees until spring, for the tiny sour apples stuck just like oak leaves waiting for next year's crop to push them off. She never noticed us, either. After a few frosts, we could get tipsy on those apples; there was not a tree in our orchard that had the spicy, teasing tang of Johnny Appleseed's apples. Then too, the limbs could be sawed off and rambo and maiden's-blush grafted on, if you wanted to; father did on some of them, so there would be good apples lying beside the road for passers-by, and they needn't steal to get them. You could graft red haws on them too, and grow great big, little haw-apples, that were the prettiest things you ever saw, and the best to eat. Father said if it didn't spoil the looks of the road, he wouldn't care how many of his neighbours straightened their fences. If they did, the birds would come to him, and the more he had, the fewer bugs and worms he would be troubled with, so he would be sure of big crops and sound fruit. He said he would much rather have a few good apples picked by robins or jays, than untouched trees, loaded with wormy falling ones he could neither use nor sell. He always patted my head and liked every line of it when I recited, sort of cheerful-like and pathetic:

"Don't kill the birds! the happy birds,
*   That bless the field and grove;*
* So innocent to look upon,*
*   They claim our warmest love."*

The roads crossing our land were all right, and most of the others near us; and a road is wonderful, if it is taking you to the woods or a creek or meadow; but when it is walking you straight to a stuffy little schoolhouse where you must stand up to see from a window, where a teacher is cross as fire, like Miss Amelia, and where you eternally *hear* things you can't see, there comes a time about the middle of April when you had quite as soon die as to go to school any longer; and what you learn there doesn't amount to a hill of beans compared with what you can find out for your-self outdoors.

Schoolhouses are made wrong. If they must be, they should be built in a woods pasture beside a stream, where you could wade, swim, and be comfortable in summer, and slide and skate in winter. The windows should be cut to the floor, and stand wide open, so the birds and butterflies could pass through. You ought to learn your geography by climbing a hill, walking through a valley, wading creeks, making islands in them, and promontories, capes, and peninsulas along the bank. You should do your arith-metic sitting under trees adding hickorynuts, subtracting walnuts, multiplying butternuts, and dividing hazelnuts. You could use apples for fractions, and tin cups for liquid measure. You could spell everything in sight and this would teach you the words that are really used in the world. Every single one of us could spell incompatibility, but I never heard father, or the judge, or even the Bishop, put it in a speech.

If you simply can't have school *that* way, then you should be shut in black cells, deep under the ground, where you couldn't see, or hear a sound, and then if they'd give you a book and candle and Miss Amelia, and her right-hand man, Mister Ruler, why you might learn something. This way, if you sat and watched the windows you could see a bird cross our woods pasture to the redbird swamp every few minutes; once in a while one of my big hawks took your breath as he swept, soared, sailed, and circled, watching the ground below for rabbits, snakes, or chickens. The skinny old blue herons crossing from the Wabash to hunt frogs in the cowslips swale in our meadow, sailed so slow and so low, that you could see their sharp bills stuck out in front, their uneven, ragged looking feathers, and their long legs trailing out behind. I bet if Polly Martin wore a blue calico dress so short her spindle-shanks showed, and flew across our farm, you couldn't tell her from a heron.

There were so many songs you couldn't decide which was which to save you; it was just a pouring jumble of robins, larks, doves, blackbirds, sparrows, everything that came that early; the red and yellow birds had not come yet, or the catbirds or thrushes. You could hear the thumping wings of the roosters in Sills' barnyard nearest the schoolhouse, and couldn't tell which was whipping, so you had to sit there and wonder; the worst of all you must stand Miss Amelia calmly telling you to pay attention to your books or you would be kept in, and all the time you were forced to bear torments, while you watched her walk from window to window to see every speck of the fight. One day they had thumped and fought for half an hour; she had looked from every window in the room, and at last there was an awful whacking, and then a silence. It grew so exciting I raised my hand, and almost before she nodded permission, "Which whipped?" I asked.

Miss Amelia turned red as a beet. Gee, but she was mad!

"I did!" she said. "Or at least I will. You may remain for it after school is dismissed."

Now if you are going to be switched, they never do it until they are just so angry anyway, and then they always make it as hard as they dare not to stripe you, so it isn't much difference *how* provoked they are, it will be the same old thrashing, and it's sure to sting for an hour at least, so you might as well be beaten for a little more as hardly anything at all. At that instant from the fence not far from my window came a triumphant crow that fairly ripped across the room.

"Oh, it was the Dorking!" I said. "No wonder you followed clear around the room to see him thrash a Shanghai three times his size! I bet a dollar it was great!"

Usually, I wouldn't have put up more than five cents, but at that time I had over six dollars from my Easter eggs, and no girl of my age at our school ever had half that much. Miss Amelia started toward me, and I braced my feet so she'd get a good jolt herself, when she went to shake me; she never struck us over the head since Laddie talked to her that first day; but John Hood's foot was in the aisle. I thought maybe I'd have him for my beau when we grew up, because I bet he knew she was coming, and stuck out his foot on purpose; anyway, she pitched, and had to catch a desk to keep off the floor, and that made her so mad at him, that she forgot me, while he got his scolding; so when my turn came at last, she had cooled down enough that she only marched past to her desk, saying I was to remain after school. I had to be careful after that to be mighty good to May and Leon.

When school was out they sat on the steps before the door and waited. Miss Amelia fussed around and there they sat. Then her face grew more gobblerish than usual, and she went out and told them to go home. Plain as anything I heard May say it: "She's been awful sick, you know, and mother wouldn't allow it." And then Leon piped up: "You *did* watch the roosters, all the time they fought, and of course all of us wanted to see just as badly as you did."

She told them if they didn't go right home she'd bring them back and whip them too; so they had to start, and leave me to my sad fate. I was afraid they had made it sadder, instead of helping me; she was so provoked when she came in she was crying, and over nothing but the plain truth too; if we had storied on her, she'd have had some cause to beller. She arranged her table, cleaned the board, emptied the water bucket, and closed the windows. Then she told me I was a rude, untrained child. I was rude, I suppose, but goodness knows, I wasn't untrained; that was hard on father and mother; I had a big notion to tell them; and then, she never whipped me at all. She said if I wanted her to love me, I mustn't be a saucy, impudent girl, and I should go straight home and think it over.

I went, but I was so dazed at her thinking I wanted her to love me, that I hardly heard May and Leon calling; when I did I went to the cemetery fence and there they lay in the long grass waiting.

"If you cried, we were coming back and pitch into her," said Leon.

There was a pointer. Next time, first cut she gave me, I decided to scream bloody murder. But that would be no Crusader way. There was one thing though. No Crusader ever sat and heard a perfectly lovely fight going on, and never even wondered which whipped.

I wished we lived in the woods the way it was when father and mother were married and moved to Ohio. The nearest neighbours were nine miles, and there wasn't a dollar for school funds, so of course the children didn't have to go, and what their fathers and mothers taught them was all they knew. That would not have helped me much though, for we never had one single teacher who knew anything to compare with what father and mother did, and we never had one who was forever reading books, papers, and learning more things that help, to teach other people. I wished father had time to take our school. It would have been some fun to go to him, because I just knew he would use the woods for the room, and teach us things it would do some good to know about.

I began debating whether it was a big enough thing to bother the Lord with: this being penned up in the schoolhouse droning over spelling and numbers, when you could smell tree bloom, flower bloom, dozens of birds were nesting, and everything was beginning to hum with life. I couldn't think for that piece about "Spring" going over in my head:

> *"I am coming, I am coming:*
> *Hark! the little bee is humming:*
> *See! the lark is soaring high,*
> *In the bright and sunny sky;*
> *All the birds are on the wing:*
> *Little maiden, now is spring."*

I made up my mind that it was of enough importance to call for the biggest prayer I could think of and that I would go up in the barn to the top window, stand on a beam, and turn my face to the east, where Jesus used to be, and I'd wrestle with the Lord for freedom, as Jacob wrestled with the Angel on the banks of the Jabbok in the land of Ammon. I was just getting up steam to pray as hard as ever I could; for days I'd been thinking of it, and I was nearly to the point where one more killdeer crying across the sky would have sent me headlong from the schoolhouse anywhere that my feet were on earth, and the air didn't smell of fried potatoes, kraut, sweat, and dogs, like it did whenever you sat beside Clarissa Polk. When I went to supper one night, father had been to Groveville, and he was busy over his papers. After he finished the blessing, he seemed worried, at last he said the funds were all out, and the county would make no appropriation, so school would have to close next week.

Well that beats me! I had faith in that prayer I was going to make, and here the very thing I intended to ask for happened before I prayed. I decided I would save the prayer until the next time I couldn't stand anything another minute, and then I would try it with all my might and see if it really did any good. After supper I went out the back door, spread my arms wide, and ran down the orchard to the fence in great bounds, the fastest I ever went in my life. I climbed my pulpit in the corner and tried to see how much air my lungs would hold without bursting, while I waved my arms and shouted at the top of my voice: "Praise ye the Lord! Praised be His holy name!"

"Ker-awk!" cried an old blue heron among the cowslips below me. I had almost scared it to death, and it arose on flapping wings and paid me back by frightening me so I screamed as I dodged its shadow.

"What is all this?" asked father behind me.

"Come up and take a seat, and I'll try to tell you," I said.

So he stepped on my pulpit and sat on the top rail, while I stood between his knees, put my arms around his neck, took off his hat and loosened his hair so the wind could wave it, and make his head feel cool and good. His hair curled a little and it was black and fine. His cheeks were pink and his eyes the brightest blue, with long lashes, and heavier brows than any other man I ever have seen. He was the best looking—always so clean and fresh, and you never had to be afraid of him, unless you had been a bad, sinful child. If you were all right, you could walk into his arms, play with his hair, kiss him all you pleased, and there wasn't a thing on earth you couldn't tell him, excepting a secret you had promised to keep.

So I explained all this, and more too. About how I wanted to hunt for the flowers, to see which bloomed first, and watch in what order the birds came, and now it was a splendid time to locate nests, because there were no leaves, so I could see easily, and how glad mother would be to know where the blue goose nested, and her white turkey hen; because she wanted her geese all blue, and the turkeys all white, as fast as she could manage. Every little thing that troubled me or that I wanted, I told him. He sat there and he couldn't have listened with more interest or been quieter if I had been a bishop, which is the biggest thing that ever happened at our house: his name was Ninde and he came from Chicago to dedicate our church when it was new. So father listened and thought and held his arms around me, and kept asking questions until I had not a thing more to tell, then he inquired: "And what were you praising the Lord for, child?"

"Because school is so near out! Because I got what I was going to pray for before I asked."

"And you think the Lord was at the bottom of the thing that makes you happy?"

"Well, you always go to Him about what concerns you, and you say, 'Praise the Lord,' when things go to please you."

"I do indeed!" said father. "But I had thought of this running short of school funds as a calamity. If I had been praying about it, I would have asked Him to show me a way to raise money to continue until middle May at least."

"Oh father!"

I just crumpled up in his arms and began to cry; to save me I couldn't help it. He held me tight. At last he said: "I think you are a little overstrained this spring. Maybe you were sicker than we knew, or are growing too fast. Don't worry any more about school. Possibly father can fix it."

Next morning when I wakened, my everyday clothes lay across the foot of the bed, so I called mother and asked if I should put them on; she took me in her arms, and said father thought I had better be in the open, and I needn't go to school any more that spring. I told her I thought I could bear it a few more days, now it was going to be over so soon; but she said I might stay at home, father and Laddie would hear me at night, and I could take my books anywhere I pleased and study when I chose, if I had my spelling and reading learned at evening. *Now,* say the Lord doesn't help those who call on Him in faith believing!

Think of being allowed to learn your lessons on the top of the granary, where you could look out of a window above the tree-tops, lie in the cool wind, and watch swallows and martins. Think of studying in the pulpit when the creek ran high, and the wild birds sang so sweetly you seemed to hear them for the first time in all your life, and hens, guineas, and turkeys made prime music in the orchard. You could see the buds swell, and the little blue flags push through the grass, where Mrs. Mayer had her flower-bed, and the cowslips greening under the water of the swale at the foot of the hill, while there might be a Fairy under any leaf. I was so full, so swelled up and excited, that when I got ready to pick up a book, I could learn a lesson in a few minutes, tell all about it, spell every word, and read it back, front, and sideways. I never learned lessons so quick and so easy in all my life; father, Laddie, and every one of them had to say so. One night, father said to Laddie: "This child is furnishing evidence that our school system is wrong, and our methods of teaching far from right."

"Or is it merely proof that she is different," said Laddie, "and you can't run her through the same groove you could the rest of us?"

"A little of both," said father, "but most that the system is wrong. We are not going at children in a way to gain and hold their interest, and make them love their work. There must be a better way of teaching, and we should find different teachers. You'll have to try the school next year yourself, Laddie."

"I have a little plan about a piece of land I am hoping to take before then," answered Laddie. "It's time for me to try my wings at making a living, and land is my choice. I have fully decided. I stick to the soil!"

"Amen!" cried father. "You please me mightily. I hate to see sons of mine thriving on law, literally making their living out of the fruit of other men's discord. I dislike seeing them sharpen their wits in trade, buying at the lowest limit, extorting the highest. I don't want their horizons limited by city blocks, their feet on pavements, everything under the sun in their heads that concerns a scheme to make money; not room for an hour's thought or study in a whole day, about the really vital things of life. After all, land and its products are the basis of everything; the city couldn't exist a day unless we feed and clothe it. In the things that I consider important, you are a king among men, with your feet on soil you own."

"So I figure it," said Laddie.

"And you are the best educated man I have reared," said father. "Take this other thought with you: on land, the failure of the bank does not break you. The fire another man's carelessness starts, does not wipe out your business or home. You are not in easy reach of contagion. Any time you want to branch out, your mother and I will stand back of you."

"Thank you!" said Laddie. "You backed none of the others. They would resent it. I'll make the best start I can myself, and as they did, stand alone."

Father looked at him and smiled slowly.

"You are right, as always," he said. "I hadn't thought so far. It would make trouble. At any rate, let me inspect and help you select your land."

"That of course!" said Laddie.

I suspect it's not a very nice thing for me to tell, but all of us were tickled silly the day Miss Amelia packed her trunk and left for sure. Mother said she never tried harder in all her days, but Miss Amelia was the most distinctly unlovable person she ever had met. She sympathized with us so, she never said a word when Leon sang:

> "Believe me, if all those endearing young charms,
>   Which I gaze on so fondly to-day,
>   Were to change by to-morrow, and fleet in my arms,
>   Like fairy-gifts fading away,
>   Thou wouldst still be adored, as this moment thou art,
>   Let thy loveliness fade as it will,
>   And around the dear ruin each wish of my heart
>   Would entwine itself verdantly still—"

while Miss Amelia drove from sight up the Groveville road.

As he sang Leon stretched out his arms after her vanishing form. "I hope," he said, "that you caught that touching reference to 'the dear ruin,' and could anything be expressed more beautifully and poetically than that 'verdantly still?' "

I feel sorry for a snake. I like hoptoads, owls, and shitepokes. I envy a buzzard the way it can fly, and polecats are beautiful; but I never could get up any sort of feeling at all for Miss Amelia, whether she was birdlike or her true self. So no one was any gladder than I when she was gone.

After that, spring came pushing until you felt shoved. Our family needed me then. If they never had known it before, they found out there was none too many of us. Every day I had to watch the blue goose, and bring in her egg before it was chilled, carrying it carefully so it would not be jarred. I had to hunt the turkey nests and gather their eggs so they would be right for setting. There had to be straw carried from the stack for new nests, eggs marked, and hens set by the dozen. Garden time came, so leaves had to be raked from the beds and from the dooryard. No one was busier than I; but every little while I ran away, and spent some time all by myself in the pulpit, under the hawk oak, or on the roof.

Coming from church that Sunday, when we reached the top of the Big Hill, mother touched father's arm. "Stop a minute," she said, and he checked the horses, while we sat there and wondered why, as she looked and looked all over the farm, then, "Now drive to the top of the Little Hill and turn, and stop exactly on the place from which we first viewed this land together," she said. "You know the spot, don't you?"

"You may well believe I know it," said father. "I can hit it to the inch. You see, children," he went on, "your mother and I arranged before the words were said over us"—he always put it that way—I never in my life heard him say, "when we were married"; he read so many books he talked exactly like a book—"that we would be partners in everything, as long as we lived. When we decided the Ohio land was not quite what we wanted, she sent me farther west to prospect, while she stayed at home and kept the baby. When I reached this land, found it for sale, and within my means, I bought it, and started home happy. Before I'd gone a mile, I turned to look back, and saw that it was hilly, mostly woods, and there was no computing the amount of work it would require to make it what I could see in it; so I began to think maybe she wouldn't like it, and to wish I had brought her, before I closed the deal. By the time I returned home, packed up, and travelled this far on the way back with her, there was considerable tension in my feelings—considerable tension," repeated father as he turned the horses and began driving carefully, measuring the distance from Hoods' and the bridge. At last he stopped, backed a step, and said: "There, mommy, did I hit the spot?"

"You did!" said mother, stepping from the carriage and walking up beside him. She raised one hand and laid it on the lamp near him. He shifted the lines, picked up her hand, and held it tight. Mother stood there looking, just silently looking. May jabbed me in the side, leaned over and whispered:

> "Could we but stand where Moses stood,
> And view the landscape o'er,
> Not our Little Creek, nor dinner getting cold,
> Could fright us from that shore."

I couldn't help giggling, but I knew that was no proper time, so I hid my head in her lap and smothered the sound the best I could; but they were so busy soft-soddering each other they didn't pay a bit of attention to us.

It was May now, all the leaves were fresh and dustless, everything that flowered at that time was weighted with bloom, bees hummed past, butterflies sailed through the carriage, while birds at the tops of their voices, all of them, every kind there was, sang fit to split; friendly, unafraid bluebirds darted around us, and talked a blue streak from every fence rider. Made you almost crazy to know what they said. The Little Creek flowed at our feet across the road, through the blue-flag swamp, where the red and the yellow birds lived. You could see the sun flash on the water where it emptied into the stream that crossed Deams', and flowed through our pasture; and away beyond the Big Hill arose, with the new church on top, the graveyard around it, the Big Creek flashing at its base. In the valley between lay our fields, meadows, the big red barn, the white house with the yard filled with trees and flowering shrubs, beyond it the garden, all made up, neat and growing; and back of it the orchard in full bloom.

Mother looked and looked. Suddenly she raised her face to father. "Paul," she said, "that first day, did you ever dream it could be made to look like this?"

"No!" said father. "I never did! I saw houses, barns, and cleared fields; I hoped for comfort and prosperity, but I didn't know any place could grow to be so beautiful, and there is something about it, even on a rainy November day, there is something that catches me in the breast, on the top of either of these hills, until it almost stifles me. What is it, Ruth?"

"The Home Feeling!" said mother. "It is in my heart so big this morning I am filled with worship. Just filled with the spirit of worship."

She was rocking on her toes like she does when she becomes too happy at the Meeting House to be quiet any longer, and cries, "Glory!" right out loud. She pointed to the orchard, an immense orchard of big apple trees in full bloom, with two rows of peach trees around the sides. It looked like a great, soft, pinkish white blanket, with a deep pink border, spread lightly on the green earth.

'We planted that way because we thought it was best; how could we know how it would look in bloom time? It seems as if you came to these hilltops and figured on the picture you would make before you cleared, or fenced a field."

"That's exactly what I did," said father. "Many's the hour, all told, that I have stopped my horse on one of these hilltops and studied how to make the place beautiful, as well as productive. That was a task you set me, my girl. You always considered *beauty* as well as *use* about the house and garden, and wherever you worked. I had to hold my part in line."

"You have made it all a garden," said mother. "You have made it a garden growing under the smile of the Master; a very garden of the Lord, father."

Father drew up her hand and held it tight against his heart.

"Your praise is sweet, my girl, sweet!" he said. "I have tried, God knows I have tried, to make it first comfortable, then beautiful, for all of us. To the depths of my soul I thank Him for this hour. I am glad, Oh I am so glad you like your home, Ruth! I couldn't endure it if you complained, found fault and wished you lived elsewhere."

"Why, father!" said my mother in the most surprised voice. "Why, father, it would kill me to leave here. This is ours. We have made it by and through the strength of the Lord and our love for each other. All my days I want to live here, and when I die, I want to lie beside my blessed babies and you, Paul, down by the church we gave the land for, and worked so hard to build. I love it, Oh I love it! See how clean and white the dark ever-greens make the house look! See how the big chestnuts fit in and point out the yellow road. I wish we had a row the length of it!"

"They wouldn't grow," said father. "You mind the time I had finding the place those wanted to set their feet?"

"I do indeed!" said mother, drawing her hand and his with it where she could rub her cheek against it. "Now we'll go home and have our dinner and a good rest. I'm a happy woman this day, father, a happy, happy woman. If only one thing didn't worry me——"

"Must there always be a 'fly in the ointment,' mother?"

She looked at him with a smile that was like a hug and kiss, and she said: "I have found it so, father, and I have been happy in spite of it. Where one has such wide interests, at some point there is always a pull, but in His own day, in His own way, the Lord is going to make everything right."

" 'Thy faith hath made thee whole,' " quoted father.

Then she stepped into the carriage, and he waited a second, quite long enough to let her see that he was perfectly willing to sit there all day if she wanted him to, and then he slowly and carefully drove home, as he always did when she was in the car-riage. Times when he had us children out alone, he went until you couldn't see the spokes in the wheels. He just loved to "speed up" once in a while on a piece of fine road to let us know how going fast felt.

Mother sat there trembling a little, smiling, misty-eyed. I was thinking, for I knew what the "fly in the ointment" was. She had a letter from Shelley yesterday, and she said there wasn't a reason on earth why father or Laddie should spend money to come to Chicago, she would soon be home, she was counting the hours, and she never wanted to leave again. In the start she didn't want to go at all, unless she could stay three years, at the very least.

Of course it was that dreadful man, who had made her so beautiful and happy, and then taken away all the joy; how *could* a man do it? It was the hardest thing to understand.

Next morning mother was feeling fine, the world was lovely, Miss Amelia was gone, May was home to help, so she began housecleaning by washing all the curtains. She had been in the kitchen to show Candace how. I had all my work done, and was making friends with a robin brooding in my very own catalpa tree, when Mr. Pryor rode up, tied his horse, and started toward the gate. I knew he and father had quarrelled; that is, father had told him he couldn't say "God was a myth" in this house, and he'd gone home mad as hops; so I knew it would be something mighty important that was bringing him back. I slid from the tree, ran and opened the gate, and led the way up the walk. I opened the front door and asked him in, and then I did the wrong thing. I should have taken his hat, told him to be seated, and said I would see if I could find father; I knew what to do, and how to do it, but because of that about God, I was so excited I made a mistake. I never took his hat, or offered him a chair; I just bolted into the dining-room, looking for father or mother, and left the door wide open, so he thought that wasn't the place to sit, because I didn't give him a chair, and he followed me. The instant I saw mother's face, I knew what I had done. The dining-room was no place for particular company like him, and bringing him in that way didn't give her time to smooth her hair, pull shut her dress band at the neck, put on her collar, and shiny goldstone pin, her white apron, and rub her little flannel rag, with rice flour on it, on her nose to take away the shine. I had made a mess of it.

There she came right in the door, just as she was from the tub. Her hair was damp and crinkled around her face, her neckband had been close in stooping, so she had unfastened it, and tucked it back in a little V-shaped place to give her room and air. Her cheeks were pink, her eyes bright, her lips red as a girl's, and her neck was soft and white. The V-shaped place showed a little spot like baby skin, right where her neck went into her chest. Sure as father kissed her lips, he always tipped back her head, bent lower and kissed that spot too. I had seen hundreds of them go there, and I had tried it myself, lots of times, and it *was* the sweetest place. Seeing what I had done, I stopped breathless. You have to beat most everything you teach a child right into it properly to keep it from making such a botch of things as that. I hardly dared to peep at mother, but when I did, she took my breath worse than the mistake I had made.

Caught, she stood her ground. She never paused a second. Straight to him she went, holding out her hand, and I could see that it was red and warm from pressing the lace in the hot suds. A something flashed over her, that made her more beautiful than she was in her silk dress going to town to help Lucy give a party, and her voice was sweet as the bubbling warbler on the garden fence when he was trying to coax a mate into the privet bush to nest.

Mother asked him to be seated, so he took one of the chairs nearest him, and sat holding his hat in one hand, his whip in the other. Mother drew a chair beside the dining table, dropped her hands on each other, and looking in his eyes, she smiled at him. I tell the same thing over about people's looks, but I haven't told of this smile of mother's; because I never saw exactly how it was, or what it would do to people, until that morning. Then as I watched her—for how she felt decided what would happen to me, after Mr. Pryor was gone—I saw something I never had noticed until that minute. She could laugh all over her face, before her lips parted until her teeth showed. She was doing it now. With a wide smile running from cheek to cheek, pushing up a big dimple at each end, her lips barely touching, her eyes dancing, she sat looking at him.

"This *is* the most blessed season for warming up the heart," she said. "If you want the half of my kingdom, ask quickly. I'm in the mood to bestow it."

How she laughed! He just had to loosen up a little, and smile back, even though it looked pretty stiff.

"Well, I'll not tax you so far," he said. "I only want Mr. Stanton."

"But he is the whole of the kingdom, and the King to boot!" she laughed, dimpled, and flamed redder.

Mr. Pryor stared at her wonderingly. You could even see the wonder, like it was something you could take hold of. I suppose he wondered what could make a woman so happy, like that.

"Lucky man!" he said. "All of us are not so fortunate."

"Then it must be you don't covet the place or the title," said mother more soberly. "Any woman will crown the man she marries, if he will allow her. Paul went farther. He compelled it."

"I wonder how!" said Mr. Pryor, his eyes steadily watching mother's face.

"By never failing in a million little things, that taken as a whole, make up one mighty big thing, on which he stands like the Rock of Ages."

"Yet they tell me that you are the mother of twelve children," he said, as if he marvelled at something.

"Yes!" cried mother, and the word broke right through a bubbling laugh. "Am I not fortunate above most women? We had the grief to lose two little daughters at the ages of eight and nine, all the others I have, and I rejoice in them."

She reached out, laid a hand on me, drew me to her, and lightly touched my arm, sending my spirits sky-high. She wasn't going to do a thing to me, not even scold! Mr. Pryor stared at her like Jacob Hood does at Laddie when he begins rolling Greek before him, so I guess what mother said must have been Greek to Mr. Pryor.

"I came to see Mr. Stanton," he said suddenly, and crosslike as if he didn't believe a word she said, and had decided she was too foolish to bother with any longer; but he kept on staring. He couldn't quit that, no matter how cross he was. The funniest thing came into my mind. I wondered what on earth he'd have done if she'd gone over, sat on his lap, put her arms around his neck, took his face between her hands and kissed his forehead, eyes, lips, and tousled his hair, like she does father and our boys. I'll bet all I got, he'd have turned to stonier stone than Sabethany. You could see that no one ever served *him* like that in all his old, cold, hard, cross, mysterious, shut-in life. I was crazy to ask, "Say, did anybody ever kiss you?" but I had such a close escape bringing him in wrong, I thought it would be wise not to take any risks so soon after. It was enough to stand beside mother, and hear every word they said. What was more, she wanted me, because she kept her hand on mine, or touched my apron every little while.

"I'm so sorry!" she said. "He was called to town on business. The County Commissioners are sitting to-day."

"They are deciding about the Groveville bridge, and pike?"

"Yes. He is working so hard for them."

"The devil you say! I beg pardon! But it was about that I came. I'm three miles from there, and I'm taxed over sixty pounds for it."

"But you cross the bridge every time you go to town, and travel the road. Groveville is quite a resort on account of the water and lovely country. Paul is very anxious to have the work completed before the summer boarders come from surrounding cities. We are even farther from it than you; but it will cost us as much."

"Are you insane?" cried Mr. Pryor, not at all politely; but you could see that mother was bound she wouldn't become provoked about anything, for she never stopped a steady beam on him. "Spend all that money for strangers to lazy around on a few weeks and then go!"

"But a good bridge and fine road will add to their pleasure, and when they leave, the improvements remain. They will benefit us and our children through all the years to come."

"Talk about 'the land of the free'!" cried Mr. Pryor. "This is a tax-ridden nation. It's a beastly outrage! Ever since I came, it's been nothing but notice of one assessment after another. I won't pay it! I won't endure it. I'll move!"

Mother let go of me, gripped her hands pretty tight together on the table, and she began to talk.

"As for freedom—no man ever was, or is, or will be free," she said, quite as forcibly as he could speak. "You probably knew when you came here that you would find a land tax-ridden from a great civil war of years' duration, and from newness of vast territory to be opened up and improved. You certainly studied the situation."

" 'Studied the situation'!" His whip beat across his knee. " 'Studied the situation'! My leaving England was—er—the result of intolerable conditions there—in the nature of flight from things not to be endured. I had only a vague idea of the States."

"If England is intolerable, and the United States an outrage, I don't know where in this world you'll go," said mother softly.

Mr. Pryor stared at her sharply.

"Madame is pleased to be facetious," he said sneeringly.

Mother's hands parted, and one of them stretched across the table toward him.

"Forgive me!" she cried. "That was unkind. I know you are in dreadful trouble. I'd give—I'd almost give this right hand to comfort you. I'd do nearly anything to make you feel that you need bear no burden alone; that we'd love to help support you."

"I believe you would," he said slowly, his eyes watching her again. "I believe you would. I wonder why!"

"All men are brothers, in the broader sense," said mother, "and if you'll forgive me, your face bears marks of suffering almost amounting to torture."

She stretched out the other hand.

"You couldn't possibly let us help you?"

Slowly he shook his head.

"Think again!" urged mother. "A trouble shared is half over to start with. You lay a part of it on your neighbours, and your neighbours in this case would be glad, glad indeed, to see you care-free and happy as all men should be."

"We'll not discuss it," he said. "You can't possibly imagine the root of my trouble."

"I shan't try!" said mother. "But let me tell you this: I don't care if you have betrayed your country, blasphemed your God, or killed your own child! So long, as you're a living man, daily a picture of suffering before me, you're a burden on my heart. You're a load on my shoulders, without your consent. I have implored God, I shall never cease to implore Him, until your brow clears, your head is lifted, and your heart is at rest. You can't prevent me! This hour I shall go to my closet and beg Him to have mercy on your poor soul, and when His time comes, He will. You can't help yourself, or you would have done so, long ago. You must accept aid! This must end, or there will be tragedy in your house."

"Madame, there has been!" said Mr. Pryor, shaking as he sat.

"I recognize that," said mother. "The question is whether what has passed is not enough."

"You simply cannot understand!" he said.

"Mr. Pryor," she said, "you're in the position of a man doubly bereft. You are without a country, and without a God. Your face tells every passer-by how you are enjoying that kind of life. Forgive me, if I speak plainly. I admire some things about you so much, I am venturing positive unkindness to try to make you see that in shutting out your neighbours you will surely make them think more, and worse things, than are true. I haven't a doubt in my mind but that your trouble is not one half so dreadful as you imagine while brooding over it. We will pass that. Let me tell you how we feel about this road matter. You see we did our courting in Pennsylvania, married and tried Ohio, and then came on here. We took this land when it was mostly woods. I could point you to the exact spot where we stopped; we visited it yesterday, looked down the hill and selected the place where we would set this house, when we could afford to build it. We moved into the cabin that was on the land first, later built a larger one, and finally this home as we had planned it. Every fruit tree, bush, vine, and flower we planted. Here our children have been born, lived, loved, and left us; some for the graveyard down yonder, some for homes of their own. Always we have planned and striven to transform this into the dearest, the most beautiful spot on earth. In making our home the best we can, in improving our township, county, and state, we are doing our share toward upbuilding this nation."

She began at the a b c's, and gave it to him straight: the whole thing, just as we saw it; and he listened, as if he were a prisoner, and she a judge telling him what he must do to gain his freedom. She put in the birds to keep away the worms, the trees to break the wind, the creeks to save the moisture. She whanged him, and she banged him, up one side, and down the other. She didn't stop to be mincy. She shot things at him like a man talking to another man who had plenty of sense but not a particle of reason. She gave him the reason. She told him exactly why, and how, and where, and also just *what* he must do to feel *right* toward his neighbours, his family, and his God. No preacher ever talked half so well. Yea verily, she was as interesting as the Bishop himself, and far pleasanter to look at. When she ran short of breath, and out of words, she reached both hands toward him again.

"Oh do please think of these things!" she begged. "Do try to believe that I am a sensible person, and know what I am talking about."

"Madame," said Mr. Pryor, "there's no doubt in my mind but you are the most wonderful woman I ever have met. Surely I believe you! Surely I know your plan of life is the true, the only right way. It is one degree added to my humiliation that the ban I am under keeps me from friendly intercourse with so great a lady."

" 'Lady'?" said my mother, her eyes widening. " 'Lady'? Now it is you who are amused."

"I don't understand!" he said. "Certainly you are a lady, a very great lady."

"Goodness, gracious me!" cried my mother, laughing until her dimples would have held water. "That's the first time in all my life I was ever accused of such a thing."

"Again, I do not comprehend," said Mr. Pryor, as if vexed about all he would endure.

Mother laughed on, and as she did so she drew back her hands and studied them. Then she looked at him again, one pink dimple flashing here and there, all over her face.

"Well, to begin at the root of the matter," she said, "that is an enormous big word that you are using lightly. Any one in petticoats is not a lady—by no means! A lady must be born of unsullied blood for at least three generations, on each side of her house. Think for a minute about where you are going to fulfil that condition. Then she must be gentle by nature, and rearing. She must know all there is to learn from books, have wide experience to cover all emergencies, she must be steeped in social graces, and diplomatic by nature. She must rise unruffled to any emergency, never wound, never offend, always help and heal, she must be perfect in deportment, virtue, wifehood and motherhood. She must be graceful, pleasing and beautiful. She must have much leisure to perfect herself in learning, graces and arts——"

"Madame, you draw an impossible picture!" cried Mr. Pryor.

"I draw the picture of the only woman on earth truly entitled to be called a lady. You use a good word lightly. I have told you what it takes to make a lady—now look at me!"

How she laughed! Mr. Pryor looked, but he didn't laugh.

"More than ever you convince me that you are a lady, indeed," he said.

Mother wiped her eyes.

"My dear man!" she cried, "I'm the daughter of a Dutch miller, who lived on a Pennsylvania mountain stream. There never was a school anywhere near us, and father and mother only taught us to work. Paul Stanton took a grist there, and saw me. He married me, and brought me here. He taught me to read and write. I learned my lessons with my elder children. He has always kept school in our house, every night of his life. Our children supposed it was for them; I knew it was quite as much for me. While I sat at knitting or sewing, I spelled over the words he gave out. I know nothing of my ancestors, save that they came from the lowlands of Holland, down where there were cities, schools, and business. They were well educated, but they would not take the trouble to teach their children. As I have spoken to you, my husband taught me. All I know I learn from him, from what he reads aloud, and places he takes me. I exist in a twenty-mile radius, but through him, I know all lands, principalities and kingdoms, peoples and customs. I need never be ashamed to go, or afraid to speak, anywhere."

"Indeed not!" cried Mr. Pryor.

"But when you think on the essentials of a real lady—and then picture me patching, with a First Reader propped before me; facing Indians, Gypsies, wild animals—and they used to be bad enough—why, I mind one time in Ohio when our first baby was only able to stand beside a chair, and through the rough puncheon floor a copperhead stuck up its gleam of bronzy gold, and shot its darting tongue within a foot of her bare leg. By all accounts, a lady would have reached for her smelling salts and gracefully fainted away; in fact, a lady never would have been in such a place at all. It was my job to throw the first thing I could lay my hands on so straight and true that I would break that snake's neck, and send its deadly fangs away from my baby. I did it with Paul's plane, and neatly too! Then I had to put the baby on the bed and tear up every piece of the floor to see that the snake had not a mate in hiding there, for copperheads at that season were going pairs. Once I was driven to face a big squaw, and threatened the life of her baby with a red-hot poker while she menaced mine with a hunting knife. There is not one cold, rough, hard experience of pioneer life that I have not endured. Shoulder to shoulder, and heart to heart, I've stood beside my man, and done what had to be done, to build this home, rear our children, save our property. Many's the night I have shivered in a barn doctoring sick cattle and horses we could ill afford to lose. Time and again I have hung on and brought things out alive, after the men gave up and quit. A lady? How funny!"

"The amusement is all on your part, Madame."

"So it seems!" said mother. "But you see, I know so well how ridiculous it is. When I think of the life a woman must lead in order to be truly a lady, when I review the life I have been forced to live to do my share in making this home, and rearing these children, the contrast is too great. I thank God for any part I have been able to take. Had I life to live over, I see now where I could do more; but neighbour, believe me, my highest aspiration is to be a clean, thrifty housekeeper, a bountiful cook, a faithful wife, a sympathetic mother. That is life work for any woman, and to be a good woman is the greatest thing on earth. Never mind about the ladies; if you can honestly say of me, she is a good woman, you have paid me the highest possible tribute."

"I have nothing to change, in the face of your argument," said Mr. Pryor. "Our loved Queen on her throne is no finer lady."

That time mother didn't laugh. She looked straight at him a minute and then she said: "Well, for an Englishman, as I know them, you have said the last word. Higher praise there is none. But believe me, I make no such claim. To be a good wife and mother is the end toward which I aspire. To hold the respect and love of my husband is the greatest object of my life."

"Then you have succeeded. You stand a monument to wifehood; your children prove your idea of motherhood," said Mr. Pryor. "How in this world have you managed it? The members of your family whom I have seen are fine, interesting men and women, educated above the average. It is not idle curiosity. I am deeply interested in knowing how such an end came to be accomplished here on this farm. I wish you would tell me just how you have gone about schooling your children."

"By educating ourselves before their coming, and with them afterward. Self-control, study, work, joy of life, satisfaction with what we have had, never-ending strife to go higher, and to do better—Dr. Fenner laughs when I talk of these things. He says he can take a little naked Hottentot from the jungle, and educate it to the same degree that I can one of mine. I don't know; but if these things do not help before birth, at least they do not hinder; and afterward, you are in the groove in which you want your children to run. With all our twelve there never has been one who at nine months of age did not stop crying if its father lifted his finger, or tapped his foot and told it to. From the start we have rigorously guarded our speech and actions before them. From the first tiny baby my husband has taught all of them to read, write and cipher some, before they went to school at all. He is always watching, observing, studying: the earth, the stars, growing things; he never comes to a meal but he has seen something that he has or will study out for all of us. There never has been one day in our home on which he did not read a new interesting article from book or paper; work out a big problem, or discuss some phase of politics, religion, or war. Sometimes there has been a little of all of it in one day, always reading, spelling, and memory exercises at night. He has a sister who twice in her life has repeated the Bible as a test before a committee. He, himself, can go through the New Testament and all of the Old save the books of the generations. He always says he considers it a waste of gray matter to learn them. He has been a schoolmaster, his home his schoolroom, his children, wife and helpers his pupils; the common things of life as he meets them every day, the books from which we learn.

"I was ignorant at first of bookish subjects, but in his atmosphere, if one were no student, and didn't even try to keep up, or forge ahead, they would absorb much through association. Almost always he has been on the school board and selected the teachers; we have made a point of keeping them here, at great inconvenience to ourselves, in order to know as much of them as possible, and to help and guide them in their work. When the children could learn no more here, for most of them we have managed the high school of Groveville, especially after our daughter moved there, and for each of them we have added at least two years of college, music school, or whatever the peculiar bent of the child seemed to demand.

"Before any daughter has left our home for one of her own, she has been taught all I know of cleanliness about a house, cookery, sewing, tending the sick, bathing and dressing the new born. She has to bake bread, pie, cake, and cook any meat or vegetable we have. She has had her bolt of muslin to make as she chose for her bedding, and linen for her underclothing. The quilts she pieced and the blankets she wove have been hers. All of them have been as well provided for as we could afford. They can knit, darn, patch, tuck, hem, and embroider, set a hen and plant a garden. I go on a vacation and leave each of them to keep house for her father a month, before she enters a home of her own. They are strong, healthy girls; I hope all of them are making a good showing at being useful women, and I know they are happy, so far at least."

"Wonderful!" said Mr. Pryor.

"Father takes the boys in hand and they must graduate in a straight furrow, an even fence, planting and tending crops, trimming and grafting trees, caring for stock, and handling plane, auger and chisel. Each one must select his wood, cure, fashion, and fit his own ax with a handle, grind and swing it properly, as well as cradle, scythe and sickle. They must be able to select good seed grain, boil sap, and cure meat. They must know animals, their diseases and treatment, and when they have mastered all he can teach them, and done each thing properly, they may go for their term at college, and make their choice of a profession. As yet I'm sorry to say but one of them has come back to the land."

"You mean Laddie?"

"Yes."

"He has decided to be a farmer?"

"He is determined to make the soil yield his living."

"I am sorry—sorry indeed to hear it," said Mr. Pryor. "He has brain and education to make a brilliant figure at law or statesmanship; he would do well in trade."

"What makes you think he would *not* do well on land?"

"Wasted!" cried Mr. Pryor. "He would be wasted!"

"Hold a bit!" said mother, her face flushing as it did when she was very provoked. "My husband is, and always has been, on land. He is far from being wasted. He is a power in this community. He has sons in cities in law and in trade. Not one of them has the friends, and the influence on his time, that his father has. Any day he says the word, he can stand in legislative halls, and take any part he chooses in politics. He prefers his home and family, and the work he does here, but let me tell you, no son of his ever had his influence or opportunity, or ever will have."

"All this is news to me," said Mr. Pryor.

"You didn't expect us to come over, force our way in and tell you?"

It was his turn to blush and he did.

"Laddie has been at our house often," he said. "He might have mentioned———"

Mother laughed. She was the gayest that morning.

"He 'might,' but he never would. Neither would I if you hadn't seemed to think that the men who do the things Mr. Stanton *refuses* to do are the ones worth while."

"He could accomplish much in legislative halls."

"He figures in the large. He thinks that to be a commissioner, travel his county and make all of it the best possible, to stand in primaries and choose only worthy men for all offices, is doing a much bigger work than to take one place for himself, and strive only for that. Besides, he really loves his land, his house, and family. He says no man has a right to bring twelve children into the world and not see personally to rearing and educating them. He thinks the farm and the children too much for me, and he's sure he is doing the biggest thing for the community at large, to go on as he does."

"Perhaps so," said Mr. Pryor slowly. "He should know best. Perhaps he is."

"I make no doubt!" said mother, lifting her head proudly. "And as Laddie feels and has fitted himself, I look to see him go head and shoulders above any other son I have. Trade is not the only way to accumulate. Law is not the only path to the legislature. Comfort, independence, and freedom, such as we know here, is not found in any city I ever have visited. We think we have the best of life, and we are content on land. We have not accumulated much money; we have spent thousands; we have had a big family for which to provide, and on account of the newness of the country, taxes always have been heavy. But we make no complaint. We are satisfied. We could have branched off into fifty different things after we had a fair start here. We didn't, because we preferred life as we worked it out for ourselves. Paul says when he leaves the city, and his horses' hoofs strike the road between our fields, he always lifts his head higher, squares his shoulders, and feels a man among men. To own land, and to love it, is a wonderful thing, Mr. Pryor."

She made me think of something. Ever since I had added to my quill and arrow money, the great big lot at Easter, father had shared his chest till with me. The chest stood in our room, and in it lay his wedding suit, his every Sunday clothes, his best hat with a red silk handkerchief in the crown, a bundle of precious newspapers he was saving on account of rare things in them he wanted for reference, and in the till was the wallet of ready money he kept in the house for unexpected expense, his deeds, insurance papers, all his particular private papers, the bunches of lead pencils, slate pencils, and the box of pens from which he supplied us for school. Since I had grown so rich, he had gone partners with me, and I might lift the lid, open the till and take out my little purse that May bought from the huckster for my last birthday. I wasn't to touch a thing, save my own, and I never did; but I knew precious well what was there. If Mr. Pryor thought my father didn't amount to much because he lived on land; if it made him think more of him, to know that he could be in the legislature if he chose, maybe he'd think still more——

I lifted the papers, picked it up carefully, and slipping back quietly, I laid it on Mr. Pryor's knee. He picked it up and held it a minute, until he finished what he was saying to mother, and then he looked at it. Then he looked long and hard. Then he straightened up and looked again.

"God bless my soul!" he cried.

You see when he was so astonished he didn't know what he was saying, he called on God, just as father says every one does. I took a side look at mother. Her face was a little extra flushed, but she was still smiling; so I knew she wasn't angry with me, though of course she wouldn't have shown the thing herself. She and father never did, except as each of us grew big enough to be taught about the Crusaders. Father said he didn't care the snap of his finger about it, except as it stood for hardihood and bravery. But Mr. Pryor cared! He cared more than he could say. He stared, and stared, and over and over he wonderingly repeated: "God bless my soul!"

"Where did you get the crest of the Earl of Eastbrooke, the master of Stanton house?" he demanded. "Stanton house!" he repeated. "Why—why, the name! It's scarcely possible, but——"

"But there it is!" laughed mother. "A mere bauble for show and amounting to nothing on earth save as it stands a mark for brave men who have striven to conquer."

"Surgere tento!" read Mr. Pryor, from the little shield. "Four shells! Madame, I know men who would give their lives to own this, and to have been born with the right to wear it. It came to your husband in straight line?"

"Yes," said mother, "but generations back. He never wore it. He never would. He only saves it for the children."

"It goes to your eldest son?"

"By rights, I suppose it should," said mother. "But father mentioned it the other night. He said none of his boys had gone as he tried to influence them, unless Laddie does now in choosing land for his future, and if he does, his father is inclined to leave it to him, and I agree. At our death it goes to Laddie I am quite sure."

"Well, I hope—I hope," said Mr. Pryor, "that the young man has the wit to understand what this would mean to him in England."

"His wit is just about level with his father's," said mother. "He never has been in England, and most probably he never will be. I don't think it means a rap more to Laddie than it does to my husband. Laddie is so busy developing the manhood born in him, he has no time to chase the rainbow of reflected glory, and no belief in its stability if he walked in its light. The child of my family to whom that trinket really means something is Little Sister, here. When Leon came in with the thief, I thought he should have it; but after all, she is the staunchest little Crusader I have."

Mr. Pryor looked me over with much interest.

"Yes, yes! No doubt!" he said. "But the male line! This priceless treasure should descend to one of the male line! To one whose name will remain Stanton! To Laddie would be best, no doubt! No doubt at all!"

"We will think about it," said mother serenely as Mr. Pryor arose to go.

He apologized for staying so long, and mother said it hadn't been long, and asked him the nicest ever to come again. She walked in the sunlight with him and pointed out the chestnuts. She asked what he thought of a line of trees to shade the road, and they discussed whether the pleasure they would give in summer would pay for the dampness they would hold in winter. They wandered around the yard and into the garden. She sent me to bring a knife, trowel, and paper, so when he started for home, he was carrying a load of cuttings, and roots to plant.

When father came from town that evening, at the first sight of him, she went straight into his arms, her face beaming; she had been like a sun all that day. Some of it must have been joy carried over from yesterday.

"Praise God, the wedge is in!" she cried.

Father held her tight, stroked her hair, and began smiling without having the least idea why, but he very well knew that whatever pleased her like that was going to be good news for him also.

"What has happened, mother?" he asked.

"Mr. Pryor came over about the road and bridge tax, and oh Paul! I've said every word to him I've been bursting to say from the very start. Every single word, Paul!"

"How did he take it?"

"Time will tell. Anyway, he heard it, all of it, and he went back carrying a load of things to plant. Only think of that! Once he begins planting, and watching things grow, the home feeling is bound to come. I tell you, Paul, the wedge is in! Oh I'm so happy!"

CHAPTER XIV

The Crest of Eastbrooke

"Sow;—and look onward, upward,
    Where the starry light appears,—
Where, in spite of coward's doubting,
    Or your own heart's trembling fears,
You shall reap in joy the harvest
    You have sown to-day in tears."

Any objections to my beginning to break ground on the west eighty to-day?" asked Laddie of father at breakfast Monday morning.

"I had thought we would commence on the east forty, when planning the work."

"So had I," said Laddie. "But since I thought that, a very particular reason has developed for my beginning to plow the west eighty at once, and there is a charming little ditty I feel strongly impelled to whistle every step of the way."

Father looked at him sharply, and so, I think, did all of us. And because we loved him deeply, we saw that his face was a trifle pale for him; his clear eyes troubled, in spite of his laughing way. He knew we were studying him too, but he wouldn't have said anything that would make us look and question if he had minded our doing it. That was exactly like Laddie. He meant it when he said he hated a secret. He said there was no place on earth for a man to look for sympathy and love if he couldn't find it in his own family; and he never had been so happy since I had been big enough to notice his moods as he had been since all of us knew about the Princess. He didn't wait for father to ask why he'd changed his mind about the place to begin.

"You see," he said, "a very charming friend of mine expressed herself strongly last night about the degrading influence of farming, especially that branch of agriculture which evolves itself in a furrow; hence it is my none too happy work to plow the west eighty where she can't look our way without seeing me; and I have got to whistle my favourite 'toon' where she must stop her ears if she doesn't hear; and then it will be my painful task, I fear, to endeavour to convince her that I am still clean, decent, and not degraded."

"Oh Laddie!" cried mother.

"Abominable foolishness!" roared father like he does roar once in about two years.

"Isn't it now?" asked Laddie sweetly. "I don't know what has got into her head. She has seen me plowing fifty times since their land has joined ours, and she never objected before."

"I can tell you blessed well!" said mother. "She didn't care two hoots how much my son plowed, but it makes a difference when it comes to her lover."

"Maw, you speak amazing reckless," said Laddie, "if I thought there was anything in *that* feature of the case, I'd attempt a Highland fling on the ridgepole of our barn."

"Be serious!" said father sternly. "This is no laughing matter."

"That's precisely why I am laughing," said Laddie. "Would it help me any to sit down and weep? I trow not! I have thought most of the silent watches—by the way they are far from silent in May—and as I read my title clear, it's my job to plow the west eighty immejit."

Father tried to look stern, but he just had to laugh.

"All right then, plow it!" he said.

"What did she say?" asked mother.

"Phew!" Laddie threw up both hands. "She must have been bottled some time on the subject. The ferment was a spill of considerable magnitude. The flood rather overwhelmed me, because it was so unexpected. I had been taking for granted that she accepted my circumstances and surroundings as she did me. But no, kind friends, far otherwise! She said last night, in the clearest

English I ever heard spoken impromptu, that I was a man suitable for her friend, but I would have to change my occupation
before I could be received on more than a friendly footing."

" 'On more than a friendly footing'?" repeated mother.

"You have her exact words," said Laddie. "Kindly pass the
ham."

"What did you say?"

"Nothing! I am going to plow the answer. Please don't object
to my beginning this morning."

"You try yourself all winter to get as far as you have, and then
upset the bowl like this?" cried mother.

"Softly, mummy, softly!" said Laddie. "What am I to do? I've
definitely decided on my work. I see land and life, as you and
father taught me, in range and in perspective far more than
you've got from it. You had a first hand wrestle. The land I covet
has been greatly improved already. I can do what I choose with
it, making no more strenuous effort than plowing; and I am
proud to say that I *love* to plow. I like my feet in the soil. I want
my head in the spring air. I can become almost tipsy on the
odours that fill my nostrils. Music evolved by the Almighty is
plenty good enough for me. I'm proud of a spanking big team,
under the control of a touch or a word. I enjoy farming, and I
am going to be a farmer. Plowing is one of the most pleasing parts
of the job. Sowing the seed beats it a little, from an artistic stand-
point, either is preferable to haying, threshing, or corn cutting: all
are parts of my work, so I'm going to begin. Mother, I hope you
don't mind if I take your grays. I'll be very careful; but the picture I present to my girl to-day is going to go hard with her at
best, so I'd like to make it level best."

He arose, went around and knelt beside mother. He took her,
chair and all, in his arms:

> *"Best of mothers! on my breast*
> *Lean thy head, and sink to rest."*

he quoted. Mother laughed.

"Mammy," he asked bending toward her, "am I clean?"

"You goose!" she said, putting her arms around him and holding him tight.

"Gander love," said Laddie, turning up his face for a kiss. "Honest mother, you have been through nigh unto forty years of it, tell me, can a man be a farmer and keep neat enough not to be repulsive to a refined woman?"

"Your father is the answer," said mother. "All of you know how perfectly repulsive he is and always has been to me."

" 'Repulsive,' " said father. "That's an ugly word!"

"There are a whole lot of unpleasant things that peep around corners occasionally," said Laddie. "But whoever of you dear people it was that showed Mr. Pryor the Crest of Eastbrooke, brought out this particular dragon for me to slay."

"Tut, tut! Now what does that mean?" said father. "Have we had a little exhibition of that especial brand of pride that goes before a fall?"

"We have! and I take the tumble," said Laddie. "Watch me start! 'Jack fell down and broke his crown.' Question—will 'Jill come tumbling after?' "

My heart stopped and I was shaking in my bare feet, because I wore no shoes to shake in. Oh my soul! No matter how Laddie jested I knew he was almost killed; the harder he made fun, the worse he was hurt. I opened my mouth to say I did it, I had to, but Leon began to talk.

"Well, I think she's smart!" he cried. "If she was going to give you the mitten, why didn't she do it long ago?"

"She had to find out first whether there were a possibility of her wanting to keep it," said Laddie.

"You're sure you are all signed, sealed, and delivered on this plowing business, are you?" asked Leon.

"Dead sure!" said Laddie.

"All right, if you like it!" said Leon. "None for me after college! But say, you can be a farmer and not plow, you know. You go trim the trees, and work at cleaner, more gentlemanly jobs. I'll plow that field. I'd just as soon as not. I plowed last year and you said I did well, didn't you, father?"

"Yes, on the potato patch," said father. "A cornfield is a different thing. I fear you are too light."

"Oh but that was a year ago!" cried Leon.

He pushed back his chair and went to father.

"Just feel my biceps now! Most like steel!" he boasted. "A fellow can grow a lot in a year, and all the riding I've been doing, and all the exercise I've had. Cert' I can plow that meadow."

"You're all right, shaver," said Laddie. "I'll not forget your offer; but in this case it wouldn't help. Either the Princess takes her medicine or I take mine. I'm going to live on land: I'm going to plow in plain sight of the Pryor house this week, if I have to hire to Jacob Hood to get the chance. May I plow, and may I take the grays, father?"

"Yes!" said father roundly.

"Then here goes!" said Laddie. "You needn't fret, mother. I'll not overheat them. I must give a concert simultaneous with this plowing performance, and I'm particular about the music, so I can't go too fast. Also, I'll wrap the harness."

"Goodness knows I'm not thinking about the horses," said mother.

"No, but if they turned up next Sunday, wind-broken, and with nice large patches of hair rubbed from their sides, you would be! If you were me, would you whistle, or vocalize to start on?"

Mother burst right out crying and laid her face all tear-wet against him. Laddie kissed her, and wiped away the tears, teased her, and soon as he could he bolted from the east door; but I was closest, so I saw plainly that his eyes were wet too. My soul and body! *And I had done it!* I might as well get it over.

"I showed Mr. Pryor the trinket," I said.

"How did you come to do that?" asked father sternly.

"When he was talking with mother. He told her Laddie would be 'wasted' farming——"

"Wasted?"

"That's what he said. Mother told him you had always farmed and you were a 'power in this community.' She told him about what you did, because you wanted to, and what you *could* do if you chose, about holding office, you know, and that seemed to make him think heaps more of you, so I thought it would be a good thing for him to know about the Crusaders too, and I ran and got the crest. I *thought* it would help——"

"And so it will," said mother. "They constantly make the best showing they can, we might as well, too. The trouble is they got more than they expected. They thought they could look down on us, and patronize us, if they came near at all; when they found we were quite as well educated as they, had as much land, could hold prominent offices if we chose, and had the right to that bauble, they veered to the other extreme. Now they seem to demand that we quit work——"

"Move to the city, 'sit on a cushion and sew a fine seam,' " suggested father.

"Exactly!" said mother. "They'll have to find out we are running our own business; but I'm sorry it fell to Laddie to show them. You could have done it better. It will come out all right. The Princess is not going to lose a man like Laddie on account of how he makes his money."

"Don't be too confident," said father. "With people of their stripe, how much money a man can earn, and at what occupation, constitute the whole of life."

She wasn't too confident. Yesterday she had been so happy she almost flew. To-day she kept things going, and sang a lot, but nearly every time you looked at her you could see her lips draw tight, a frown cross her forehead, and her head shake. Pretty soon we heard a racket on the road, so we went out. There was Laddie with the matched team of carriage horses and a plow. Now, in dreadfully busy times, father let Ned and Jo work a little, but not very much. They were not plow horses; they were roadsters. They liked to prance, and bow their necks and dance to the carriage. It shamed them to be hitched to a plow. They drooped their heads and slunk along like dogs caught sucking eggs. But they were a sight on the landscape. They were lean and slender and yet round too, matched dapple gray on flank and side, with long snow-white manes and tails. No wonder mother didn't want them to work. Laddie had reached through the garden fence and hooked a bunch of red tulips and yellow daffodils. The red was at Jo's ear, and the yellow at Ned's, and they did look fine. So did he! Big, strong, clean, a red flower in his floppy straw hat band; and after he drove through the gate, he began a shrill, fifelike whistle you could have heard a half mile:

"See the merry farmer boy, tramp the meadows through,
Swing his hoe in careless joy, while dashing off the dew.
Bobolink in maple high, trills a note of glee,
Farmer boy in gay reply now whistles cheerily."

The chorus was all whistle, and it was written for folks who could. It went up until it almost split the echoes, and Laddie could easily sail a measure above the notes. He did it too. As for me, I kept from sight. For a week Laddie whistled and plowed. He wore that tune threadbare, and got an almost continuous pucker on his lips. Leon said if he didn't stop whistling, and sing more, the girls would think he was doing a prunes and prisms stunt. So after that he sang the words, and whistled the chorus. But he made no excuse to go, and he didn't go, to Pryors'. When Sunday came, he went to Westchester to see Elizabeth, and stayed until Monday morning. Not once that week did the Princess ride past our house, or her father either. By noon Monday Laddie was back in the field, and I had all I could bear. He was neither whistling nor singing so much now, because he was away at the south end, where he couldn't be seen or heard at Pryors'. He almost scoured the skin from him, and he wore his gloves more carefully than usual. If he soiled his clothing in the least, and it looked as if he would make more than his share of work, he washed the extra pieces at night.

Tuesday morning I hurried with all my might, and then I ran to the field where he was. I climbed on the fence, sat there until he came up, and then I gave him some cookies. He stopped the horses, climbed beside me and ate them. Then he put his arms around me and hugged me tight.

"Laddie, do you know I did it?" I wailed.

"Did you now?" said Laddie. "No, I didn't know for sure, but I had suspicions. You always have had such a fondness for that particular piece of tinware."

"But Laddie, it means so much!"

"Doesn't it?" said Laddie. "A few days ago no one could have convinced me that it meant anything at all to me, or ever could. Just look at me now!"

"Don't joke, Laddie! Something must be done."

"Well, ain't I doing it?" asked Laddie. "Look at all these acres and acres of Jim-dandy plowing!"

"Don't!" I begged. "Why don't you go over there?"

"No use, Chicken," said Laddie. "You see her exact stipulation was that I must *change my occupation* before I came again."

"What does she want you to do?"

"Law, I think. Unfortunately, I showed her a letter from Jerry asking me to enter his office this fall."

"Hadn't you better do it, Laddie?"

"How would you like to be shut in little, stuffy rooms, and set to droning over books and papers every hour of the day, all your life, and to spend the best of your brain and bodily strength straightening out other men's quarrels?"

"Oh Laddie, you just couldn't!" I cried.

"Precisely!" said Laddie. "I just couldn't, and I just won't!"

"What can you do?"

"I might compromise on stock," he said. "I could follow the same occupation as her father, and with better success. Neither he nor his men get the best results from horses. They don't understand them, especially the breeds they are attempting to handle. Most Arab horsemen are tent dwellers. They travel from one oasis to another with their stock. At night their herds are gathered around them as children. As children they love them, pet them, feed them. Each is named for a divinity, a planet or a famous ruler, and the understanding between master and beast is perfect. Honestly, Little Sister, I think you have got to believe in the God of Israel, in order to say the right word to an Arabian horse; and I know you must believe in the God of love. A beast of that breed, jerked, kicked, and scolded is a fine horse ruined. If I owned half the stock Mr. Pryor has over there, I could put it in such shape for market that I could get twice from it what his men will."

"Are Thomas and James rough with the horses?"

" 'Like master, like man,' " quoted Laddie. "They are! They are foolish with the Kentucky strain, and fools with the Arab; and yet, that combination beats the world. But I must get on with the P.C. job."

He slid from the fence, took a drink from his water jug, and pulled a handful of grass for each horse. As he stood feeding them, I almost fell from the top rail.

"Laddie!" I whispered. "Look! Mr. Pryor is halfway across the field on Ranger."

"So?" said Laddie. "Now I wonder——"

"Shall I go?"

"No indeed!" said Laddie. "Stay right where you are. It can't be anything of much importance."

At first it didn't seem to be. They talked about the weather, the soil, the team. Laddie scooped a handful of black earth, and holding it out, told Mr. Pryor all about how good it was, and why, and he seemed interested. Then they talked about everything; until if he had been Jacob Hood, he would have gone away. But just at the time when I expected him to start, he looked at Laddie straight and hard.

"I missed you Sabbath evening," he said.

Then I looked at him. He had changed, some way. He seemed more human, more like our folks, less cold and stern.

"I sincerely hope it was unanimous," said Laddie.

Mr. Pryor had to laugh.

"It was a majority, at any rate."

Laddie stared dazed. You see that was kind of a joke. An easy one, because I caught it; but we were not accustomed to expecting a jest from Mr. Pryor. Not one of us dreamed there was a joke between his hat crown and his boot soles. Then Laddie laughed; but he sobered quickly.

"I'm mighty sorry if Mrs. Pryor missed me," he said. "I thought of her. I have grown to be her devoted slave, and I hoped she liked me."

"You put it mildly," said Mr. Pryor. "Since you didn't come when she expected you, we've had the worst time with her that we have had since we reached this da—ah—er—um—this country."

"Could you make any suggestion?" asked Laddie.

"I could! I would suggest that you act like the sensible fellow I know you to be, and come as usual, at your accustomed times."

"But I'm forbidden, man!" cried Laddie.

Ugh! Such awful things as Mr. Pryor said.

"Forbidden!" he cried. "Is a man's roof his own, or is it not? While I live, I propose to be the head of my family. I invite you! I ask you! Mrs. Pryor and I want you! What more is necessary?"

"*Two* things," said Laddie, just as serenely. "That Miss Pryor wants me, and that I want to come."

"D'ye mean to tell me that you *don't* want to come, eh? After the fight you put up to force your way in!"

Laddie studied the sky, a whimsy smile on his lips.

"Now wasn't that a good fight?" he inquired. "I'm mighty proud of it! But not now, or ever, do I wish to enter your house again, if Miss Pryor doesn't want, and welcome me."

Then he went over, took Mr. Pryor's horse by the head, and began working with its bridle. It didn't set right some way, and Mr. Pryor had jerked, spurred, and mauled, until there was a big space tramped to mortar. Laddie slid his fingers beneath the leather, eased it a little, and ran his hands over the fretful creature's head. It just stopped, stood still, pushed its nose under his arm, and pressed against his side. Mr. Pryor arose in one stirrup, swung around and alighted. He looped an arm through the bridle rein, and with both hands gripped his whipstock.

"How the devil do you do it?" he asked, as if he were provoked.

"First, the bridle was uncomfortable; next, you surely know, Mr. Pryor, that a man can transfer his mental state to his mount."

Laddie pointed to the churned up earth.

"*That* represents your mental state; *this*"—he slid his hand down the neck of the horse—"portrays mine."

Mr. Pryor's face reddened, but Laddie was laughing so heartily he joined in sort of sickly-like.

"Oh I doubt if you are so damnably calm!" he cried.

"I'm *calm* enough, so far as that goes," said Laddie. "I'm not denying that I've got about all the heartache I can conveniently carry."

"Do you mind telling me how far this affair has gone?"

"Wouldn't a right-minded man give the woman in the case the first chance to answer that question? I greatly prefer that you ask Miss Pryor."

If ever I felt sorry for any one, I did then for Mr. Pryor. He stood there gripping the whip with both hands and he looked exactly as if the May wind might break him into a thousand tiny pieces, and every one of them would be glass.

"Um—er——" he said at last. "You're right, of course, but unfortunately, Pamela and her mother did not agree with my motives, or my course in coming to this country; and while there is no outward demonstration—er—um—other than Mrs. Pryor's seclusion; yet, er—um!—I am forced to the belief that I'm *not* in their confidence."

"I see!" said Laddie. "And of course you love your daughter as any man would love so beautiful a child, and when she is all he has——" I thought the break was coming right there, but Mr. Pryor clenched his whip and put it off; still, any one watching with half an eye could see that it was only put off, and not for long at that,—"It has been my idea, Mr. Pryor, that the proper course for me was to see if I could earn any standing with your daughter. If I could, and she gave me permission, then I intended coming to you the instant I knew how she felt. But in such a case as this, I don't think I shall find the slightest hesitation in telling you anything you want to know, that I am able."

"You don't know how you stand with her?"

Laddie took off his hat and ran his fingers through his hair.

His feet were planted widely apart, and his face was sober enough for any funeral now. At last he spoke.

"I've been trying to figure that out," he said slowly. "I believe the situation is as open to you as it is to me. She was a desperately lonely, homesick girl, when she caught my eye and heart; and I placed myself on her horizon. In her case the women were slow in offering friendship, because, on account of Mrs. Pryor's seclusion, none was felt to be wanted; then Miss Pryor was different in dress and manner. I found a way to let her see that I wanted to be friends, and she accepted my friendship, and at the same time allowed it go only so far. On a few rare occasions, I've met her alone, and we've talked out various phases of life together; but most of our intercourse has taken place in your home, and in your presence. You probably have seen her meet and entertain her friends frequently. I should think you would be more nearly able to gauge my standing with her than I am."

"You haven't told her that you love her?"

"Haven't I though?" cried Laddie. "Man alive! What do you think I'm made of? Putty? Told her? I've told her a thousand times. I've said it, and sung it and whistled it, and looked it, and lived it. I've written it, and ridden it, and this week I've plowed it! Your daughter knows as she knows nothing else, in all this world, that she has only to give me one glance, one word, one gesture of invitation, to find me before her six feet of the worst demoralized beefsteak a woman ever undertook to handle. Told her? Ye Gods! I should say I've told her!"

If any of Pryors had been outdoors they certainly could have heard Mr. Pryor. How he laughed! He shook until he tottered. Laddie took his arm and led him to the fence. He lifted a broad top rail, pushed it between two others across a corner and made a nice comfortable seat for him. After a while Mr. Pryor wiped his eyes. Laddie stood watching him with a slow grin on his face.

"And she hasn't given the signal you are waiting for?" he asked at last.

Laddie slowly shook his head.

"Nary the ghost of a signal!" he said. "Now we come to Sunday before last. I only intimated, vaguely, that a hint of where I stood would be a comfort—and played Jonah. The whale swallowed me at a gulp, and for all my inches, never batted an eye. You see, a few days before I showed her a letter from my brother Jerry, because I thought it might interest her. There was something in it to which I had paid little or no attention, about my going to the city and beginning work in his law office; to cap that, evidently you had mentioned before her our prize piece of family tinware. There was a culmination like a thunder clap in a January sky. She said everything that was on her mind about a man of my size and ability doing the work I am, and then she said I must change my occupation before I came again."

"And for answer you've split the echoes with some shrill, abominable air, and plowed, before her very eyes, for a week!"

Then Laddie laughed.

"Do you know," he said; "that's a good one on me! It never occurred to me that she would not be familiar with that air, and understand its application. Do you mean to crush me further by telling me that all my perfectly lovely vocalizing and whistling was lost?"

"It was a dem irritating, challenging sort of thing," said Mr. Pryor. "I listened to it by the hour, myself, trying to make out exactly what it did mean. It seemed to combine defiance with pleading, and through and over all ran a note of glee that was really quite charming."

"You have quoted a part of it, literally," said Laddie. "'A note of glee'—the cry of a glad heart, at peace with all the world, busy with congenial work."

"I shouldn't have thought you'd have been so particularly joyful."

"Oh, the joy was in the music," said Laddie. "That was a whistle to keep up my courage. The joy was in the song, not in me! Last week was black enough for me to satisfy the most exacting pessimist."

"I wish you might have seen the figure you cut! That fine team, flower bedecked, and the continuous concert!"

"But I did!" cried Laddie. "We have mirrors. That song can't be beaten. I know this team is all right, and I'm not dwarfed or disfigured. That was the pageant of summer passing in review. It represented the tilling of the soil; the sowing of seed, garnering to come later. You buy corn and wheat, don't you? They are vastly necessary. Much more so than the settling of quarrels that never should have taken place. Do you think your daughter found the spectacle at all moving?"

"Damn you, sir, what I should do, is to lay this whip across your shoulders!" cried Mr. Pryor.

But if you will believe it, he was laughing again.

"I prefer that you don't," said Laddie, "or on Ranger either. See how he likes being gentled."

Then he straightened and drew a deep breath.

"Mr. Pryor," he said, "as man to man, I have got this to say to you—and you may use your own discretion about repeating it to your daughter: I can offer her six feet of as sound manhood as you can find on God's footstool. I never in my whole life have had enough impure blood in my body to make even one tiny eruption on my skin. I never have been ill a day in my life. I never have touched a woman save as I lifted and cared for my mother, and hers, or my sisters. As to my family and education she can judge for herself. I offer her the first and only love of my heart. She objects to farming, because she says it is dirty, offensive work. There are parts of it that are dirty. Thank God, it only soils the body, and that can be washed. To delve and to dive into, and to study and to brood over the bigger half of the law business of any city is to steep your brain in, and smirch your soul with, such dirt as I would die before I'd make an occupation of touching. Will you kindly tell her that word for word, and that I asked you to?"

Mr. Pryor was standing before I saw him rise. He said those awful words again, but between them he cried: "You're right! It's the truth! It's the eternal truth!"

"It *is* the truth," said Laddie. "I've only to visit the offices, and examine the business of those of my family living by law, to *know* that it's the truth. Of course there's another side! There are times when there are great opportunities to do good; I recognize that. To some these may seem to overbalance that to which I object. If they do, all right. I am merely deciding for myself. Once and for all, for me it is land. It is born in me to love it, to handle it easily, to get the best results from stock. I am going to take the Merriweather place adjoining ours on the west, and yours on the south. I intend to lease it for ten years, with purchase privilege at the end, so that if I make of it what I plan, my work will not be lost to me. I had thought to fix up the place and begin farming. If Miss Pryor has any use whatever for me, and prefers stock, that is all right with me. I'll go into the same business she finds suitable for you. I can start in a small way and develop. I can afford a maid for her from the beginning, but I couldn't clothe her as she has been accustomed to being dressed, for some time. I would do my best, however. I know what store my mother sets by being well gowned. And as a husband, I can offer your daughter as loving consideration as woman ever received at the hands of man. Provided by some miracle I could win her consent, would you even consider me, and such an arrangement?"

"Frankly sir," said Mr. Pryor, "I have reached the place where I would be——" whenever you come to a long black line like that, it means that he just roared a lot of words father never said, and never will—"glad to! To tell the truth, the thing you choose to jestingly refer to as 'tinware'—I hope later to convince of the indelicacy of such allusion—would place you in England on a social level above any we ever occupied, or could hope to. Your education equals ours. You are a physical specimen to be reckoned with, and I believe what you say of yourself. There's something so clean and manly about you, it amounts to confirmation. A woman should set her own valuation on that; and the height of it should correspond with her knowledge of the world."

"Thank you!" said Laddie. "You are more than kind! more than generous!"

"As to the arrangements you could make for Pamela," said Mr. Pryor, "she's all we have. Everything goes to her, ultimately. She has her stipulated allowance now; whether in my house or yours, it would go with her. Surely you wouldn't be so callous as to object to our giving her anything that would please us!"

"Why should I?" asked Laddie. "That's only natural on your part. Your child is your child; no matter where or what it is, you expect to exercise a certain amount of loving care over it. My father and mother constantly send things to their children absent from home, and they take much pleasure in doing it. That is between you and your daughter, of course. I shouldn't think of interfering. But in the meantime, unless Miss Pryor has been converted to the beauties of plowing through my continuous performance of over a week, I stand now exactly where I did before, so far as she is concerned. If you and Mrs. Pryor have no objection to me, if you feel that you could think of me, or find for me any least part of a son's place in your hearts, I believe I should know how to appreciate it, and how to go to work to make myself worthy of it."

Mr. Pryor sat down so suddenly, the rail almost broke. I thought the truth was, that he had heart trouble, himself. He stopped up, choked on things, flopped around, and turned so white. I suppose he thought it was womanish, and a sign of weakness, and so he didn't tell, but I bet anything that he had it—bad!

"I'll try to make the little fool see!" he said.

"Gently, gently! You won't help me any in that mood," said Laddie. "The chances are that Miss Pryor repeated what she heard from you long ago, and what she knows you think and feel, unless you've changed recently."

"That's the amount of it!" cried Mr. Pryor. "All my life I've had a lot of beastly notions in my head about rank, and class, and here they don't amount to a damn! There's no place for them. Things are different. Your mother, a grand, good woman, opened my eyes to many things recently, and I get her viewpoint —clearly, and I agree with her, and with you, sir!—I agree with you!"

"I am more than glad," said Laddie. "You certainly make a friend at court. Thank you very much!"

"And you will come——?"

"The instant Miss Pryor gives me the slightest sign that I am wanted, and will be welcomed by her, I'll come like a Dakota blizzard! Flos can hump herself on time for once."

"But you won't come until she does?"

"Man alive! I can't!" cried Laddie. "Your daughter said positively exactly what she meant. It was unexpected and it hit me so hard I didn't try to argue. I simply took her at her word, her very explicit word."

"Fool!" cried Mr. Pryor. "The last thing on earth any woman ever wants or expects is for a man to take her at her word."

"What?" cried Laddie.

"She had what she said in her mind of course, but what she wanted was to be argued out of it! She wanted to be convinced!"

"I think not! She was entirely too convincing herself," said Laddie. "It's my guess that she has thought matters over, and that her mind is made up; but I would take it as a mighty big favour if you would put that little piece of special pleading squarely up to her. Will you?"

"Yes," said Mr. Pryor, "I will. I'll keep cool and do my best, but I am so unfortunate in my temper. I could manage slaves better than women. This time I'll be calm, and reason things out with her, or I'll blow out my brains."

"Don't you dare!" laughed Laddie. "You and I are going to get much pleasure, comfort and profit from this world, now that we have come to an understanding."

Mr. Pryor arose and held out his hand. Laddie grasped it tight, and they stood there looking straight at each other, while a lark on the fence post close by cried, "Spring o' ye-ar!" at them, over and over, but they never paid the least attention.

"You see," said Mr. Pryor, "I've been thinking things over deeply, deeply! ever since talking with your mother. I've cut myself off from going back to England, by sacrificing much of my property in hasty departure, if by any possibility I should ever want to return, and there is none, not the slightest! There's no danger of any one crossing the sea, and penetrating to this particular spot so far inland; we won't be molested! And lately—lately, despite the rawness, and the newness, there is something about the land that takes hold, after all. I should dislike leaving now! I found in watching some roots your mother gave me, that I wanted them to grow, that I very much hoped they would develop, and beautify our place with flowers, as yours is. I find myself watching them, watching them daily, and oftener, and there seems to be a sort of home feeling creeping around my heart. I wish Pamela would listen to reason! I wish she would marry you soon! I wish there would be little children. Nothing else on earth would come so close to comforting my wife, and me also. Nothing! Go ahead, lad, plow away! I'll put your special pleading up to the girl."

He clasped Laddie's hand, mounted and rode back to the gate he had entered when he came. Laddie sat on the rail, so I climbed down beside him. He put his arm around me.

"Do I feel any better?" he asked dubiously.

"Of course you do!" I said stoutly. "You feel whole heaps, and stacks, and piles better. You haven't got *him* to fight any more, or Mrs. Pryor. It's now only to convince the Princess about how it's all right to plow."

"Small matter, that!" said Laddie. "And easy! Just as simple and easy!"

"Have you asked the Fairies to help you?"

"Aye, aye, sir," said Laddie. "Also the winds, the flowers, the birds and the bees! I have asked everything on earth to help me except you, Little Sister. I wonder if I have been making a mistake there?"

"Are you mad at me, Laddie?"

"'Cause for why?"

"About the old crest thing!"

"Forget it!" laughed Laddie. "I have. And anyway, in the long run, I must be honest enough to admit that it may have helped. It seems to have had its influence with Mr. Pryor, no doubt it worked the same on Mrs. Pryor, and it may be that it was because she had so much more to bank on than she ever expected, that the

Princess felt emboldened to make her demand. It may be, you can't tell! Anyway, it's very evident that it did no real harm. And forget my jesting, Chicken. A man can't always cry because there are tears in his heart. I think quite as much of that crest as you do. In the sum of human events, it is a big thing. No one admires a Crusader more than I. No one likes a good fight better. No Crusader ever put up a stiffer battle than I have in the past week while working in these fields. Every inch of them is battlefield, every furrow a separate conflict. Gaze upon the scene of my Waterloo! When June covers it with green, it will wave over the resting place of my slain heart!"

"Oh Laddie!" I sobbed. "There you go again! How can you?"

"Whoo-pee!" cried Laddie. "That's the question! How can I? Got to, Little Sister! There's no other way."

"No," I was forced to admit, "there isn't. What are we going to do now?"

"Life-saver, we'll now go to dinner," said Laddie. "Nothing except the partnership implied in 'we' sustains me now. *You'll find a way to help me out, won't you, Little Sister?*"

"*Of course I will!*" I promised, without ever stopping a minute to think what kind of a job that was going to be.

Did you ever wish with all your might that something would happen, and wait for it, expect it, and long for it, and nothing did, until it grew so bad, it seemed as if you had to go on another minute you couldn't bear it? Now I thought when Mr. Pryor talked to her, maybe she'd send for Laddie that very same night; but send nothing! She didn't even ride on our road any more. Of course her father had made a botch of it! Bet I could have told her Laddie's message straighter than he did. I could think it over, and see exactly how he'd do. He'd talk nicely about one minute, and the first word she said, that he didn't like, he'd be ranting, and using unsuitable words. Just as like as not he told her that he'd lay his whip across her shoulders, like he had Laddie. Any one could see that as long as she was his daughter, she might be slightly handy with whips herself; at least she wouldn't be likely to stand still and tell him to go ahead and beat her.

Sunday Laddie went to Lucy's. He said he was having a family reunion on the installment plan. Of course we laughed, but none of us missed the long look he sent toward Pryors' as he mounted to start in the opposite direction.

Everything went on. I didn't see how it could, but it did. It even got worse, for another letter came from Shelley that made matters concerning her no brighter, and while none of us talked about Laddie, all of us knew mighty well how we felt; and what was much worse, how he felt. Father and mother had quit worrying about God; especially father. He seemed to think that God and Laddie could be trusted to take care of the Princess, and I don't know exactly what mother thought. No doubt she saw she couldn't help herself, and so she decided it was useless to struggle.

The plowing on the west side was almost finished, and some of the seed was in. Laddie went straight ahead flower-trimmed and whistling until his face must have ached as badly as his heart. In spite of how hard he tried to laugh, and keep going, all of us could see that he fairly had to stick up his head and stretch his neck like the blue goose, to make the bites go down. And you couldn't help seeing the roundness and the colour go from his face, a little more every day. My! but being in love, when you couldn't have the one you loved, was the worst of all. I wore myself almost as thin as Laddie, hunting a Fairy to ask if she'd help me to make the Princess let Laddie go on and plow, when he was so crazy about it. I prayed beside my bed every night, until the Lord must have grown so tired He quit listening to me, for I talked right up as impressively as I knew how, and it didn't do the least bit of good. I hadn't tried the one big prayer toward the east yet; but I was just about to the place where I intended to do it soon.

CHAPTER XV

Laddie, the Princess, and the Pie

"O whistle, and I'll come to you, my lad."

CANDACE was baking the very first batch of rhubarb pies for the season and the odour was so tempting I couldn't keep away from the kitchen door. Now Candace was a splendid cook about chicken gizzards—the liver was always mother's—doughnuts and tarts, but I never really did believe she would cut into a fresh rhubarb pie, even for me. As I reached for the generous big piece I thought of Laddie—poor Laddie, plowing away at his Crusader fight, and not a hint of victory. No one in the family liked rhubarb pie better than he did. I knew there was no use to ask for a plate.

"Wait—oh wait!" I cried.

I ran to the woodshed, pulled a shining new shingle from a bale stacked there, and held it for Candace. Then I slipped around the house softly. I didn't want to run any one's errands that morning. I laid the pie on the horseblock and climbed the catalpa carefully, so as not to frighten my robins. They were part father's too, because robins were his favourite birds; he said their song through and after rain was the sweetest music on earth, and mostly he was right; so they were not all my robins, but they were most mine after him; and I owned the tree. I hunted the biggest leaf I could see, and wiped it clean on my apron, although it was early for much dust. It covered the pie nicely, because it was the proper shape, and I held the stem with one hand to keep it in place.

If I had made that morning myself I couldn't have done better. It was sunny, spring air, but it was that cool, spicy kind that keeps you stopping every few minutes to see just how full you can suck your lungs without bursting. It seemed to wash right through and through and make you all over. The longer you breathed it the clearer your head became, and the better you felt, until you would be possessed to try and see if you really couldn't fly. I tried that last summer, and knocked myself into jelly. You'd think once would have been enough, but there I was going down the road with Laddie's pie, and wanting with all my heart to try again.

Sometimes I raced, but I was a little afraid the pie would shoot from the shingle and it was like pulling eye teeth to go fast that morning. I loved the soft warm dust, that was working up on the road. Spat! Spat! I brought down my bare feet, already scratched and turning brown, and laughed to myself at the velvety feel of it. There were little puddles yet, where May and I had "dipped and faded" last fall, and it was fun to wade them. The roadsides were covered with meadow grass and clover that had slipped through the fence. On slender green blades, in spot after spot, twinkled the delicate bloom of blue-eyed grass. Never in all this world was our Big Creek lovelier. It went slipping, and whispering, and lipping, and lapping over the stones, tugging at the rushes and grasses as it washed their feet; everything beside it was in masses of bloom, a blackbird was gleaming and preening on every stone, as it plumed after its bath. Oh there's no use to try —it was just *Spring* when it couldn't possibly be any better.

But even spring couldn't hold me very long that morning, for you see my heart was almost sick about Laddie; and if he couldn't have the girl he wanted, at least I could do my best to comfort him with the pie. I was going along being very careful the more I thought about how he would like it, so I was not watching the road so far ahead as I usually did. I always kept a lookout for Paddy Ryan, Gypsies, or Whitmore's bull. When I came to an unusually level place, and took a long glance ahead, my heart turned right over and stopped still, and I looked long enough to be sure, and then right out loud some one said, "I'll *do* something!" and as usual, I was the only one there.

For days I'd been in a ferment, like the vinegar barrel when the cider boils, or the yeast jar when it sets too close to the stove. To have Laddie and the Princess separated was dreadful, and knowing him as I did, I knew he never really would get over it. I had tried to help once, and what I had done started things going wrong; no wonder I was slow about deciding what to try next. That I was going to do something, I made up my mind the instant Laddie said he was not mad at me; that I was his partner, and asked me to help; but exactly *what* would do any good, took careful thought.

Here was my chance coming right at me. She was far up the road, riding Maud like racing. I began to breathe after a while, like you always do, no matter how you are worked up, and with my brain whirling, I went slowly toward her. How would I manage to stop her? Or what could I say that would help Laddie? I was shaking, and that's the truth; but through and over it all, I was watching her too. I only wish you might have seen her that morning. Of course the morning was part of it. A morning like that would make a fence post better looking. Half a mile away you could see she was tipsy with spring as I was, or the song sparrows, or the crazy babbling old bobolinks on the stakes and riders. She made such a bright splash against the pink fence row, with her dark hair, flushed cheeks, and red lips, she took my breath. Father said she was the loveliest girl in three counties, and Laddie stretched that to the whole world. As she came closer, smash! through me went the thought that she looked precisely as Shelley had at Christmas time; and Shelley had been that way because she was in love with the Paget man. Now if the Princess was gleaming and flashing like that, for the same reason, there wasn't any one for her to love so far as I knew, except Laddie.

Then smash! came another thought. She *had* to love him! She couldn't help herself. She had all winter, all last summer, and no one but themselves knew how long before that, and where was there any other man like Laddie? Of course she loved him! Who so deserving of love? Who else had his dancing eyes of deep tender blue, cheeks so pink, teeth so white, such waving chestnut hair, and his height and breadth? There was no other man who could ride, swim, leap, and wrestle as he could. None who could sing the notes, do the queer sums with letters having little figures at the corners in the college books, read Latin as fast as English, and even the Greek Bible. Of course she loved him! Every one did! Others might plod and meander, Laddie walked the tired, old road that went out of sight over the hill, with as prideful a step as any king; his laugh was as merry as the song of the gladdest thrush, while his touch was so gentle that when mother was in dreadful pain I sometimes thought she would a little rather have him hold her than father.

Now, he was in this fearful trouble, the colour was going from his face, his laugh was a little strained, and the heartache almost more than he could endure—and there she came! I stepped squarely in the middle of the road so she would have to stop or ride over me, and when she was close, I stood quite still. I was watching with my eyes, heart, and brain, and I couldn't see that she was provoked, as she drew rein and cried: "Good morning, Little Queer Person!"

I had supposed she would say Little Sister, she had for ages, just like Laddie, but she must have thought it was queer for me to stop her that way, so she changed. I was in for it. I had her now, so I smiled the very sweetest smile that I could think up in such a hurry, and said, "Good morning," the very politest I ever did in all my life. Then I didn't know what to do next, but she helped me out.

"What have you there?" she asked.

"It's a piece of the very first rhubarb pie for this spring, and I'm carrying it to Laddie," I said, as I lifted the catalpa leaf and let her peep, just to show her how pie looked when it was right. I bet she never saw a nicer piece.

The Princess slid her hand down Maud's neck to quiet her prancing, and leaned in the saddle, her face full of interest. I couldn't see a trace of anything to discourage me; her being on our road again looked favourable. She seemed to think quite as much of that pie as I did. She was the finest little thoroughbred. She understood so well, I was sorry I couldn't give it to her. It made her mouth water all right, for she drew a deep breath that sort of quivered; but it was no use, she didn't get that pie.

"I think it looks delicious," she said. "Are you carrying it for Candace?"

"No! She gave it to me. It's my very own."

"And you're doing without it yourself to carry it to Laddie, I'll be bound!" cried the Princess.

"I'd much rather," I said.

"Do you love Laddie so dearly?" she asked.

My heart was full of him right then; I forgot all about when I had the fever, and as I never had been taught to lie, I told her what I thought was the truth, and I guess it *was:* "Best of any one in all this world!"

The Princess looked across the field, where she must have seen him finishing the plowing, and thought that over, and I waited, sure in my mind, for some reason, that she would not go for a little while longer.

"I have been wanting to see you," she said at last. "In fact I think I came this way hoping I'd meet you. Do you know the words to a tune that goes like this?"

Then she began to whistle "The Merry Farmer Boy." I wish you might have heard the flourishes she put to it.

"Of course I do," I answered. "All of us were brought up on it."

"Well, I have some slight curiosity to learn what they are," she said. "Would you kindly repeat them for me?"

"Yes," I said. "This is the first verse:

" 'See the merry farmer boy tramp the meadows through,
   Swing his hoe in careless joy while dashing off the dew.
   Bobolink in maple high——'

"Of course you can see for yourself that they're not. There isn't a single one of them higher than a fence post. The person who wrote the piece had to put it that way so high would rhyme with reply, which is coming in the next line."

"I see!" said the Princess.

> *"'Bobolink in maple high, trills a note of glee*
> *Farmer boy a gay reply now whistles cheerily.'*

"Then you whistle the chorus like you did it."

"You do indeed!" said the Princess. "Proceed!"

> *"'Then the farmer boy at noon, rests beneath the shade,*
> *Listening to the ceaseless tune that's thrilling through*
> *the glade.*
> *Long and loud the harvest fly winds his bugle round,*
> *Long, and loud, and shrill, and high, he whistles back*
> *the sound.'"*

"He does! He does indeed! I haven't a doubt about that!" cried the Princess. " 'Long, and loud, and shrill, and high,' he whistles over and over the sound, until it becomes maddening. Is that all of that melodious, entrancing production?"

"No, evening comes yet. The last verse goes this way:

> *"'When the busy day's employ, ends at dewy eve,*
> *Then the happy farmer boy, doth haste his work to leave,*
> *Trudging down the quiet lane, climbing o'er the hill,*
> *Whistling back the changeless wail, of plaintive whip-poor-will,'—*

and then you do the chorus again, and if you know how well enough you whistle in, 'whip-poor-will,' 'til the birds will answer you. Laddie often makes them."

"My life!" cried the Princess. "Was that he doing those bird cries? Why, I hunted, and hunted, and so did father. We'd never seen a whip-poor-will. Just fancy us!"

"If you'd only looked at Laddie," I said.

"My patience!" cried the Princess. "Looked at him! There was no place to look without seeing him. And that ear-splitting thing will ring in my head forever, I know."

"Did he whistle it too high to suit you, Princess?"

"He was perfectly welcome to whistle as he chose," she said, "and also to plow with the carriage horses, and to bedeck them and himself with the modest, shrinking red tulip and yellow daffodil."

Now any one knows that tulips and daffodils are *not* modest and shrinking. If any flowers just blaze and scream colour clear across a garden, they do. She was provoked, you could see that.

"Well, he only did it to please you," I said. "He didn't care anything about it. He never plowed that way before. But you said he mustn't plow at all, and he just had to plow, there was no escaping that, so he made it as fine and happy as possible to show you how nicely it could be done."

"Greatly obliged, I'm sure!" cried the Princess. "He showed me! He certainly did! And so he feels that there's 'no escaping' plowing, does he?"

Then I knew where I was. I'd have given every cent of mine in father's chest till, if mother had been in my place. Once, for a second, I thought I'd ask the Princess to go with me to the house, and let mother tell her how it was; but if she wouldn't go, and rode away, I felt I couldn't endure it, and anyway, she had said she was looking for me; so I gripped the shingle, dug in my toes and went at her just as nearly like mother talked to her father as I could remember, and I'd been put through memory tests, and descriptive tests, nearly every night of my life, so I had most of it as straight as a string.

"Well, you see, he *can't* escape it," I said. "He'd do anything in all this world for you that he possibly could; but there are some things no man *can* do."

"I didn't suppose there was anything you thought Laddie couldn't do," she said.

"A little time back, I didn't," I answered. "But since he took the carriage horses, trimmed up in flowers, and sang and whistled so bravely, day after day, when his heart was full of tears, why I learned that there was something he just *couldn't do; not to save his life, or his love, or even to save you.*"

"And of course you don't mind telling me what that is?" coaxed the Princess in her most wheedling tones.

"Not at all! He told our family, and I heard him tell your father. The thing he can't do, not even to win you, is to be shut up in a little office, in a city, where things roar, and smell, and nothing is like this——"

I pointed out the orchard, hill, and meadow, so she looked where I showed her—looked a long time.

"No, a city wouldn't be like this," she said slowly.

"And that isn't even the beginning," I said. "Maybe he could bear that, men have been put in prison and lived through years and years of it, perhaps Laddie could too; I doubt it! but anyway the worst of it is that he just couldn't, not even to save you, spend all the rest of his life trying to settle other people's old fusses. He despises a fuss. Not one of us ever in our lives have been able to make him quarrel, even one word. He simply won't. And if he possibly could be made to by any one on earth, Leon would have done it long ago, for he can start a fuss with the side of a barn. But he can't make Laddie fuss, and nobody can. He *never* would at school, or anywhere. Once in a while if a man gets so overbearing that Laddie simply can't stand it, he says: 'Now, you'll take your medicine!' Then he pulls off his coat, and carefully, choosing the right spots, he just pounds the breath out of that man, but he never stops smiling, and when he helps him up he always says: 'Sorry! hope you'll excuse me, but you *would* have it.' That's what he said about you, that you had to take your medicine——"

I made a mistake there. That made her too mad for any use.

"Oh," she cried, "I do? I'll jolly well show the gentleman!"

"Oh, you needn't take the trouble," I cried. "He's showing you!"

She just blazed like she'd break into flame. Any one could fuss with her all right; but that was the last thing on earth I wanted to do.

"You see he already knows about you," I explained as fast as I could talk, for I was getting into an awful mess. "You see he knows that you want him to be a lawyer, and that he must quit plowing before he can be more than friends with you. That's what he's plowing for! If it wasn't for that, probably he wouldn't be plowing at all. He asked father to let him, and he borrowed mother's horses, and he hooked the flowers through the fence. Every night when he comes home, he kneels beside mother and asks her if he is 'repulsive,' and she takes him in her arms and the tears roll down her cheeks and she says: 'Father has farmed all his life, and you know how repulsive he is.' "

I ventured an upward peep. I was doing better. Her temper seemed to be cooling, but her face was a jumble. I couldn't find any one thing on it that would help me, so I just stumbled ahead guessing at what to say.

"He didn't *want* to do it. He perfectly *hated* it. Those fields were his Waterloo. Every furrow was a *fight,* but he was *forced* to show you."

"Exactly *what* was he trying to show me?"

"I can think of three things he told me," I answered. "That plowing could be so managed as not to disfigure the land-scape——"

"The dunce!" she said.

"That he could plow or do dirtier work, and not be repul-sive——"

"The idiot!" she said.

"That if he came over there, and plowed right under your nose, when you'd told him he mustn't, or he couldn't be more than friends; and when you knew that he'd much rather die and be laid beside the little sisters up there in the cemetery than to *not* be more than friends, why, you'd see, if he did *that,* he couldn't help it, that he just *must.* That he was *forced*——"

"The soldier!" she said.

"Oh Princess, he didn't want to!" I cried. "He tells me secrets he doesn't any one else, unless you. He told me how he hated it; but he just had to do it."

"Do you know *why?*"

"Of course! It's the way he's *made!* Father is like that! He has chances to live in cities, make big business deals, and go to the legislature at Indianapolis; I've seen his letters from his friend Oliver P. Morton, our Governor, you know; they're in his chest till now; but father can't do it, because he is made so he stays at home and works for us, and this farm, and township, and county where he belongs. He says if all men will do that the millennium will come to-morrow. I 'spose you know what the millennium is?"

"I do!" said the Princess. "But I don't know what your father and his friend Oliver P. Morton have to do with Laddie."

"Why, everything on earth! Laddie is father's son, you see, and he is made like father. None of our other boys is. Not one of them loves land. Leon is going away as quick as ever he finishes college; but the more you educate Laddie, the better he likes to make things grow, the more he loves to make the world beautiful, to be kind to every one, to gentle animals—why, the biggest fight he ever had, the man he whipped 'til he most couldn't bring him back again, was one who kicked his horse in the stomach. Gee, I thought he'd killed him! Laddie did too for a while, but he only said the man deserved it."

"And so he did!" cried the Princess angrily. "How beastly!"

"That's one reason Laddie sticks so close to land. He says he doesn't meet nearly so many two-legged beasts in the country. Almost every time he goes to town he either gets into a fight or he sees something that makes him fighting mad. Princess, you think this beautiful, don't you?"

I just pointed anywhere. All the world was in it that morning. You couldn't look right or left and not see lovely places, hear music, and smell flowers.

"Yes! It is altogether wonderful!" she said.

"Would you like to live among this all your life, and have your plans made to fix you a place even nicer, and then be forced to leave it and go to a little room in the city, and make all the money you earned off of how much other men fight over business, and land and such perfectly awful things, that they always have to be whispered when Jerry tells about them? Would you?"

"You little dunce!" she cried.

"I know I'm a fool. I know I'm not telling you a single thing

I should! Maybe I'm hurting Laddie far more than I'm helping him, and if I am, I wish I would die before I see him; but oh! Princess, I'm trying with all my might to make you understand how he feels. He *wants* to do every least thing you'd like him to. He will, almost any thing else in the world, he would this— he would in a minute, but he just *can't*. All of us know he can't! If you'd lived with him since he was little and always had known him, you wouldn't ask him to; you wouldn't want him to! You don't know what you're doing! Mother says you don't! You'll kill him if you send him to the city to live, you just will! You are doing it now! He's getting thinner and whiter every day. Don't! Oh please don't do it!"

The Princess was looking at the world. She was gazing at it so dazed-like she seemed to be surprised at what she saw. She acted as if she'd never really seen it before. She looked and she looked. She even turned her horse a full circle to see all of it, and she went around slowly. I stepped from one foot to the other and sweat; but I kept quiet and let her look. At last when she came around, she glanced down at me, and she was all melted, and lovely as any one you ever saw, exactly like Shelley at Christmas, and she said: "I don't think I ever saw the world before. I don't know that I'm so crazy about a city myself, and I perfectly hate lawyers. Come to thing of it, a lawyer helped work ruin in our family, and I never have believed, I never will believe——"

She stopped talking and began looking again. I gave her all the time she needed. I was just straining to be wise, for mother says it takes the very wisest person there is to know when to talk, and when to keep still. As I figured it, now was the time not to say another word until she made up her mind about what I had told her already. If Pryors didn't know what we thought of them by that time, it wasn't mother's fault or mine. As she studied things over she kept on looking. What she saw seemed to be doing her a world of good. Her face showed it every second plainer and plainer. Pretty soon it began to look like she was going to come through as Amos Hurd did when he was redeemed. Then, before my very eyes, it happened! I don't know how I ever held on to the pie or kept from shouting, "Praise the Lord!" as father does at the Meeting House when he is happiest. Then she leaned toward me all wavery, and shining eyed, and bloomful, and said: "Did you ever hurt Laddie's feelings, and make him angry and sad?"

"I'm sure I never did," I answered.

"But suppose you had! What would you do?"

"Do? Why, I'd go to him on the run, and I'd tell him I never intended to hurt his feelings, and how sorry I was, and I'd give him the very best kiss I could."

The Princess stroked Maud's neck a long time and thought while she studied our farm, theirs beyond it, and at the last, the far field where Laddie was plowing. She thought, and thought, and afraid to cheep, I stood gripping the shingle and waited. Finally she said: "The last time Laddie was at our house, I said to him those things he repeated to you. He went away at once, hurt and disappointed. Now, if you like, along with your precious pie, you may carry him this message from me. You may tell him that I said I am sorry!"

I could have cried "Glory!" and danced and shouted there in the road, but I didn't. It was no time to lose my head. That was all so fine and splendid, as far as it went, but it didn't quite cover the case. I never could have done it for myself; but for Laddie I would venture anything, so I looked her in the eyes, straight as a dart, and said: "He'd want the kiss too, Princess!"

You could see her stiffen in the saddle and her fingers grip the reins, but I kept on staring right into her eyes.

"I could come up, you know," I offered.

A dull red flamed in her cheeks and her lips closed tight. One second she sat very still, then a dancing light leaped sparkling into her eyes; a flock of dimples chased each other around her lips like swallows circling their homing place at twilight.

"What about that wonderful pie?" she asked me.

I ran to the nearest fence corner, and laid the shingle on the gnarled roots of a Johnny Appleseed apple tree. Then I set one foot on the arch of the Princess' instep and held up my hands.

One second I thought she would not lift me, the next I was on her level and her lips met mine in a touch like velvet woven from threads of flame. Then with a turn of her stout little wrist, she dropped me, and a streak went up our road. Nothing so amazing and so important ever had happened to me. It was an occasion that demanded something unusual. To cry, "Praise the Lord!" was only to repeat an hourly phrase at our house; this demanded something out of the ordinary, so I said just exactly as father did the day the brown mare balked with the last load of seed clover, when a big storm was breaking—"Jupiter Ammon!"

When I had calmed down so I could, I climbed the fence, and reached through a crack for the pie. As I followed the cool, damp furrow, and Laddie's whistle, clear as the lark's above the wheat, thrilled me, I was almost insane with joy. Just joy! Pure joy! Oh what a good world it was!—most of the time! Most of the time! Of course, there *were* Paget men in it. But anyway, *this* couldn't be beaten. I had a message for Laddie from the Princess that would send him to the seventh heaven, wherever that was; no one at our house spent any time thinking farther than the first one. I had her kiss, that I didn't know what would do to him, and I also had a big piece of juicy rhubarb pie not yet entirely cold. If that didn't wipe out the trouble I had made showing the old crest thing, nothing ever could. I knew even then, that men were pretty hard to satisfy, but I was quite certain that Laddie would be satisfied that morning. As I hurried along I wondered whether it would be better to give him my gift first, or the Princess'. I decided that joy would keep, while the pie was cold enough, with all the time I had stopped; and if I told him about her first, maybe he wouldn't touch it at all, and it wasn't so easy as it looked to carry it to him and never even once stick in my finger for the tiniest lick—joy would keep; but I was going to feed him; so with shining face, I offered the pie and stood back to see just how happy I could get.

"Mother send it?" asked Laddie.

People were curious that morning, as if I had a habit of stealing pie. I only took pieces of cut ones from the cellar when mother didn't care. So I explained again that Candace gave it to me, and I was free to bring it.

"Oh I see!" said Laddie.

After nearly two weeks of work, the grays had sobered down enough to stand without tying; so he wound the lines around the plow handle, sat on the beam, and laid aside his hat, having a fresh flower in the band. Once he started a thing, he just simply wouldn't give up. He unbuttoned his neckband until I could see his throat where it was white like a woman's, took out his knife and ate that pie. Of course we knew better than to use a knife at the table, but there was no other way in the field. He ate that pie, slowly and deliberately, and between bites he talked. I watched him with a wide grin, wondering what in this world he *would* say, in a minute. I don't think I ever had quite such a good time in all my life before, and I never expect to again. He was saying: "Talk about nectar and ambrosia! Talk about the feasts of Lucullus! Talk about food for the Gods!"

I put on his hat, sat on the ground in front of him, and was the happiest girl in the world, of that I am quite sure. When the last morsel was finished, Laddie looked at me steadily.

"I wonder," he said, "I wonder if there's another man in the world who is blest with quite such a loving, unselfish little sister as mine?" Then he answered himself: "No! By all the Gods, and half-Gods, I swear it— No!"

It was grand as a Fourth of July oration or the most exciting part when the Bishop dedicated our church. I couldn't hold in another second, I could hear my heart beat.

"Oh Laddie!" I shouted, jumping up, "that pie is only the beginning of the good things I have brought you. I have a message, and a gift besides, Laddie!"

"A message and a gift?" Laddie repeated. "What! More?"

"Truly I have a message and a gift for you," I cried, "and Laddie—they are from the Princess!"

His eyes raised to mine now, and slowly he turned Sabethany-like.

"From the Princess!" he exclaimed. "A message and a gift for me, Little Sister? You never would let Leon put you up to serve me a trick?"

That hurt. He should have *known* I wouldn't, and besides, "Leon feels just as badly about this as any of us," I said. "Have you forgotten he offered to plow, and let you do the clean, easy work?"

"Forgive me! I'm overanxious," said Laddie, his arms reaching for me. "Go on and tell carefully, and if you truly love me, don't make a mistake!"

Crowding close, my arms around his neck, his crisp hair against my lips, I whispered my story softly, for this was such a fine and splendid secret, that not even the shining blackbirds, and the pert robins in the furrows were going to get to hear a word of it. Before I had finished Laddie was breathing as Flos does when he races her the limit. He sat motionless for a long time, while over his face slowly crept a beauty that surpassed that of Apollo in his Greek book.

"And her gift?"

It was only a breath.

"She helped me up, and she sent you this," I answered.

Then I set my lips on his, and held them there a second, trying my level best to give him her very kiss, but of course I could only try.

"Oh, Laddie," I cried. "Her eyes were like when stars shine down in our well! Her cheeks were like mother's damask roses! She smelled like flowers, and when her lips touched mine little stickers went all over me!"

Then Laddie's arms closed around me and I thought sure every bone in my body was going to be broken; when he finished there wasn't a trace of that kiss left for me. Remembering it would be all I'd ever have. It made me see what would have happened to the Princess if she had been there; and it was an awful pity for her to miss it, because he'd sober down a lot before he reached her, but I was sure as shooting that he wouldn't be so crazy as to kiss her hands again. Peter wasn't a patching to him!

That night Laddie rode to Pryors'. When he brought Flos to

the gate you could see the shadow of your face on her shining flank; her mane and tail were like ravelled silk, her hoofs bright as polished horn, and her muzzle was clean as a ribbon. I broke one of those rank green sprouts from the snowball bush and brushed away the flies, so she wouldn't fret, stamp, and throw dust on herself. Then Laddie came, fresh from a tubbing, starched linen, dressed in his new riding suit, and wearing top hat and gauntlets. He looked the very handsomest I ever had seen him; and at the same time, he seemed trembling with tenderness, and bursting with power. Goodness sake! I bet the Princess took one good look and "came down" like Davy Crockett's coon. Mother was on his arm and she walked clear to the gate with him.

"*Laddie, are you sure enough to go?*" I heard her ask him whisper-like.

"*Sure as death!*" Laddie answered.

Mother looked, and she had to see how it was with him; no doubt she saw more than I did from having been through it herself, so she smiled kind of a half-sad, half-glad smile. Then she turned to her damask rose bush, the one Lucy brought her from the city, and that she was so precious about, that none of us dared touch it, and she searched all over it and carefully selected the most perfect rose. When she borrowed Laddie's knife and cut the stem as long as my arm, I knew exactly how great and solemn the occasion was; for always before about six inches had been her limit. She held it toward him, smiling bravely and beautifully, but the tears were running straight down her cheeks.

"Take it to her," she said. "I think, my son, it is very like."

Laddie took her in his arms and wiped away the tears; he told her everything would come out all right about God, and the mystery, even. Then he picked me clear off the ground, and he tried to see how near he could come to cracking every bone in my body without really doing it, and he kissed me over and over. It hadn't been so easy, but I guess you'll admit that paid. Then he rode away with the damask rose waving over his heart. Mother and I stood beside the hitching rack and looked after him, with our arms tight around each other while we tried to see which one could bawl the hardest.

CHAPTER XVI

The Homing Pigeon

"A millstone and the human heart,
Are ever driven round,
And if they've nothing else to grind,
They must themselves be ground."

It SEEMED to me that my mother was the person who really could
have been excused for having heart trouble. The more I watched
her, the more I wondered that she didn't. There was her own
life, the one she and father led, where everything went exactly
as she wanted it to; and if there had been only themselves to
think of, no people on earth could have lived happier, unless the
pain she sometimes suffered made them trouble, and I don't think
it would, for neither of them were to blame for that. They
couldn't help it. They just had it to stand, and fight the stiffest
they could to cure it, and mother always said she was better;
every single time any one asked, she was better. I hoped soon it
would all be gone. Then they could have been happy for sure,
if some of us hadn't popped up and kept them in hot water all
the time.

I can't tell you about Laddie when he came back from Pryors'.
He tore down the house, then tore it up, and then threw around
the pieces, and none of us cared. Every one was just laughing,
shouting, and every bit as pleased as he was, while I was the
Queen Bee. Laddie said so, himself, and if he didn't know, no
one did. Pryors had been lovely to him. When mother asked him
how he made it, he answered: "I rode over, picked up the Princess and helped myself. After I finished, I remembered the little
unnecessary formality of asking her to marry me; and she said

right out loud that she *would*. When I had time for them, I reached Father and Mother Pryor, and maybe it doesn't show, but somewhere on my person I carry their blessing, genially and heartily given, I am proud to state. Now, I'm only needing yours, to make me a king among men."

They gave it quite as willingly, I am sure, although you could see mother scringe when Laddie said "Father and Mother Pryor." I knew why. She adored Laddie, like the Bible says you must adore the Almighty. From a tiny baby Laddie had taken care of her. He used to go back, take her hand, and try to help her over rough places while he still wore dresses. Straight on, he had been like that; always seeing when there was too much work and trying to shield her; always knowing when a pain was coming and fighting to head it off; always remembering the things the others forgot, going to her last at night, and his face against hers on her pillow the first in the morning, to learn how she was before he left the house. If you were the mother of a man like that, how would you like to hear him call some one else mother, and have the word slip from his tongue so slick you could see he didn't even realize that he had used it? The answer would be, if you were honest, that you wouldn't have liked it any more than she did. She knew he had to go. She wanted him to be happy. She was as sure of the man he was going to be as she was sure of the mercy of God. That is the strongest way I know to tell it. She was unshakably sure of the mercy of God, but I wasn't. There were times when it seemed as if He couldn't hear the most powerful prayer you could pray, and when instead of mercy, you seemed to get the last torment that could be piled on. Take right now. Laddie was happy, and all of us were, in a way; and in another we were almost stiff with misery.

I dreaded his leaving us so, I would slip to the hawk oak and cry myself sick, more than once; whether any of the others were that big babies I don't know; but anyway, *they* were not his Little Sister. I was. I always had been. I always would be, for that matter; but there was going to be a mighty big difference. I had the poor comfort that I'd done the thing myself. Maybe if it hadn't been for stopping the Princess when I took him that pie, they never would have made up, and she might have gone across the sea and stayed there. Maybe she'd go yet, as mysteriously as she had come, and take him along. Sometimes I almost wished I hadn't tried to help him; but of course I didn't really. Then, too, I had sense enough to know that loving each other as they did, they wouldn't live on that close together for years and years, and not find a way to make up for themselves, like they had at the start. I liked Laddie saying I had made his happiness for him; but I wasn't such a fool that I didn't know he could have made it for himself just as well, and no doubt better. So everything was all right with Laddie; and what happened to us, the day he rode away for the last time, when he went to stay—what happened to us, then, was our affair. We had to take it, but every one of us dreaded it, while mother didn't know how to bear it, and neither did I. Once I said to her: "Mother, when Laddie goes we'll just have to make it up to each other the best we can, won't we?"

"Oh my soul, child!" she cried, staring at me so surprised-like. "Why, how unspeakably selfish I have been! No little lost sheep ever ran this farm so desolate as you will be without your brother. Forgive me baby, and come here!"

Gee, but we did cry it out together! The God she believed in has wiped away her tears long ago; this minute I can scarcely see the paper for mine. If you could call anything happiness, that was mixed with feeling like that, why, then, we were happy about Laddie. But from things I heard father and mother say, I knew they could have borne his going away, and felt a trifle better than they did. I was quite sure they had stopped thinking that he was going to lose his soul, but they couldn't help feeling so long as that old mystery hung over Pryors that he *might* get into trouble through it. Father said if it hadn't been for Mr. Pryor's stubborn and perverted notions about God, he would like the man immensely, and love to be friends; and if Laddie married into the family we would have to be as friendly as we could anyway. He said he had such a high opinion of Mr. Pryor's integrity that he didn't believe he'd encourage Laddie to enter his family if it would involve the boy in serious trouble. Mother didn't know. Anyway, the thing was done, and by fall, no doubt, Laddie would leave us.

Just when we were trying to keep a stiff upper lip before him, and whistling as hard as ever he had, to brace our courage, a letter came for mother from the head of the music school Shelley attended, saying she was no longer fit for work, so she was being sent home at once, and they would advise us to consult a specialist immediately. Mother sat and stared at father, and father went to hitch the horses to drive to Groveville.

There's only one other day of my life that stands out as clearly as that. The house was clean as we could make it. I finished feeding early, and had most of the time to myself. I went down to the Big Hill, and followed the top of it to our woods. Then I turned around, and started toward the road, just idling. If I saw a lovely spot I sat down and watched all around me to see if a Fairy really would go slipping past, or lie asleep under a leaf. I peeked and peered softly, going from spot to spot, watching everything. Sometimes I hung over the water, and studied tiny little fish with red, yellow, and blue on them, bright as flowers. The dragonflies would alight right on me, and some wore bright blue markings and some blood red. There was a blue beetle, a beautiful green fly, and how the blue wasps did flip, flirt and glint in the light. So did the blackbirds and the redwings. That embankment was left especially to shade the water, and to feed the birds. Every foot of it was covered with alders, wild cherry, hazelbush, mulberries, everything having a berry or nut. There were several scrub apple trees, many red haws, the wild strawberries spread in big beds in places, and some of them were colouring.

Wild flowers grew everywhere, great beds were blue with calamus, and the birds flocked in companies to drive away the water blacksnakes that often found nests, and liked eggs and bird babies. When I came to the road at last, the sun was around so the big oak on the top of the hill threw its shadow across the bridge, and I lay along one edge and watched the creek bottom, or else I sat up so the water flowed over my feet, and looked at the embankment and the sky. In a way, it was the most peculiar day of my life. I had plenty to think of, but I never thought at all. I only lived. I sat watching the world go past through a sort of golden haze the sun made. When a pair of kingbirds and three crows chased one of my hawks pell-mell across the sky, I looked on and didn't give a cent what happened. When a big blacksnake darted its head through sweet grass and cattails, and caught a frog that had climbed on a mossy stone in the shade to dine on flies, I let it go. Any other time I would have hunted a stick and made the snake let loose. To-day I just sat there and let things happen as they did.

At last I wandered up the road, climbed the back garden fence, and sat on the board at the edge of a flowerbed, and to-day, I could tell to the last butterfly about that garden: what was in bloom, how far things had grown, and what happened. Bobby flew under the Bartlett pear tree and crowed for me, but I never called him. I sat there and lived on, and mostly watched the bees tumble over the bluebells. They were almost ready to be cut to put in the buttered tumblers for perfume, like mother made for us. Then I went into the house and looked at Grace Greenwood, but I didn't take her along. Mother came past and gave me a piece of stiff yellow brocaded silk as lovely as I ever had seen, enough for a dress skirt; and a hand-embroidered chemise sleeve that only needed a band and a button to make a petticoat for a Queen doll, but I laid them away and wandered into the orchard.

I dragged my bare feet through the warm grass, and finally sat under the beet red peach tree. If ever I seemed sort of lost and sorry for myself, that was a good place to go; it was so easy to feel abused there because you didn't dare touch those peaches. Fluffy baby chickens were running around, but I didn't care; there was more than a bird for every tree, bluebirds especially; they just loved us and came early and stayed late, and grew so friendly they nested all over the wood house, smoke house, and any place we fixed for them, and in every hollow apple limb. Bobby came again, but I didn't pay any attention to him.

Then I heard the carriage cross the bridge. I knew when it was father, every single time his team touched the first plank. So I ran like an Indian, and shinned up a cedar tree, scratching myself until I bled. Away up I stood on a limb, held to the tree and waited. Father drove to the gate, and mother came out, with May, Candace, and Leon following. When Shelley touched the ground and straightened, any other tree except a spruce having limbs to hold me up, I would have fallen from it. She looked exactly as if she had turned to tombstone with eyes and hair alive. She stopped a second to brush a little kiss across mother's lips, to the others she said without even glancing at them: "Oh do let me lie down a minute! The motion of that train made me sick."

Well, I should say it did! I quit living, and began thinking in a hooray, and so did every one else at our house. Once I had been sick and queened it over them for a while, now all of us strained ourselves trying to wait on Shelley; but she wouldn't have it. She only said she was tired to death, to let her rest, and she turned her face to the wall and lay there. Once she said she never wanted to see a city again so long as she lived. When mother told her about Laddie and the Princess to try to interest her, she never said a word; I doubted if she even listened. Father and mother looked at each other, when they thought no one would see, and their eyes sent big, anxious questions flashing back and forth. I made up my mind I'd keep awake that night and hear what they said, if I had to take pins to bed with me and stick myself.

Once mother said to Shelley that she was going to send for Dr. Fenner, and she answered: "All right, if *you* need him. Don't you dare for me! I'll not see him. All I want is a little peace and rest."

The idea! Not one of us ever had spoken to mother like that before in all our born days. I held my breath to see what she would do, but she didn't seem to have heard it, or to notice how rude it had been. Well, *that* told about as plain as anything what we had on our hands. I wandered around and *now* there was no trouble about thinking things. They came in such a jumble I could get no sense from them; but one big black thought came over, and over, and over, and wouldn't be put away. It just stood, stayed, forced you, and made you look it in the face. If Shelley weren't stopped quickly she was going up on the hill with the little fever and whooping cough sisters. There it was! You could try to think other things, to play, to work, to talk it down in the pulpit, to sing it out in a tree, to slide down the haystack away from it—there it stayed! And every glimpse you had of Shelley made it surer.

There was no trouble about keeping awake that night; I couldn't sleep. I stood at the window and looked down the Big Hill through the soft white moonlight, and thought about it, and then I thought of mother. I guess *now* you see what kind of things mothers have to face. All day she had gone around doing her work, every few minutes suggesting some new thing for one of us to try, or trying it herself; all day she had talked and laughed, and when Sarah Hood came she told her she thought Shelley must be bilious, that she had travelled all night and was sleeping: but she would be up the first place she went, and then they talked all over creation and Mrs. Hood went home and never remembered that she hadn't seen Shelley. She worked Mrs. Freshett off the same way, but you could see she was almost too tired to do it, so by night she was nearly as white as Shelley, yet keeping things going. When the house was still, she came into the room, and stood at the window as I had, until father entered, then she turned, and I could see they were staring at each other in the moonlight, as they had all day.

"She's sick?" asked father, at last.

"Heartsick!" said mother bitterly.

"We'd better have Doc come?"

"She says she isn't sick, and she won't see him."

"She will if I put my foot down."

"Best not, Paul! She'll feel better soon. She's so young! She must get over it."

They were silent for a long time and then father asked in a

harsh whisper: "Ruth, can she possibly have brought us to shame?"

"God forbid!" cried mother. "Let us pray."

Then those two people knelt on each side of that bed, and I could hear half the words they muttered, until I was wild enough to scream. I wished with all my heart that I hadn't listened. I had always known it was no nice way. I must have gone to sleep after a while, but when I woke up I was still thinking about it, and to save me, I couldn't quit. All day, wherever I went, that question of father's kept going over in my head. I thought about it until I was almost crazy, and I just couldn't see where anything about shame came in.

She was only mistaken. She *thought* he loved her, and he didn't. She never could have been so bloomy, so filled with song, laughter, and lovely like she was, if she hadn't truly believed with all her heart that he loved her. Of course it would almost finish her to give him up, when she felt like that; and maybe she did wrong to let herself care so much, before she was sure about him; but that would only be foolish, there wouldn't be even a shadow of shame about it. Besides, Laddie had done exactly the same thing. He loved the Princess until it nearly killed him when he thought he had to give her up, and he loved her as hard as ever he could, when he hadn't an idea whether she would love him back, even a tiny speck; and the person who wasn't foolish, and never would be, was Laddie.

The more I thought, the worse I got worked up, and I couldn't see how Shelley was to blame for anything at all. Love just came to her, like it came to Laddie. She would hardly have knelt down and beseeched the Lord to make her fall in love with a man she scarcely knew, and when she couldn't be sure what he was going to do about it—not the Lord, the man, I mean. You could see for yourself she wouldn't do that. I finished my work, and then I tried to do things for her, and she wouldn't let me. Mother told me to ask her to make Grace Greenwood the dress she had promised when I was so sick; so I took the Scotch plaid to her and reminded her, and she pushed me away and said: "Some time!"

I even got Grace, and showed Shelley the spills on her dress, and how badly she needed a new one, but she never looked, she said: "Oh bother! My head aches. Do let me be!"

Mother was listening. I could see her standing outside the door. She motioned to me to come away, so I went to her and she was white as Shelley. She was sick too, she couldn't say a word for a minute, but after a while she kissed me, I could feel the quivers in her lips, and she said stifflike: "Never mind, she'll be better soon, then she will! Run play now!"

Sometimes I wandered around looking at things and living dully. I didn't try to study out anything, but I must have watched closer than I knew, for every single thing I saw then, over that whole farm, I can shut my eyes and see to-day; everything, from the old hawk tilting his tail to steer him in soaring, to a snake catching field mice in the grass, lichens on the fence, flowers, butterflies, every single thing. Mostly I sat to watch something that promised to become interesting, and before I knew it, I was back on the shame question. That's the most dreadful word in the dictionary. There's something about it that makes your face burn, only to have it in your mind.

Laddie said he never had met any man who knew the origin of more words than father. He could even tell every clip what nationality a man was from his name. Hundreds of time I have heard him say to stranger people, "From your name you'd be of Scotch extraction," or Irish, or whatever it was, and every time the person he was talking with would say, "Yes." Some day away out in the field, alone, I thought I would ask him what people first used the word "shamc," and just exactly what it did mean, and what the things were that you could do that would make the people who loved you until they would die for you, ashamed of you.

Thinking about that and planning out what it was that I wanted to know, gave me another idea. Why not ask her? She was the only one who knew what she had done away there in the city, alone among strangers; I wasn't sure whether all the music a girl could learn was worth letting her take the chances she would have to in a big city. From the way Laddie and father hated them, they were a poor place for men, and they must have been much worse for girls. Shelley knew, why not ask *her?* Maybe I could coax her to tell me, and it would make my life much easier to know; and only think what was going on in father's and mother's heads and hearts, when I felt that way, and didn't even know what there was to be ashamed about. She wouldn't any more than slap me; and sick as she was, I made up my mind not to get angry at her, or ever to tell, if she did. I'd rather have her hit me when she was so sick than to have Sally beat me until she couldn't strike another lick, just because she was angry. But I forgave her that, and I was never going to think of it again—only I did.

Mother kept sending Leon to the post-office, and she met him at the gate half the time herself and fairly snatched the letters from his hands. Hum! She couldn't pull the wool over my eyes. I knew she hoped somehow, some way, there would be a big fat one with Paget, Legal Adviser, or whatever a Chicago lawyer puts on his envelopes. Jerry's just say: "Attorney at Law."

No letter ever came that had Paget in the corner, or anything happened that did Shelley any good. Far otherwise! Just before supper Leon came from Groveville one evening, and all of us could see at a glance that he had been crying like a baby. He had wiped up, and was trying to hold in, but he was killed, next. I nearly said, "Well, for heaven's sake, another!" when I saw him. He slammed down a big, long envelope, having printing on it, before father, and glared at it as if he wanted to tear it to smithereens, and he said: "If you want to know why it looks like that, I buried it under a stone once; but I had to go back, and then I threw it as far as I could send it, into Ditton's gully, but after a while I hunted it up again!"

Then he keeled over on the couch mother keeps for her in the dining-room, and sobbed until he looked like he'd come apart.

Of course all of us knew exactly what that letter was from the way he acted. Mother had told him, time and again, not to set his heart so; father had, too, and Laddie, and every one of us, but that little half-Arab, half-Kentucky mare was the worst tempation a man who loved horses could possibly have; and while father and mother stopped at good work horses, and matched roadsters for the carriage, they managed to prize and tend them so that every one of us had been born horse-crazy, and we had been allowed to ride, care for, and taught to love horses all our lives. Treat a horse ugly, and we'd have gone on the thrashing floor ourselves.

Father laid the letter face down, his hand on it, and shook his head. "This is too bad!" he said. "It's a burning shame, but the money, the exact amount, was taken from a farmer in Medina County, Ohio, by a traveller he sheltered a few days, because he complained of a bad foot. The description of the man who robbed us is perfect. The money was from the sale of some prize cattle. It will have to be returned."

"Just let me see the letter a minute," said Laddie.

He read it over thoughtfully. He was long enough about it to have gone over it three times; then he looked at Leon, and his forehead creased in a deep frown. The tears slid down mother's cheeks, but she didn't know it, or else she'd have wiped them away. She was never mussy about the least little thing.

"Father!" she said. "Father——!"

That was as far as she could go.

"The man must have his money," said father, "but we'll look into this——"

He pushed back the plates and tablecloth, and cleared his end of the table. Mother never budged to stack the plates, or straighten the cloth so it wouldn't be wrinkled. Then father brought his big account book from the black walnut chest in our room, some little books, and papers, sharpened a pencil and began going up and down the columns and picking out figures here and there that he set on a piece of paper. I never had seen him look either old or tired before; but he did then. Mother noticed it too, for her lips tightened, she lifted her head, wiped her eyes, and pretended that she felt better. Laddie said something about doing the feeding, and slipped out. Just then Shelley came into the room, stopped, and looked questioningly at us. Her eyes opened wide, and she stared hard at Leon.

"Why what ails him?" she asked mother.

"You remember what I wrote you about a man who robbed us, and the money Leon was to have, provided no owner was found in a reasonable time; and the horse the boy had planned to buy, and how he had been going to Pryors'— Oh, I think he's slipped over there once a day, and often three times, all this spring! Mr Pryor encouraged him, let him take his older horses to practise on, even went out and taught him cross-country riding himself——"

"I remember!" said Shelley.

Leon sobbed out loud. Shelley crossed the room swiftly, dropped beside him and whispered something in his ear. Quick as a shot his arm reached out and went around her She hid her head deep in the pillow beside him, and they went to pieces together. Clear to pieces! Pretty soon father had to take off his glasses and wipe them so he could see the figures. Mother took one long look at him, a short one at Leon and Shelley, then she arose, her voice as even and smooth, and she said: "While you figure, father, I'll see about supper. I have tried to plan an extra good one this evening."

She left the room. *Now,* I guess you know about all I can tell you of mother! I can't see that there's a thing left. That was the kind of soldier she was. Talk about Crusaders, and a good fight! All the blood of battle in our family wasn't on father's side, not by any means! The Dutch could fight too!

Father's pencil scraped a little, a bee that had slipped in buzzed over the apple butter, while the clock ticked as if it used a hammer. It was so loud one wanted to pitch it from the window. May and I sat still as mice when the cat is near. Candace couldn't keep away from the kitchen door to save her, and where mother went I hadn't an idea, but she wasn't getting an extra good supper. Shelley and Leon were quieter now. May nudged me, and I saw that his arm around her was gripping her tight, while her hand on his head was patting him and fingering his hair.

Ca-lumph! Ca-lumph! came the funniest sound right on the stone walk leading to the east door, then a shrill whicker that made father drop his pencil. Leon was on his feet, Shelley beside him, while at the door stood Laddie grinning as if his face would split, and with her forefeet on the step and her nose in the room, stood the prettiest, the very prettiest horse I ever saw. She was sticking her nose toward Leon, whinnying softly, as she lifted one foot, and if Laddie hadn't backed her, she would have walked right into the dining-room.

"Come on, Weiscope, she's yours!" said Laddie. "Take her to the barn, and put her in one of the cow stalls, until we fix a place for her."

Leon crossed the room, but he never touched the horse. He threw his arms around Laddie's neck.

"Son! Son! Haven't you let your feelings run away with you? What does this mean?" asked father sternly.

"There's nothing remarkable in a big six-footer like me buying a horse," said Laddie. "I expect to purchase a number soon, and without a cent to pay, in the bargain. I contracted to give five hundred dollars for this mare. She is worth more; but that should be satisfactory all around. I am going to earn it by putting five of Mr. Pryor's fancy, pedigreed horses in shape for market, taking them personally, and selling them to men fit to own and handle real horses. I get one hundred each, and my expenses for the job. I'll have as much fun doing it as I ever had at anything. It suits me far better than plowing, even."

Mother entered the room at a sweep, and pushed Leon aside.

"Oh you man of my heart!" she cried. "You man after my own heart!"

Laddie bent and kissed her, holding her tight as he looked over her head at father.

"It's all right, of course?" he said.

"I never have known of anything quite so altogether right," said father. "Thank you, lad, and God bless you!"

He took Laddie's hand, and almost lifted him from the floor, then he wiped his glasses, gathered up his books with a big, deep breath of relief, and went into his room. If the others had looked to see why he was gone so long, they would have seen him on his knees beside his bed thanking God, as usual. Leon couldn't have come closer than when he said, "The same yesterday, to-day, and forever," about father.

Leon had his arms around the neck of his horse now, and he was kissing her, patting her, and explaining to Shelley just why no other horse was like her. He was pouring out a jumble all about the oasis of the desert, the tent dwellers, quoting lines from "The Arab to His Horse," bluegrass, and gentleness combined with spirit, while Shelley had its head between her hands, stroking it and saying, "Yes," to every word Leon told her. Then he said: "Just hop on her back from that top step and ride her to the barn, if you want to see the motion she has."

Shelley said: "Has a woman ever been on her back? Won't she shy at my skirts?"

"No," explained Leon. "I've been training her with a horse blanket pinned around me, so Susie could ride her! She'll be all right."

So Shelley mounted, and the horse turned her head, and tried to rub against her, as she walked away, tame as a sheep. I wondered if she could be too gentle. If she went "like the wind," as Leon said, it didn't show then. I was almost crazy to go along, and maybe Leon would let me ride a little while; but I had a question that it would help me to know the answer and I wanted to ask father before I forgot; so I waited until he came out. When he sat down, smiled at me and said, "Well, is the girl happy for brother?" I knew it was a good time, and I could ask anything I chose, so I sat on his knee and said: "Father, when you pray for anything that it's all perfectly right for you to have, does God come down from heaven and do it Himself, or does He send a man like Laddie to do it for him?"

Father hugged me tight, smiling the happiest.

"Why, you have the whole thing right there in a nutshell, Little Sister," he said. "You see it's like this: the Book tells us most distinctly that 'God is love.' Now it was love that sent Laddie to bind himself for a long, tedious job, to give Leon his horse, wasn't it?"

"Of course!" I said. "He wouldn't have been likely to do it if he hated him. It was love, of course!"

"Then it was God," said father, "because 'God is love.' They are one and the same thing."

Then he kissed me, and *that* was settled. So I wondered when you longed for anything so hard you really felt it was worth bothering God about, whether the quickest way to get it was to ask Him for it, or to try to put a lot of love into the heart of some person who could do what you wanted. I decided it all went back to God though, for most of the time probably we wouldn't know who the right one was to try to awaken love in. I was mighty sure none of us ever dreamed Laddie could walk over to Pryors', and come back with that horse, in a way perfectly satisfactory to every one, slick as an eel.

You should have seen Leon following around after Laddie, trying to do things for him, taking on his work to give him more time with the horses, getting up early to finish his own stunts, so he could go over to Pryors' and help. Mother said it had done more to make a man of him than anything that ever happened. It helped Shelley, too. Something seemed to break in her, when she cried so with Leon, because he was in trouble. Then he was so crazy to show off his horse he had Shelley ride up and down the lane, while he ran along and led, so she got a lot of exercise, and it made her good and hungry. If you don't think by this time that my mother was the beatenest woman alive, I'll prove it to you. When the supper bell rang there was strawberry preserves instead of the apple butter, biscuit, fried chicken, and mashed potatoes. She must have slapped those chickens into the skillet before they knew their heads were off. When Shelley came to the table, for the first time since she'd been home, had pink in her cheeks, and talked some, and ate too, mother forgot her own supper. She fumbled over her plate, but scarcely touched even the livers, and those delicious little kidneys in the tailpiece like Leon and I had at Sally's wedding. When we finished, and it was time for her to give the signal to arise, no one had asked to be excused, she said: "Let us have a word with the Most High." Then she bowed her head, so all of us did too. "O Lord, we praise Thee for all Thy tender mercies, and all Thy loving kindness. Amen!"

Of course father always asked the blessing to begin with, and mostly it was the same one, and that was all at meal time, but this was a little extra that mother couldn't even wait until night to tell the Almighty, she was so pleased with Him. Maybe I haven't told everything about her, after all. Father must have thought that was lovely of her; he surely felt as happy as she did, to see Shelley better, for he hugged and kissed her over and over, finishing at her neck like he always did, and then I be-hanged, if he didn't hug and kiss every last one of us—tight, even the boys. Shelley he held long and close, and patted her a little when he let her go. It made me wonder if the rest of us didn't get ours, so he'd have a chance at her without her noticing it. One thing was perfectly clear. If shame came to us, they were going to love her, and stick tight to her right straight through it.

Now that everything was cleared up so, Shelley seemed a little more like herself every day, although it was bad enough yet; I thought I might as well hurry up the end a little, and stop the trouble completely, so I began watching for a chance to ask her. But I wanted to get her away off alone, so no one would see if she slapped me. I didn't know how long I'd have to wait. I tried coaxing her to the orchard to see a bluebird's nest, but she asked if bluebirds were building any different that year, and I had to admit they were not. Then I tried the blue-eyed Mary bed, but she said she supposed it was still under the cling peach tree, and the flower, two white petals up, two blue down, and so it was. Just as I was beginning to think I'd have to take that to the Lord in prayer, I got my chance by accident.

May and Candace were forever going snake hunting. You would think any one with common sense would leave them alone and be glad of the chance, but no indeed! They went nearly every day as soon as the noon work was finished, and stayed until time to get supper. They did have heaps of fun and wild excitement.

May was gentle, and tender with everything else on earth; so I 'spose she had a right to bruise the serpent with her heel—really she used sticks and stones—if she wanted to. I asked her how she *could,* and she said there was a place in the Bible that told how a snake coaxed Eve to eat an apple, that the Lord had told her she mustn't touch; and so she got us into most of the trouble there was in the world. May said it was all the fault of the *snake* to begin with, and she meant to pay up every one she could find, because she had none of the apple, and lots of the trouble. Candace cried so much because Frederick Swartz had been laid in the tomb, that mother was pleased to have her cheer up, even enough to go snake hunting.

That afternoon Mehitabel Heasty had come to visit May, so she went along, and I followed. They poked around the driftwood at the floodgate behind the barn, and were giving up the place. Candace had crossed the creek and was coming back, and May had started, when she saw a tiny little one and chased it. We didn't know then that it was a good thing to have snakes to eat moles, field mice, and other pests that bother your crops; the Bible had no mercy on them at all, so we were not saving our snakes; and anyway we had more than we needed, while some of them were too big to be safe to keep, and a few poison as could be. May began to bruise the serpent, when out of the driftwood where they hadn't found anything came its mammy, a great big blacksnake, maddest you ever saw, with its pappy right after her, mad as ever too. Candace screamed at May to look behind her, but May was busy with the snake and didn't look quick enough, so the old mammy struck right in her back. She just caught in the hem of May's skirt, and her teeth stuck in the goods—you know how a snake's teeth turn back—so she couldn't let go. May took one look and raced down the bank to the crossing, through the water, and toward us, with the snake dragging and twisting, and trying her best to get away. May was screaming at every jump for Candace, and Mehitabel was flying up and down crying: "Oh there's snakes in my shoes! There's snakes in my shoes!"

That was a fair sample of how much sense a Heasty ever had.

It took all Mehitabel's shoes could do to hold her feet, for after one went barefoot all week, and never put on shoes except on Sunday or for a visit, the feet became so spread out, shoes had all they could do to manage them, and then mostly they pinched until they made one squirm. But she jumped and said that, while May ran and screamed, and Candace gripped her big hickory stick and told May to stand still. Then she bruised that serpent with her whole foot, for she stood on it, and swatted it until she broke its neck. Then she turned ready for the other one, but when it saw what happened to its mate, it decided to go back. Even snakes, it doesn't seem right to break up families like that; so by the time Candace got the mammy killed, loose from May's hem, and stretched out with the back up, so she wouldn't make it rain, when Candace wasn't sure that father wanted rain, I had enough. I went down the creek until I was below the orchard, then I crossed, passed the cowslip bed, climbed the hill and fence, and stopped to think what I would do first; and there only a few feet away was Shelley. She was sitting in the shade, her knees drawn up, her hands clasped around them, staring straight before her across the meadow at nothing in particular, that I could see. She jumped as if I had been a snake when she saw me, then she said, "Oh, is it you?" like she was half glad of it. My chance had come.

I went to her, sat close beside her and tried snuggling up a little. It worked. She put her arm around me, drew me tight, rubbed her cheek against my head and we sat there. I was wondering how in the world I could ask her, and not get slapped. I was growing most too big for that slapping business, anyway. We sat there; I was looking across the meadow as she did, only I was watching everything that went on, so when I saw a grosbeak fly from the wild grape where Shelley had put the crock for sap, it made me think of her hair. She used to like to have me play with it so well, she'd give me pennies if I did. I got up, and began pulling out her pins carefully. I knew I was getting a start because right away she put up her hand to help me.

"I can get them," I said just as flannel-mouthed as ever I

could, like all of us talked to her now, so I got every one and never pulled a mite. When I reached over her shoulder to drop them in her lap, being so close I kissed her cheek. Then I shook down her hair, spread it out, lifted it, parted it, and held up strands to let the air on her scalp. She shivered and said: "Mercy child, how good that does feel! My head has ached lately until it's a wonder there's a hair left on it."

So I was pleasing her. I never did handle hair so carefully. I tried every single thing it feels good to you to have done with your hair, rubbed her head gently, and to cheer her up I told her about May and the snake, and what fool Mehitabel had said, and she couldn't help laughing; so I had her feeling about as good as she could, for the way she actually felt, but still I didn't really get ahead. Come right to the place to do it, that was no very easy question to ask a person, when you wouldn't hurt their feelings for anything; I was beginning to wonder if I would lose my chance, when all at once a way I could manage popped into my mind.

"Shelley," I said, "they told you about Laddie and the Princess, didn't they?"

I knew they had, but I had to make a beginning some way.

"Yes," she said. "I'm glad of it! I think she's pretty as a picture, and nice as she looks. Laddie may have to hump himself to support her, but if he can't get her as fine clothes as she has, her folks can help him. They seem to have plenty, and she's their only child."

"They're going to. I heard Mr. Pryor ask Laddie if he'd be so unkind as to object to them having the pleasure of giving her things."

"Well, the greenhorn didn't say he would!"

"No. He didn't want to put his nose to the grindstone quite that close. He said it was between them."

"I should think so!"

"Shelley, there's a question I've been wanting to ask some one for quite a while."

"What?"

"Why, this! You know, Laddie was in love with the Princess, like you are when you want to marry folks, for a long, long time, before he could be sure whether she loved him back."

"Yes."

"Well, now, 'spose she never had loved him, would he have had anything to be ashamed of?"

"I can't see that he would. Some one must start a courtship, or there would be no marrying, and it's conceded to be the place of the man. No. He might be disappointed, or dreadfully hurt, but there would be no shame about it."

"Well, then, suppose she loved him, and wanted to marry him, and he hadn't loved her, or wanted her, would *she* have had anything to be ashamed of?"

"I don't think so! If she was attracted by him, and thought she would like him, she would have a right to go to a certain extent, to find out if he cared for her, and if he didn't, why, she'd just have to give him up. But any sensible girl waits for a man to make the advances, and plenty of them, before she allows herself even to dream of loving him, or at least, I would."

Now I was getting somewhere!

"Of course you would!" I said. "That would be the way mother would, wouldn't it?"

"Surely!"

"If that Paget man you used to write about had seemed to be just what you liked, you'd have waited to know if he wanted you, before you loved him, wouldn't you?"

"I certainly would!" answered Shelley. "Or at least, I'd have waited until I *thought* sure as death, I knew. It seems that sometimes you can be fooled about those things."

"But if you thought sure you knew, and then found out you had been mistaken, you wouldn't have anything to be *ashamed* of, would you?"

"Not-on-your-life-I-wouldn't!" cried Shelley, hammering each word into her right knee with her doubled fist. "What are you driving at, Blatherskite? What have you got into your head?"

"Oh just studying about things," I said, which was exactly the truth. "Sally getting married last fall, and Laddie going to this, just started me to wondering."

Fooled her, too!

"Oh well, there's no harm done," she said. "The sooner you get these matters straightened out, the better able you will be to take care of yourself. If you ever go to a city, you'll find out that a girl needs considerable care taken of her."

"You could look out for yourself, Shelley?"

"Well, I don't know as I made such a glorious fist of it," she said, "but at least, as you say, I've nothing to be ashamed of!"

I almost hugged her head off.

"Of course you haven't!" I cried. "Of course you wouldn't have!"

I just kissed her over and over for joy; I was so glad my heart hurt for father and mother. Shame had not come to them!

"Now, I guess I'll run to the house and get a comb," I told her.

"Go on," said Shelley. "I know you are tired."

"I'm not in the least," I said. "Don't you remember I always use a comb when I fuss with your hair?"

"It *is* better," said Shelley. "Go get one."

As I got up to start I took a last look at her, and there was something in her face that I couldn't bear. I knelt beside her, and put both arms around her neck.

"Shelley, it's a secret," I said in a breathless half whisper. "It's a great, big secret, but I'm going to tell you. Twice now I've had a powerful prayer all ready to try. It's the kind where you go to the barn, all alone, stand on that top beam below the highest window and look toward the east. You keep perfectly still, and just think with all your might, and you look away over where Jesus used to be, and when the right feeling comes, you pray that prayer as if He stood before you, and it will come true. I *know* it will come true. The reason I know is because twice now I've been almost ready to try it, and what I intended to ask for happened before I had time; so I've saved that prayer; but Shelley, shall I pray it about the Paget man, for you?"

She gripped me, and she shook until she was all twisted up; you could hear her teeth click, she chilled so. The tears just gushed, and she pulled me up close and whispered right in my ear: "Yes!"

It was only pretend about the comb; what I really wanted was to get to father and mother quick. I knew he was at the barn and he was going to be too happy for words in a minute. But as I went up the lane, I wasn't sure whether I'd rather pray about that Paget man or bruise him with my heel like a serpent. The only way I could fix it was to remember if Shelley loved him so, he *must* be mighty nice. Father was in the wagon shovelling corn from it to a platform where it would be handy to feed the pigs, so I ran and called him, and put one foot on a hub and raised my hands. He pulled me up and when he saw how important it was, he sat on the edge of the bed, so I told him: "Father, you haven't got a thing in the world to be ashamed of about Shelley."

"Praise the Lord!" said father like I knew he would, but you should have seen his face. "Tell me about it!"

I told him and he said: "Well, I don't know but this is the gladdest hour of my life. Go straight and repeat to your mother exactly what you've said to me. Take her away all alone, and then forget about it, you little blessing."

"Father, have you got too many children?"

"No!" he said. "I wish I had a dozen more, if they'd be like you."

When I went up the lane I was so puffed up with importance I felt too dignified to run. I strutted like our biggest turkey gobbler. The only reason you couldn't hear my wings scrape, was because through mistake they grew on the turkey. If I'd had them, I would have dragged them sure, and cried "Ge-hobble-hobble!" at every step.

I took mother away alone and told her, and she asked many more questions than father, but she was even gladder than he. She almost hugged the breath out of me. Sometimes I get things *right*, anyway! Then I took the comb and ran back to Shelley.

"I thought you'd forgotten me," she said.

She had wiped up and was looking better. If ever I combed carefully I did then. Just when I had all the tangles out, there came mother. She had not walked that far in a long time. I thought maybe she could comfort Shelley, so I laid the comb in her lap and went to see how the snake hunters were coming on. It must be all right, when the Bible says so, but the African Jungle will do for me, and a popgun is not going to scatter families. I never felt so strongly about breaking home ties in my life as I did then. There was nothing worse. It was not where I wanted to be, so I thought I'd go back to the barn, and hang around father, hoping maybe he'd brag on me some more. Going up the lane I saw a wagon passing with the biggest box I ever had seen, and I ran to the gate to watch where it went. It stopped at our house and Frank came toward me as I hurried up the road.

"Where are the folks?" he asked, without paying the least attention to my asking him over and over what was in the box.

"May and Candace are killing every snake in the driftwood behind the barn, Shelley and mother are down in the orchard, and father and the boys are hauling corn."

"Go tell the boys to come quickly and keep quiet," he said. "But don't let any one else know I'm here."

That was so exciting I almost fell over my feet running, and all three of them came quite as fast. I stood back and watched, and I just danced a steady hop from one foot to the other while those men got the big box off the wagon and opened it. On the side I spelled Piano, so of course it was for Shelley. It was so heavy it took all six of them, father and the three boys, the driver and another very stylish looking man to carry it. They put it in the parlour, screwed a leg on each corner, and a queer harp in the middle, then they lifted it up and set it on its feet, under the whatnot, and it seemed as if it filled half the room. Then Frank spread a beauteous wine coloured cover all embroidered in pink roses with green leaves over it, and the stylish man opened a lid, sat down and spread out his hands. Frank said: "Soft pedal! Mighty soft!" So he smothered it down, and tried only enough to find that it had not been hurt coming, and then he went away on the wagon. Father and the boys gathered up every scrap, swept the walk, and put all the things they had used back where they got them, like we always did.

Then Frank took a card from his pocket and tied it to the music rack, and it read: "For Shelley, from her brothers in fact, and in law." To a corner of the cover he pinned another card that read: "From Peter."

"What is that?" asked father.

"That's from Peter," said Frank. "Peter is great on finishing touches. He had to outdo the rest of us that much or bust. Fact is, none of us thought of a cover except him."

"How about this?" asked father, staring at it as if it were an animal that would bite.

"Well," said Frank, "it was apparent that practising her fingers to the bone wouldn't do Shelley much good unless she could keep it up in summer, and you and mother always have done so much for the rest of us, and now mother isn't so strong and the expenses go on the same with these youngsters; we know you were figuring on it, but we beat you. Put yours in the bank, and try the feel of a surplus once more. Haven't had much lately, have you, father?"

"Well, not to speak of," said father.

"Now let's shut everything up, ring the bell to call them, and get Shelley in here and surprise her."

"She's not very well," said father. "Mother thinks she worked too hard."

"She's all right now, father," I said. "She is getting pink again and rounder, and this will fix her grand."

Wouldn't it though! There wasn't one anywhere, short of the city. Even the Princess had none. Father hunted up a song book, opened it and set it on the rack. Then all of us went out.

"We'll write to the boys, mother and I, and Shelley also," said father. "I can't express myself just now. This is a fine thing for all of you to do."

Frank seemed to think so too, and looked rather puffed up, until Leon began telling about his horse. When Frank found out that Laddie, who had not yet branched out for himself, had given Leon much more than any one of them had Shelley, he looked a little disappointed. He explained how the piano cost eight hundred dollars, but by paying cash all at once, the man took seven hundred and fifty, so it only cost them one hundred and fifty a piece, and none of them felt it at all.

"Sometimes the clouds loom up pretty black, and mother and I scarcely know how to go on, save for the help of the Lord, but we certainly are blest with good children, children we can be proud of. Your mother will like that instrument as well as Shelley, son," said father.

Frank went out and rang the bell, tolled it, and made a big noise like he always did when he came unexpectedly, and then sat on the back fence until he saw them coming, and went to meet them. He walked between mother and Shelley, with an arm around each one. If he thought Shelley looked badly, he didn't mention it. What he did say was that he was starved, and to fly around and get supper. I thought I'd burst. They began to cook, and the boys went to feed and see Leon's horse, and then we had supper. I just sat and stared at Frank and grinned. I couldn't eat.

"Do finish your supper," said mother. "I never saw anything take your appetite like seeing your brother. You'll be wanting a piece before bedtime."

I didn't say a word, because I was afraid to, but I kept looking at Leon and he smiled back, and we had great fun. Secrets are lovely. Mother couldn't have eaten a bite if she'd known about that great shining thing, all full of wonderful sound, standing in our parlour. When the last slow person had finished, father said: "Shelley, won't you step into the front room and bring me that book I borrowed from Frank on 'Taxation.' I want to talk over a few points."

All of us heard her little breathless cry, and mother said, "There!" as if she'd been listening for something, and she beat all of us to the door. Then she cried out too, and such a time as we did have. At last after all of us had grown sensible enough to behave, Shelley sat on the stool, spread her fingers over the keys and played at the place father had selected, and all of us sang as hard as we could: "Be it ever so humble, There's no place like home;" and there *was* no place like ours, of *that* I'm quite sure.

CHAPTER XVII

In Faith Believing

"Nor could the bright green world around
A joy to her impart,
For still she missed the eyes that made
The summer of her heart."

Soon as she had the piano, Shelley needed only the Paget man to make her happy as a girl could be; and having faith in that prayer, I decided to try it right away. So I got Laddie to promise surely that he'd wake me when he got up the next morning. I laid my clothes out all ready; he merely touched my foot, and I came to, slipped out with him, and he helped me dress. We went to the barn when the morning was all gray.

"What the dickens have you got in your head now, Chicken?" he asked. "Is it business with the Fairies?"

"No, this is with the Most High," I said solemnly, like father. "Go away and leave me alone."

"Well of all the queer chickens!" he said, but he kissed me and went.

I climbed the stairs to the threshing floor, then the ladder to the mow, walked a beam to the wall, there followed one to the east end, and another to the little, high-up ventilator window. There I stood looking at the top of the world. A gray mist was rising like steam from the earth, there was a curious colour in the east, stripes of orange and flames of red, where the sun was coming. I folded my hands on the sill, faced the sky, and stood staring. Just stood, and stood, never moving a muscle. By and by I began to think how much we loved Shelley, how happy she had been at Christmas, the way she was now, and how much all of us would give in money, or time, or love, to make her sparkling, bubbling, happy again; so I thought and thought, gazing at the sky, which every second became a grander sight. Little cold chills began going up my back, and soon I was talking to the Lord exactly as if He stood before me on the reddest ray that topped our apple trees.

I don't know all I said. That's funny, for I usually remember to the last word; but this time it was so important, I wanted it so badly, and I was so in earnest that words poured in a stream. I began by reminding Him that He knew everything, and so He'd understand if what I asked was for the best. Then I told Him how it looked to us, who knew only a part; and then I went at Him and implored and beseeched, if it would be best for Shelley, and would make her happy, to send her the Paget man, and to be quick about it. When I had said the last word that came to me, and begged all I thought becoming—I don't think with His face, that Jesus wants us to grovel to Him, at least He looks too dignified to do it Himself—I just stood there, still staring.

I didn't expect to see a burning bush, or a pillar of fire, or a cloud of flame, or even to hear a small, still voice; but I watched, so I wouldn't miss it if there should be anything different in that sunrise from any other I ever had seen, and there was not. Not one thing! It was so beautiful, and I was so in earnest my heart hurt; but that was like any other sunrise on a fine July morning. There wasn't the least sign that Jesus had heard me, and would send the man; yet before I knew it, I was amazed to find the feeling creeping over me that he was coming. If I had held the letter in my hand saying he would arrive on the noon train, I couldn't have grown surer. Why, I even looked down the first time I moved, to see if I had it; but I was certain anyway. So I looked steadily toward the east once more and said, "Thank you, with all my heart, Lord Jesus," then I slowly made my way down and back to the house.

Shelley was at the orchard gate, waiting; so I knew they had missed me, and Laddie had told them where I was and not to call. She had the strangest look on her face, as she asked: "Where have you been?"

I looked straight and hard at her and said, "It's all right, Shelley. He's going to come soon"; but I didn't think it was a thing to mouth over, so I twisted away from her, and ran to the kitchen to see if breakfast had all been eaten. I left Shelley standing there with her eyes wide, also her mouth. She looked about as intelligent as Mehitabel Heasty, and it wouldn't have surprised me if she had begun to jump up and down and say there were snakes in *her* shoes. No doubt you have heard of people having been knocked silly; I knew she was, and so she had a perfect right to look that way, until she could remember what she was doing, and come back to herself. Maybe it took her longer, because mother wasn't there, to remind her about her mouth, and I didn't propose to mention it.

At breakfast, mother said father was going to drive Frank home in the carriage, and if I would like, I might go along. I would have to sit on the back seat alone, going; but coming home I could ride beside and visit with father. I loved that, for you could see more from the front seat, and father would stop to explain every single thing. He always gave me the money and let me pay the toll. He would get me a drink at the spring, let me wade a few minutes at Enyard's riffles, where their creek, with the loveliest gravel bed, ran beside the road; and he always raced like wildfire at the narrows, where for a mile the railroad ran along the turnpike.

We took Frank to his office, stopped a little while to visit Lucy, and give her the butter and cream mother sent, went to the store to see Peter, and then to the post-office. From there we could see that the veranda of the hotel across the street was filled with gayly dressed people, and father said that the summer boarders from big cities around must be pouring in fast. When he came out with the mail he said he better ask if the landlord did not want some of mother's corn and milk fed spring chickens, because last year he had paid her more than the grocer. So he drove across the street, stopped at the curb, and left me to hold the team.

Maybe you think I wasn't proud! I've told you about Ned and Jo, with their sharp ears, dappled sides, and silky tails, and the carriage almost new, with leather seats, patent leather trimmings, and side lamps, so shiny you could see yourself in the brass. We never drove into the barn with one speck of mud or dust on it. That was how particular mother was.

I watched the team carefully; I had to if I didn't want my neck broken; but I also kept an eye on that veranda. You could see at a glance that those were stylish women. Now my mother liked to be in fashion as well as any one could; so I knew she'd be mightily pleased if I could tell her a new place to set her comb, a different way to fasten her collar, or about an unusual pattern for a frock.

I got my drink at the spring, father offered to stop at the riffle, but I was enjoying the ride so much, and I could always wade at home, although our creek was not so beautiful as Enyard's, but for common wading it would do; we went through the narrows, like two shakes of a sheep's tail, then we settled down to a slow trot, and were having the loveliest visit possible, when in the bundle on my lap, I saw the end of something that interested me. Mr. Agnew always made our mail into a roll with the *Advocate* and the *Agriculturist* on the outside, and because every one was so anxious about their letters, and some of them meant so much, I felt grown and important while holding the package.

I was gripping it tight when I noticed the end of one letter much wider and fatter than any I ever had seen, so when father was not looking I began pushing it a little at one end, and pulling it at the other, to work it up, until I could read the address. I got it out so far I thought every minute he'd notice, and tell me not to do that, but I could only see Stanton. All of us were Stanton, so it might be for me, for that matter. Jerry might be sending me pictures, or a book, he did sometimes, but there was an exciting thing about it. Besides being fatter than it looked right at the end, it was plastered with stamps—lots of them, enough to have brought it clear around the world. I pushed that end back, pulled out the other, and took one good look. I almost fell from the carriage. I grabbed father's arm and cried: "Stop! Stop this team quick. Stop them and see if I can read."

"Are you crazy, child?" asked father, but he checked the horses.

"No, but you are going to be in a minute," I said. "Look at that!"

I yanked the letter from the bundle, and held it over. I *thought* I could read, but I was too scared to be sure. I thought it said in big, strong, upstanding letters, Miss Shelley Stanton, Groveville, Indiana. And in the upper corner, Blackburn, Yeats and *Paget,* Counsellors of Law, 37 to 39 State St., Chicago. I put my finger on the Paget, and looked into father's face. I was no fool after all. He was not a bit surer that *he* could read than I was, from the dazed way he stared.

"You see!" I said.

"It says Paget!" he said, like he would come nearer believing it if he heard himself pronounce the word.

"I *thought* it said 'Paget,' " I gasped, "but I wanted to know if you thought so too."

"Yes, it's Paget plain enough," said father, but he acted like there was every possibility that it might change to Jones any minute. "It says 'Paget,' plain as print."

"Father!" I cried, clutching his arm, "father, see how fat it is! There must be pages and pages! Father, it wouldn't take all that to tell her he didn't like her, and he never wanted to see her again. Would it, father?"

"It doesn't seem probable," said father.

"Father, don't you think it means there's been some big mistake, and it takes so much to tell how it can be fixed?"

"It seems reasonable."

I gripped him tighter, and maybe shook him a little.

"Father!" I cried. "Father, doesn't it just look *hurry,* all over? Can't you speed up a little? They have all day to cool off. Oh father, won't you speed a little?"

"That I will!" said father. "Get a tight hold, and pray God it is good word we carry."

"But I prayed the one big prayer to get this," I said. "It

wouldn't be sent if it wasn't good. The thing to do now is to thank the Lord for 'all his loving kindnesses,' like mother said. Drive father! Make them go!"

At first he only touched them up; I couldn't see that we were getting home so fast; but in a minute a cornfield passed like a streak, a piece of woods flew by a dark blur, a bridge never had time to rattle, and we began to rock from side to side a little. Then I gripped the top supports with one hand, the mail with the other, and hung on for dear life. I took one good look at father.

His feet were on the brace, his face was clear, even white, his eyes steely, and he never moved a muscle. When Jo thought it was funny, that he was loose in the pasture, and kicked up a little behind, father gave him a sharp cut with the whip and said: "Steady boy! Get along there!"

Sometimes he said, "Aye, aye! Easy!" but he never stopped a mite. We whizzed past the church and cemetery, and scarcely touched the Big Hill. People ran to their doors, even to the yards, and I was sure they thought we were having a runaway, but we were not. Father began to stop at the lane gate, he pulled all the way past the garden, and it was as much as he could do to get them slowed down so that I could jump out by the time we reached the hitching rack. He tied them, and followed me into the house instead of going to the barn. I ran ahead calling: "Shelley! Where is Shelley?"

"What in this world has happened, child?" asked mother, catching my arm.

"Her letter has come! Her Paget letter! The one *you* looked for until you gave up. It's come at last! Oh, where is she?"

"Be calmer, child, you'll frighten her," said mother.

May snatched the letter from my fingers and began to read all that was on it aloud. I burst out crying.

"Make her give that back!" I sobbed to father. "It's mine! I found it. Father, make her let me take it!"

"Give it to her!" said father. "I rather feel that it is her right to deliver it."

May passed it back, but she looked so disappointed, that by how she felt I knew how much I wanted to take it myself; so I reached my hand to her and said: "You can come along! We'll both take it! Oh where is she?"

"She went down in the orchard," said mother. "I think probably she's gone back where she was the other day."

Gee, but we ran! And there she was! As we came up, she heard us and turned.

"Shelley!" I cried. "Here's your letter! Everything is all right! He's coming, Shelley! Look quick, and see when! Mother will want to begin baking right away!"

Shelley looked at me, and said coolly: "Paddy Ryan! What's the matter?"

"Your letter!" I cried, shoving it right against her hands. "Your letter from Robert! From the Paget man, you know! I *told* you he was coming! Hurry, and see when!"

She took it, and sat there staring at it, so much like father, that it made me think of him, so I saw that she was going to have to come around to it as we did, and that one couldn't hurry her. She just had to take her time to sense it.

"Shall I open it for you?" I asked, merely to make her see that it was time she was doing it herself.

Blest if she didn't reach it toward me!—sort of woodenlike. I stuck my finger under the flap, gave it a rip across and emptied what was inside into her lap. Bet there were six or seven letters in queer yellow envelopes I never before had seen any like, and on them was the name, Robert Paget, while in one corner it said, "Returned Dead Letter"; also there was a loose folded white sheet. She sat staring at the heap, touching one, another, and repeating "Robert Paget?" as she picked each up in turn.

"What do you suppose it means?" she asked May. May examined them.

"You must read the loose sheet," she advised. "No doubt that will explain."

But Shelley never touched it. She handled those letters and stared at them. Father and mother came through the orchard and stood together behind us, so father knelt down at last, reached across Shelley's shoulder, picked one up and looked at it.

"Have you good word, dear?" asked mother of Shelley.

"Why, I don't understand at all," said Shelley. "Just look at all these queer letters, addressed to Mr. Paget. Why should they be sent to me? I mustn't open them. They're not mine. There must be some mistake."

"These are *dead letters*," said father. "They've been written to you, couldn't be delivered, and so were sent to the Dead Letter Office at Washington, which returned them to the writer, and unopened he has forwarded them once more to you. You've heard of dead letters, haven't you?"

"I suppose so," said Shelley. "I don't remember just now; but there couldn't be a better name. They've come mighty near killing me."

"If you'd only read that note!" urged May, putting it right into her fingers.

Shelley still sat there.

"I'm afraid of it," she said exactly like I'd have spoken if there had been a big rattlesnake coming right at me, when I'd nothing at hand to bruise it.

Laddie and Leon came from the barn. They had heard me calling, seen May and me run, and then father and mother coming down, so they walked over.

"What's up?" asked Leon. "Has Uncle Levi's will been discovered, and does mother get his Mexican mines?"

"What have you got, Shelley?" asked Laddie, kneeling beside her, and picking up one of the yellow letters.

"I hardly know," said Shelley.

"I brought her a big letter with all those little ones and a note in it, and they are from the Paget man," I explained to him. "But she won't even read the note, and see what he writes. She says she's afraid."

"Poor child! No wonder!" said Laddie, sitting beside her and putting his arm around her. "Suppose I read it for you. May I?"

"Yes," said Shelley. "You read it. Read it out loud. I don't care."

She leaned against him, while he unfolded the white sheet.

"Umph!" he said. "This *does* look bad for you. It begins: 'My own darling Girl.' "

"Let me see!" cried Shelley, suddenly straightening, and reaching her hand.

Laddie held the page toward her, but she only looked, she didn't offer to touch it.

" 'My own darling Girl:' " repeated Laddie tenderly, making it mean just all he possibly could, because he felt so dreadfully sorry for her—" 'On my return to Chicago, from the trip to England I have so often told you I intended to make some time soon——' "

"Did he?" asked mother.

"Yes," answered Shelley. "He couldn't talk about much else. It was his first case. It was for a friend of his who had been robbed of everything in the world; honour, relatives, home, and money. If Robert won it, he got all that back for his friend and enough for himself—that he could—a home of his own, you know! Read on, Laddie!"

" 'I was horrified to find on my desk every letter I had written you during my absence returned to me from the Dead Letter Office, as you see.' "

"Good gracious!" cried mother, picking up one and clutching it tight as if she meant to see that it didn't get away again.

"Go on!" cried Shelley.

" 'I am enclosing some of them as they came back to me, in proof of my statement. I drove at once to your boarding place and found you had not been there for weeks, and your landlady was distinctly crabbed. Then I went to the college, only to find that you had fallen ill and gone to your home. That threw me into torments, and all that keeps me from taking the first train is the thought that perhaps you refused to accept these letters, for some reason. Shelley, you did not, did you? There is some mistake somewhere, is there not——' "

"One would be led to think so," said father sternly. "Seems as if he might have managed some way——"

"Don't you blame him!" cried Shelley. "Can't you see it's all my fault? He'd been coming regularly, and the other girls envied me; then he just disappeared, and there was no word or anything, and they laughed and whispered until I couldn't endure it; so I moved in with Peter's cousin, as I wrote you; but that left Mrs. Fleet with an empty room in the middle of the term, and it made her hopping mad. I bet anything she wouldn't give the postman my new address, to pay me back. I left it, of course. But if I'd been half a woman, and had the confidence I should have had in myself and in him—— Oh how I've suffered, and punished all of you——!"

"Never you mind about that," said mother, stroking Shelley's hair. "Likely there isn't much in Chicago to give a girl who never had been away from her family before, 'confidence' in herself or any one else. As for him—just disappearing like that, without a word or even a line—— Go on Laddie!"

" 'Surely, you knew that I was only waiting the outcome of this trip to tell you how dearly I love you. Surely, you encouraged me in thinking you cared for me a little, Shelley. Only a little will do to begin with——' "

"You see, I *did* have something to go on!" cried Shelley, wiping her eyes and straightening up.

" 'No doubt you misunderstood and resented my going without coming to explain, and bid you good-bye in person, but Shelley, *I simply dared not.* You see, it was this way: I got a cable about the case I was always talking of, and the only man who could give the testimony I *must have* was dying!' "

"For land's sake! The poor boy!" cried mother, patting Shelley's shoulder.

" 'An hour's delay might mean the loss of everything in the world to me, even you. For if I lost any time, and the man escaped me, there was no hope of winning my case, and everything, even you, as I said before, depended on him——' "

"Good Lord! I mean land!" cried Leon.

" 'If I could catch the train in an hour, I could take a boat at New York, and go straight through with no loss of time. So I wrote you a note that probably said more than I would have ventured in person, and paid a boy to deliver it.' "

"Kept the money and tore up the note, I bet!" said May.

" 'I wrote on the train, but found after sailing that I had rushed so I had failed to post it in New York. I kept on writing every day on the boat, and mailed you six at Liverpool. All the time I have written frequently; there are many more here that this envelope will not hold, that I shall save until I hear from you.' "

"Well, well!" said father.

" 'Shelley, I beat death, reached my man, got the testimony I had to have, and won my case.' "

"Glory!" cried mother. "Praise the Lord!"

" 'Then I scoured England, and part of the continent, hunting some interested parties; and when I was so long finding them, and still no word came from you, I decided to come back and get you, if you would come with me, and go on with the work together.' "

"Listen to that! More weddings!" cried Leon. He dropped on his knees before Shelley. "Will you marry me, my pretty maid?" he begged.

"Young man, if you cut any capers right now, I'll cuff your ears!" cried father. "This is no proper time for your foolishness!"

" 'Shelley, I beg that you will believe me, and if you care for me in the very least, telegraph if I may come. Quick! I'm half insane to see you. I have many things to tell you, first of all how dear you are to me. Please telegraph. Robert.' "

"Saddle a horse, Leon!" father cried as he unstrapped his wallet. "Laddie, take down her message."

"Can you put it into ten words?" asked Laddie.

"Mother, what would you say?" questioned Shelley.

Leon held up his fingers and curled down one with each word. "Say, 'Dear Robert. Well and happy. Come when you get ready.' "

"But then I won't know when he's coming," objected Shelley. "You don't need to," said Leon. "You can take it for granted from that epistolary effusion that he won't let the grass grow under his feet while coming here. That's a bully message! It sounds as if you weren't crazy over him, and it's a big compliment to mother. Looks as if she didn't have to know when people are coming—like she's ready all the time."

"Write it out and let me see," said Shelley.

So Laddie wrote it, and she looked at it a long time, it seemed to me, at last she said: "I don't like that 'get.' It doesn't sound right. Wouldn't 'are' be better?"

"Come when you are ready," repeated Laddie. "Yes, that's better. 'Get' sounds rather saucy."

"Why not put it, 'Come when you choose?' " suggested mother. "That will leave a word to spare, so it won't look as if you had counted them and used exactly ten on purpose, and it doesn't sound as if you expected him to make long preparations, like the other. That will leave it with him to start whenever he likes."

"Yes! yes!" cried Shelley. "That's much better! Say, 'Come when you choose!' "

"Right!" said Laddie as he wrote it. "Now I'll take this!"

"Oh no you won't!" cried Leon. "Father told me to saddle my horse. She's got enough speed in her to beat yours a mile. I take that! Didn't you say for me to saddle, father?"

"Such important business, I think I better," said Laddie, and Leon began to cry.

"I think you should both go," said Shelley. "It is so important, and if one goes to make a mistake, maybe the other will notice it."

"Yes, that's the best way," said mother.

"Yes, both go," said father.

It was like one streak when they went up the Big Hill. Father shook his head. "Poor judgment—that," he said. "Never run a horse up hill!"

"But they're in such a hurry," Shelley reminded him.

"So they are," said father. "In this case I might have broken the rule myself. Now come all of you, and let the child get at her mail."

"But I want you to stay," said Shelley. "I'm so addle-pated this morning. I need my family to help me."

"Of course you do, child," said mother. "Families were made to cling together, and stand by each other in every circumstance of life—joy or sorrow. Of course you need your family."

May began sorting the letters by dates so Shelley could start on the one that had been written first. Father ran his knife across the top of each, and cut all the envelopes, and Shelley took out the first and read it; that was the train one. In it he told her about sending the boy with the note again, and explained more about how it was so very important for him to hurry, because the only man who could help him was so sick. We talked it over, and all of us thought the boy had kept the money and torn up the note. Father said the way would have been to send the note and pay the boy when he came back; but Shelley said Mr. Paget would have been gone before the boy got back, so father saw that wouldn't have been the way, in such a case.

Next she read one written on the boat. He told more about sending the boy; how he loved her, what it would mean to both of them if he got the evidence he wanted and won his first case; and how much it would bring his friend. The next one told it all over again, and more. In that he wrote a little about the ocean, the people on board the ship, and he gave Shelley the name of the place where he was going and begged her to write to him. He told her if the ship he was on passed another, they were going to stop and send back the mail. He begged her to write often, and to say she forgave him for starting away without seeing her, as he had been forced to.

The next one was the same thing over, only a little more yet. In the last he had reached England, the important man was still living, but he was almost gone, and Mr. Paget took two good witnesses, all the evidence he had, and went to see him; and the man saw it was no use, so he made a statement, and Robert had it all written out, signed and witnessed. For the real straight sense there was in that letter, I could have done as well myself. It was a wild jumble, because Robert was so crazy over having the evidence that would win his case; and he told Shelley that now he was perfectly free to love her all she would allow him. He said he had to stay a while longer to find his friend's people so they would get back their share of the money, but it was not going to be easy to locate them. You wouldn't think the world so big, but maybe it seemed smaller to me because as far as I could see from the top of our house, was all I knew about it. After Shelley had read the letters, and the note again, father heaved a big sigh that seemed to come clear from his boot soles and he said: "Well Shelley, it looks to me as if you had found a *man*. Seems to me that's a mighty important case for a young lawyer to be trusted with, in a first effort."

"Yes, but it was for Robert's best friend, and only think, he has won!"

"I don't see how he could have done better if he'd been old as Methuselah, and wise as Solomon," boasted mother.

"But he hasn't found the people who must have back their money," said May. "He will have to go to England again. And he wants to take you, Shelley. My! You'll get to sail on a big steamer, cross the Atlantic Ocean, and see London. Maybe you'll even get a peep at the Queen!"

Shelley was busy making a little heap of her letters; when the top one slid off I reached over and put it back for her. She looked straight at me, and smiled the most wonderful and the most beautiful smile I ever saw on any one's face, so I said to her: "You see! I *told* you he was coming!"

"I can't understand it!" said Shelley.

"You *know* I told you."

"Of course I do! But what made you think so?"

"That was the answer. Just that he was coming."

"What are you two talking about?" asked mother.

Shelley looked at me, and waited for me to tell mother as much as I wanted to, of what had happened. But I didn't think things like that were to be talked about before every one, so I just said:

"Oh nothing! Only, I told Shelley this very morning that the Paget man was coming soon, and that everything was going to be all right."

"You did? Well of all the world! I can't see why."

"Oh something told me! I just *felt* that way."

"More of that Fairy nonsense?" asked father sharply.

"No. I didn't get that from the Fairies."

"Well, never mind!" said Shelley, rising, because she saw that I had told all I wanted to. "Little Sister *did* tell me this morning that he was coming, that everything would be made right, and it's the queerest thing, but instantly I believed her. Didn't I sing all morning, mother? The first note since Robert didn't come when I expected him in Chicago, weeks ago."

"Yes," said mother. "That's a wonderfully strange thing. I can't see what made you think so."

"Anyway, I did!" I said. "Now let's go have dinner. I'm starving."

I caught May's hand, and ran to get away from them. Father and mother walked one on each side of Shelley, while with both hands she held her letters before her. When we reached the house we just talked about them all the time. Pretty soon the boys were back, and then they told about sending the telegram. Leon vowed he gave the operator a dime extra to start that message with a shove, so it would go faster.

"It will go all right," said Laddie, "and how it will go won't be a circumstance to the way he'll come. If there's anything we ought to do, before he gets here, we should hustle. Chicago isn't a thousand miles away. That message can reach him by two o'clock, it's probable he has got ready while he was waiting, so he will start on the first train our way. He could reach Groveville on the ten, to-morrow. We better meet it."

"Yes, we'll meet it," said mother. "Is the carriage perfectly clean?"

Father said: "It must be gone over. Our general manager here ordered me to speed up, and we drove a little coming from town."

Mother went to planning what else should be done.

"Don't do anything!" cried Shelley. "The house is all right. There's no need to work and worry into a sweat. He won't notice or care how things look."

"I miss my guess if he docsn't notice and care very much indeed," said mother emphatically. "Men are not blind. No one need think they don't see when things are not as they should be, just because they're not cattish enough to let you know it, like a woman always does. Shelley, wouldn't you like to ride over and spend the afternoon with the Princess?"

"Nope!" said Shelley. "It's her turn to come to see me. Besides, you don't get me out of the way like that. I know what you'll do here, and I intend to help."

"Do you need one of the boys at the house?" asked father, and if you'll believe it, both of them wanted to stay.

Father said he must have one to help wash the carriage and do a little fixing around the barn; so he took Leon, but he didn't like to go. He said: "I don't see what all this fuss is about, anyway. Probably he'll be another Peter."

Shelley looked at him: "Oh Mr. Paget isn't nearly so large as Peter," she said, "and his hair is whiter than yours, while his eyes are not so blue."

"Saints preserve us!" cried Leon. "Come on, father, let's only dust the carriage! He's not worth washing it for."

"Is he like that?" asked mother anxiously.

"Wait and see!" said Shelley. "Looks don't make a man. He has proved what he can do."

Then all of us went to work. Before night we were hunting over the yard, and beside the road, to see if we could find anything to pick up. Six chickens were in the cellar, father was to bring meat and a long list of groceries from town in the morning. He was to start early, get them before train time, put them under the back seat, and take them out after he drove into the lane, when he came back. That made a little more trouble for father, but there was not the slightest necessity for making Mr. Paget feel that he had ridden in a delivery wagon.

Next morning I wakened laughing softly, because some one

was fussing with my hair, patting my face, and kissing me, so I put up my arms and pulled that loving person down on my pillow, and gave back little half-asleep kisses, and slept on; but it was Shelley, and she gently shook me and began repeating that fool old thing I have been waked up with half the mornings of my life:

> *"Get up, Little Sister, the morning is bright,*
> *The birds are all singing to welcome the light,*
> *Get up; for when all things are merry and glad,*
> *Good children should never be lazy and sad;*
> *For God gives us daylight, dear sister, that we*
> *May rejoice like the lark and work like the bee."*

Usually I'd have gone on sleeping, but Shelley was so sweet and lovely, and she kissed me so hard, that I remembered it was going to be a most exciting day, so I came to quick as snap and jumped right up, for I didn't want to miss a single thing that might happen.

The carriage was shining when it came to the gate, so was father. I thought there was going to be a vacant seat beside him, and I asked if I might go along. He said: "Yes, if mother says so." He always would stick that in. So I ran to ask her, and she didn't care, if Shelley made no objections. I was just starting to find her, when here she came, all shining too, but Laddie was with her. I hadn't known that he was going, and I was so disappointed I couldn't help crying.

"What's the matter?" asked Shelley.

"Father and mother both said I might go, if you didn't care."

"Why, I'm dreadfully sorry," said Shelley, "but I have several things I want Laddie to do for me."

Laddie stooped down to kiss me good-bye and he said: "Don't cry, Little Sister. The way to be happy is to be good."

Then they drove to Groveville, and we had to wait. But there was so much to do, it made us fly to get all of it finished. So mother send Leon after Mrs. Freshett to help in the kitchen, while Candace wore her white dress, and waited on the table. Mother cut flowers for the dining table, and all through the house. She left the blinds down to keep the rooms cool, chilled buttermilk to drink, and if she didn't think of every single, least little thing, I couldn't see what it was. Then all of us put on our best dresses. Mother looked as glad and sweet as any girl, when she sat to rest a little while. I didn't dare climb the catalpa in my white dress, so I watched from the horse block, and when I saw the grays come over the top of the hill, I ran to tell. As mother went to the gate, she told May and me to walk behind, to stay back until we were spoken to, and then to keep our heads level, and remember our manners. I don't know where Leon went. He said he lost all interest when he found there was to be another weak-eyed towhead in the family, and I guess he was in earnest about it, because he wasn't even curious enough to be at the gate when Mr. Paget came.

Father stopped with a flourish, Laddie hurried around and helped Shelley, and then Mr. Paget stepped down. Goodness, gracious, sakes alive! Little? Towhead? He was taller than Laddie. His hair was most as black as ink, and wavy. His eyes were big and dark; he was broad and strong and there was the cleanest, freshest look about him. He put his arm spang around Shelley, right there in the road, and mother said: "Hold there! Not so fast, young man! I haven't given my consent to that."

He laughed, and he said: "Yes, but you'ah going to!" And he put his other arm around mother, so May and I crowded up, and we had a family reunion right between the day lilies and the snowball bush. We went into the house, and he *liked* us, his room, and everything went exactly right. He was crazy about the cold buttermilk, and while he was drinking it Leon walked into the dining-room, because he thought of course Mr. Paget and Shelley would be on the davenport in the parlour. When he saw Robert he said lowlike to Shelley: "Didn't Mr. Paget come? Who's that?"

Shelley looked so funny for a minute, then she remembered what she had told him and she just laughed as she said: "Mr. Paget, this is my brother."

Robert went to shake hands, and Leon said right to his teeth: "Well a divil of a towhead you are!"

"Towhead?" said Robert, bewildered-like.

"Shelley said you were a little bit of a man, with watery blue eyes, and whiter hair than mine."

"Oh I say!" cried Robert. "She must have been stringin' you!"

Leon just whooped; because while Mr. Paget didn't talk like the 'orse, 'ouse people, he made you think of them in the way he said things, and the sound of his voice. Then we had dinner, and I don't remember that we ever had quite such a feast before. Mother had put on every single flourish she knew. She used her very best dishes, and linen, and no cook anywhere could beat Candace alone; now she had Mrs. Freshett to help her, and mother also. If she tried to show Mr. Paget, she did it! No visitor was there except him, but we must have been at the table two hours talking, and eating from one dish after another. Candace *liked* to wear her white dress, and carry things around, and they certainly were good.

And talk! Father, Laddie, and Robert talked over all creation. Every once in a while when mother saw an opening, she put in her paddle, and no one could be quicker, when she watched sharp and was trying to make a good impression. Shelley was very quiet; she scarcely spoke or touched that delicious food. Once the Paget man turned to her, looking at her so fondlike, as he picked up one of her sauce dishes and her spoon and wanted to feed her. And he said: "Heah child, eat your dinnah! You have nawthing to be fussed ovah! I mean to propose to you, and your parents befowr night. That is what I am heah for."

Every one laughed so, Shelley never got the bite; but after that she perked up more and ate a little by herself.

At last father couldn't stand it any longer, so he began asking Robert about his trip to England, and the case he had won. When the table was cleared for dessert, Mr. Paget asked mother to have Candace to bring his satchel. He opened it and spread papers all over, so that father and Laddie could see the evidence, while he told them how it was.

It seemed there was a law in England, all of us knew about it, because father often had explained it. This law said that a man who had lots of money and land must leave almost all of it to his eldest son; and the younger ones must go into law, the army, be clergymen, or enter trade and earn a living, while the eldest kept up the home place. Then he left it to his eldest son, and his other boys had to work for a living. It kept the big estates together; but my! it was hard on the younger sons, and no one seemed even to think about the daughters. I never heard them mentioned.

Now there was a very rich man; he had only two sons, and each of them married, and had one son. The younger son died, and sent his boy for his elder brother to take care of. He pretended to be good, but for sure, he was bad as ever he could be. He knew that if his cousin were out of the way, all that land and money would be his when his uncle died. So he went to work and he tried for years, and a lawyer man who had no conscience at all, helped him. At last when they had done everything they could think of, they took a lot of money and put it in the pocket of the son they wanted to ruin; then when his father missed the money, and the house was filled with policemen, detectives, and neighbours, the bad man said he'd feel more comfortable to have the family searched too, merely as a formality, so he stepped out and was gone over, and when the son's turn came, there was the money on him! That made him a public disgrace to his family, and a criminal who couldn't inherit the estate, and his father went raving mad and tried to kill him, so he had to run away. At first he didn't care what he did, so he came over here. Robert said that man was his best friend, and as men went, he was a decent fellow, so he cheered him up all he could, and went to work with all his might to prove he was innocent, and to get back his family, and his money for him.

When Robert had enough evidence that he was almost ready to start to England, his man got a cable from an old friend of his father's, who always had believed in him, and it said that the bad man was dying—to come quick. So Robert went all of a sudden, like the Dead Letters told about. Now, he described how he reached there, took the old friend of the father of his friend with him, and other witnesses, and all the evidence he had, and went to see the sick man. When Robert showed him what he could prove, the bad man said it was no use, he had to die in a few days, so he might as well go with a clean conscience, and he told about everything he had done. Robert had it all written out, signed and sworn to. He told about all of it, and then he said to father: "Have I made it clear to you?"

Leon was so excited he forgot all the manners he ever had, for he popped up before father could open his head, and cried: "Clear as mud! I got that son business so plain in my mind, I'd know the party of the first part, from the party of the second part, if I met him promenading on the Stone Wall of China!"

Father and Laddie knew so much law they asked dozens of questions; but that Robert man wasn't a smidgin behind, for every clip he had the answer ready, and then he could go on and tell much more than he had been asked. He said as a Case, it was a pretty thing to work on; but it was much more than a case to him, because he always had known that his friend was not guilty; that he was separated from his family, suffering terribly under the disgrace, and they must be also. He had worked for life for his friend, because the whole thing meant so much to both of them. He said he must go back soon and finish up a little more that he should have done while he was there, if it hadn't been that he received no word from Shelley.

"When I didn't heah from heh for so long, and wrote so many letters, and had no reply, I thought possibly some gay 'young Lochinvah had come out from the west,' and taken my sweet-'eart," he said, "and while I had my armour on, I made up my mind that I'd give him a fight too. I didn't propose to lose Shelley, if it were in my powah to win heh. I hadn't been able to say to heh exactly what I desiahed, on account of getting a start alone in this country; but if I won this case, I would have ample means. When I secuahed the requiahed evidence, I couldn't wait to finish, so I came straight ovah, to make sure of heh."

He arose and handed the satchel to father.

"I notice you have a very good looking gun convenient," he

said. "Would you put these papahs where you consider them safe until I'm ready to return? Our home, our living, and the honah of a man are there, and we are mighty particular about that bag, are we not, Shelley?"

"Well I should think we are!" cried Shelley. "For goodness sake, father, hang to it! Is the man still living? Could you get that evidence over again?"

"He was alive when I left, but the doctors said ten days would be his limit, so he may be gone befowr this."

Father picked up the satchel, set it on his knees, and stroked it as if it were alive.

"Well! Well!" he said. "Now would any one think such a little thing could contain so much?"

Shelley leaned toward Robert.

"Your friend!" she cried, "Your friend! What *did* he say to you? What did he *do?*"

"Well, for a time he was wildly happy ovah having the stain removed from his honah, and knowing that he would have his family and faw'tn back; but there is an extremely sad feature to his case that is not yet settled, so he must keep his head level until we work that out. Now about that hoss you wanted to show me——" he turned to Leon.

Mother gave the signal, and we left the table. Father carried the satchel to his chest, made room for it, locked it in and put the key in his pocket. Then our men started to the barn to show the Arab-Kentucky horse. Mr. Paget went to Shelley and took her in his arms exactly like Peter did Sally before the parlour door that time when I got into trouble, and he looked at mother and laughed as he said: "I hope you will excuse me, but I've been having a very nawsty, anxious time, and I cawn't conform to the rules for a few days, until I become accustomed to the fawct that Shelley is not lost to me. It was beastly when I reached Chicago, had back all my letters, and found she had gone home ill. I've much suffering to recompense. I'll atone for a small portion immediately."

He lifted Shelley right off the floor—that's how big and strong he was—he hugged her tight, and kissed her forehead, cheeks, and eyes.

"When I've gone through the fahmality of asking your parents for you, and they have said a gracious 'yes,' I'll put the fust one on your lips," he said, setting her down carefully. "In the meantime, you be fixing your mouth to say, 'yes,' also, when I propose to you, because it's coming befowr you sleep."

Shelley was like a peach blossom. She reached up and touched his cheek, while she looked at mother all smiling, and sparkling, as she said: "You see!"

Mother smiled back.

"I do, indeed!" she answered.

Leon pulled Mr. Paget's sleeve.

"Aw quit lally-gaggin' and come see a real horse," he said.

Robert put his other arm around Leon, drew him to his side and hugged him as if he were a girl. "I'm so glad Shelley has a lawge family," he said. "Big families are jolly. I'm so proud of all the brothers I'm going to have. I was the only boy at home."

"You haven't told us about your family," said mother.

"No," said Robert, "but I intend to. I have a family! One of the finest on uth. We'll talk about them after this hoss is inspected."

He let Shelley go and walked away, his arm still around Leon. Shelley ran to mother and both of them sobbed out loud.

"Now you see how it was!" she said.

"You poor child!" cried mother. "Indeed I *do* see how it was. You've been a brave girl. A good, brave girl! Father and I are mighty proud of you!"

"Oh mother! I thought you were ashamed of me!" sobbed Shelley.

"Oh my child!" said mother quavery-like. "Oh my child! You surely see that none of us could understand, as we do now."

She patted Shelley, and told her to run upstairs and lie down for a while, because she was afraid she would be sick.

"We mustn't have a pale, tired girl right now," said mother.

"Well!" said Shelley, but she just stood there holding mother.

"Well?" said mother gripping her.

"You see!" said Shelley.

"Child," said mother, "I *do* see! I see six feet of as handsome manhood as I ever have seen anywhere. His manner is perfect, and I find his speech most attractive. I am delighted with him. I do see indeed! Your father is quite as proud and pleased as I am. Now go to bed."

Shelley held up her lips, and then went. I ran to the barn, where the men were standing in the shade, while Leon led his horse up and down before them, told about its pedigree, its record, how he came to have it. The Paget man stood there looking and listening gravely, as he studied the horse. At last he went over her, and gee! but he knew horse! Then Laddie brought out Flos and they talked all about her, and then went into the barn. Father opened the east doors to show how much land he had, which were his lines; and while the world didn't look quite so pretty as it had in May, still it was good enough. Then they went into the orchard, sat under the trees and began talking about business conditions. That was so dry I went back to the house. And maybe I didn't strike something interesting there!

As I came up the orchard path to a back yard gate, I saw a carriage at the hitching rack in front of the house, so I took a peep and almost fell over. It was the one the Princess had come to Sally's wedding in; so I knew she was in the house visiting Shelley. I went to the parlour and there I had another shock; for lo and behold! in our big rocking chair, and looking as well as any one, so far as you could see—of course you can't see heart trouble, though—sat Mrs. Pryor. The Princess and mother were there, all of them talking, laughing and having the best time, while on the davenport enjoying himself as much as any one, was Mr. Pryor. They talked about everything, and it was easy to see that the Pryor door was *open* so far as we were concerned, anyway. Mrs. Pryor was just as nice and friendly as she could be, and so was he. Shelley sat beside him, and he pinched her cheek and said: "Something seems to make you especially brilliant to-day, young woman!"

Shelley flushed redder, laughed, and glanced at mother, so she said: "Shelley is having a plain old-fashioned case of beau. She met a young man in Chicago last fall and he's here now to ask our consent. All of us are quite charmed with him. That's why she's so happy."

Then the Princess sprang up and kissed Shelley, so did Mrs. Pryor, while such a chatter you never heard. No one could repeat what they said, for as many as three talked at the same time.

"Oh do let's have a double wedding!" cried the Princess when the excitement was over a little. "I think it would be great fun; do let's! When are you planning for?"

"Nothing is settled yet," said Shelley. "We've had no time to talk!"

"Mercy!" cried the Princess. "Go make your arrangements quickly! Hurry up, then come over, and we'll plan for the same time. It will be splendid! Don't you think that would be fine, Mrs. Stanton?"

"I can't see any objections to it," said mother.

"Where is your young man? I'm crazy to see him," cried the Princess. "If you have gone and found a better looking one than mine, I'll never speak to you again."

"She hasn't!" cried Mrs. Pryor calmly, like that settled it. I like her. "They're not made!"

"I am not so sure of that," said Shelley proudly. "Mother, isn't my man quite as good looking, and as nice in every way, as Laddie?"

"Fully as handsome, and so far as can be seen in such a short time, quite as fine," said mother.

I was perfectly amazed at her; as if any man could be!

"I don't believe it, I won't stand it, and I shan't go home until I have seen for myself!" cried the Princess, laughing, and yet it sounded as if she were half-provoked, and I knew I was. The Paget man was all right, but I wasn't going to lose my head over him. Laddie was the finest, of course!

"Well, he's somewhere on the place with our men, this minute," said Shelley, "but you stay for supper, and meet him."

"When you haven't your arrangements made yet! You surely are unselfish! Of course I won't do that, but I'd love to have one little peep, then you bring him and come over to-morrow, so all of us can become acquainted, and indeed, I'm really in earnest about a double wedding."

"Go see where the men are," said Shelley to me.

I went to the back door, and their heads were bobbing far down in the orchard.

"They're under the greening apple tree," I reported.

"If you will excuse us," said Shelley to Mr. and Mrs. Pryor, "we'll walk down a few minutes and prove that I'm right."

"Don't stay," said Mrs. Pryor. "This trip is so unusual for me that I'm quite tired. For a first venture, in such a long time, I think I've done well. But now I'm beginning to feel I should go home."

"Go straight along," said the Princess. "I'll walk across the fields, or Thomas can come back after me."

So Mr. and Mrs. Pryor went away, while the Princess, Shelley, May, and I walked through the orchard toward the men. They were standing on the top of the hill looking over the meadow, and talking with such interest they didn't hear us or turn until Shelley said: "Mr. Paget, I want to present you to Laddie's betrothed— Miss Pamela Pryor."

He swung around, finishing what he was saying as he turned, the Princess took a swift step toward him, then, at the same time, both of them changed to solid tombstone, and stood staring, and so did all of us, while no one made a sound. At last the Paget man drew a deep, quivery breath and sort of shook himself as he gazed at her.

"Why, Pam!" he cried. "Darling Pam, cawn it possibly be you?"

If you ever heard the scream of a rabbit when the knives of a reaper cut it to death, why that's exactly the way she cried out. She covered her eyes with her hands. He drew back and smiled, the red rushed into his face, and he began to be alive again. Laddie went to the Princess and took her hands.

"What does this mean?" he begged.

She pulled away from him, and went to the Paget man slowly, her big eyes wild and strained.

"Robert!" she cried. "Robert! how did you get here? Were you hunting us?"

"All ovah England, yes," he said. "Not heah! I came heah to see Shelley. But you? How do you happen to be in this country?"

"We've lived on adjoining land for two years!"

"You moved heah! To escape the pity of our friends?"

"Father moved! Mother and I had no means, and no refuge. We were forced. We never believed it! Oh Robert, we never—not for a minute! Oh Robert, say you never did it!"

"Try our chawming cousin Emmet your next guess!"

"That devil! Oh that devil!"

She cried out that hurt way again, so he took her tight in his arms; but sure as ever Laddie was my brother, he was hers, so that was all right. When they were together you wondered why in this world you hadn't thought of it the instant you saw him alone. They were like as two peas. They talked exactly the same, only he sounded much more so, probably from having just been in England for weeks, while in two years she had grown a little as we were. We gazed at them, open-mouthed, like as not, and no one said a word.

At last Mr. Paget looked over the Princess' shoulder at father and said: "I can explain this, Mr. Stanton, in a very few wuds. *I am my friend. The case was my own. The evidence I secuahed was for myself. This is my only sisteh. Heh people are mine——*"

"The relationship is apparent," said father. "There is a striking likeness between you and your sister, and I can discern traces of your parents in your face, speech and manner."

"If you know my father," said Robert, "then you undehstand what happened to me when I was found with his money on my pehson, in the presence of our best friends and the police. He went raving insane on the instant, and he would have killed me if he hadn't been prevented; he tried to; has he changed any since, Pam?"

The Princess was clinging to him with both hands, staring at him, wonder, joy, and fear all on her lovely face.

"Worse!" she cried. "He's much worse! The longer he broods, the more mother grieves, the bitterer he becomes. Mr. Stanton, he is always armed. He'll shoot on sight. Oh what shall we do?"

"Miss Pamela," said Leon, "did your man Thomas know your brother in England?"

"All his life."

"Well, then, we'd better be doing something quick. He tied the horses and was walking up and down the road while he waited, and he saw us plainly when we crossed the wood yard a while ago. He followed us and stared so, I couldn't help noticing him."

"Jove!" cried Robert. "I must have seen him in the village this morning. A man reminded me of him, then I remembered how like people of his type are, and concluded I was mistaken. Mr. Stanton, you have agreed that the evidence I hold is sufficient. Pam cawn tell you that while I don't deny being full of tricks as a boy, they weh not dirty, not low, and while father always taking Emmet's paht against me drove me to recklessness sometimes, I nevah did anything underhand or disgraceful. She knows what provocation I had, and exactly what happened. Let heh tell you!"

"I don't feel that I require any further information," said father. "You see, I happen to be fairly well acquainted with Mr. Pryor."

"Pryor?"

"He made us use that name here," explained the Princess.

"*Well, his name is Paget!*" said Robert angrily.

Laddie told me long ago he didn't believe it was Pryor.

"Then, if you are acquainted with my father, what would you counsel? Unless I'm prepahed to furnish the central figyah of interest in a funeral, I dare not meet him, until he has seen this evidence, had time to digest it, and calm himself."

Shelley caught him by the arm. No wonder! She hadn't been proposed to, or even had a kiss on her lips. She pulled him.

"You come straight to the house," she said. "Thomas may tell your father he thought he saw you."

That was about as serious as anything could be, but nothing ever stopped Leon. He sidled away from father, repeating in a low voice:

> " 'For sore dismayed, through storm and shade
> His child he did discover;
> One lovely hand she stretched for aid,
> And one was round her lover—' "

Shelley just looked daggers at him, but she was too anxious to waste any time.

"Would Thomas tell your father?" she asked the Princess.

"The instant he saw him alone, yes. He wouldn't before mother."

"Hold one minute!" cried father. "We must think of our mother, just a little. Shelley, you and the girls run up and explain how this is. Better all of you go to the house, except Mr. Paget. He'll be safe here as anywhere. Mr. Pryor will stop there, if he comes. So it would be best for you to keep out of sight, Robert, until I have had a little talk with him."

"I'll stay here," I offered. "We'll talk until you get Mr. Pryor cooled off. He can be awful ragesome when he's excited, and it doesn't take much to start him."

"You're right about that!" agreed Robert.

So we sat under the greening and were having a fine visit while the others went to break the news gently to mother that the Pryor mystery had gone up higher than Gilderoy's kite. My! but she'd be glad! It would save her many a powerful prayer. I was telling Robert all about the time his father visited us, and what my mother said to him, and he said: "She'd be the one to talk with him now. Possibly he'd listen to her, until he got it through his head that his own son is not a common thief."

"Maybe he'll have to be held, like taking quinine, and made to listen," I said.

"That would be easy, if he were not a walking ahsenal," said Robert. "You have small chance to reason with a half-crazy man while he is handling a pistol."

He meant revolver.

"But he'll shoot!" I cried. "The Princess said he'd shoot!"

"So he will!" said Robert. "Shoot first, then find out how things are, and kill himself and every one else with remorse, afterward. He is made that way."

"Then he doesn't dare see you until he finds out how mistaken he has been," I said, for I was growing to like Robert better every minute longer I knew him. Besides, there was the Princess, looking like him as possible, and loving him of course, like I did Laddie, maybe. And if anything could cure Mrs. Pryor's heart trouble, having her son back would, because that was what made it in the first place, and even before them, there was Shelley to be thought of, and cared for.

CHAPTER XVIII

The Pryor Mystery

"And now old Dodson, turning pale,
Yields to his fate—so ends my tale."

It DIDN'T take me long to see why Shelley liked Robert Paget. He
was one of the very most likeable persons I ever had seen. We
were sitting under the apple tree, growing better friends every
minute, when we heard a smash, so we looked up, and it was the
sound made by Ranger as Mr. Pryor landed from taking our
meadow fence. He had ridden through the pasture, and was coming down the creek bank. He was a spectacle to behold. A mile
away you could see that Thomas had told him he had seen Robert, and where he was. Father had been mistaken in thinking Mr.
Pryor would go to the house. He had lost his hat, his white hair
was flying, his horse was in a lather, and he seemed to be talking
to himself. Robert took one good look. "Ye Gods!" he cried.
"There he comes now, a chattering madman!"

"The Station," I panted. "Up that ravine! Roll back the stone
and pull the door shut after you. Quick!"

He never could have been inside, before Mr. Pryor's horse was
raving along the embankment beside the fence.

"Where is he?" he cried. "Thomas saw him here!"

I didn't think his horse could take the fence at the top of the
hill, but it looked as if he intended trying to make it, and I had
to stop him if I could.

"Saw who?" I asked with clicking teeth.

"A tall, slender man, with a handsome face, and the heart of a
devil."

"Yes, there was a man here like that in the face. I didn't see his heart," I said.

"Which way?" raved Mr. Pryor. "Which way? Is he at your house?"

Then I saw that he had the reins in his left hand, and a big revolver in his right. So there was no mistake about whether he'd really shoot. But that gun provoked me. People have no business to be careless with those things. They're dangerous!

"He didn't do what you think he did," I cried, "and he can prove he didn't, if you'll stop cavorting, and listen to reason."

Mr. Pryor leaned over the fence, dark purple like a beet now.

"You tell me where he is, or I'll choke it out of you," he said.

I guess he meant it. I took one long look at his lean, clawlike fingers, and put both hands around my neck.

"He knew Thomas saw him. He went that way," I said, waving off toward the north.

"Hah! striking for petticoats, as usual!" he cried, and away he went in the direction of his house. Then I flew for the Station.

"Come from there, quick!" I cried. "I've sent him back to his house, but when he finds you're not there, he will come here again. Hurry, and I'll put you in the woodshed loft. He'd never think of looking there."

He came out and we started toward the house, going pretty fast. Almost to the back gate we met Shelley.

"Does mother know?" I asked.

"I just told her," she said.

"Father," I cried, going in the back dining-room door. "Mr. Pryor was down in the meadow on Ranger. Thomas did see Robert, and his father is hunting him with a gun. We saw him coming, so I hid Robert in the Station and sent Mr. Pryor back home—I guess I told him a lie, father, or at least part of one, I said he went 'that way,' and he did, but not so far as I made his father think; so he started back home, but when he gets there and doesn't find Robert he'll come here again, madder than ever. Oh father, he'll come again, and he's crazy, father! Clear, raving crazy! I know he'll come again!"

"Yes," said father calmly. "I think it very probable that he will come again."

Then he started around shutting and latching windows, closing and locking the doors, and he carefully loaded his gun, and leaned it against the front casing. Then he put on his glasses, and began examining the papers they had brought out again. Robert stood beside him, and explained and showed him.

"You see with me out of the way, the English law would give everything to my cousin," he said, and he explained it all over again.

"And to think how he always posed for a perfect saint!" cried the Princess. "Oh I hope the devil knows how to make him pay for what all of us have suffered!"

"Child! Child!" cried mother.

"I can't help it!" said the Princess. "Let me tell you, Mr. Stanton."

Then *she* told everything all over again, but it was even more interesting than the way Robert explained it, because what she said was about how it had been with her and her mother.

"It made father what he is," she said. "He would have killed Robert, if our friends hadn't helped him away. He will now, if he isn't stopped. I tell you he will! He sold everything he could legally control, for what any one chose to give him, and fled here stricken in pride, heartbroken, insane with anger, the creature you know. In a minute he'll be back again. Oh what are we going to do?"

Father was laying out the papers that he wanted to use very carefully.

"These constitute all the proof any court would require," he said to Robert. "If he returns, all of you keep from sight. This is *my* house; I'll manage who comes here, in my own way."

"But you must be allowed to take no risk!" cried Robert. "I cawn't consent to youah facing danger for me."

"There will be no risk," said father. "There is no reason why he should want to injure me. As the master of this house, I am accustomed to being obeyed. If he comes, step into the parlour there, until I call you."

He was busy with the papers when he saw Mr. Pryor coming. I wondered if he would jump the yard fence and ride down mother's flowers, but he left his horse at the hitching rack, and pounded on the front door.

"Did any of you notice whether he was displaying a revolver?" asked father.

"Yes father! Yes!" I cried. "And he's shaking so I'm afraid he'll make it go, when he doesn't intend to."

Father picked up and levelled his rifle on the front door.

"Leon," he said, "you're pretty agile. Open this door, keep yourself behind it, and step around in the parlour. The rest of you get out, and stay out of range."

Those nearest hurried into the parlour. Candace, May, and I crouched in the front stairway, but things were so exciting we just had to keep the door open a tiny crack so we could see plain as anything. There had been nothing for Mrs. Freshett to do all afternoon, so she had gone over to visit an hour with Amanda Deam. Now Mr. Pryor probably thought father would meet him with the Bible in his hand, and read a passage about loving your neighbour as yourself. I'll bet anything you can mention that he never expected to find himself looking straight down the barrel of a shining big rifle when that door swung open. It surprised him so, he staggered, and his arm wavered. If he had shot and hit anything then, it would have been an accident.

"Got you over the heart," said father, in precisely the same voice he always said, "This is a fine day we are having." "Now why are you coming here in such a shape?" This was a little cross. "I'm not the man to cringe before you!" This was quite boastful. "You'll get bullet for bullet, if you attempt to invade my house with a gun." This pinged as if father shot words instead of bullets.

"I want my daughter to come home," said Mr. Pryor. "And if you're sheltering the thief she is trying to hide, yield him up, if you would save yourself."

"Well, I'm not anxious about dying, with the family I have on my hands, neighbour," said father, his rifle holding without a waver, "but unless you put away that weapon, and listen to reason, you cannot enter my house. Calm yourself, man, and hear what there is to be said! Examine the proof, that is here waiting to be offered to you."

"Once and but once, send them out, or I'll enter over you!" cried Mr. Pryor.

"Sorry," said father, "but if only a muscle of your trigger finger moves, you fall before I do. I've the best range, and the most suitable implement for the work."

"Implement for the work!" Well, what do you think of father? Any one who could not see, to have heard him, would have thought he was talking about a hoe. We saw a shadow before we knew what made it; then, a little at a time, wonderingly, her jolly face a bewildered daze, her mouth slowly opening, Mrs. Freshett, half-bent and peering, stooped under Mr. Pryor's arm and looked in our door. She had come back to help get supper, and because the kitchen was locked, she had gone around the house to see if she could get in at the front. What she saw closed her mouth, and straightened her back.

"*Why, you two old fools!*" she cried. "*If ye ain't drawed a bead on each other!*"

None of us saw her do it. We only knew after it was over what must have happened. She had said she'd risk her life for mother. She never stopped an instant when her chance came. She must have turned, and thrown her big body against Mr. Pryor. He was tired, old, and shaking with anger. They went down together, she gripping his right wrist with both hands, and she was strong as most men. Father set the gun beside the door, and bent over them. A minute more and he handed the revolver to Leon, and helped Mrs. Freshett to her feet. Mr. Pryor lay all twisted on the walk, his face was working, and what he said was a stiff jabber no one could understand. He had broken into the pieces we often feared he would.

Robert and Laddie came running to help father carry him in, and lay him on the couch.

"I hope, Miss Stanton," said Mrs. Freshett, "that I wa'n't too rough with him. He was so shaky-like, I was 'feered that thing would go off without his really makin' it, and of course I couldn't see none of yourn threatened with a deadly weepon, 'thout buttin' in and doin' the best I could."

Mother put her arms around her as far as they would reach. She would have had to take her a side at a time to really hug all of her, and she said: "Mrs. Freshett, you are an instrument in the hands of the Lord this day. Undoubtedly you have kept us from a fearful tragedy; possibly you have saved my husband for me. None of us ever can thank you enough."

"Loosen his collar and give him air," said Mrs. Freshett pushing mother away. "I think likely he has bust a blood vessel."

Father sent Leon flying to bring Dr. Fenner. Laddie took the carriage and he and Robert went after Mrs. Pryor, while father, mother, Mrs. Freshett, the Princess, May, and I, every last one, worked over Mr. Pryor. We poured hot stuff down his throat, put warm things around him, and rubbed him until the sweat ran on us, trying to get his knotted muscles straightened out. When Dr. Fenner came he said we were doing all he could; *maybe* Mr. Pryor would come to and be all right, and maybe his left side would be helpless forever; it was a stroke. Seemed to me having Mrs. Freshett come against you like that, could be called a good deal more than a stroke, but I couldn't think of the right word then. And after all, perhaps stroke was enough. He couldn't have been much worse off if the barn had fallen on him. I didn't think there was quite so much of Mrs. Freshett; but then she was scared, and angry; and he was about ready to burst, all by himself, if no one had touched him. He had much better have stayed at home and listened to what was to be said, reasonably, like father would; and then if he really had to shoot, he would have been in some kind of condition to take aim.

After a long hard fight we got him limber, straightened out, and warm, it didn't rip so when he breathed, then they put him in the parlour on the big davenport. Leon said if the sparkin' bench didn't bring him to, nothing would. Laddie sat beside him and mother kept peeping. She wouldn't let Dr. Fenner go, because she said Mr. Pryor just must come out of it right, and have a few years of peace and happiness.

Mrs. Pryor came back with Laddie and Robert. He carried her in, put her in the big rocking chair again, and he sat beside her, stroking and kissing her, while she held him with both hands. You could see *now* why his mother couldn't sleep, walked the road, and held her hands over her heart. She was a brave woman, and she had done well to keep alive and going in any shape at all. You see we knew. There had been only the few hours when it seemed possible that one of our boys had taken father's money and was gone. I well remembered what happened to our mother then. And if she had been disgraced before every one, dragged from her home away across a big sea to live among strangers, and not known where her boy was for years, I'm not a bit sure that she'd have done better than Mrs. Pryor. Yes, she would too; come to think it out—she'd have kept on believing the Lord had something to do with it, and that He'd fix it some way; and I know she and father would have held hands no matter what happened or where they went. I guess the biggest thing the matter with Pryors was that they didn't know how to go about loving each other right; maybe it was because they didn't love God, so they couldn't know exactly what *proper love* was; because God is love, like father said.

Mrs. Pryor didn't want to see Mr. Pryor—I can't get used to calling them Paget—and she didn't ask anything about him. I guess she was pretty mad at him. She never had liked the Emmet cousin, and she'd had nothing but trouble with him all the time he had been in her family, and then that awful disgrace, that she always *thought* was all him, but she couldn't prove it, and she had no money.

That's a very bad thing. A woman should always have some money. She works as hard as any one, and usually she has more that worries her, so it's only fair for her to have part of what the work and worry bring. Mother always has money. Why, she has so much, she can help father out when he is pushed with bills, as she did last fall, to start Shelley to music school. It's no way to be forced to live with a man, just to get a home, food, and clothing. I don't believe mother ever would do it in all this world. But then mother has worked all her life, and so if father doesn't do as she wants him to, she'd know exactly how to go about taking care of herself.

After all Mrs. Pryor didn't need to sit back on her dignity and look so abused. He couldn't knock her down, and drag her clear here. Why didn't she say right out, in the beginning, that her son *couldn't* be a thief, that she knew it, and she'd stay at home and wait for him to come back? She could have put a piece in the paper saying she knew her boy was all right, and for him to come back, so they could go to work and *prove* it. I bet if she'd had one tenth of the ginger mother has, she'd have stopped the whole fuss in the start. I looked at her almost steadily, trying to figure out just what mother would have done in her place. Maybe I'm mistaken about exactly how she would have set to work, but this I *know:* she'd have stuck to the Lord; she'd have loved father, so dearly, he just *couldn't* have wanted her to do things that hurt her until it gave her heart trouble; and she never, never would have given up one of us, and sat holding her heart for months, refusing to see or to speak to any one, while she waited for some one else to do something. Mother never waits. She always thinks a minute, if she's in doubt she asks father; if he can't decide, both of them ask God; and then you ought to see things begin to fly.

The more I watched Mrs. Pryor, the more I began to think she was a lady; and just about when I was sure that was what ailed her, I heard father say: "Perhaps the lady would like a cup of tea." I had a big notion to tell her to come on, and I would show her where the cannister was, but I thought I better not. I wanted to, though. She'd have felt much better if she had got up and worked like the rest of us. With all the excitement, and everything happening at once, you'd have thought mother would be flat on her back, but flat nothing! Everything was picked up and slid back, fast as it was torn down; she found time to flannel her nose and brush her hair, her collar was straight, and the goldstone pin shone in the light, while her starched white apron fluttered as she went through the doors. She said a few words to Candace and Mrs. Freshett, May took out a linen cloth and began to set places for all the grown people, so I knew there'd be strawberry preserves and fried ham, but in all that, would you ever have thought that she'd find a second to make biscuit, and tea cakes herself? Plain as preaching I heard her say to Mrs. Freshett: "I do hope and pray that Mr. Pryor will come out of it right, so we can take him home, and teach him to behave himself; but if he's gone this minute, I intend to have another decent meal for Shelley to offer her young man; and I don't care if I show Mrs. Pryor that we're not hungry over here, if we do lack servants to carry in food on silver platters."

"That I jest would!" said Mrs. Freshett. "Even if he turns up his toes, 'tain' *your* funeral, thank the Lord! an' looky here, I'd jest as soon set things in a bake pan an' pass 'em for you, myself. I'll do it, if you say the word."

Mother bit her lip, and fought her face to keep it straight, as she said confidential-like: "No, I'm not going to toady to her. I only want her to see that a meal really consists of food after all; I don't mind putting my best foot foremost, but I won't ape her."

"Huccome they to fuss like this, peaceable as Mr. Stanton be, an' what's Shelley's beau to them?"

"I should think you could tell by looking at Pryors," said mother. "He's their mystery, and also their son. Shelley met him in Chicago, he came here to see her, and ran right into them. I'll tell you about it before you go. Now, I must keep these applications hot, for I've set my head on pulling Mr. Pryor out so that he can speak, and have a few decent years of life yet."

"But why did the old devil—*ex*-cuse me, I mean the old *gentleman,* want to shoot your man?"

"He didn't! I'll tell you all about it after they're gone."

"I bet you don't get shet of them the night," said Mrs. Freshett.

"All right!" said mother. "Whatever Dr. Fenner thinks. I won't have Mr. Pryor moved until it can't hurt him, if he stays a week. I blame her quite as much as I do him; from what I know.

If a woman is going to live with a man, there are times when she's got to put her foot down—flat—most unmercifully flat!"

"Ain't she though!" said Mrs. Freshett; then she and mother just laughed.

There! What did I tell you? I feel as good as if father had patted me on the head and bragged on me a lot. I *thought* mother wouldn't think that Mr. Pryor was *all* to blame, and she didn't. I figured that out by myself, too.

Every minute Mr. Pryor grew better. He breathed easier, and mother tilted on her toes and waved her hands, when he moved his feet, threw back his head, lifted his hand to it, and acted like he was almost over it, and still in shape to manage himself. She hurried to tell Mrs. Pryor, and I know mother didn't like it when she never even said she was glad, or went to see for herself.

Laddie and the Princess watched him, while every one else went to supper. Laddie picked up Mrs. Pryor's chair, carried her to the dining-room, and set her in my place beside father. He placed Dr. Fenner next her, and left Robert to sit with Shelley. I don't think Mrs. Pryor quite liked that, but no one asked her.

I watched and listened until everything seemed to be going right there, and then I slipped into the parlour, where Laddie and the Princess were caring for Mr. Pryor. With one hand Laddie held hers, the other grasped Mr. Pryor's wrist. Laddie never took his eyes from that white, drawn face, except to smile at her, and squeeze her hand every little while. At last Mr. Pryor turned over and sighed, pretty soon he opened his eyes, and looked at Laddie, then at the Princess, and it was nothing new to see them, so he smiled and dozed again. After a while he opened them wider, then he saw the piano—that was an eye-opener for any one— and the strange room, so he asked, most as plain as he ever talked, why he was at our house again, and then he began to remember. He struggled to sit up and the colour came into his face. So Laddie let go the Princess, and held him down while he said: "Mr. Pryor, answer me this. Do you want to spend the remainder of your life in an invalid's chair, or would you like to walk abroad and sit a horse again?"

He glared at Laddie, but he heard how things were plainly enough. Laddie held him, while he explained what a fight we had to unlock his muscles, and start him going again, and how, if we hadn't loved him, and wanted him so, and had left him untouched until the Doctor came, very likely he'd have been paralyzed all the rest of his life, if he hadn't died; and he said he wished he *had,* and he didn't *thank* any one for saving him.

"Oh yes you do!" said Laddie, the same as he'd have talked to Leon. "You can't stuff me on that, and you needn't try. Being dead is a cold, clammy proposition, that all of us put off as long as we can. You know you want to see Pamela in her own home. You know you are interested in how I come out with those horses. You know you want the little people you spoke of, around you. You know the pain and suspense you have borne have almost driven you insane, and it was because you cared so deeply. Now lie still, and keep quiet! All of us are tired and there's no sense in making us go through this again, besides the risk of crippling yourself that you run. Right here in this house are the papers to prove that your nephew took your money, and hid it in your son's clothing, as he already had done a hundred lesser things, before, purposely to estrange you. Hold steady! You must hear this! The sooner you know it, the better you'll feel. You remember, don't you, that before your nephew entered your home, you idolized your son. You thought the things he did were amusing. A boy is a boy, and if he's alive, he's very apt to be lively. Mother could tell you a few pranks that Leon has put us through; but they're only a boy's foolishness, they are not unusual or unforgivable. I've gone over the evidence your son brings, with extreme care, so has father. Both of us are quite familiar with common law. He has every proof you can possibly desire. You can't get around it, even if your heart wasn't worn out with rebellion, and you were not crazy to have the loving sympathy of your family again."

"I don't believe a word of it!"

"You have got to! I tell you it is *proof,* man! The documents are in this house now."

"He forged them, or stole them, as he took the money!"

Laddie just laughed.

"How you do long, and fight, to be convinced!" he said. "I don't blame you! When anything means this much, of course you must be sure. But you'll know your nephew's signature; also your lawyer's. You'll know letters from old friends who are above ques- tion. Sandy McSheel has written you that he was with Robert through all of it, and he gives you his word that everything is all right. You will believe him, won't you?"

Big tears began to squeeze from under Mr. Pryor's lids, until Laddie and the Princess each tried to see how much of him they could hold to keep him together-like.

"Tell me!" he said at last, so they took turns explaining every- thing plain as day, and soon he listened without being held. When they had told him everything they could think of, he asked: "Did Robert kill Emmet?"

"I am very happy to be able to tell you that he did not. It would have been painful, and not helped a bad matter a particle. Your nephew had dissipated until he was only a skeleton just breathing his last. It's probable that his fear of death helped your son out, so that he got the evidence he wanted easier than he hoped to in the beginning. I don't mean that he is dead now; but he is passing slowly, and loathsomely. Robert thinks word that he has gone will come any hour. Think how pleasant it will be to have your son! Think how happy your home will be now! Think how you will love to see Sandy, and all your old friends! Think how glad you'll be to go home, and take charge of your estate!"

"Think!" cried Mr. Pryor, pushing Laddie away and sitting up: "Think how I shall enjoy wringing the last drop of blood from that craven's body with these old hands!"

What a sight he did look to be sure! Sick, half-crazy, on the very verge of the grave himself, and wanting to kill a poor man already dying. Aren't some people too curious?

Laddie carefully laid him down, straightened him out and held him again. Mother always said he was "patient as Job," and that day it proved to be a good thing.

"You're determined to keep yourself well supplied with trouble," laughed Laddie. I don't believe any one else would have dared. "Now to an unbiased observer, it would seem that you'd be ready to let well enough alone. You have your son back, you have him fully exonerated, you have much of your property, you are now ready for freedom, life, and love, with the best of us; you have also two weddings on your hands in the near future. Why in the name of sense are you anxious for more?"

"I should have thought that Sandy McSheel, if he's a real friend of mine——"

"Sandy tells you all about it in the letter he has sent. He went with Robert fully intending to do that very thing for you, but the poor creature was too loathsome. The sight of him made Sandy sick. He writes you that when he saw the horrible spectacle, all he could think of was to secure the evidence needed and get away."

Suddenly the Princess arose and knelt beside the davenport. She put her arms around her father's neck and drew his wrinkled, white old face up against her lovely one.

"Daddy! Dear old Daddy!" she cried. "I've had such a hard spot in my heart against you for so long. Oh do let's forget everything, and begin all over again; begin away back where we were before Emmet ever came. Oh Daddy, do let's forget, and begin all over new, like other people!"

He held her tight a minute, then his lips began whispering against her ear. Finally he said: "Take yourselves off, and send Robert here. I want my son. Oh I want my boy!"

It was a long time before Robert came from the parlour; when he did, it was only to get his mother and take her back with him; then it was a still longer time before the door opened; but when it did, it was perfectly sure that they were all friends again. Then Leon went to tell Thomas, and he came with the big carriage. White and shaking, Mr. Pryor was lifted into it and they went home together, taking Shelley with them to stay that night; so no doubt she was proposed to and got her kiss before she slept.

That fall there were two weddings at our church at the same time. Sally's had been fine; but it wasn't worth mentioning beside Laddie and the Princess, and Robert and Shelley. You should have seen my mother! She rocked like a kingbird on the top twig of the winesap, which was the tallest tree in our orchard, and for once there wasn't a single fly in her ointment, not one, she said so herself, and so did father. As we watched the big ve-hi-acklé, as Leon called it, creep slowly down the Little Hill, it made me think of that pathetic poem, "The Three Warnings," in McGuffey's Sixth. I guess I gave Mr. Pryor the first, that time he got so angry he hit his horse until it almost ran away. Mother delivered the second when she curry-combed him about the taxes, and Mrs. Freshett finished the job. The last two lines read as if they had been especially written about him:

> *"And now old Dodson, turning pale,*
> *Yields to his fate—so ends my tale."*

THE END